Seduced by the Rich Man
by Maureen Child

ಠ ೫ ೧ ಅ

"You're going to ask me to be your mistress. I swear, rich men are all alike."

"What an interesting mind you have," Max said. "But no. That is not the plan."

He had looked surprised when she levelled her accusation, so she'd apparently been wrong about what he was up to. She couldn't imagine anything else, though, that he would need to pay her money for.

"Then what?" Janine asked.

"Why, I want to hire you to be my wife."

Iron Cowboy
DIANA PALMER

Seduced by the Rich Man
MAUREEN CHILD

MILLS & BOON®
Pure reading pleasure™

First published in Great Britain 2008
by Harlequin Mills & Boon Limited,
Eton House, 18-24 Paradise Road, Richmond, Surrey TW9 1SR

The publisher acknowledges the copyright holders of the individual works as follows:

Iron Cowboy © Diana Palmer 2008
Seduced by the Rich Man © Maureen Child 2007

ISBN: 978 0 263 85915 7

51-1008

Printed and bound in Spain
by Litografia Rosés S.A., Barcelona

IRON COWBOY
by
Diana Palmer

Dear Reader,

I still don't know where this book came from. It was all very mysterious, and I think Tony the Dancer (you'll meet him inside the book) had something to do with it.

I laughed a lot when I saw it unfolding on my computer screen, and I also cried a little along the way. It's not a melancholy book, but, like life itself, it has some heartbreak in it. The hero and heroine are both a bit mysterious. Both have secrets. Both have tragedies in their pasts. As usual, in my eccentric way, I have built false trails, so nothing is quite what it seems at the beginning. I do like surprises, as long as they're nice ones. These are. Trust me.

I hope you enjoy reading *Iron Cowboy* as much as I enjoyed writing it for you.

Love to my fans.

As always, I am your biggest fan,

Diana Palmer

DIANA PALMER

has a gift for telling the most sensual tales with charm and humour. With over forty million copies of her books in print, Diana Palmer is one of North America's most beloved authors and considered one of the top ten romance authors in the US.

Diana's hobbies include gardening, archaeology, anthropology, iguanas, astronomy and music. She has been married to James Kyle for over twenty-five years, and they have one son.

To Ann Painter in Massachusetts with love

One

It was a lovely spring day, the sort of day that makes gentle, green, budding trees and white blossoms look like a spring fantasy has been painted. Sara Dobbs stared out the bookstore's side window wistfully, wishing she could get to the tiny flower bed full of jonquils and buttercups to pick a bouquet for the counter. The flowers were blooming on the street that ran beside the Jacobsville Book Nook, where she worked as assistant manager to Dee Harrison, the owner.

Dee was middle-aged, a small, thin, witty woman who made friends wherever she went. She'd been looking for someone to help her manage the store, and Sara had just lost her bookkeeping position at the small print shop that was going out of business. It was a match made in heaven. Sara spent a good portion of her meager salary on books. She loved to read. Living with her grandfather, a retired college professor, had predisposed her to education. She'd had plenty of time to read when she was with her parents, in one of the most dangerous places on earth.

Sara's father, with her maternal grandfather's assistance, had talked her mother into the overseas work. Her father had died violently. Her mother changed, lost her faith, turned to alcohol. She brought Sara to Jacobsville and moved in with her father. She then launched herself into one scandal after another, using her behavior to punish her father without caring about the cost to her only child. Sara and Grandad had suffered for her blatant immorality. It wasn't until Sara had come home in tears, with bruises all over her, that her mother faced the consequences of what she'd done. The children of one of her mother's lovers had caught her alone in the gym and beaten her bloody. Their father had divorced their mother, who was now facing eviction from their home and the loss of every penny they had; their father had spent it on jewels for Sara's mother.

That had led to worse tragedy. Her mother stopped drinking and seemed to reform. She even went back to church. She seemed very happy, until Sara found her one morning, a few days later…

The sound of a vehicle pulling up in the parking lot just in front of the bookstore stopped her painful reveries. At least, she thought, she had a good job and made enough to keep a roof over her head.

Her grandfather's little two-bedroom house outside of town had been left to Sara, along with a small savings account. But there was a mortgage on the house.

She missed the old man. Despite his age, he was young in mind and heart, and adventurous. It was lonely without him, especially since she had no other living family. She had no siblings, no aunts or uncles, or even cousins that she knew about. She had nobody.

The ringing of the electronic bell over the door caught her attention. A tall, grim-looking man came into the small bookstore. He glowered at Sara. He was dressed in an expensive-looking three-piece gray suit and wore hand-tooled black boots and a creamy Stetson. Under the hat was straight, thick, conventionally cut black hair. He had the sort of physique that usually was only seen in motion pictures. But he was no movie star. He looked like a businessman. She glanced out the door and saw a big, black pickup truck with a white horse in a white circle on the truck's door. She knew about the White Horse Ranch outside town. This newcomer, Jared Cameron, had bought it from its previous owner, lock, stock, manager and resident cowboys. Someone said he'd been in town several months earlier for a funeral of some sort, but nobody knew who he was related to that had died. So many old people had out-of-town relatives these days, even in Jacobsville, Texas, a town of less than two thousand inhabitants.

Standing outside next to the driver's side of the black pickup was a tall, husky man with wavy black hair in a ponytail and an olive complexion, wearing a dark suit and sunglasses. He looked like a professional wrestler. He was probably a sort of bodyguard. Maybe his employer had enemies. She wondered why.

The man in the gray suit was glaring at the magazine counter with both hands deep in his pockets, muttering to himself.

Sara wondered what he was looking for. He hadn't asked for assistance, or even looked her way. But the muttering was getting darker by the minute. She couldn't afford to turn away a potential customer. No small town business was that secure.

"May I help you?" she asked with a smile.

He gave her a cold look from pale green eyes in a tanned

face that seemed to be all hard lines and angles. His eyes narrowed on her short, straight blond hair, moved over her wide forehead, down over her own green eyes and straight nose and high cheekbones, to her pretty mouth and rounded chin. He made a sound, as if she didn't live up to his specifications. She didn't dare make a comment, but she was really tempted to tell him that if he was shopping for pretty women, a designer boutique in a big city would be a better place to look than a small bookstore.

"You don't carry financial magazines." He made it sound like a hanging offense.

"Nobody around here reads them much," she defended.

His eyes narrowed. "I read them."

She did occasionally have to bite her tongue to save her job. This looked like one of those times. "I'm very sorry. We could order them for you, if you like."

"Forget it. I can subscribe." He glanced toward the mystery paperbacks and scowled again. "I hate paperbacks. Why don't you carry hardcover novels?"

Her tongue was stinging. She cleared her throat. "Well, most of our clientele are working people and they can't afford them."

Both thick black eyebrows arched. "I don't buy paperbacks."

"We can special order any sort of hardcover you want," she said. The smile was wavering, and she was trying hard not to offend him.

He glanced toward the counter at the computer. "Do you have Internet access?"

"Of course." He must think he'd landed in Borneo. She frowned. They probably even had computers in the jungles these days. He seemed to consider Jacobsville, Texas, a holdover from the last century.

"I like mystery novels," he said. "Biographies. I like first-person adventure novels and anything factual on the North African campaign of World War II."

Her heart jumped at the subject he'd mentioned. She cleared her throat. "Would you like all of them at once, then?"

One eyebrow went up. "The customer is always right," he said shortly, as if he thought she was making fun of him.

"Of course he is," she agreed. Her teeth hurt from being clenched in that smile.

"Get me a sheet of paper and a pen. I'll make you a list."

She wouldn't kick him, she wouldn't kick him, she wouldn't kick him… She found paper and pencil and handed them to him, still smiling.

He made a list while she answered a phone call. She hung up, and he handed her the list.

She frowned as she read it.

"Now what's wrong?" he asked impatiently.

"I don't read Sanskrit," she began.

He muttered something, took the list back and made minor modifications before handing it back. "It's the twenty-first century. Nobody handwrites anything," he said defensively. "I've got two computers and a PDA and an MP3 player." He gave her a curious look. "Do you know what an MP3 player is?" he asked, just to irritate her.

She reached in her jeans pocket, produced a small iPod Shuffle and earphones. The look that accompanied the action could kill.

"How soon can you get those books here?" he asked.

She could, at least, make out most of the titles with his so-called handwriting corrections. "We order on Mondays," she said. "You'll have as many of these as are in stock at the distributors by next Thursday or Friday."

"The mail doesn't come by horse anymore," he began.

She took a deep breath. "If you don't like small towns,

maybe you could go back to wherever you came from. If you can get there by conventional means, that is," with an edge to the smile that accompanied the words.

The insinuation wasn't lost on him. "I'm not the devil."

"Are you sure?" she queried, all wide-eyed.

One eye narrowed. "I'd like these books delivered. I'm usually too busy to make a special trip into town."

"You could send your bodyguard."

He glanced out the door at the big man who was leaning back against the driver's door of the pickup with his arms folded. "Tony the Dancer doesn't run errands."

Her eyes widened more. "Tony the Dancer? Are you in the mob?"

"No, I'm not in the mob!" he growled. "Tony's last name is Danzetta. Tony the Dancer. Get it?"

"Well, he looks like a hit man to me," she returned.

"Known a few of them, have you?" he asked sarcastically.

"If I did, you'd be double-checking your locks tonight," she said under her breath.

"Can you deliver the books?"

"Yes, but it will cost you ten dollars. Gas is expensive."

"What do you drive?" he asked. "A Greyhound bus?"

"I have a VW, thank you very much, but your place is six miles out of town."

"You can tell me the amount when you call to say the books are here. I'll have my accountant cut the check. You can pick it up when you deliver the books."

"All right."

"I'd better give you the number. It's unlisted."

She turned over the sheet of paper with his list of titles on it and copied down the number he gave her.

"I'd also like to get two financial magazines," he added, naming them.

"I'll see if our distributor carries them. He might not."

"Serves me right for moving to Outer Cowpasture," he muttered aloud.

"Well, excuse us for not having malls on every street!" she shot back.

He glowered. "You're the rudest clerk I've seen yet."

"Get your bodyguard to loan you his shades and you won't have to see me at all."

He pursed his lips. "You might get yourself a book on manners."

She smiled sarcastically. "I'll see if I can find one on ogres for you."

His pale eyes swept over her with calculation. "Just the ones I listed, if you please. I'll expect to hear from you late next week."

"Yes, sir."

He cocked his head. "Your boss must have been pretty desperate to leave you in charge of his sole means of support."

"It's a she, not a he. And my boss likes me very much."

"Good thing someone does, I guess." He turned to leave, pausing at the door. "You're wearing two different shades of hose under those slacks, and your earrings don't match."

She had problems with symmetry. Most people knew her background and were kind enough not to mention her lapses. "I'm no slave to popular fashion," she informed him with mock hauteur.

"Yes. I noticed."

He left before she came up with a suitable reply. Lucky for him there wasn't anything expendable that she could have thrown after him.

Dee Harrison rolled in the aisles laughing when she heard Sara's biting description of their new customer.

"It wasn't funny," Sara protested. "He called Jacobsville 'Outer Cowpasture,'" she grumbled.

"Obviously the man has no taste." Dee grinned. "But he did want us to order a lot of books for him, so your sacrifice wasn't in vain, dear."

"But I have to deliver the books to him," she wailed. "He's probably got people-eating dogs and machine guns out there. You should have seen the guy driving him! He looked like a hit man!"

"He's probably just eccentric," Dee said calmingly. "Like old man Dorsey."

She gave her employer a narrow glance. "Old man Dorsey lets his German shepherd sit at the table and eat with him. This guy would probably eat the dog!"

Dee just smiled. A new customer was just what she needed, especially one with expensive tastes in reading. "If he orders a lot of books, you might get a raise," Dee ventured.

Sara just shook her head. Dee didn't understand the situation. If Sara had to be around that particular customer very often, she'd probably end up doing time for assault and battery.

She went home to her small house. Morris met her at the door. He was an old, battle-scarred yellow tabby cat. Part of his tail was missing, and he had slits in his ears from fights. He'd been a stray who came crying to Sara's back door in a thunderstorm. She'd let him in. That had been eight years ago. Her grandfather had commented that he looked like trouble. Sara defended him.

She never agreed with her grandfather, even after she had to replace a chair and a throw rug that Morris had ripped to shreds. She bought the old cat a scratching post and herself a water pistol. Morris hated water. When he did something he wasn't supposed to, she let him have it. Over

the years, he'd calmed down and stopped clawing furniture.
Now, he just ate and sprawled in the sun. Occasionally he
sat in Sara's lap while she watched her small color television. But he wasn't a cuddling cat, and you couldn't pick
him up. He bit.

She stroked him while they watched the latest episode of her
favorite forensic show. "I guess it's just as well that we're not
overrun with visitors, Morris," she mused softly. "You're definitely an antisocial personality." She pursed her lips as she looked
down at him. "I know a guy you'd like," she added on a chuckle.
"I must attract animals and people with bad attitudes."

The end of the next week came all too soon. Dee had
placed Jared Cameron's order on Monday. Sara was hoping
the ogre's order wouldn't come in, allowing her a reprieve to
work on her social skills. But all the books in the order arrived
like clockwork on Friday.

She phoned the number Jared Cameron had given her.

"Cameron ranch," came a gruff reply.

"Mr. Cameron?" she asked hesitantly, because this didn't
sound like the man who'd come into the store earlier.

"He's not here," a gravelly deep voice replied.

She pictured the face that would have gone with that voice,
and figured it must be the hit man. "Mr....Danzetta?"

There was a shocked pause. "Yeah. How'd you know?"

"I read minds," she lied.

"No kidding?" He sounded as if he actually believed her.

"Mr. Cameron ordered a lot of books…"

"Yeah, he said they were due today. He said for you to
bring them out tomorrow about ten. He'll be here."

Tomorrow was Saturday, and she didn't work Saturdays.
"Couldn't I leave them with you, and he can send us the check?"

"Tomorrow at ten, he said. He'll be here."

There was no arguing with stone walls. She sighed. "Okay. I'll see him tomorrow."

"Good."

The line went dead. The voice had a decidedly Southern accent. Not a Texas accent. A Georgia one, if she were guessing. She had an ear for accents. Her grandfather had taught students from all over the country and around the world at the Jacobsville Community College, and he often brought them home. Sara had learned a lot about other places.

She put the phone down belatedly. If the bodyguard was part of the mob, it must be the Southern branch. She chuckled. But now she didn't know what to do. Should she call him tomorrow before she started out, to let him know how much he owed? Surely his bookkeeper didn't work weekends.

"You look unsettled," Dee remarked as she started for the front door. "What's wrong?"

"I have to take the ogre's order out to him tomorrow morning."

"On your day off." Dee smiled. "You can have a half day next Wednesday to make up for it. I'll come in at noon and work until closing time."

"You will?" Sara asked, beaming.

"I know how you look forward to your drawing time," Dee replied. "I just know you're going to sell that children's book you're working on. Call Lisa Parks and tell her you'll come next Wednesday to draw her new puppies instead of tomorrow. They'll make a gorgeous page in your story," she added.

Sara grinned. "They're the cutest puppies I've ever seen. Their father was one of the puppies Tom Walker's dog Moose fathered, and their mother is Cy Parks's collie, Bob."

"Bob is a girl dog?" Dee exclaimed.

"Yes. The puppies look like both their parents. Tom asked for one of them. He lost Moose just last month," she added sadly. "They have another dog a little younger than Moose, but Tom loved that old dog. He had him cremated and put in an urn. He's still grieving, though. Lisa e-mailed a picture of the puppies to Tom and said he could have one. He and his oldest daughter went over to pick it out. They'll be ready to go to new homes in a week or so. They're just precious at this age. I'm going to draw them in a big Easter basket."

"You could sell drawings," Dee said.

"I guess so. But I'd never make a living at it," she replied, smiling. "I want to sell books."

"I think you're going to be selling your own books pretty soon," Dee told her. "You have a wonderful talent."

Sara beamed. "Thanks. It's the only thing I inherited from my father. He loved the work he did, but he could draw beautiful portraits." She grimaced. "It was hard, losing him like that."

"Wars are terrible," Dee agreed. "But at least you had your grandfather. He was your biggest fan. He was always bragging about you, to anybody who'd listen."

"I still get letters from Grandad's former students," Sara said. "He taught military history. I guess he had every book ever written on World War II. Especially the campaign in North Africa." She frowned. "Funny, that's what the ogre likes to read about."

"Maybe the ogre is like that lion who got a thorn in his paw, and when the mouse pulled it out, they were friends for life."

Sara glowered at her boss. "No mouse in his right mind would go near that man," she said.

"Except you," came the amused reply.

"Well, I don't have a choice. What do we do about the check?" she asked Dee. "Do I call him before I go over there, or…"

Dee picked up the slip of paper with his phone number on it. "I'll call him in the morning. You can put the books in a bag and take them home with you tonight. That way you won't have to come in to town."

"You're sweet, Dee."

The older woman smiled. "So are you." She checked her watch. "I've got to pick Mama up at the beauty parlor and take her home, then I'm going to do paperwork. You know my cell phone number. Call me if you need me."

"I won't, but thanks all the same."

Dee looked uneasy. "You need to have a cell phone, Sara. You can get a prepaid one for next to nothing. I don't like you having to drive home after dark on that dirt road."

"Most of the drug traffickers are in prison now," she reminded her boss.

"That isn't what Cash Grier says," Dee replied. "They locked up the Dominguez woman, and her successor, but there's a man in charge now, and he killed two Mexican policemen at a border crossing, as well as a Border Patrol agent and even a reporter. They say he killed a whole family over near Nuevo Laredo for ratting on him."

"Surely he wouldn't come here," Sara began.

"Drug dealers like it here," Dee returned. "We don't have federal agents—well, except for the DEA agent, Cobb, who works out of Houston and has a ranch here. Our police and sheriff's departments are underfunded and understaffed. That's why that man Lopez tried to set up a distribution network here. They say this new drug lord has property around town that he bought with holding companies, so nobody would know who really owned the land. A farm or ranch way out in the country would be a perfect place to transport drugs to."

"Like they tried once, behind Cy Parks's place and at the old Johnson place."

Dee sighed. "It makes me uneasy, that's all."

"You worry too much," Sara said gently. "Besides, I'm

only a mile out of town and I lock all my doors." She looked at the clock on the wall opposite. "You'd better get moving, or your mother's going to be worried about you!"

Dee chuckled. "I guess so. Well, if you need me…"

"I'll call."

Dee went out with a wave, leaving Sara alone.

Later in the afternoon, Harley Fowler came in, dusty and sweaty and half out of humor. He pushed his hat back over wet hair.

"What in the world happened to you?" Sara exclaimed. "You look like you've been dragged down a dirt road behind a horse!"

He glowered. "I have."

"Ouch," she sympathized.

"I need a book on Spanish slang. Ranch Spanish slang, if you've got one."

"We have every Spanish dictionary ever published, including slang ones. I'll show you."

She pointed out a rack with dozens of paperback dictionaries, including specific books just on verbs.

"Just the thing," Harley murmured, reading titles. "Mr. Parks still has an account, doesn't he?"

"He and Lisa both do."

"Well, you can put these on his tab." He picked out four and handed them to her.

"Would it be safe to ask why you want them?" she mused as she went behind the counter to the cash register.

"Why not?" he sighed. "I thought I was telling Lanita, Juan's wife, that it was hot outside. She blushed, Juan jumped me, and we rolled around in the dirt until I finally convinced him that I was just talking about the weather. We got up and shook hands, and then he told me what I'd actually said to her. I was just sick." He groaned. "I speak a little Spanish, but I learned it in high school, and I've forgotten how *not* to say embarrassing things." He groaned. "Juan and the rest of the workers speak English, but I thought I might get along better with them if I spoke a little Spanish. And this happens!"

She pursed her lips. "If you want to remark on the weather, in Spanish you say 'there is heat,' not 'I am hot.' Especially in front of a woman."

"Thanks, I do know that now," he replied, soothing his jaw. "That Juan hits like a mule kicking."

"So I've heard."

She totaled the books on the cash register and wrote down the tally in a book of accounts that Dee kept. "We'll bill Mr. Parks."

"Thanks." He took the bag with the books. "If Mr. Parks wants to argue about me buying them, I'll tell him to go talk to Juan."

She grinned. "Good idea."

He smiled back, and hesitated, as if he wanted to say something more. Just then, the phone rang, and it was one of her long-winded customers. She shrugged and waved at Harley. He waved back as he left. She wondered later what he'd been about to say.

He was handsome and well-known in the community for being a hardworking cowboy. He'd actually gone on a mission with three of the town's ex-mercenaries to help stop Manuel Lopez's drug-smuggling operation. He'd earned a lot of respect for his part in it. Sara liked him a lot, but he didn't date much. Rumor was that he'd had a real case on a local girl who'd made fun of his interest in her and threw him over. But he didn't look like a man with a broken heart.

Sara knew about broken hearts. She'd been sweet on a boy in the community college she attended to learn accounting. So had Marie, her best friend. The boy had dated both of them, but finally started going steady with Marie. A good loser, Sara had been maid of honor at their wedding. Marie and her new husband had moved to Michigan to be near his parents. Sara still wrote to Marie. She was too kindhearted to hold a grudge. Probably, she realized, the boy had only dated her because she was best friends with Marie. She recalled that he spent most of their time together asking her questions about Marie.

She was old-fashioned. Her grandfather had firm opinions about the morality deprived state of modern society. He and Sara went to church regularly and she began to share his views. She wasn't the sort of girl who got invited to wild parties, because she didn't drink or smoke or do drugs. Everyone knew that her grandfather was good friends with one of Police Chief Cash Grier's older patrol officers, too. Her law enforcement connections made the party crowd cautious. It also got around that Sara didn't "give out" on dates. There were too many girls who had no such hang-ups. So Sara and Morris spent most of their Friday and Saturday nights together with Sara's grandfather, watching movies on television.

She wondered where the ogre had gone, and why Tony the Dancer hadn't gone with him. Maybe he was off on a hot date somewhere. She wondered about the sort of woman who might appeal to a man with his gloomy outlook. But then she remembered that he'd been wearing an expensive suit, and driving a new truck, and he owned one of the bigger ranches in the county. Some women wouldn't mind how gloomy and antisocial he was, as long as he had lots of money to spend on them.

He did look like a cold fish. But maybe he was different around people he liked. He'd made it obvious that he didn't like Sara. The feeling was mutual. She hated having to give up her Saturday to his whim.

She phoned Lisa to tell her that she wouldn't be able to come until the following Wednesday.

"That's okay," Lisa replied. "Cy and I wanted to take the baby to the mall in San Antonio on Saturday, but I was going to stay home and wait for you. There's lots of sales on baby clothes and toys."

Like Lisa needed sales, when her husband owned one of the most productive ranches in Texas, she thought, but she didn't say it. "You're always buying that baby clothes," Sara teased. "He's going to be the best-dressed little boy in town."

"We go overboard, I know," Lisa replied, "but we're so happy to have him. Cy and I took a long time to get over losing our first one."

"I remember," Sara said softly. "But birth defects turn up sometimes in the healthiest families, you know. I read about it in one of the medical books we sell. This little boy is going to grow up and be a rancher, just like his parents."

Lisa laughed softly. "Thanks, Sara," she said gently. "You make me feel better every time I talk to you."

"I'll call you Wednesday, okay? Dee's giving me a half-day, so I'll have the afternoon off."

"That will work out fine," Lisa said.

"Thanks."

"You're very welcome."

Sara hung up. Poor Lisa. Her first husband had been killed not long after their wedding. He'd been an undercover DEA agent, whom one of the drug dealer, Lopez's, men had killed. Cy had taken her under his wing and protected her while she waited for the birth of her child. Harley said the baby she was carrying wasn't her husband's, because he had a vasectomy, but she'd thought she was pregnant. Only weeks after marrying Cy, she really was pregnant. But the baby was born with birth defects that were beyond a physician's ability to cure. He'd died when he was only a week old, leaving two devastated parents to grieve. They hadn't rushed into another pregnancy. But this one had worked out without any health issues at all. Their little boy, Gil, was a toddler, and very active.

Sara wondered if she'd ever get married and have a family, but it wasn't something she dwelled on. She was young and the world would have been wide-open for her, except for her one small secret that she wasn't anxious to share with anyone. Still, she was optimistic about the future. Well, except for the ogre.

She sighed. Every life had to have a few little irritations, she decided. And who knew? The ogre might turn out to be a handsome prince inside.

Two

It was pouring rain when Sara reluctantly crawled out of bed the next morning. She looked out the window and sighed.

"Boy, I'd love to go back under the covers and sleep, Morris," she mused as she fed the old cat.

He rubbed up against her pajama-clad legs and purred.

She yawned as she made a pot of coffee and some buttered toast to go with it. Her grandfather had insisted on a balanced breakfast, but Sara couldn't manage a lot of food early in the morning.

She nibbled toast and watched the rain bounce down over the camellia bush next to the window. She was going to get wet.

She dressed in jeans and a cotton blouse and threw her ancient tan raincoat over her clothes. It was embarrassing to wear such a tacky coat to a rich man's house, but it was all she had. Her salary didn't cover many new things. Mostly she shopped at thrift stores. The coat had a stained neck and two or three tears where Sara—never the world's most graceful woman—had tripped over garden stakes or steps or her own feet and brushed against nails and a barbed-wire fence. She looked down and noticed that she was wearing socks that didn't match. Well, it was something she just had to learn to live with. The doctor told her she'd cope. She hoped he was right. She was nineteen, and sometimes she felt fifty when she tried to force her mind to comprehend matching colors.

Groaning, she checked her watch. It was fifteen to ten, and it would take her almost all that time to get to the White Horse Ranch. Well, the ogre would just have to make fun of her. She didn't have time to unload her sock drawer and find mates. They were hidden under her jeans, anyway, and maybe he wouldn't notice.

She stepped right into a hole filled with muddy water getting to her car. Her sneakers and her socks were immediately soaked. She groaned again as she unlocked the little car and quickly climbed in. The seats were leather, thank goodness, and they'd shed water. Her VW was seven years old, but the mechanics at Turkey Sanders's used car lot kept it in good repair. Despite his reputation for bad car sales, Turkey prided himself on his mechanics.

She patted its cracked dash. The VW had been wrecked, so she got it very cheaply. Probably it would fall apart if she tried to drive it as far as San Antonio. But she never left the Jacobsville area, and it was dependable transportation.

It started on the first go, making that lovely race car sound that made her think of luxury racers as she gunned the engine. If she closed her eyes and did that, sometimes it sounded just like a Formula 1 challenge car.

"In my dreams," she laughed to herself. She wouldn't earn enough in her lifetime to make six months of payments on one of those fancy sports cars. But it was just as well. The little black VW suited her very well.

She pulled out of her driveway onto the dirt road that led out to the state highway. It had been recently scraped and a little new gravel had been laid down, but it was still slippery in the rain. She gritted her teeth as she felt the car slide around in the wet mud. At least it was flat land, and even if she did go into a ditch, it wouldn't be a deep one. All the same, she didn't look forward to walking for help in that molasses-thick mud. She remembered a long walk in similar red mud, overseas, with the sound of guns echoing… She drew her mind back to the present. Dwelling on the past solved nothing.

By downshifting, not hitting the brakes and going slowly, she managed to get to the paved highway. But she was going to be late getting to the ogre's house. She grimaced. Well, it couldn't be helped. She'd just have to tell him the truth and hope he was understanding about it.

"I specifically said ten o'clock," he shot at her when he opened the front door.

He was wearing jeans and a chambray shirt and working boots—you could tell by the misshapen contours of them that many soakings had caused—and a ratty black Stetson pulled low over his forehead. Even in working garb, he managed to look elegant. He looked like a cowboy, but they could have used him as a model for one made of metal. An iron cowboy.

She had to fight a laugh at the comparison.

"And you're dripping wet all over," he muttered, glaring at her clothes. "What the hell did you do, swim through mud holes on your way here?"

"I stepped in a mud puddle on the way to my car," she began, clutching a plastic bag that held his books.

He looked past her. "I don't know what the hell that thing is, but I wouldn't dignify it by calling it a car."

Her eyes began to glitter. "Here," she said, thrusting the books at him.

"And your manners could use some work," he added bitingly.

"'Cast not your pearls before swine!'" she quoted angrily.

Both eyebrows went up under the hat. "If that raincoat is any indication of your finances, you'd be lucky to be able to toss a cultured pearl at a pig. Which I am not one of," he added firmly.

"My boss said she'd call you…"

"She did." He took a folded check out of his shirt pocket and handed it to her. "Next time I order books, I'll expect you at the stated time. I'm too busy to sit in the house waiting for people to show up."

"The road I live on is six inches thick in wet mud," she began.

"You could have phoned on the way and told me that," he retorted.

"With what, smoke signals?" she asked sourly. "I don't have a cell phone."

"Why am I not surprised?" he asked with pure sarcasm.

"And my finances are none of your business!"

He glanced down. "If they were, I'd quit. No accountant is going to work for a woman who can't afford two matching socks."

"I have another pair just like this one at home!"

He frowned. He leaned closer. "What in the world is *that*?" he asked, indicating her left sleeve.

She looked down. "Aahhhhhh!" she screamed, jumping from one leg to the other. "Get it off, get it off! Aaaahhhh!"

The large man in the house came out onto the porch, frowning. When he followed his employer's pointed finger, he spotted the source of the uproar. "Oh," he said.

He walked forward, caught Sara's arm with a big hand, picked up the yellow hornet on her sleeve, slammed it to the porch and stepped on it with a shoe the size of a shoebox.

"It's just a hornet," Mr. Danzetta said gently.

Sara stared down at the smashed insect and drew in a deep breath. "It's a yellow hornet. I got stung by one of them once, on my neck. It swelled up and I had to be taken to the emergency room. I've been scared of them ever since." She smiled up at him. "Thank you." Odd, she thought, how familiar he looked. But she was almost certain she'd never seen him before. Her condition made it difficult for her to remember the past.

The ogre glared at his employee, who was smiling at Sara and watching her with something like recognition. He noted the glare, cleared his throat and went back into the house.

"Don't start flirting with the hired help," he told her firmly after the front door had closed behind Tony.

"I said thank you! How can you call that flirting?" she asked, aghast.

"I'll call the store when I need a new supply of books," he replied, ignoring her question.

She read quickly herself, but he had eight books there. But he might not be reading them, she thought wickedly. He might be using them for other purposes: as doorstops, maybe.

"You brought the books. I gave you a check. Was there something else?" he asked with a cold smile. "If you're lonely and need companionship, there are services that advertise on television late at night," he added helpfully.

She drew herself up to her full height. "If I were lonely, this is the last place in the world that I'd look for relief!" she informed him.

"Then why are you still here?"

She wouldn't kick him, she wouldn't kick him…

"And don't spin out going down my driveway," he called after her. "That's new gravel!"

She hoped he was watching her the whole way. She dislodged enough gravel to cover a flower bed on her way down the driveway.

It was a long, wet weekend. She knew that nobody around Jacobs County would be complaining about the rain. It was a dry, unusually hot spring. She read in the market bulletins online that ranchers were going to pay high prices for corn. Floods in the Midwest and Great Plains were killing the corn there, and drought was getting it in the South and Southwest. Considering the vast amounts of the grain that were being used as biofuel, and the correspondingly higher prices it was commanding, it looked as if some small ranchers and farmers might go broke because they couldn't afford to feed it to their cattle. Not to mention the expense of running farm machinery, which mostly burned gasoline.

She was glad she wasn't a farmer or rancher. She did feel sorry for the handful of small ranchers around town. One day, she thought, there would be no more family agriculture in the country. Everything would be owned by international corporations, using patented seed and genetically enhanced produce. It was a good thing that some small farmers were holding on to genetically pure seeds, raising organic crops. One day, the agricultural community might be grateful, if there was ever a wholesale dying out of the genetically modified plants.

"Well, you're deep in thought, aren't you?" Dee teased as she walked in the door the following Wednesday, just before noon.

Sara blinked, startled by her boss's appearance. "Sorry," she said, laughing. "I was thinking about corn."

Dee stared at her. "OOOOOkay," she drawled.

"No, I'm not going mad," Sara chuckled. "I read an article in this farm life magazine." She showed it to the older woman. "It's about the high prices corn is going to get this year."

Dee shook her head. "I don't know what the smaller ranchers are going to do," she said. "Gas prices are so high that it's hard to afford enough fuel to run tractors and trucks, and now they'll have to hope the hay crop is good or they'll have to sell off cattle before winter rather than having to feed them stored corn." She sighed. "I expect even the Ballengers will be feeling a pinch, with their feedlot."

"It must be tough, having your livelihood depend on the weather," she remarked.

"Yes, it is. I grew up on a little truck farm north of here," Dee told her. "One year, we had a drought so bad that everything we grew died. Dad had to borrow on the next year's profits to buy seed and fertilizer." She shook her head. "Finally he couldn't deal with the uncertainty anymore. He got a job fixing engines at one of the car dealerships."

"It's so bad, you know—floods in the Midwest and drought here and in the Southeast. Too much water or not enough. They need to build aqueducts like the Romans did and share that water with places that need it."

"Not a bad idea, but who'd pay for it?"

Sara laughed. "I don't guess anybody could. But it was a nice thought."

Dee checked her watch. "You'd better get a move on, before we get swamped with customers and you're late leaving."

"I'll do that. Thanks, Dee."

The older woman smiled. "Good luck with those drawings."

Lisa Parks had blond hair and a sweet smile. She was carrying Gil, her eighteen-month-old toddler, when she came to the door to let Sara in. The baby had brownish colored hair and his eyes were green, like his father's. He was wearing a two-piece sailor suit.

"Doesn't he look cute!" Sara enthused over the little boy, while Lisa beamed.

"Our pride and joy," Lisa murmured, kissing the child on his soft nose. "Come in."

Sara stepped into the cool confines of the house. It had been a bachelor house for years, but Lisa's feminine touches made it into a home.

"Want coffee before you start?" Lisa asked, shifting Gil on her hip while he chanted happy noises.

"After, if you don't mind," came the smiling reply. "I always try to avoid work if it's at all possible."

"Don't we all? I've got the puppies out in the barn." She led the way down the back steps, pausing at the sound of a horse approaching. Gil was still making happy baby sounds, cradled on his mother's hip.

Harley Fowler was just riding into the yard. He spotted Sara with Lisa and smiled hugely. "Hi, Sara."

"Hello, Harley. How's the Spanish coming along?"

He glanced at Lisa, who grinned at him. He shrugged. "Well, I guess I'm learning some. But Juan is a better teacher than any book."

"How's your jaw?" Sara asked with twinkling eyes.

He fingered it. "Much better." He smiled back.

"Uh oh, Mama," Gil said, frowning. "Uh oh." He squirmed.

"Uh oh means somebody needs a diaper change," Lisa laughed. She glanced at Harley and, sensing something, concealed a smile. "Harley, if you've got a minute, would you mind showing Sara the pups while I change Gil? We're working on potty training, but it's early days yet," she added on a laugh.

Harley beamed. "I'd be happy to!" He climbed down

gracefully out of the saddle and held the reins, waiting for Sara. "Are you going to adopt one of the puppies?"

She blinked. "Well, I hadn't thought about that. I have a cat, you know, and he really doesn't like dogs much. I think one tried to eat him when he was younger. He's got scars everywhere and even dogs barking on television upsets him."

He frowned. "But you came to see the puppies…?"

She showed him her drawing pad. "I came to sketch the puppies," she corrected, "for the children's book I'm writing."

"Someday she's going to be famous, and we can all say we knew her back when," Lisa teased. "I'll have coffee ready when you're done, Sara. I made a pound cake, too."

"Thanks," Sara called after her.

Lisa waved as she took the baby back into the house.

Harley tied his horse to the corral fence and walked into the dim confines of the barn with Sara. In a stall filled with fresh hay were five puppies and Bob the Collie. She was nursing the babies. In the stall beside hers was Puppy Dog, Lisa's dog, no longer a puppy. He looked exactly like Tom Walker's dog, Moose.

"A girl dog named Bob," Sara mused.

"Boss said if Johnny Cash could have a boy named 'Sue,' he could have a girl dog named Bob."

"She's so pretty," Sara said. "And the puppies are just precious!"

"Three males, two females," he said. "Tom's got first choice, since they're Moose's grandkids." He shook his head. "He's taking Moose's loss hard. He loved that old dog, even though he was a disaster in the house."

"Moose saved Tom's daughter from a rattler," Sara reminded him. "He was a real hero."

"You want a chair?" he asked.

"This old stool will do fine. Thanks anyway." She pulled

up the rickety stool, opened her pad and took her pencils out of her hip pocket.

"Will it make you nervous if I watch?"

She grinned up at him. "Of course not."

He lolled against the stall wall and folded his arms, concentrating on the way her hand flew over the page, the pencil quickly bringing the puppies to life on the off-white sheet. "You're really good," he said, surprised.

"Only thing I was ever good at in school," she murmured while she drew. She was also noting the pattern of colors on the pups and shading her drawing to match. Then she wrote down the colors, so she wouldn't forget them when she started doing the illustrations for her book in pastels.

"I can fix anything mechanical," he said, "but I can't draw a straight line."

"We all have our talents, Harley," she said. "It wouldn't do for all of us to be good at the same thing."

"No, it wouldn't, I guess."

She sketched some more in a personable silence.

"I wanted to ask you in the bookstore, but we got interrupted," he began. "There's going to be a concert at the high school this Saturday. They're hosting a performance by the San Antonio Symphony Orchestra. I wondered if, well, if you'd like to go. With me," he added.

She looked up, her soft eyes smiling. "Well, yes, I would," she said. "I'd thought about it, because they're doing Debussy, and he's my favorite composer. But I didn't have the nerve to go by myself."

He chuckled, encouraged. "Then it's a date. We could leave earlier and have supper at the Chinese place. If you like Chinese?"

"I love it. Thanks."

"Then I'll pick you up about five on Saturday. Okay?"

She smiled at him. He was really nice. "Okay."

He glanced out of the barn at his horse, which was getting restless. "I'd better get back out to the pasture. We're dipping cattle and the vet's checking them over. I'll see you Saturday."

"Thanks, Harley."

"Thank *you.*"

She watched him walk away. He was good-looking, local and pleasant to be around. What a difference from that complaining, bad-tempered rancher who hadn't even sympathized with her when she'd almost drowned delivering his stupid books!

Now why had she thought about Jared Cameron? She forced herself to concentrate on the puppies.

Harley picked her up at five on Saturday in his aged, but clean, red pickup truck. He was wearing a suit, and he looked pretty good. Sara wore a simple black dress with her mother's pearls and scuffed black high-heeled shoes that she hoped wouldn't be noticed. She draped a lacy black mantilla around her shoulders.

"You look very nice," Harley said. "I figure there will be people there in jeans and shorts, but I always feel you should dress up to go to a fancy concert."

"So do I," she agreed. "At least it isn't raining," she added.

"I wish it would," he replied. "That nice shower we got last Saturday is long gone, and the crops are suffering. We're still in drought conditions."

"Don't mention that shower," she muttered. "I was out in it, sliding all over Jeff Bridges Road in my VW, bogged up to my knees in mud, just to deliver Jared Cameron's books!"

He glanced at her. "Why didn't he go to the store and get them himself?"

"He's very busy."

He burst out laughing. "Hell! Everyone's very busy. He could spare thirty minutes to drive into town. God knows, he's got half a dozen cars. That big fella who works for him is something of a mechanic in his spare time. He keeps the fleet on the road."

"What sort of cars?" she asked curiously.

"There's a sixties Rolls-Royce Silver Shadow, a thirties Studebaker and several assorted sports cars, mostly classics. He collects old cars and refurbishes them."

"He arrived at our store in a truck," she said flatly.

"From time to time that big fella wearing fancy suits drives him around."

"Do you know where he came from?"

Harley shook his head. "Somebody said he was from Montana, but I'm not sure. He came here for a funeral about eight months ago. Nobody can remember whose."

"A relative, you think?"

He shrugged. "It was at one of the old country churches. Mount Hebron Baptist, I think."

"That's where I go to church," she said, frowning. "Grandad's buried there. But I don't remember reading about any funeral in the bulletin for out-of-town people."

"It was a private service, they said. Just ashes, not even a coffin."

She pursed her lips and whistled softly. "I wouldn't like to be burned."

"I would," he said, grinning at her. "A true Viking's funeral. Nothing wrong with that. Then they can put you in a nice-looking urn and set you on the mantel above the fireplace. Nice and neat. No upkeep."

She laughed. "Harley, you're terrible!"

"Yes, but I do have saving graces. I can whistle and carry a tune. Oh, and I can gather eggs. Just ask the boss's wife!"

* * *

They had a nice meal at the local Chinese restaurant and then Harley drove them to the high school. There were a lot of people on hand for the rare big city musical talent. Both Ballengers and their wives and teenaged kids, and a few of the Tremaynes and two Hart brothers and their families.

Harley caught Sara's arm gently to help her up onto the sidewalk from the parking lot, and then let his fingers accidentally catch in hers. She didn't object. She'd always liked Harley. It was nice, to have a man find her attractive, even if it was just in a friendly way.

He was smiling down at her when they almost collided with a man in line. The man, nicely dressed in a suit and a wide-brimmed top-of-the-line John B. Stetson cowboy hat, turned his head back toward them and green eyes glared belligerently.

"Sorry, Mr. Cameron," Harley said at once.

Jared Cameron gave them both a speaking glance and turned his attention back to the line, which was rapidly moving inside. When he was out of earshot, Sara muttered, "He ran into us. You didn't have to apologize."

He chuckled. "It isn't the place for a skirmish, you know," he teased.

She grimaced. "Sorry, Harley. I don't like him, that's all. He's too full of himself."

"He's just bought that huge ranch," he reminded her. "He must live on a higher level than most of us. I guess he thinks he's above normal courtesies."

She only nodded. She hadn't liked the antagonism in the tall man's eyes when he'd looked at Harley.

They got their tickets and found seats as far away from Jared Cameron as Sara could possibly manage. Then she lost herself in the beautiful musical landscapes created by the themes of Claude Debussy. Harley seemed to enjoy the concert as much as she did. It was nice to have something in common.

On the way out, they noticed Jared Cameron speaking earnestly with Police Chief Cash Grier, who'd shown up just after the concert began and stood at the back of the room. Sara wondered what they were talking about. But it was none of her business.

It was ten o'clock when Harley dropped her off at her home. She smiled up at him. "Thanks, Harley. I had a really nice time."

"So did I. Want to go to a movie next Friday?"

Her heart jumped pleasantly. He liked her! She beamed. "Yes. I would."

He chuckled. "That's great!"

He hesitated. So did she. Her experience of men was extremely limited. Her upbringing had been strict and unrelenting on the issue of morals. Her past wasn't widely known around Jacobsville, but her reputation was rock-solid. It was why she hadn't dated much. Harley knew that. But it didn't seem to bother him overmuch. After a minute's deliberation, he bent and brushed his mouth briefly, softly over hers. "Good night, Sara."

She smiled. "Good night, Harley."

He jumped back into the truck, waved and took off down the driveway,

She watched the truck disappear into the distance, frowning as she considered that brief kiss. It hadn't touched her. She liked Harley. She'd have loved having a steady boyfriend, just for the novelty of the thing. But she hadn't felt anything when he kissed her. Maybe you just had to work up to those feelings, she told herself as she unlocked her door and went inside. It was early days in their relationship. They had plenty of time to experiment.

* * *

It was the week after the concert before her nemesis placed another order. This time he did it on the telephone, and to Dee, who got to the telephone first early Monday morning.

"What a selection," Dee exclaimed when she hung up. She read down the list, shaking her head. "Greek and Roman writers of the classics, some science fiction, two books on drug interdiction and two on South American politics. Oh, and one on independent contractors. Mercenaries."

"Maybe he's thinking of starting a war," Sara offered. "In some other country, of course." She pursed her lips and her eyes twinkled. "Maybe he's anxious to skip town because he's so fascinated by me!"

Dee looked at her over her glasses. "Excuse me?"

"It's just a theory I'm working on," she said facetiously. "I mean, I'm growing into a femme fatale. Harley Fowler can't resist me. What if my fatal charm has worked its magic on Mr. Cameron and he's running scared? He might feel a need to escape before he gets addicted to me!"

"Sara, do you feel all right?"

Sara just grinned. "I never felt better."

"If you say so. I'll get these ordered." She glanced at Sara. "He wants you to take them out to him on Saturday."

Sara grimaced. "He just likes ruining my weekends."

"He hardly knows you, dear. I'm sure it's not that."

Sara didn't answer her.

On Thursday, Harley phoned with bad news. "I have to fly to Denver on business for the boss, and I'll be gone a week or more," he said miserably. "So we can't go to the movies on Friday."

"That's all right, Harley," she assured him. "There will be a movie left when you get back that we can see. Honest."

He laughed. "You make everything so easy, Sara."

"You have a safe trip."

"I'll do my best. Take care."

"You, too."

She hung up and wondered idly why Harley had to go out of town just before they went on another date. It was as if fate was working against her. She'd looked forward to it, too. Now all she had to anticipate was delivering books to the ogre. It wasn't a happy thought. Not at all.

Well, she told herself, it could always be worse. She could be dating HIM—the ogre.

Three

Sara took the ogre's books home with her on Friday, just as she had the last time, so that she didn't have to go to town. At least it wasn't pouring rain when she went out to her car early Saturday morning to make the drive to the White Horse Ranch.

This time, he was waiting for her on the porch. He was leaning against one of the posts with his hands in his jean pockets. Like last time, he was wearing working garb. Same disreputable boots and hat, same unpleasant expression. Sara tried not to notice what an incredible physique he had, or how handsome he was. It wouldn't do to let him know how attractive she found him.

He looked pointedly at his watch as she came up the steps. "Five minutes late," he remarked.

Her eyebrows arched. "I am not," she shot back. "My watch says ten, exactly."

"My watch is better than yours," he countered.

"I guess so, if you judge it by the amount of gold on the band instead of the mechanics inside it," she retorted.

"You're testy for a concert goer," he returned. He smiled, and it wasn't sarcastic. "You like Debussy, do you?"

"Yes."

"Who else?"

She was taken aback by the question. "I like Resphigi, Rachmaninoff, Haydn and some modern composers like the late Basil Poledouris and Jerry Goldsmith. I also like James Horner, Danny Elfman, Harry Gregson-Williams and James Newton Howard."

He eyed her curiously. "I thought a country girl like you would prefer fiddles to violins."

"Well, even here in Outer Cowpasture, we know what culture is," she countered.

He chuckled deeply. "I stand corrected. What came in?" he asked, nodding toward the books she was carrying.

She handed the bag to him. He looked over the titles, nodding and pulled a check out of his pocket, handing it to her.

"Is it serious?" he asked abruptly.

She just stared at him. "Is what serious?"

"You and the cowboy at the concert. What's his name, Fowler?"

"Harley Fowler. We're friends."

"Just friends?"

"Listen, I've already been asked that question nine times this week. Just because I go out with a man, it doesn't mean I'm ready to have his children."

Something touched his eyes and made them cold. His faintly friendly air went into eclipse. "Thanks for bringing the books out," he said abruptly. He turned and went in the house without another word, closing the door firmly behind him.

Sara went back to her car, dumbfounded. She couldn't imagine what she'd said to make him turn off like a blown lightbulb.

The next day she went to church and then treated herself to a nice lunch at Barbara's Café in town. The ogre's odd behavior had disturbed her. She couldn't understand what she'd said to put that look on his lean face. She was upset because she didn't understand. She wasn't a woman who went around trying to hurt other people, even when they deserved it.

After lunch, on an impulse she drove back to her church, parked her car and walked out into the cemetery. She wanted to see her grandfather's grave and make sure the silk flowers she'd put there for Father's Day—today—were still in place. Sometimes the wind blew them around. She liked talking to him as well; catching him up on all the latest news around town. It would probably look as if she were crazy if anyone overheard her. But she didn't care. If she wanted to think her grandfather could hear her at his grave, that was nobody else's business.

She paused at his headstone and stooped down to remove a weed that was trying to grow just beside the tombstone. Her grandmother was buried beside him, but Sara had never known her. She'd been a very small child when she died.

She patted the tombstone. "Hello, Grandad," she said softly. "I hope you're in a happy place with Granny. I sure do miss you. Especially in the summer. Remember how much fun we had going fishing together? You caught that big bass the last time, and fell in the river trying to get him reeled in." She laughed softly. "You said he was the tastiest fish you'd ever eaten."

She tugged at another weed. "There's this new guy in town. You'd like him. He loves to read and he owns a big ranch. He's sort of like an ogre, though. Very antisocial. He thinks I look like a bag lady…"

She stopped talking when she realized she wasn't alone in the cemetery. Toward the far corner, a familiar figure was tugging weeds away from a tombstone, patting it with his hand. Talking to it. She hadn't even heard him drive up.

Without thinking of the consequences, she went toward him. Here, among the tombstones, there was no thought of causing trouble. It was a place people came to remember, to honor their dead.

She stopped just behind him and read the tombstone. "Ellen Marist Cameron," it said. She would have been nine years old, today.

He felt her there and turned. His eyes were cold, full of pain, full of hurt.

"Your daughter," she guessed softly.

"Killed in a wreck," he replied tonelessly. "She'd gone to the zoo with a girlfriend and her parents. On the way back, a drunk driver crossed the median and t-boned them on the side my daughter was occupying. She died instantly."

"I'm sorry."

He cocked his head. "Why are you here?"

"I come to talk to my grandad," she confessed, avoiding his eyes. "He died recently of a massive coronary. He was all the family I had left."

He nodded slowly. "She—" he indicated the tombstone "—was all the family I had left. My parents are long dead. My wife died of a drug overdose a week after Ellen was killed." He looked out across the crop of tombstones with blank eyes. "My grandfather used to live here. I thought it was a good place to put her, next to him."

So that was the funeral he'd come here to attend. His child. No wonder he was bitter. "What was she like?" she asked.

He looked down at her curiously. "Most people try to avoid the subject. They know it's painful, so they say nothing."

"It hurts more not to talk about them," she said simply. "I miss my grandfather every day. He was my best friend. He taught history at the local college. We went fishing together on weekends."

"She liked to swim," he said, indicating the tombstone. "She was on a swim team at her elementary school. She was a whiz at computers," he added, laughing softly. "I'd be floundering around trying to find a Web site, and she'd make two keystrokes and bring it up on the screen. She was…a child…of great promise." His voice broke.

Without counting the cost, Sara stepped right up against him and put her arms around him. She held on tight.

She felt the shock run through him. He hesitated, but only for a minute. His own arms slid around her. He held her close while the wind blew around them, through the tall trees that lined the country cemetery. It was like being alone in the world. Tony Danzetta was out of sight watching, of course, even if he couldn't be seen. Jared couldn't be out of his sight, even at a time like this.

He let out a long breath, and some of the tension seemed to drain out of him. "I couldn't talk about her. There's a hole in my life so deep that nothing fills it. She was my world, and while she was growing up, I was working myself to death making money. I never had time to go to those swim meets, or take her places on holidays. I wasn't even there last Christmas, because I was working a deal in South America and I had to fly to Argentina to close it. She was supposed to spend Christmas with me. She had Thanksgiving with her mother." He drew in a ragged breath and his arms involuntarily contracted around Sara's slim figure. "She never complained. She was happy with whatever time I could spare for her. I wish I'd done more. I never thought we'd run out of time. Not this soon."

"Nobody is ever ready for death," Sara said, eyes closed

as she listened to the steady, reassuring heartbeat under her ear. "I knew Grandad was getting old, but I didn't want to see it. So I pretended everything was fine. I lost my parents years ago. Grandad and I were the only family left."

She felt him nodding.

"Did she look like you?" she asked.

"She had my coloring. But she had her mother's hair. She wasn't pretty, but she made people feel good just being around her. She thought she was ugly. I was always trying to explain to her that beauty isn't as important as character and personality."

There was a long, quiet, warm silence.

"Why did you decide to live here?" she asked suddenly.

He hesitated. "It was a business decision," he replied, withdrawing into himself. "I thought new surroundings might help."

She pulled back and his arms fell away from her. She felt oddly chilled. "Does it help?"

He searched her eyes quietly. After a minute, the intensity of the look brought a flaming blush to her cheeks and she looked down abruptly.

He laughed softly at her embarrassment. "You're bashful."

"I am not. It's just hot," she protested, putting a little more distance between them. Her heart was racing and she felt oddly hot. That wouldn't do at all. She didn't dare show weakness to the enemy.

"It wasn't an insult," he said after a minute. "There's nothing wrong with being shy." His eyes narrowed. "Who looks after you, if you get sick? Your boss?"

"Dee's wonderful, but she's not responsible for me. I look out for myself." She glanced at him. "How about you?"

He shrugged. "If it looked like I was dying, Tony the Dancer would probably call somebody if he was around—if he wasn't on holiday or having days off. My lawyer might send a doctor out, if it was serious and somebody called."

"But would they take care of you?" she persisted.

"That's not their job."

She drew in a long breath. "I know you don't like me. But maybe we could look out for each other."

His dark eyebrows lifted. "Be each other's family, in other words."

"No ties," she said at once. "We'd just be there if one of us was sick."

He seemed to be seriously considering it. "I had flu and almost died last winter," he said quietly. "It was just after I lost my daughter. If Tony hadn't come back early from Christmas holidays, I guess I'd have died. It went into pneumonia and I was too sick and weak to get help."

"Something like that happened to me this year," she said. "I got sick and I had this horrible pain in my stomach. I stayed in bed for days until I could get up and go back to work. It was probably just the stomach bug that was going around, but I thought, what if it was something serious? I couldn't even get to the phone."

He nodded. "I've had the same thoughts. Okay. Suppose we do that?"

She smiled. "It's not such a bad idea, is it?"

"Not bad at all."

"I would be more amenable to the plan if you'd stop treating me like a bag lady," she added.

"Stop dressing like one," he suggested.

She glowered up at him. "I am not dressed like a bag lady."

"Your socks never match. Your jeans look like they've been worn by a grizzly bear. Your T-shirts all have pictures or writing on them."

"When you're working, you don't look all that tidy

yourself," she countered, not comfortable with telling him the truth about her odd apparel, "and I wouldn't dare ask what you got on your boots to make them smell so bad."

His eyes began to twinkle. "Want to know? It was," and he gave her the vernacular for it so wickedly that she blushed.

"You're a bad man."

He studied her closely. "If you want to be my family, you have to stop saying unkind things to me. Give a dog a bad name," he said suggestively.

"I'd have to work on that," she replied.

He drew in a long breath as he glanced back at the small grave. "Why did you come out here today?"

She smiled sadly. "Today is Father's Day. I put some new silk flowers on Grandad's grave. Sometimes the wind blows them away. I wanted to make sure they were still there."

"I meant to call one of the local florists and get them to come out and put a fresh bouquet on her grave. But I've had some business problems lately," he added without specifying what they were. "I write myself notes about things like that." He smiled wryly. "Then I misplace the notes."

"I do that all the time," she confessed.

He cocked his head, staring at her. "Why can't you wear things that match?" he asked, noting that she had on mismatched earrings.

She grimaced. It was much too early in their ambiguous relationship to tell him the real reason. She lied instead. "I'm always in a hurry. I just put on whatever comes to hand. Around town, people know I do it and nobody makes fun of me." She hesitated. "That's not quite true. When I came here to live with Grandad, some of the local kids made it hard on me."

"Why?"

"Well, my mother wasn't exactly pure as the driven snow," she confessed. "She had affairs with three or four local men, and broke up marriages. The children of those divorces couldn't get to her, but I was handy."

She said it matter-of-factly, without blame. He scowled. "You should sound bitter, shouldn't you?" he queried.

She smiled up at him. "Giving back what you get sounds good, but these days you can end up in jail for fighting at school. I didn't want to cause Grandad any more pain than Mom already had. You see, he was a college professor, very conservative. What she did embarrassed and humiliated him. One of her lovers was his department head at college. She did it deliberately. She hated Grandad."

His eyes narrowed. "Can I ask why?"

That was another question she didn't feel comfortable answering. Her eyes lowered to his tie. "I'm not really sure," she prevaricated.

He knew she was holding something back. Her body language was blatant. He wondered if she realized it.

Another question presented itself. He frowned. "Just how old are you?"

She looked up, grinning. "I'm not telling."

He pursed his lips, considering. "You haven't lost your illusions about life, yet," he mused, noting the odd flicker of her eyelids when he said it. "I'd say you haven't hit your mid-twenties yet, but you're close."

He'd missed it, but she didn't let on. "You're not bad," she lied.

He stuck his hands in the pockets of his slacks and looked at the sky. "No rain yet. Probably none for another week, the meteorologists say," he remarked. "We need it badly."

"I know. We used to have this old guy, Elmer Randall, who worked at the newspaper office helping to run the presses. He was part Comanche. Every time we had a drought, he'd get into his tribal clothes and go out and do ceremonies outside town."

"Did it work?" he asked with real interest.

She laughed. "One time after he did it, we had a flood. It almost always rained. Nobody could figure it out. He said his grandfather had been a powerful shaman and rode with Quanah Parker." She shrugged. "People believe what they want to, but I thought he might really have a gift. Certainly, nobody told him to stop."

"Whatever works," he agreed. He checked his watch. "I'd better get home. I'm expecting a phone call from Japan."

"Do you speak the language?"

He laughed. "I try to. But the company I'm merging with has plenty of translators."

"I'll bet Japan is an interesting place," she said with dreamy eyes. "I've never been to Asia in my whole life."

He looked surprised. "I thought everybody traveled these days."

"We never had the money," she said simply. "Grandad's idea of international travel was to buy Fodor's Guides to the countries that interested him. He spent his spare cash on books, hundreds of books."

"He taught history, you said. What was his period?"

She hesitated as she looked up at his lean, handsome face. Wouldn't it sound too pat and coincidental to tell him the truth?

He frowned. "Well?"

She grimaced. "World War II," she confessed. "The North African theater of war."

His intake of breath was audible. "You didn't mention that when I ordered books on the subject."

"I thought it would sound odd," she said. "I mean, here you were, a total stranger looking for books on that subject, and my grandfather taught it. It seems like some weird coincidence."

"Yes, but they do happen." He moved restlessly. "Did he have autobiographies?"

"Yes, all sorts of first person accounts on both sides of the battle. His favorite subjects were German Field Marshal Erwin Rommel and General George Patton, but he liked the point of view of the 9th Australian Division, as well as British General Bernard Montgomery's memoirs."

"I asked the high school age son of one of my vice presidents which of the generals he liked to read about when he was studying history. He said they hadn't taught him about any individual officers. He didn't even know who Rommel was."

The allusion to vice presidents went right by her. She smiled sheepishly. She'd only graduated from high school two years before, and he didn't know that. "I didn't, either, from high school courses," she confessed. "But Grandad was good for a two-hour lecture on any subject I mentioned."

He pursed his lips, really interested. "Who was the last commander of the British Eighth Army before Montgomery in North Africa?"

She chuckled. "You don't think I know, do you? It was Auchinleck—Sir Claude. He was a big, redheaded man, and his wife was from America."

His eyebrows arched. "You're good. What was Rommel's wife called?"

"Her name was Lucie, but he called her Lu. They had a son, Manfred, who eventually became Lord Mayor of Stuttgart, Germany." She wiggled her eyebrows at him. "Want to know what sort of anti-tank field artillery Rommel used that confounded the British generals? It was the 88 millimeter anti-aircraft gun. He camouflaged them and then lured the British tanks within firing range. They thought it was some sort of super weapon, but they were just regular antiaircraft weapons. One captured officer told Rommel that it wasn't fair to use them against tanks. But it was war."

"It was." He was looking at her in a totally different way than he had before. "Do you ever loan books?"

She frowned. "Well, I never have before. But I might make an exception for you. Grandad would have loved talking with you about North Africa."

"I would have enjoyed it, too." He glanced again at his watch. "Lord, I'm late!"

"I have to get back home, too." She looked down at the tombstone. "I'm sorry about your daughter."

He sobered. "I'm sorry about your grandfather. Holidays are the worst times, aren't they? I stayed drunk for two days last Christmas. It was my first without her."

"I don't drink," she replied. "But my heart wasn't in celebrating. I spent Christmas day at one of the senior citizen homes, reading to a lady who didn't get any company."

He reached out unexpectedly and touched her hair. "I wouldn't have guessed you had so many soft spots. Sara. Isn't it?"

She nodded, thrilled by the faint caress. "Sara Dobbs."

He smiled tenderly. "I'll be in touch."

She smiled back, her eyes twinkling with emotion. "See you."

He drove off in a fancy red sports car like ones she'd seen on televised auto shows. She smiled as she considered his interest in her because of Grandad's favorite subject. First Harley, now the iron cowboy. She felt better than she had in years.

But she wondered if her ogre would still be interested if he found out how young she was. She'd just keep that to herself, she decided, like her past. There was no need for him to know anything about either subject yet. And by the time there was…well, maybe it wouldn't matter anymore.

* * *

On Thursday, when she got home from work, she sorted out Grandad's books, carefully pairing subject matter with time period, in case Jared Cameron wanted to borrow one. She knew her grandfather wouldn't have minded. He enjoyed teaching students about the amazing contradictions of the North African theater, where what many called a "gentleman's war" was fought. Rommel had actually called a truce during one bloody battle and sent his men to help move Allied wounded off the battlefield.

Patton had entered the campaign too late to face off against Rommel, but he had read Rommel's book about the strategy and tactics of World War I. The general was known for his own lightning strike sort of attack; he said that fewer soldiers were lost when battles were won quickly. Both soldiers led from the front, and both were respected by not only their own men, but by the enemy as well.

Her hands touched a book by a missionary who'd worked in Africa and stilled. This had been one of Grandad's favorite biographies, although it had nothing to do with World War II. The author of the book was a physician. He'd gone to Africa, sanctioned as a missionary, and remained there for many years treating natives. The book had inspired Grandad to missionary work, but he'd chosen to become a college educator instead. He'd regretted his decision later in life and had sold the idea wholesale to his daughter's husband.

Sara put the book aside, shoving it into a bookcase with undue savagery. If only he'd realized what the consequences of his fervor for mission work would be…

She stacked the books she was through sorting and got up. Morris was crying to be fed.

As she moved into the kitchen, she felt suddenly nauseous, and that pain in her stomach came back full force. She managed to get the sack of dry cat food and poured some of it into his bowl. Then she sat down and groaned. She was so sick she could barely move. It hurt to move, anyway.

She rested her forehead on her forearm, draped across the scarred little kitchen table where she and Grandad always had meals. She was sweating. It wasn't that hot in the house. She had a window air conditioner, and it was running full tilt.

These sick spells were getting closer together. Could she be having the same virus week after week? she wondered. Or could it be something else?

Her grandmother had suffered from gallbladder disease. She remembered, barely, the old lady being taken to the hospital when Sara was about four years old to have an operation. Doctors had removed it. She recalled that old Mrs. Franklin had complained of terrible pain in her stomach and feeling nauseous.

But gallbladder problems were in the upper right area of the abdomen. This felt like it was dead-center. Could she possibly have an ulcer?

It would pass, she told herself. She'd just sit very still and not move around and it would go away, like it always did.

But it didn't go away. An hour later, it hurt to walk and nausea washed over her unexpectedly. She barely made it to the bathroom in time to lose her breakfast. The pain was horrible. She'd never felt anything like it. She felt feverish as well. Something was wrong. Something bad.

She crawled to the phone in the living room and pulled it down on the floor with her. She pressed in 911.

When the dispatcher answered, she gave her symptoms and then her name and address. The lady told her to stay on the line while she sent the paramedics out.

Sara leaned back against the wall, so sick she couldn't bear the thought of being moved. The pain was in her side, her right side. It was so bad that even the lightest touch of her fingers caused her to jump.

Morris, sensing that something was wrong, came into the living room and rubbed against her, purring. She petted him, but she couldn't let him get into her lap.

Fortunately she hadn't locked up for the night. She'd managed to reach up and turn on the porch light. When the paramedics knocked, she shouted for them to come in.

One of them was a girl she'd gone to high school with, a brunette with short hair who'd been kind to her when other students hadn't been.

"Hi, Lucy," Sara managed as the woman bent over her with a stethoscope.

"Hi, Sara. Where does it hurt?"

Sara showed her. When Lucy pressed her fingers against it, Sara came up off the floor, groaning.

The three paramedics looked at each other.

Lucy put the thermometer into Sara's ear. "A hundred and two," she remarked. "Any nausea?"

"Yes," Sara groaned.

"Okay, we're taking you in to the hospital. What do you need us to do?"

"Get my purse on the sofa and make sure I've turned off everything and then lock the door with the key that's in this side of the dead bolt," she said weakly.

"Will do. Curt, can you check the appliances and turn off the lights?"

"Sure. What about the cat?"

"He can stay here, he's been fed and he has a litter box. I'll get my boss to run out and feed him tomorrow..." She sat back with a sigh. "My goodness, it stopped hurting," she said, smiling at Lucy. "I may not need to go to the hospital..."

"Get her loaded, stat!" Lucy said at once, and moved away

to speak into the microphone on her shoulder so that Sara couldn't hear. She nodded as the reply came back. When she turned, Sara was on her way into the ambulance, arguing all the way. She wouldn't know until hours later that the cessation of pain had been a signal that her appendix had perforated. If she'd argued successfully to stay home, she'd have been dead by morning.

Four

It was all a blur to Sara. She was surprised that they'd prepped her for surgery and had her sign a consent form only minutes after she arrived at the hospital.

Dr. "Copper" Coltrain, the redheaded local surgeon, was already masked and gowned when they wheeled her in.

"Hi, Dr. Coltrain," Sara said, her voice drowsy from the preop meds. "Are you going to carve me up?"

"Only your appendix, Sara," he replied with a chuckle. "You won't even miss it, I promise."

"But it feels fine now."

"I imagine so. That's a very bad sign. It means it's perforated."

"What's that?" she asked, while a capped, gowned and masked woman beside her put something in a syringe into the drip that led down to the needle in her arm.

"It's something to make you comfortable," came the reply. "Count backward from a hundred for me, will you?"

Sara smiled, sleepy. "Sure. One hundred, ninety-nine, ninety-eight, ninety…"

She came to in the recovery room, dazed and completely confused. She wanted to ask them what they'd done to her, but her lips wouldn't work.

A nurse came in and checked her. "Awake, are we?" she asked pleasantly. "Good!"

"Did Dr. Coltrain take out my appendix?"

"Yes, dear," the nurse replied.

Sara closed her eyes again and went back to sleep.

One of the great unsolved mysteries of small town life is how quickly word gets around if someone local is injured or killed. The process seems to consist largely of word of mouth. Someone who works at the hospital is related to someone who owns a small business, and phone traffic increases exponentially. Soon after the incident, it's an open secret.

Exactly how Jared Cameron found out that Sara's appendix had gone ballistic was never known. But he showed up about the time they'd moved Sara into a semi-private room.

Tony Danzetta came with him and stood quietly outside the hospital room while Jared walked into it. The nurse who was making Sara comfortable and checking her vitals did a double take when she saw him and his companion.

"Don't mind Tony," Jared told her. "He goes everywhere with me."

Sara peered at him past the nurse. "Don't worry about it," she told the nurse in a still-drowsy tone. "He's not the only man who carries protection around with him."

The nurse burst out laughing. So did Jared.

Sara closed her eyes and drifted off again.

* * *

The second time she awoke, it was to find Jared lounging in the chair beside her bed. He was wearing working clothes. He looked really good in denim, she considered through a mixture of drugs and pain. He was very handsome. She didn't realize she'd said it out loud until he raised both eyebrows.

"Sorry," she apologized.

He smiled. "How do you feel?"

"I'm not sure how to put it into words." She looked past him at Tony, still standing patiently outside her room. "I seem to have lost my appendix. Do you suppose you could send Tony the Dancer out to look for it?"

"It's long gone by now. You'll improve. While you're improving, I'm taking you home with me."

She blinked. "That will cause gossip."

"It won't matter to your friends and what your enemies think doesn't matter to you. Or it shouldn't."

"Put that way," she agreed, "I guess you're right."

"You can't stay at your house alone, in this condition."

"What about Morris?"

"Tony the Dancer drove over to your house and fed him on his way here," he said carelessly. "He'll look after your cat until you're able to go home."

She was too groggy to wonder how Tony had gotten inside her house. The EMTs had locked it. She moved and grimaced. "I didn't realize that an appendix could kill you."

"It can if it perforates. Those stomach pains you were having were probably a symptom of chronic appendicitis," he said.

"I guess so. I never thought it might be dangerous. How long have you been here?"

"Since they took you in to surgery," he said surprisingly. "Tony and I went out to supper until you were in recovery, then we sat in the waiting room until they put you in a room."

Her eyelids felt heavy. "It was nice of you to come."

"We're each other's family, remember?" he asked, and he didn't smile. "I take responsibilities seriously."

"Thanks," she said weakly.

"Not necessary. Try to go back to sleep. The more rest you get, the faster you'll heal."

She stared at him a little drowsily. "Will you be here, when I wake up?"

"Yes," he said quietly.

She tried to smile, but she wasn't able to get her lips to move. She fell back into the comfortable softness of sleep.

It hurt to move. She tried to turn over, and it felt as if her stomach was going to come apart. She groaned.

The big man who went around with the ogre came and stood over her. He had large dark eyes, and heavy black eyebrows. His dark, wavy hair was in a ponytail. He had an olive complexion. He was frowning.

"Do you need something for pain?" he asked in a voice like rumbling thunder.

Her eyes managed to focus. He looked foreign. But he had that Georgia drawl. Maybe he was of Italian heritage and raised in the South.

He grinned, showing perfect white teeth. "I'm not Italian. I'm Cherokee."

She hadn't realized that she'd spoken her thoughts aloud. The painkilling drugs seemed to be affecting her in odd ways. "You're Mr. Danzetta," she said. "I thought you were a hit man."

He laughed out loud. "I prevent hits," he replied. "I'm Tony. Nobody calls me Mr. Danzetta." The frown was back. "It hurts, huh?"

"It does," she managed weakly.

He touched the call button. A voice came over it. "May I help you?"

"This young lady could use something for pain," he replied.

"I'll be right there."

Minutes later, a nurse came into the room, smiling. "Dr. Coltrain left orders so that you could have something for pain."

"It feels like my body's been cut in half," Sara confessed.

"This will help you feel better," she said, adding something to the drip that was feeding her fluids. "It will be automatic now."

"Thanks," Sara said, grimacing. "I sure never thought losing a tiny little thing like an appendix would hurt so much."

"You were in bad shape when you came in," she replied. She glanced at Tony the Dancer curiously. "Are you a relative?"

"Who, me? No. I work for Mr. Cameron."

The nurse was confused. "Is he related to Miss Dobbs?"

Tony hesitated. "Sort of."

"No, he's not," Sara murmured, smiling. "But Mr. Cameron doesn't have any family left, and neither do I. So we said we'd take care of each other if one of us got sick."

"The boss said that?" Tony asked, his dark eyebrows arching.

The nurse frowned. "How can you be deaf with ears like that?" she wondered.

Tony glared at her. "I am not deaf."

"I should think not," she agreed, paying deliberate attention to his large ears.

"Listen, I may have big ears, but you've got a big mouth," he shot right back.

The pert little brunette gave him a gimlet stare. "The better to bite you with, my dear," she drawled. "You've been warned."

She wiggled her eyebrows at him before she turned back to Sara. "If you need me, just call. I'm on until midnight."

"Thanks," Sara told her.

She winked, gave the bodyguard a glance and waltzed out of the room.

Tony made a rough sound in his throat. "My ears are not big," he muttered.

Sara wouldn't have dared disagree.

He glowered. "People are supposed to be nice to you in hospitals."

"Only when you're sick," Sara told him, smiling. "Thanks, Tony," she said as the pain began to diminish, just a little.

"No problem."

"Where's Mr. Cameron?"

"He had a phone call to return," he said, and looked worried.

"Do you go everywhere with him?"

"Well, not everywhere," he replied. "He gets antsy if I follow him into the restroom."

"I never knew anybody who had a bodyguard," she told him. She moved drowsily. "In fact, I never knew a bodyguard."

"First time for everything," he said, and he smiled.

She smiled back. He'd looked frightening the first time she saw him, standing beside Jared's truck outside the bookstore. But now he was starting to resemble a big teddy bear. She closed her eyes and went to sleep, but not before she heard a soft, deep chuckle. She'd said it aloud.

Jared walked in with a scowl, pausing to stare at Sara, who was fast asleep. "Did they give her something for pain?" he asked Tony.

The big man nodded. He wasn't smiling now. He looked both intelligent and dangerous. "Is something going on?"

Jared looked toward the door, paused to push it shut and

put his cell phone away. "Max thinks they may have tracked me here."

"That isn't good," Tony replied.

"We expected it," Jared reminded him. "We'll have to be extravigilant is all. I told the foreman to put a man with a rifle at the front gate and keep him there, even if he has to have catered meals." He cursed under his breath. "I hate hiding out," he said harshly. "If they'd let me do what I please, we could have handled this on our own, and more efficiently. They're going to protect me to death!"

"Not here," Tony said slowly. "You know they're doing the best they can. Meanwhile, this is the best place to be."

Jared let out a long breath. "It's the waiting."

Tony nodded. He glanced toward the bed. "What about her?" he asked. "She isn't going to be in the line of fire, is she?"

The other man stuck his hands in his pockets and looked stern. "She hasn't got anybody else."

"Yes, but she has no idea what's going on. She could become a target."

Jared glared at him. "Then you'll just have to call in a marker and get some backup, won't you?"

Tony sighed. "I gave up a hot tub and HD TV to come down here."

The glare got worse. "Don't blame me. I was willing to come alone. Your *boss* decided I needed baby-sitting," Jared said irritably.

"My boss was right," Tony replied. He shrugged. "I guess I can live without the hot tub for a few weeks."

Jared put a hand on his shoulder. "Sure you can. You need to reread Sun Tzu."

"I can quote it verbatim," Tony told him. "This isn't my first job."

Jared chuckled. "No. Of course it's not." He stared back at Sara. "We can't let them hurt her."

"We won't," Tony replied. "I promise."

Jared relaxed a little. But just a little.

Sara woke up and it was dark again. She'd slept for a long time. She looked around curiously. She was alone, but there was a cowboy hat occupying the seat beside her bed. It looked familiar.

The door opened, and Harley Fowler walked in, carrying a foam cup of coffee. "You're awake," he exclaimed, smiling.

"Hi, Harley," she replied, returning the smile. "Nice of you to come check up on me."

"I had tonight free."

"No date?" she asked with mock surprise as he moved his hat and sat down.

He chuckled. "Not tonight."

"No exciting missions, either?" she teased, recalling that he'd helped some of the local mercs shut down a drug dealer two years before.

"Interesting that you should mention that," he replied, his eyes twinkling. "We've had word that the drug cartel has re-organized again and been taken over by a new group. We don't know who they are. But there's some buzz that we may have trouble here before long."

"That's not encouraging," she said.

"I know." He sipped coffee. He looked somber. "Two DEA agents bought it on the border this week. Execution-style. Cobb's fuming. My boss is calling in contacts for a confab." His boss was Cy Parks, one of the small town's retired professional soldiers.

Cobb was Alexander Cobb, a senior Houston DEA agent who lived in Jacobsville with his wife and sister.

"Does anybody know who the new people are?"

He shook his head. "We can't find out anything. We think somebody's gone undercover in the organization, but we can't verify it. It's unsettling to have drug dealers who'll pop a cap on cops. They killed a reporter, too, and a member of the Border Patrol."

She whistled softly. "They're arrogant."

He nodded. "Dangerous," he said. "There's something worse. They're kidnapping rich Americans for ransom, to increase their cash flow reserves. They got an heiress last week. Her people are scrambling to meet the deadline, without knowing for sure if they'll return her even so."

She moved restlessly on the pillow. She was sore, but the pain was better. "Aren't most kidnap victims killed in the first twenty-four hours?"

"I don't know, honestly," he said. "Cash Grier is working with the FBI, trying to get informants who might know something about the heiress."

"Our police chief?" she asked

He grinned. "Like a lot of our local citizens, he's not quite what he seems."

"Oh."

He stretched. "Mr. Parks had me working on our tractor all day. I'm stiff. I guess I'm getting old."

She laughed. "No, you aren't, Harley."

He leaned forward with the cup in both hands. "I heard you had a close call," he said.

"I didn't know I had an appendix until yesterday," she said wistfully. "They brought me in by ambulance."

"What about Morris?"

"Mr. Danzetta fed him for me," she said complacently.

"Cameron's bodyguard?" He looked strange.

"What is it?" she asked curiously.

"One of our cowboys was driving past your house last night and saw lights on inside. He knew you were here, so he called the sheriff's department."

"And?"

"When they got there, the lights were off, the doors were all locked and there was nobody around."

She pursed her lips, wondering.

"Did you give the bodyguard a key?" he persisted.

She hesitated. "Well…"

Before she could speak, the door opened and Jared walked in. He stopped when he saw Harley and his eyes began to glitter.

Harley had great reflexes. He exercised them by getting out of the chair, wishing Sara well, promising to check on her later. He walked out with a nod to Cameron. He passed by Tony, who didn't say a word.

"You had company," Jared said quietly.

She wondered what he was thinking. His face gave little away. "Harley came to tell me about my house."

He frowned. "What about your house?"

"He said one of the Parks cowboys saw lights on inside and knew I wasn't there, so he called the sheriff," she began. "But when the deputy got there, all the lights were out and nobody was anywhere around."

He managed to look innocent. "How odd."

He looked too innocent. She frowned. "I didn't give Mr. Danzetta a key to my house, so how did he get in to feed Morris?"

He sat down in the chair beside the bed, looking thoughtful for a minute. "Tony has some, shall we say, unexpected skills."

"Like breaking and entering?" she probed with a grin.

"This is a conversation we shouldn't have right now," he replied with a quiet smile.

Her eyebrows lifted. "Is he wanted by the law?" she asked, keeping her voice low so that Tony wouldn't overhear her.

"Only in two countries," he said absently. "Or was it three?"

She looked shocked.

He scowled at her. "I'm kidding!"

She relaxed. "Okay," she said. "That's a relief."

Outside the door, a tall, dark-eyed man was chuckling silently.

"I talked to Dr. Coltrain," Jared said. "He told me if you're still improving like this, you can be released Monday."

She grimaced. "I'll miss work." Her eyes widened. "Oh, gosh. Dee! I didn't even phone her…!"

"I did," Jared said lazily. "She's coming to see you tonight."

"Thanks," she told him.

"She already knew, of course," he added ruefully. "It's amazing how gossip gets around here."

"We're a very small town," she reminded him.

"You're a very large family," he contradicted. "I've never lived in a place where people knew so much about each other."

She smiled. "I know. I love it here. I can't imagine living anywhere else."

"Well, you'll be living with me for a few days," he replied, crossing his long legs. "My attorney's coming down Monday, so we'll be chaperoned. Less gossip."

"Does your attorney come to stay?"

"Only when I have legal matters to discuss," he said easily. "I've had the same attorney for two years."

She was picturing a tall lawyer like Blake Kemp. Jared must be very well-to-do if he could get a live-in attorney, she was thinking.

"Don't mention anything about Tony feeding your cat, okay?" he asked abruptly. "I don't want the police asking any embarrassing questions. I need Tony."

"Of course I won't," she agreed, but she couldn't help wondering what all the secrecy was about.

"I can't stay long tonight," he said apologetically. "I'm trying to do business by phone, fax and modem, and it's damned hard."

Her eyes were curious. "Where do you live when you're not here?"

He smiled. "That's need-to-know. You don't."

"Well!" she exclaimed. "What a lot of cloak-and-dagger stuff!"

"You have no idea," he replied absently.

The door opened. Tony came in, flipping his phone shut. "Max needs to talk to you again. It's going to take a while."

"We'll go home." He got up, pausing to smile down at Sara. "Get better. I'll be back in the morning."

"Thanks," she said.

He shrugged. "We're family."

He went out with Tony and closed the door behind him.

Max was not happy to learn that Jared was keeping company with some sick girl in the little hick town.

"You need your head read," she muttered on the phone. "You've got enough problems without adding a penniless, clinging cowgirl to them."

"She's not a cowgirl," he replied. "She sells books."

"An egghead isn't much better," she scoffed. "They want you to come back out here and let them give you around-the-clock security."

"We'll never catch the perpetrators if we hide in a fortress," he said. "And we've had this damned argument before!"

"Somebody's getting testy," she purred. "No pillow talk down there, I guess?"

"What do you want?" he interrupted.

She hesitated. "I wanted to tell you that they've tracked three men as far as San Antonio. We're not sure if they're connected to the other, or not, but they're the right nationality."

"What's their cover?"

"How should I know?" she muttered.

"I pay you to know everything," he countered.

"Oh, all right, I'll ask questions. Honestly, Jared, you're getting to be a grouch. What's this girl doing to you?"

"Nothing," he said tersely. "She's just a friend."

"You're spending a lot of time at the hospital."

"Neither of us has family," he said absently. "We decided we'd look after each other if we got sick."

The pause was heated. "You know I'd take care of you if you got sick! I'd have doctors and nurses all over the place."

Of course she would, he thought. She'd hire people to care for him, but she wouldn't do it herself. Max hated illness.

"I'm tired and I've got a lot of work to do."

"I'm flying down there Monday," she told him. "I'll bring some contracts for you to look over. Need anything from the big city?"

"Nothing at all. I'll talk to you later."

"Okay. Sleep well."

"Sure." He hung up. Max was possessive of him. He hadn't noticed it before, and he didn't like it. She was sleek, elegant, aggressive and intelligent. But she did nothing for him physically. He did have occasional liaisons, but never with Max. He hoped she wasn't going to come down to Texas and upset things. He knew that she wasn't going to like Sara. Not at all.

Monday morning, Sara was on the mend. Dee had come twice, on Friday night and Sunday afternoon, bearing baskets of flowers and magazines for Sara to read. She absolutely forbade her to come back to work until the end of the next week. That made Sara feel a little better. She knew Dee was shorthanded when she wasn't there.

Jared had been back to visit, staying for a few minutes at

a time, with Tony always in the background. She wondered why he needed a full-time bodyguard. He changed the subject every time she asked.

Dr. Coltrain released her after lunch. She was wheeled out to the hospital entrance, where Jared was waiting in the big black pickup truck. He bent and lifted her like a sack of flour, putting her gently into the passenger seat and belting her in.

She didn't expect the sudden rush of breath that escaped her lips when he paused in the act of fastening the seat belt and looked straight into her eyes at point-blank range. She felt the world shift ten degrees. His eyes narrowed and dropped to her blouse.

It didn't take an expert to realize that he saw her heartbeat shaking the fabric and knew that she was attracted to him.

"Well, well," he murmured in a deep, sultry tone. And he smiled.

Five

Jared's green eyes burned into Sara's, probing and testing. They dropped to her full mouth and lingered there until she caught her breath audibly. He only chuckled. It had a vaguely predatory sound.

He went around to his own side of the truck, climbed in, fastened his seat belt and started the engine. He was still smiling when he pulled out of the hospital parking lot.

Sara had liked the White Horse Ranch from her first close-up look at it, the first time she'd delivered Jared's books to him. She admired the sprawling white ranch house with its hanging baskets of flowers and the white wooden fences that surrounded a well-manicured pasture. Jared ran purebred Santa Gertrudis cattle here, not horses. Sara enjoyed watching the calves. Pastures were full of them in spring, just in time for the lush new grass to pop up. Or, at least, that would have been the case if the drought hadn't hit this part of Texas so hard.

"How do you have green grass in a drought?" she asked suddenly.

He smiled. "I sank wells and filled up tanks in every pasture," he replied, using the Texas term for small ponds.

"Not bad," she remarked. "Do those windmills pump it?" she added, nodding toward two of them—one near the barn and another far out on the horizon.

He glanced at her amusedly. "Yes. It may be an old-fashioned idea, but it was good enough for the pioneers who settled this country."

"Your grandfather, was he born here?"

He shook his head. "One of his distant cousins inherited a piece of property and left it to him. He ranched for a while, until his health got bad." His face seemed to harden. "He took a hard fall from a bucking horse and hit his head on a fence. He was never quite right afterward. He put a manager in charge of the ranch and moved up to Houston with his wife. One summer day, he shot my grandmother with a double-barreled shotgun and then turned it on himself."

Her gasp was audible.

He noted her surprise. "My father brought him down here to be buried, although nobody knew how he died. None of the family ever came back here after that," he said. "I guess we all have something in the past that haunts us. I shouldn't have been so blunt about it," he added, when he realized that she was upset. "I forget that you grew up in a small town, sheltered from violence."

Obviously he considered her a lightweight, she mused. But it was too soon for some discussions. "It's all right."

He pulled up in front of the house, cut the engine and went around to pick Sara up in his strong arms and carry her up the three wide steps to the front porch. He grinned at her surprise.

"Coltrain's nurse said to keep you off your feet for another day," he mused, looking down into her wide, soft green eyes.

"So you're becoming public transportation?" she teased, and her smile made her whole face radiant.

It made her look beautiful. He was captivated by the feel of her soft, warm little body in his arms, pressed close to his chest. He loved that smile that reminded him of a warm fire in winter. He liked the surge of excitement that ran through his hard body at the proximity. His eyes narrowed and the smile faded as he held her attention.

"Listen, don't you get any odd ideas," she cautioned with breathless humor. "He didn't do that buttonhole surgery, he split me open at least six inches and sewed me back up with those stitches that you don't have to take out later. We wouldn't want my guts to spill out all over your nice clean floor, now, would we?"

The comment, so unexpected, caused him to burst out laughing.

"Good God!" he chuckled. He bent and brushed his hard mouth over her lips in a whisper of sensation that caused her entire body to clench. It was a rush of sensation so overwhelming that she felt her breath catch in her throat.

His eyebrows arched at her response. He pursed his lips and his green eyes twinkled. "What a reaction," he murmured deeply. "And I barely touched you." The twinkle faded. "Suppose we try that again…?"

She started to give him ten good reasons why he shouldn't, but it was already too late.

His hard mouth crushed down onto her soft lips, parting them in a sensuous, insistent way that took her breath away. Her eyes closed helplessly. Her cold hands slid farther around his neck as his arm contracted and flattened her soft breasts against the wall of his chest. The kiss grew demanding.

"Open your mouth," he bit off against her bruised lips.

She tried to answer that audacious command, but it gave him the opening he was looking for, and he took it. His tongue moved deep into her mouth, accompanied by a groan that sounded agonized.

He felt her shiver in his arms. His mouth roughened for an instant until he realized that she was just out of the hospital, and her side hadn't healed. He lifted his head. His eyes were blazing. His face was set, solemn, his gaze intent on her flushed skin.

"Wh…why?" she faltered, all eyes.

An odd expression crept over his face. "When you smile, the emptiness goes away," he said in a rough whisper.

She didn't know how to answer that. But she didn't have to. The door opened suddenly, revealing a tall, very attractive brunette in a blue business suit with a short skirt that stopped halfway between her knees and her panty line.

The brunette raised an eyebrow at the sight of Jared with Sara in his arms, and she didn't smile. "Didn't you expect me, darling?" she asked Jared in a honey-smooth tone.

Jared was still collecting his senses. "Max, this is Sara Dobbs. Sara, Max Carlton, my attorney."

Sara had never seen an attorney who looked like that. The woman could have posed for a fashion magazine. She was sophisticated, beautiful and world-wise. Sara felt like a small child trying to play with adults.

"I have to get Sara to bed. Where's Tony?"

Max shrugged. "I haven't seen him. We have several contracts to go over."

"We'll get to them later," Jared said, with an edge to his tone.

"Suit yourself, it's only money. I like the house."

The lawyer had yet to say one word to Sara. Jared noticed, and his irritation was obvious.

"Sara, you said?" Max asked, smiling at the woman in his arms. "Is something wrong with your leg?"

"She just had an emergency appendectomy and there's nobody at her house to look after her while she heals," Jared said shortly, turning toward one of the downstairs guest bedrooms.

"I see. Well, I'm sure you'll feel better soon," she told Sara as Jared carried her down the hall.

Jared ignored her. He turned into a pretty blue-themed bedroom with its own private bathroom and eased Sara down on the quilted coverlet.

He leaned over her, his big hands on either side of her head, and looked straight into her eyes. "Max is my lawyer. That's all she's ever been."

"She likes you," Sara replied.

His green eyes narrowed. "She likes my money."

"She's pretty."

He bent and brushed his mouth softly over her lips, smiling as they parted for him now. "So are you," he whispered, standing up straight. "I have to sign some contracts for Max. I'll be back in a few minutes. TV control's on the bedside table," he indicated. "We have pay-per-view. Help yourself. I'll have Mrs. Lewis bring you something to eat in a little while."

"Mrs. Lewis? I thought she worked for the Hart brothers."

"She did, but she had to retire just recently from doing heavy housework. Her arthritis got steadily worse and she had to leave them. But her doctor found a new drug that works. She still can't do heavy work, but she cooks for me three days a week."

She studied him curiously. "What do you do the other four days?"

He grinned. "I eat Italian."

"We don't have an Italian restaurant," she began.

"Tony the Dancer can cook," he told her. "He makes the best lasagna I've ever eaten."

She laughed. "He doesn't look like a cook."

"He doesn't look like a lot of things. Amuse yourself until I get Max out of here. I'll be back soon."

"Okay."

He winked at her and closed the door on his way out.

"Are you out of your mind?" Max raged. "The girl's poor! She's just after your money!"

He slid his hands deep into his pockets and glared back at her. "And you discovered that after exchanging two sentences with her, did you?"

Her lips tautened. "You can't get involved with the locals, Jared. You know that, and you know why."

He cocked his head and stared at her intently. "Why are you here?" he asked abruptly. "I can sign contracts at your office in Oklahoma City if I have to. I can't think of a single good reason for you to be underfoot."

Her eyes avoided his. "You're vulnerable right now. You might get involved with someone you'd walk away from if things were normal."

"I pay you a king's ransom of a retainer to look out for my business interests," he said, emphasizing the business. "You start poking your nose into my private life and I'll replace you with a man. After," he added deliberately, "I send a letter of explanation to the Oklahoma Bar Association."

Her anger was gone at once. She pulled herself together. "You're right, I was out of line."

"What contracts are we discussing, then?"

She seemed oddly disoriented. One hand went to her temple and she frowned. "You know, I can't remember."

"Then why don't you go back to your office and think about it?" he suggested.

She sighed. "Okay. But it's still not good sense to trust people you don't know too far," she added.

He didn't reply.

She went into the living room and picked up her attaché case. She laughed self-consciously. "I really just wanted to see how you were," she confessed.

"I'm fine."

"Take care of yourself."

He didn't answer that statement, either. He just stared at her with dark, brooding eyes until she went toward the front door.

"You'll call, if you need anything?" she asked at the door.

"If I need legal advice," he emphasized, "I will."

She grimaced. The door closed firmly behind her.

Jared stared into space as he wondered how he'd missed that possessiveness in Max. Had it been there all along, or was it just starting? She knew he didn't want involvement. He'd said so. Why had she come? Had she been checking up on him and found out about Sara?

He turned toward his study, still deep in thought. She did have a point, about Sara. He knew almost nothing about her.

Tony the Dancer came in with a bag of groceries. He paused at the open study door.

"I met a stretch limo on my way back," he told Jared. "Was it Max?"

He nodded.

"What was she doing here?" he asked.

"God knows," Jared replied curtly. "Warning me off Sara, I guess."

"I thought it would come to that," Tony mused. "Max

likes to live high, and she doesn't make quite enough to suit her tastes."

"Obviously. Her office had better be paying for that limo," he added. "I'm not picking up the tab."

"You should tell Arthur," the other man advised, naming the elderly accountant who lived in and took care of the accounts.

"I will. You cooking?"

"Unless you want to try again," Tony said warily. "I'm still trying to scrape the scrambled eggs off that iron skillet."

"You didn't say I had to grease it first," he growled.

Tony just shook his head. "How's the kid?" he asked, nodding toward the hall.

"She's a grown woman," Jared countered. "She's fine."

Grown woman? Tony wondered if his employer really thought that innocent in his spare bed was fair game. She put on a good front with Jared, but Tony could see through the camouflage, and he knew things that his boss didn't. He wondered if he should mention what he knew to the other man, but the phone rang and Jared picked up the receiver. Tony thought it must be fate, and he went off into the kitchen to cook.

Sara fussed when Mrs. Lewis had to come all that way to serve her a bowl of soup and a salad.

"I can walk, honestly," she protested gently. "You don't have to wait on me."

Mrs. Lewis just grinned as she slid the tray onto Sara's lap. "It isn't any trouble, dear. Tony will pick this up. I have to get back home. My sister's coming over to visit." She chuckled. "Tony's making supper for you and the boss tonight. He walked in with enough Italian sausage and tomato sauce to float a battleship."

Now Sara remembered that Tony cooked Italian dishes for

his boss. The big man didn't look like anybody's idea of a chef. She said as much to the older woman.

Mrs. Lewis raised an eyebrow. "Mr. Danzetta is in a class of his own as a cook. I can do basic meals, but he has a flair for improvising. He saved me a plate of spaghetti just after I came to work here. It was the best I ever tasted."

"I never thought of a bodyguard as being a cook," Sara commented.

The older woman glanced at the open door and moved a little closer. "He wears an automatic pistol under his jacket," she said softly. "I watched out the kitchen window while he was practicing with it. He stuck pennies in clothespins and strung the clothespins on an old wire that was used for a clothesline years ago. And in a heartbeat," she added, "he'd picked off the pennies without touching the clothespins."

Sara's eyes grew wide. "I'm going to make sure that I never tick him off," she murmured aloud.

"He's pretty handy with martial arts, too," Mrs. Lewis added. "He spars with Mr. Cameron."

She hesitated with the soup halfway to her mouth in a spoon. "Mr. Cameron does martial arts?"

Mrs. Lewis nodded. "Tony said he'd never met a man he couldn't throw until he started working here."

"And here I thought Mr. Cameron hired Tony because he didn't want to get his hands dirty."

"Tony isn't quite what he seems," the older woman said quietly. "And neither is his boss. They're both very secretive. And they know Cy Parks and Eb Scott."

That was interesting, because Cy and Eb were part of a group of professional soldiers who'd fought all over the world. Several of the old group lived either in Jacobs County or in Houston and San Antonio.

"Well, that sounds very mysterious, doesn't it?" Sara

murmured as she sipped the hot liquid. "This is wonderful soup, Mrs. Lewis. I can't make potato soup, but I love to eat it."

The older woman beamed. "I'm glad you like it."

Sara paused, thinking. "Mr. Cameron was in a huddle with Chief Grier at the symphony concert," she recalled. "They looked very solemn."

"Gossip says that a new group is trying to establish a drug smuggling network through here again."

"That might explain the serious faces," Sara replied. "Our police chief has solved a lot of drug cases, and made a lot of enemies to go with them."

"Good for him," Mrs. Lewis responded. "I hope they lock them all up."

Sara grinned. "Me, too." She shifted and groaned, touching her stomach under the floppy blouse she was wearing with jeans. "How can a little thing like an appendix cause so much trouble?" she wondered.

"You're lucky you were able to get to a phone," the older woman said gently. "People have died of appendicitis."

Sara nodded. She looked around the pretty blue room. "Mr. Cameron and I agreed that we'd be each others' families when we got sick, but I never expected to take him up on the offer this soon."

"He's a surprising person, isn't he?" she asked. "He seems so cold and distant when you meet him. But he's not like that at all when you get to know him. You wouldn't believe what he did to Mr. Danzetta…"

"And you can stop right there while you still have work," Jared said from the doorway. He sounded stern, but his eyes were twinkling.

Mrs. Lewis made a face at him. "I was only humanizing you for Sara, so she wouldn't think you were really an ogre…" She stopped and clapped a hand over her mouth and blushed.

"It's all right," Sara assured her between mouthfuls of soup. "I did used to call him an ogre, but he improves on closer acquaintance." She grinned at Jared.

He pursed his lips and looked pointedly at her mouth. She almost dropped her spoon, and he laughed softly.

"Well, if you don't need me for anything else, I'm going home," Mrs. Lewis told him. "Mr. Danzetta's got stuff to make supper."

"I saw the sack full of tomatoes and tomato sauce," Jared replied. "He's planted tomatoes out behind the house in what used to be a kitchen garden. Tomatoes, oregano, chives, sage and about twenty other spices I never heard of."

"He doesn't look like a gardener," Sara commented.

Jared didn't answer her. She didn't need to know about Tony just yet.

"He planted poppies in the flower garden," Mrs. Lewis said with obvious concern.

"He likes flowers," Jared began.

"You don't understand," Mrs. Lewis persisted. "He didn't plant California poppies. He planted the other kind."

He frowned. "What's your point?"

"We're barely inside the city limits," she said, "but the fact is, we are inside them. When they begin to bloom, Chief Grier will send one of his officers out here to pull them up."

Jared didn't mention that he'd like to see anyone do that with Tony watching. "Why?"

"They're opium poppies," Mrs. Lewis emphasized.

He whistled. "I'll bet Tony didn't realize it."

"Better tell him," Mrs. Lewis replied. "Before he gets in trouble with the law."

He was going to say that it was way too late for that, but he didn't dare. "I'll talk to him," he said.

"I'll see you tomorrow, then. Get better, dear," Mrs. Lewis added with a smile for Sara.

"I heal fast," Sara replied, grinning. "Thanks."

Jared went out to make some phone calls and Sara finished her soup and dozed off. When she opened her eyes again, it was getting dark outside. She hadn't thought about night-clothes, but it was obvious now that she'd arrived with only her purse and the clothes she'd had on when they transported her to the hospital. She didn't have anything to sleep in.

There was a wonderful smell of spices drifting down the hall. Seconds later, Tony stuck his head in the door.

"You like spaghetti?" he asked.

"I love it," she replied, smiling.

He smiled back. "I'm just about to take up the pasta," he said. "It fell off the wall when I threw it there, so it's got about two minutes left before it's al dente."

"Al who?" she asked.

He glowered at her. "Al dente," he repeated. "Just right for the teeth. When you throw it at the wall and it sticks, it's just right to…"

"What the hell have you done to my kitchen wall?" came a roar from down the hall.

"I have to check that the pasta's ready!" Tony called to him.

Jared stomped down the hall, glaring at his bodyguard. "You've got streaks all over the damned paint!"

"They wipe off, boss," Tony assured him. "Honest."

"You couldn't just stick a strand of it in your mouth and chew it to see if it's ready?" Jared grumbled.

Tony's eyebrows arched. "Who bit you?" he asked.

Jared's face was like iron. He looked furious. "The bread's burning."

Tony rushed back down the hall without another word.

Jared glared at Sara. "Harley Fowler's in the living room. He stopped by to see about you."

"That's nice of him."

"Nice." His green eyes were glaring. "I don't have time to run a hospital complete with visiting hours," he muttered.

She flushed with embarrassment. She hadn't expected Harley to come looking for her.

Jared backstepped at her expression. She'd just had surgery and he was acting like a jealous boyfriend. He caught himself and tried to relax. It didn't work. Harley was poaching on his preserves. "I'll send him in. Don't encourage him to stay long or drop in unexpectedly again without calling first."

"I won't," she began, but he was already halfway down the hall before she got the words out. She felt terrible. She was imposing on him. She should never have suggested that they take care of each other when they got sick. It was apparent that Jared already regretted agreeing to it.

Harley didn't look much better than Sara did. His lips were compressed and he was carrying his wide-brimmed Western straw hat.

"How're you doing?" he asked.

She sighed. "I'm feeling much better," she said.

"You don't look it. Why don't I phone Lisa and see if you can stay with her and Cy until you're back on your feet?" he suggested.

"I really don't need looking after," she replied. She felt uneasy. "Harley, do you think you could drive me to my house?" she added in a low voice.

He scowled. "You're not well enough to look after yourself, Sara. You won't even be able to lift a gallon of milk until that incision heals."

"I don't drink milk and I want to go home." She pulled herself off the bed, grimacing because it hurt. Jared had her pain capsules, but she'd be damned if she was going to ask him for them. It was clear that he didn't want her here.

She moved to the foot of the bed. She'd forgotten that Jared had carried her down the hall. Walking it was going to be an ordeal, and she didn't dare ask Harley to carry her, although she knew he would if she asked.

Harley's arm shot out and caught her as she began to weave. "Here, you're not able to do this, Sara," he said firmly.

"What the hell are you doing?"

Jared walked right around Harley, picked Sara up and put her back in the bed. "Stay there," he said shortly.

She flushed again. "I will not! I just asked Harley to drive me home."

Jared felt his height decrease. "You're not able to stay by yourself yet."

"I am so," she retorted.

Jared glared at Harley as if the whole thing was his fault.

"You'll take her out of this house over my dead body," Jared told the younger man. He said it very softly, but it was a threat. Harley had seen eyes like that over the barrel of a gun. The hair on the back of his neck stood up.

"I'm in the way here," Sara interrupted, sitting up. She winced and held her incision with her fingertips. "I've got frozen TV dinners and I need to get back and take care of Morris, anyway!"

"I fed the cat today," Tony the Dancer said from the doorway. He was wearing a huge white apron and holding a slotted spoon. He frowned. "Something wrong here?" he queried when he tallied up the taut faces.

"She's trying to escape," Jared muttered.

"Hey, don't you listen to him," Tony said firmly, pointing the spoon at Jared. "It was only the one time I dropped baking soda in the sauce by accident. This sauce is perfect. You don't need to run away on account of my cooking."

"You cook?" Harley exclaimed, looking at the tall, muscular man with the olive complexion and wavy black hair in a ponytail. He looked as dangerous as Jared Cameron. And Harley had reason to know what dangerous men looked like.

Tony glared at him. "Yeah. I cook. What's it to you?"

Harley actually moved back a step. "Nothing at all!"

"Lots of men cook," Tony said belligerently. He glanced back at Sara and frowned. She was near tears and she wouldn't look at Jared. Tony's threatening expression melted into concern. He moved to the side of the bed. "I made you a nice apple strudel for dessert," he coaxed, "with freshly whipped cream."

She bit her lower lip. "You're so nice, Tony," she said, trying to sound normal even as her lower lip quivered.

"Here, hold this." Tony put the spoon in Jared's hand and sat down beside Sara, tugging her gently against him so that he wouldn't hurt her. A hand the size of a ham rested against her back, covering almost half of it comfortingly as he drew her head to his broad shoulder. "Now, now, it's all right," he said softly.

She bawled. Jared and Harley glared daggers at the big man, but neither of them said a word.

Harley shifted on his feet. "Sara, I've got to get back home. You call me if you need anything, okay?" he added with a speaking glance at Jared.

"I will," Sara said in a thin, sad voice. "Thanks."

"No problem. See you."

He hated leaving her, but the whole situation was getting out of hand. That big fellow who cooked wasn't going to let Jared Cameron hurt Sara in any way. Harley knew she'd be safe, or he wouldn't have budged.

Jared walked out of the room behind him, totally disgusted, still carrying the spoon.

Six

Tony tugged a tissue from the box on the bedside table and dabbed it against Sara's wet eyes.

"Now you stop that," he said, smiling gently. "The boss has a nasty temper and he doesn't always choose his words before he opens his mouth. But he never would have asked you to come here if he hadn't wanted to."

She looked up at him from swollen red eyes. "He was awful to Harley."

Tony grimaced. "There's stuff going on that you don't know about," he said after a minute. "I can't tell you what it is. But it doesn't help his temper."

She blew her nose. "I'm sorry."

"What for? Everybody cries," he replied. "I bawled like a kid when my sister died."

Her green eyes met his black ones. "Was it very long ago?"

"Ten years," he said. "Our mother was still alive then. We lost our dad when we were just little kids."

"I lost my grandad a little while ago," she replied. "I still miss him. He taught history at our local college."

"I like history," he said. He would have liked to tell her that he'd minored in it during his college years, but it wasn't the time for heart-to-heart talks. The boss was already gunning for him because he'd opened the door and let Harley inside.

"How long have you worked for Jared?" she asked.

"Seems like forever, sometimes," he chuckled. "On and off, for about six years, I suppose," he said.

"You know, he really doesn't look like the sort of man who'd need a bodyguard," she ventured.

"He doesn't, does he?" he agreed. "You feel better now?"

She smiled at him with her eyes still red and swollen. "I'm better. Thanks, Tony."

He stood up, and he was smiling now, too. "You're a lot like her. My sister, I mean. She had a big heart. She loved people. She was always giving." His dark eyes grew haunted, especially when he looked at Sara. "Don't you let him push you into anything," he said out of the blue.

She was shocked, and showed it. "What do you mean?"

His black eyes narrowed. "You know what I mean. He's been around the world. You're just a sprout."

"Yes, but I can take care of myself," she assured him. "Nobody will make me do something I don't want to do."

"That's just what my sister said," he told her, and he looked down at his apron. "I'd better get back in there and rescue my sauce. You need anything?"

She shook her head. "But, thanks."

He grinned. "Goes with the job."

If she could have walked, she'd have gone home. She was hurt by Jared's sarcasm and she felt unwelcome. It was going to be an ordeal to get through the next couple of days. She wished she'd never become friendly with him. One thing was for sure. If she ever got sick or hurt again, she wouldn't turn to him for help.

He walked in a short time later with a plate of spaghetti and homemade garlic bread. He pulled a rolling table to the bed and put the meal, plus a tall glass of milk, on it.

She was rigid with wounded pride. "Thank you," she said stiffly, and in a subdued tone that betrayed, even more than her posture, how hurt she was.

He stood still, his hands in his pockets, and stared at her. "He's a good cook," he said, just to break the silence.

She put the napkin on her lap and sat sideways on the bed so that she could eat comfortably. It put him at an angle so that she didn't have to look right at him.

"All right, I was out of line," he muttered. "But it's courteous to ask me before you invite people here to see you."

"I didn't invite Harley to come," she said, eating spaghetti in tiny little bites.

He frowned. "You didn't?"

She ate another bite of Tony's delicious concoction, and never tasted a thing.

"People who live in small towns think of everyone as family. It would never occur to Harley that he wasn't welcome to visit a sick friend, no matter who she was staying with."

His eyes kindled. "It's still good manners to ask first."

"Yes," she had to agree. "It is. I'm sure he wishes he had. I know I do."

That was right on target. He felt smaller than ever. She could have died. He'd agreed to take her home and nurse her, and now he was laying down rules and regulations as fast as he could. He didn't like Harley Fowler in his home, in Sara's temporary bedroom. It made him angry. He couldn't tell her that, of course.

He noticed suddenly that she was wearing the same clothes she'd worn to the hospital before her surgery.

"Don't you have a gown, or pajamas?" he asked abruptly.

"There really wasn't time to pack a bag when the ambulance got to my house," she reminded him.

"Point taken."

"If Tony could go by my house and get me some night things," she began.

"No." It came out belligerently. He shouldn't have said that. But he didn't like the idea of Tony, who already treated her like family, poking through her underthings.

"I'll go," he said. "Where's your house key?"

"It's in the zippered compartment in my purse." She indicated it, hanging over the closet doorknob. "Can you make sure Morris has enough water while you're there?" she added, hating even to have to ask. "Tony fed him already, he said, but Morris drinks a lot of water."

He retrieved the key. "I'll take care of him."

"Thanks," she said without meeting his eyes.

He gave her one last look and left her. He'd made a stupid mistake. He hoped he'd have time to make it up to her.

Tony was just clearing away supper when Jared stopped in the kitchen doorway. "I'm going over to Sara's house to get her a few things to wear."

Tony's eyebrows arched. "You know where she lives?"

He cursed mentally. Of course he didn't know where she lived; he'd never been to her house.

"And you can't go alone," the big man added solemnly. "They'd love to catch you out alone at night. They have all the equipment we've got, and more." He took off the apron and tossed it aside. "I'm going with you."

"That will leave Sara here alone," Jared argued.

Tony pointed a device down the hall and locks slid into place audibly. "She wouldn't be any safer in Fort Knox with the alarm systems activated," Tony told his boss. "Besides, I've got Clayton out there with night vision and a Glock."

He relaxed a little. "Okay. Let's go."

Tony paused by the closet on the way out and retrieved his .45 in its shoulder holster. He took just seconds to get it in place before he opened the front door and shepherded his boss out to the truck parked in the circular driveway.

Before they got into it, Tony waved his hand and a tall, shadowy figure approached the car, going over it with electronic devices.

"All clear," the newcomer said.

"Nobody gets in or out while we're gone," Tony told him.

"Yes, sir."

Tony climbed in behind the wheel, letting Jared ride shotgun. The shadowy figure moved back into the darkness beside the house and settled in.

While Jared was gone, the phone started ringing off the hook. Sara waited for Tony to answer it, but he didn't. There didn't seem to be an answering machine, either. She didn't know what to do. The stupid instrument wouldn't stop. Finally, in desperation, she picked up the receiver by her bed.

"Cameron residence," she said, trying to sound like a secretary.

"Where's Jared?" came a biting reply.

Sara didn't have to ask who it was. That strident tone was unforgettable. "I don't know," she said. "Sorry," she added quickly.

There was a pause. "It's the little house guest, isn't it?" the horrible woman purred. "Well, don't get too comfortable. Jared wouldn't give you the time of day if you hadn't appealed to his senses, but it won't last. He has women like some men have cars, and he doesn't want anything permanent. He'll dump you the first time you sleep with him."

"I do not sleep with men!" Sara retorted harshly.

"You don't?" She laughed. "That's what his last lover said, too. She gave in just like all the rest. And he dumped her just as fast."

"What do you want?" Sara asked, trying to be polite when she felt like screaming at the woman.

"What we all want, dear," the other woman laughed. "To have Jared for keeps. But that won't happen. If he wasn't so financially secure, he might be less attractive," she added.

"I know very little about Mr. Cameron," Sara said stiffly. "And I don't think you should talk about him that way. You're supposed to be his lawyer."

"His lawyer, his lover, it's all the same," came the bored reply. "Tell him I called."

She hung up.

Sara felt sick at her stomach. Surely the horrible woman wasn't right? Jared didn't seem like a heartless seducer. But what did she really know about him? Next to nothing. Could he be a ladykiller? Sara felt insecure. She was still very young. She hadn't dated very much and she'd never had to extricate herself from a dangerously intimate situation. She knew instinctively that Jared was experienced. She'd given in to his hard kisses at once. What if he really put on the pressure? Could she save herself in time?

The thought worried her.

She was still gnawing on it when Jared opened the door and came into her bedroom with a large laundry hamper.

Her eyebrows arched. "You brought my dirty clothes back with you?" she exclaimed, aghast.

He glowered at her. "Tony's got your clothes. I brought your cat."

Her heart skipped. He had to be kidding! She sat up on the side of the bed and looked down into the basket. There was old Morris, curled up asleep and purring for all he was worth, on one of her old hand-crocheted afghans.

She looked up at Jared curiously.

"He didn't touch his supper last night. He wouldn't eat today, either. Tony thinks he's worried about you. So we brought him home with us." Gently he lifted the battle-scarred old marmalade tomcat out of the basket and placed him on the bed with Sara.

Morris opened one green eye, butted his head against Sara affectionately, and went right back to sleep.

"Tony's bringing the litter box. We can put it in your bathroom," Jared said disgustedly.

She cuddled Morris while he was in the mood. "He didn't try to bite you…? Oh!"

He displayed a hand liberally covered with colorful plastic bandages.

"I'm really sorry," she began.

"I had an old hunting dog I was fond of," he said gruffly. "He died last month at the age of fourteen years." He shrugged. "They're like family."

She managed a tiny smile. "Yes."

He heard Tony coming down the hall. "I hope we got the right things."

Tony came in grinning and put down a suitcase on the chest at the foot of Sara's bed. "Here's your stuff. I'll bring the litter box when I come back. He's nice, your cat."

"Well, of course you'd think he was nice," Jared muttered. "He didn't sink his fangs into you!"

"He's got good taste," Tony defended himself.

"Good taste the devil, he knows that you've eaten cats!" Jared shot back. "He was probably afraid you'd serve him up for lunch if he bit you!"

Tony, noting Sara's expression, scowled. "It was only one cat," he pointed out. "And we were all starving. It was a very old and very tough cat. Nobody liked it," he added, trying to hit the right note.

Sara was all eyes. "Where were you?" she asked, aghast.

"Somewhere in Malaysia," Tony said easily. "Mostly we ate snakes, but sometimes you got no choice, especially when the snakes can outrun you." He noted Sara's expression and stopped while he was ahead. "I'll just go get that litter box."

"You'd never be able to eat a snake he cooked," Jared muttered when Tony was in the hall. "He can't make anything if it doesn't go well with tomato sauce."

"I heard that!" Tony called back. "And snakes go great with tomato sauce!"

Sara smiled despite the rough time Jared had given her. He and Tony were a great act together. But she sensed undercurrents. And she thought both men were wearing masks, figuratively speaking. She wondered what they hid.

She finished her dinner and Jared still hadn't said another word.

"This was very nice," she said when she finished her last sip of milk and was pushing the rolling cart away from the bed. "Thanks." She eased back onto the bed, grimacing as the stitches pulled, and drew old Morris close to her. "He doesn't move much these days," she said as she stroked the purring old tomcat. "I've never been sure how old he is. I don't think I want to know." She looked up at Jared. "I would have told you that he doesn't like being picked up, if I'd known you planned to bring him over here."

"Well, the minute Tony picked him up he started purring."

She hid a smile. "I'll bet animals follow Tony around."

He thought of a few women he and Tony had come across in their travels. "It isn't just animals," he said thoughtfully.

She stroked Morris again. "Your lawyer called."

He hesitated. "Max?"

She nodded.

"What did she want?"

She was weighing honesty against peace on earth. Peace on earth won. "She just wanted to tell you something. She said she'd call back."

He frowned. "Was that all she said?" he asked with visible suspicion. "No comments about your presence here?"

The blush gave her away.

"I thought so," he said. "She's good at what she does, but she bores easily and she likes new experiences. She can't resist setting her cap at every presentable male client who comes along. She's already gone through three husbands and several lovers."

Including you? she wondered, but she didn't dare say it out loud.

He watched her stroking the cat and it reminded him, for some reason, of his grandmother. "My father's mother loved cats," he recalled. "She had six at one time. Then they began to get old and pass on. The last one she had was a yellow tabby, sort of like Morris. When she died, he stopped eating. We tried everything. Nothing worked. He settled down in the sun without moving and died three days later."

"And they say animals don't feel emotion," she murmured absently.

"Everything feels. Even plants."

She looked up, grinning. "Did you see that show where they put plants in little greenhouses…"

"…They yelled and praised one group, ignored another

group and played classical and rock music to two other groups," he continued, his green eyes twinkling.

"And the plants that grew biggest were the ones bombarded with hard rock."

He chuckled. "If I thought that would work on hay, I'd have loudspeakers set up in the fields." He shook his head. 'First we had drought for a year in Oklahoma, now we're having floods. The weather is no friend to the rancher this year, either."

"Our dry fields could sure use some of your floods," she agreed.

The conversation ended. He was tired and half out of humor. She was getting over surgery.

"You need your rest," he said.

"Thanks," she called after him. "For bringing Morris."

"What's a little blood between friends?" he mused, holding up his scratched hand. "Sleep well."

"You, too."

But she didn't sleep well. She had violent dreams, just as she had as a child. There was something about this house, this atmosphere, that reminded her of all she'd lost. Guns shooting. Men yelling. Fires burning. The plane almost crashing. And then her mother's fury at Grandad, her accusations, her sudden bizarre behavior. The anger and rage in her mother never abated. Sara was left with nobody except Grandad to look after her. Her mother had destroyed herself, in the end. It had started out as a grand adventure with a noble purpose. It ended in bloodshed and death.

Sara pulled Morris closer to her in the big bed, wiping angrily at the tears. She hated going to sleep. She wondered if there would ever be a night when she'd sleep until morning and there would be no more bad dreams.

She touched her head where the faint indentation marked

the most tragic part of her young life. It was under her thick blond hair, and it didn't show. But Sara felt it there. It was a constant reminder of how brief life was, and how dangerous. She thought about it when she looked at Tony Danzetta, but she couldn't understand why.

Finally, just before dawn she drifted off again. When she woke, late in the morning, it was to the realization that she was still wearing her jeans and the blouse. She'd been too preoccupied even to change into a nightgown.

She stayed with Jared for two more days. He seemed to be avoiding her. He didn't have breakfast, lunch or dinner at the table. He was always in his study or out with the cowboys on the ranch. Tony assured her that it was his normal routine, but something in the way Tony said it made her uneasy.

The fourth day after her surgery, she packed up Morris and her suitcase and asked Jared to let Tony take her home. She wasn't completely over the surgery, but she was getting around very well. There was some residual soreness, but she was already feeling better.

Jared didn't hesitate when she asked to go. It wounded her that he could let her walk away without a qualm. But, then, he was a financially secure man, from all appearances, and she was a poor woman. They'd agreed only to be each other's support in times of need, not to make the care permanent.

Sara and Morris settled back into their routine, and she went back to work.

"At least you look a little better," Dee commented, noting the dark circles under Sara's eyes. "I'll bet you didn't sleep a lot at Mr. Cameron's place."

"It was sort of awkward," she admitted. "But I saw a lot more of Tony than I did of Mr. Cameron," she added.

"Tony?"

"The big guy."

"Oh," Dee recalled. "The hit man."

Sara chuckled. "He improves on closer acquaintance," she told her boss. "And Morris let Tony pick him up. He bit Mr. Cameron. Several times." It felt good, remembering that.

"I suppose Morris is a pretty good judge of character, then," Dee said with a grin.

"Now, now," Sara chided. "Mr. Cameron took good care of me while I was getting back on my feet."

Dee grimaced. "I could have taken you home with me," she began guiltily.

"Dee, you have four kids and your mother lives with you and your husband," Sara replied gently. "You couldn't possibly take care of one more person. But thank you for offering. I'm just grateful that I still have a job."

"As if I'd fire you for being sick," the older woman scoffed. "Now don't you do any heavy lifting. I'll do that. You just sit there at the counter and ring up purchases."

"I can do that, at least," Sara replied cheerfully.

It was just before closing time when Harley Fowler turned up. Dee had gone to the bank with the day's receipts while Sara waited for her to come back and lock up.

"Hi, Harley," Sara greeted.

He smiled. "You look lots better," he said. He grimaced. "I know I got you in trouble with Cameron by just walking in to see you. I'm really sorry."

She was stunned. "How did you find out about that?"

"Mrs. Lewis is kin to one of our cowboys. She heard Tony talking about it. I never thought Mr. Cameron would mind. I guess I should have asked first."

"He's an outsider, Harley," she said gently. "He doesn't

know how people behave in small towns. Nobody else would have had a problem."

"I sort of wondered…" he began, and then stopped.

"Wondered?" she prompted.

"If Mr. Cameron might be jealous," he said.

She laughed. "Oh, that would be the day," she chuckled. "A big time rancher jealous of a piddly little clerk in a bookstore. He's got this gorgeous attorney, named Max," she added, trying to sound lighthearted. "She's educated and beautiful and crazy about him."

Harley sighed. "It must be nice to have a little money. I wouldn't know." He leaned on the counter with his forearms. "The Parks are having a barbecue at the ranch Saturday. Lisa said you might want to sketch the pups one more time before they're old enough to adopt. She says they're growing like weeds."

"A barbecue?" she echoed, smiling. "I love barbecue."

"I know," he returned, grinning. "Suppose I come and pick you up about eleven Saturday morning? I know you're still sore and all. I can drive you home whenever you need to go."

"I'd love to go, Harley," she said with genuine affection.

He smiled. She wasn't beautiful, but he liked being with her. "That's a date, then."

"Will there be dancing?" she asked.

"Oh, yes. They hired a Mariachi band to play. I understand there's going to be a major competition between the Caldwells and Cash Grier and his wife. A tango."

"Wow," Sara breathed. "Matt and Leslie were our champions hands down until Cash Grier got out on the dance floor with Christabel Gaines—I mean, Christabel Dunn, but that was before she married Judd. Can Tippy Grier do a tango?"

"Apparently. It's going to be a night to remember." He hesitated. "Your adopted family's invited, too."

"Mr. Cameron?" she asked warily.

"Yes, and the hit man, too."

"Tony is not a hit man," she said, laughing when she realized that it was her own description of him that was making the rounds in town. "I shouldn't have said that."

"He does sort of remind me of a hit man," he replied dryly. "He's big and slow-looking, though. He can't be that good a bodyguard."

Sara had doubts about how slow-moving Tony was. She had the distinct impression that he was quick as lightning and sly like a fox, hiding his light under a barrel. But she didn't say so.

"Saturday at eleven," he repeated.

"Yes." She grinned at him as he waved and went out the door.

Sara pictured the band and Jared Cameron. She wondered if he'd ask her to dance. She wondered if he could dance. It was thrilling to consider.

Harley came for her exactly at eleven. She was wearing a full skirt with a simple white cotton peasant blouse and silver jewelry. She looked like a pixie.

He was in jeans and a clean plaid cotton shirt, Western cut, with polished black boots and a cowboy hat to match.

"You look nice, Sara," he told her. "Are you feeling okay?"

She nodded. "The stitches catch a little when I walk too fast, but I feel fine."

"Can you climb up by yourself?" he added when they reached his pickup truck. It had a running board, but it was higher than a car.

"Sure, I can," she said. She held on to the inside handle over the door facing, put one foot on the running board and pulled herself up and into the passenger seat. It hurt a little, but she didn't let that show. "Piece of cake," she told him, smiling while she fastened her seat belt.

He grinned back. "Then we're off!"

* * *

Cy Parks's ranch was huge, even by Texas standards. The yard was full of tent pavilions complete with oilcloth-covered long tables and benches for people to sit on. The cowboys had barbecued a steer and their wives had prepared huge tubs of baked beans and coleslaw, and there were baking sheets full of homemade rolls and fresh butter. For dessert, there was everything from cakes to pies to soft-serve ice cream. Cy had really pulled out the stops. Across the fences, his Santa Gertrudis cattle grazed peacefully and stared at the crowds of people who'd come to enjoy the food.

All the powerful people in the county had shown up for Parks's legendary barbecue. Even the children were invited. It resembled, more than anything, a family reunion.

"Is that the Coltrains' little boy, Joshua?" Sara exclaimed, indicating a blond-headed little boy in jeans and cotton shirt and boots running from another small boy with dark hair and eyes.

"Yes, and that's J.D. and Fay Langley's little boy, Jon, chasing him."

"They've grown so fast!" she exclaimed.

"They have," he added, smiling at their antics. "Children must be a lot of fun. Their parents seem to dote on them."

"I imagine they do."

She was staring after the little boys when she spotted a familiar face. Jared Cameron was standing by one of the long tables talking to Cy Parks. With him were Tony the Dancer…and the female attorney, Max, standing with Jared's arm around her.

Sara felt as if she'd just walked into a nightmare.

Seven

At the same time Sara spotted him, Jared glanced her way and saw her with Harley Fowler. His green eyes, even at the distance, were blazing.

She averted her eyes and kept walking with Harley to where Lisa was sitting with Gil on her lap. She didn't dare look the way she felt. Jared Cameron had every right to hang out with his gorgeous attorney. It shouldn't have made Sara feel betrayed. But it did. The realization shocked her.

Lisa smiled as they joined her. "Have a seat. I could have left Gil in his playpen, but I don't really like being away from him, even for a few minutes."

"I wouldn't, either," Sara said. "He's a little doll."

Gil smiled at Sara shyly and said, "Pretty."

Sara and Lisa burst out laughing.

"Horsey, Mama, horsey!" Gil demanded, bouncing.

Lisa put him on one knee and bounced him while he laughed happily.

"He's going to be a ladies' man when he grows up," Harley drawled. "He's starting early!"

Lisa laughed. "You may be right. He likes Sara."

"Everybody likes Sara," Harley said smoothly, winking at her.

"Not everybody," Sara murmured as Jared Cameron walked toward them with Max curled close in his arm. He was smiling at Max, but his green eyes shot daggers at Harley and Sara when he came closer.

"Should you be up so soon after major surgery?" Jared demanded, glaring at Sara.

"Major surgery?" Sara gasped. "I had my appendix out! The incision was barely four inches long!"

Jared's eyes narrowed. "It ruptured," he pointed out.

"Why does he get to make comments on your surgery?" Lisa asked innocently.

"Because I took her home with me and Tony and I nursed her back to health," Jared said curtly. "We have a vested interest in her recovery."

"Like it put you out! Tony did all the work!" Sara retorted.

Jared held up his hand with all the plastic bandages on it.

"You didn't try to pick up Morris, did you?" Lisa asked the newcomer.

Jared looked around him, exasperated. "Am I the only person in this town who didn't know that he bites?"

"Looks like it," Harley chuckled.

"I hate cats," Max muttered. "They're scary, and they have fangs, like snakes."

Sara wished the other woman had been around when Morris was staying at Jared's house. She'd have loved watching him stalk the slick lawyer. He loved to attack people who were afraid of cats.

"Hi, Sara," Tony said, thickening his drawl for the group.

He was wearing his suit and his sunglasses, and he looked really big. "You doing okay?"

Sara had gotten used to him being as articulate as Jared in the privacy of the Cameron ranch. Only now did she realize what a compliment he'd paid her by not putting on what was obviously an act for the masses.

"I'm much better, Tony, thanks," she replied, and gave him a genuine smile.

Max was looking more uncomfortable by the minute. "We aren't going to eat outside, are we?" she asked uneasily. "I mean, there are flies!"

"They only land on bad people," Sara promised.

Seconds later, two huge black flies came to rest on Max's arm. She screamed, hitting at them. "Get them off!" she exclaimed.

Tony glanced at Sara and grinned. "Sound familiar?" he teased.

She burst out laughing, remembering her own horror at the yellow hornet that had landed on her shoulder at Jared's house.

But Max thought Sara was laughing at her and, without a pause, she swung her hand and slapped Sara in the face.

There was a sudden silence around them. Cy Parks, who'd been directing the cowboys cooking the beef, strode up to the small group with blood in his eye.

"Are you all right, Sara?" he asked in a menacing tone.

"I'm…fine," Sara replied. She had a huge red mark on one cheek.

Cy turned to Max. "I've never asked a guest to leave my home until now. I want you off my property."

Max fumed. "She laughed at me! I was covered up in flies and she thought it was funny!"

"She was laughing because the same thing happened to her at our place with a yellow hornet," Tony said, and he looked menacing as well. "I reminded her of it."

Max flushed. "Oh."

Jared hadn't said a word until then. But his eyes spoke volumes. "You can apologize to Sara before I take you back to the ranch," he told Max, and he wasn't smiling.

Max backed down at once. "I'm very sorry," she told the younger woman. "I hope I didn't hurt you," she added in a condescending tone.

Cash Grier joined the small group. He wasn't smiling, either. "If you'd like to press charges," he told Sara while he glared down at Max, "I'll be delighted to arrest her for you."

"Arrest me!" Max exclaimed.

"For assault," he replied coldly. "In Jacobsville, you don't strike another person physically unless you've been attacked physically. It's against the law."

"Yeah, you'd think a lawyer would know that, wouldn't you?" Tony put in his two cents' worth.

Max seemed to be suddenly aware of her whereabouts and her vulnerability in this small town. She laughed nervously. "Surely that won't be necessary…?"

Cash looked at Sara. "Sara?" he questioned softly.

Sara took a deep breath and gave Max her best glare. "I won't have you arrested," she said quietly. "But if you ever touch me again, I'll show you how much I learned in Chief Grier's self-defense course last fall."

"It won't happen again," Jared replied. He took Max firmly by the arm. "Thanks for inviting us," he told Cy, "but we have to go."

Tony grimaced. "Yeah. Sorry," he added, smiling at Sara. "That barbecue sure smelled good."

"Can't you stay?" Sara asked Tony gently.

He lit up like a Christmas tree at her tone.

Jared muttered something under his breath and Max protested as his hand tightened bruisingly on her arm.

Tony glanced at his boss and sighed. "No. I got to go, too. See you, Sara."

She smiled. "See you."

The three walked away with stiff backs. Sara could have kicked Max. She'd ruined everything.

"Thanks, Chief Grier," Sara told the town's police chief.

He shrugged. "You were my star pupil," he replied. He grinned. "I wish you'd pressed charges, though. I would have enjoyed locking her up."

"Locking who up?" Tippy Grier asked curiously, joining her husband. The "Georgia Firefly" as she'd been known in modeling circles was still gorgeous, with long reddish-gold hair and green eyes. She smiled at Sara, and then frowned when she saw the red marks on her cheek. "What in the world happened?" she exclaimed.

"Jared Cameron's lawyer hit her," Harley said angrily.

"A man hit you?" Tippy gasped.

"A woman," Sara corrected. "It was because of the flies."

Tippy stared at her, wide-eyed. "Flies. Right."

"No," Sara laughed. "I mean, she thought I was laughing at her because she attracted flies."

"Good riddance, I say," Harley muttered, watching Jared's Jaguar peel out and roar away. "The poor flies will probably drop dead now."

Sara was disappointed, because she'd hoped that she might have a chance to dance with Jared. But she hated herself for the thought. He'd been horrible to her about Harley, and now he'd sided with Max. But Tony had defended her. Sweet Tony.

"Who was the big fella with Jared?" Cash asked curiously.

"Tony the Dancer," Cy answered before Sara could.

Everybody looked at him.

He realized at once what a slip he'd made. "I heard Jared call him that," he said at once.

They still looked at him. He'd used Jared's first name, something he never did with strangers.

He cursed. "Just pretend I didn't say a word, and let's go and eat barbecue," he muttered. He bent to Lisa, smiling, and picked his little son up in his arms.

"Daddy!" Gil enthused, hugging his father around the neck.

The burned arm was still a little weak, but it didn't show. The look on his face as he held the little boy was indescribable.

"Gil's growing," Tippy said, smiling at the child.

"So is our Tris," Cash replied. "She's two now. Rory's twelve. He's crazy about his niece." Rory was Tippy's younger brother.

"Speaking of Tris," Tippy grinned, looking past her husband's shoulder.

Rory had little Tris up in his arms and was carrying her around, laughing. She looked just like her mother, with red hair and green eyes, and she was wearing a pretty little green-patterned cotton dress with white shoes. She was holding on to Rory for all she was worth, talking to him.

Rory, taller now, had dark hair and green eyes, and he obviously doted on the little girl.

"She can walk, you know," Cash told the boy with a smile.

"She likes it when I carry her, though," Rory replied, grinning. "Isn't she just the neatest thing in the world?" he added, kissing the little girl's hair.

"You're spoiling her," Tippy laughed.

Rory shook his head. "No, I'm not. I just carried her away from the ice cream. She talked Randy into giving her a bowl of it, but I made him take it back."

"Wanted ice cream, Rory," Tris pouted. "Bad Rory."

He only chuckled.

Tippy held out her arms for Tris, who got a tighter hold on her uncle. "No!" she said. "Want Rory!"

Cash looked down at his wife musingly. "So there."

She laughed, pressing close against him. "All right, Tris," she told her daughter. "Rory, when your arms get tired, bring her back."

"Okay, sis." He went off toward the fenced pasture where horses were grazing.

Harley excused them and drew Sara along with him to the tables where plates of barbecue and beans and rolls were being served up.

"You sure you're all right?" Harley asked, concerned.

Sara nodded. "It was a shock, that's all."

"I don't like that smarmy lawyer," he muttered darkly. "But she and her boss do suit one another. They're both bad company."

Sara didn't answer him. She was remembering the hard look Jared had given Max. He hadn't liked the woman's reaction to Sara. That was comforting. But her face still stung.

The Latin music played by the Mariachi band had everyone who could walk streaming up onto the wooden dance floor Cy had built for the occasion. Strings of large Japanese lanterns provided light, after the sun went down, and there was a crowd swaying to the rhythm.

Matt Caldwell and his wife, Leslie, were doing a spirited *paso doble* while Cash and Tippy Grier looked on from the sidelines. They exchanged mischievous glances, got up, held hands and moved onto the dance floor.

"Bet you can't do a tango," Cash chided.

Matt gave him a wicked grin. "You lose. Hey, Paco!" he called to the band leader. "Tango!"

The band leader and his band all laughed, stopped playing, measured the rhythm and then sailed into a Tango number that was all fire and passion.

Everybody except the two couples evacuated the dance floor, expecting a real competition.

They got one. It was a duel, and both couples put on their best form for it. As the music built to a crescendo, both couples stopped at the same time, in lingering poses, as the band finished the number.

But it was a draw, as the dancers had figured it would be. They laughed and shook hands as the audience went wild with clapping and cheering.

"Pity we don't have trophies," Cy Parks drawled.

"Next time, we have to have a waltz contest!" Harley called. He'd been studying the dance for months, and he was good at it.

"I learned to waltz in Austria," Cash called to him.

Harley flapped his hand at the police chief.

The music started again, this time a lazy two-step. Just as Harley turned to take Sara onto the dance floor, he was bypassed.

Jared Cameron lifted Sara gently into his arms, carried her onto the wooden dance platform and eased her to the floor.

"My turn," he said softly, and he smiled in a way that made her heart race.

She slid her free arm around his neck and looked up at him with her breath catching in her throat.

Harley, for one instant, thought about separating them. But when he saw Sara's face, he knew it would be almost a betrayal to interfere. Subdued, he went back to the buffet table for a beer.

"I didn't think you'd be back," Sara said to his chest. He was so much taller that her head barely came to his chin.

His big, warm hand contracted around hers. "Didn't you?" He tilted her chin up so that he could see her cheek. "At least it isn't bruised," he added quietly. "I've never wanted so badly to manhandle a woman. Max needs to take some classes in anger management."

"She thought I was laughing at her."

"Tony explained it." His hand tightened. "You keep your

distance from Tony," he added firmly. "He's not what he seems to be. He could hurt you."

"He would never lift a hand to me," she protested at once.

He stopped dancing for an instant and looked down into her wide eyes. "I don't mean physically."

She frowned. "He's very sweet to me."

He started dancing again. "You remind him of his sister."

"Yes. He said she died."

He made a slow turn, one that drew her very close to his hard-muscled body and made her tingle all over. "Tony has issues you're better off not knowing about."

"Cy Parks knows both of you."

"I've lived here several weeks," he said carelessly.

"That isn't what I mean."

He raised an eyebrow. "I've known Cy for a while."

She was really curious now. Most people knew that Cy Parks, Eb Scott and Micah Steele had been professional mercenaries, soldiers of fortune, before they settled down in Jacobsville. She knew next to nothing about Jared Cameron. She wondered what secrets he was keeping.

He saw that curiosity in her eyes and just smiled. "Never you mind," he told her, drawing her closer. "I don't plan to waste the evening with walks down memory lane. I'm much more interested," he added huskily, "in making new memories."

His hand slid gently up and down her spine in sensuous little forays that made her feel boneless. It worried her that she didn't want to protest the near intimacy of his hold. If he ever turned up the heat, she knew she wouldn't be able to resist him. She couldn't help but remember what Max had told her about Jared's easy conquests and his indifference to them afterward.

"I had Tony drive Max to the airport," he said after a minute.

Her heart skipped. "She's gone?"

"Yes. She's gone." He didn't mention the vicious things

Max had to say about Sara and Jared's interest in her, or the threat he used to get her out of town. Tony wasn't too keen on leaving Jared alone while he escorted the lawyer to the airport, either. It had been a battle.

"Is Tony coming over, then?" she asked.

He stiffened. "Yes," he said, but he didn't sound happy about it. "I meant what I said. You don't need to start looking at Tony as a prom date."

"I didn't go to the prom," she said absently. "And it's not your business who I look at. I came with Harley," she added firmly.

He drew back so that he could see her eyes. "And you're going home with me," he said softly.

How she wished that her excitement hadn't shown when he said that. She couldn't walk off with another man when Harley had brought her here. It would have been unthinkable...

"Sara," Harley said from beside them, grimacing, "I've got something to do for the boss. It can't wait."

"I'll drive her home," Jared told the younger man. "No problem."

"Sara, is that all right with you?" Harley asked gently.

She nodded. "It's okay. What is it? Or can't you say?"

Harley shrugged. "I really can't," he replied. He forced a smile. "We'll do this again, Sara."

She smiled back. "Of course."

He nodded to Jared and walked off toward the parking lot, looking forlorn even from behind.

Jared was smiling.

Sara frowned. "Did you have anything to do with that?"

"You mean, did I ask Cy to occupy Harley so that I could take you home? Of course I did. I don't like competition."

She was gaping. "Excuse me?"

His arm contracted. His eyes were strangely darkened as he met her own. "I'm possessive," he said softly. "Territorial."

"About…me?" she asked, unbelieving.

"Of course about you," he muttered.

"But Max is beautiful," she began.

"Max is the past," he said bluntly. "She knows it."

That was thrilling. Exciting. Her whole face lit up. He was serious!

He stopped dancing and traced her mouth with a long forefinger, teasing her lips apart in a sensuous tension that grew by the second. "You're tired," he whispered. "You've done too much. You need to go home, and I have to take you because Harley left early."

She nodded, wordless.

He caught her by the hand and tugged her to Cy and Lisa. They said their goodbyes. Jared asked Cy to tell Tony where he'd gone. He put Sara in the Jaguar, buckled her up and revved off toward her small house.

They didn't exchange a single word during the short drive. The tension between them was so thick it was almost tangible. Sara felt hot all over. The feel of Jared so close to her had removed all her inhibitions. She couldn't think past wanting to kiss him until her mouth hurt.

He cut off the engine in front of her house and turned to her. "We've reached the point of no return," he said curtly. "Either we go ahead, or we stop seeing each other. I'm too old to stop at kisses."

She stared at him helplessly, all her upbringing urging her to tell him to leave, to go inside by herself. All her life, she'd done the right thing, the safe thing. But she loved this man. If she said the wrong words now, she knew she'd never be in his arms again. The thought was torture. Then she caught herself. She was being overly worried. He wanted to do some heavy petting. Of course. He wasn't a kiss-at-the-front-door sort of man. And if things got too hot, well, she'd just find an excuse to get up. Easy.

He got out of the car, opened her door and locked the sleek vehicle before he followed Sara up onto her porch. Nervously she unlocked the door and went inside. She reached for the light switch, but he was right behind her. He stayed the movement, locked the dead bolt and suddenly swept her up into his arms and brought his mouth down on her soft lips.

The sofa was only a few feet away. It was long and wide, just right for two people to lie on. Sara felt his weight with a sense of destiny. It was the most glorious thing she'd ever felt, all that hard, warm muscle down the length of her body. She seemed to throb like her own runaway heartbeat while Jared made a midnight snack of her mouth.

Before long, she was as anxious as he was to have her blouse and bra out of the way so that his hands, and then his mouth, could explore the softness of her warm skin. By the time he slid his hands under her skirt and against her bare legs, she was shivering all over.

She felt his body vibrate, as if he was as electrified as she was. He whispered something under his breath that she didn't understand. Apparently it wasn't too important, because only seconds later, she felt him against her in a way that was as new as it was frightening.

She started to protest, but it was already too late. His mouth ground into hers as his body suddenly invaded the most secret place of her own. The delicious sensations she felt when they began were now absent as she felt him insistent and demanding, his big hand under her hips, holding them steady as he pushed down hard. He groaned as he felt the soft barrier give. His control was gone at once. He drove for fulfillment; abstinence and too many beers had robbed him of self-control. He felt the rush of pleasure like a hot wave over his body, leaving him to shudder in a tense arch that was like rain after the baking desert.

When he regained his control, he felt her trying to get away from the crush of his body. He was aware of broken sobs. Trembling. Audible misery.

He lifted his head. He couldn't see her in the darkness of the room, but his hand touched her face and felt the wetness.

"Please," she sobbed, pushing at his chest.

He was shocked at his lapse. He hadn't really meant to go this far, not the first time they were intimate. But it was too late now. He moved away, fastening his slacks. He heard her move, heard fabric against skin. At least she'd stopped crying.

"I'll get the light," he said gruffly.

"No!" She was standing now. "No," she added in a more controlled tone. "Please don't."

"Why not?" He moved closer to her. "We made love. What's so horrible about it?"

She was shivering with self-revulsion. "Please go," she whispered.

"Sara…"

"Please!" she sobbed.

He drew in an angry breath. "Small town girls and their damned hang-ups," he muttered. "What now? Do you think you'll go to hell for sleeping with a man you haven't married?"

It was so close to what she'd been taught all her life, that she didn't even bother to reply.

"I don't believe this!" he raged. "I can't be the first man to—" He stopped dead, remembering the barrier that he'd dealt with. "I was the first," he said slowly. "Wasn't I, Sara?"

"Please go," she pleaded tearfully.

He drew in a long breath. "Tell me you're on birth control," he demanded.

"I never needed to be," she bit off.

"Great!" he burst out, furious. "That's just great! And you

see me as a meal ticket, don't you? If I made you pregnant, you'll have a free ride for life! Except you won't," he added coldly. "I don't want children ever again. You'll have a termination or I'll take you to court and show everyone who lives here how mercenary you are!"

He was talking about a possibility she hadn't even considered. She'd tried to stop him. Why did he expect every woman to be prepared for sex? Was that the way people thought in big cities? Were they all prepared, all the time?

"Don't worry," she said through her teeth. "I promise you, there won't be any horrible consequences. Now will you please go home?"

He started for the door, still furious. But he paused with it open and looked back toward her. "I didn't mean to hurt you," he said uncomfortably.

She laughed hollowly. "My whole life has been nothing except pain. Why should this be any different?"

She turned and went into a room down the hall, closed the door and audibly locked it.

He left, frowning, curious about the remark. He didn't want to think about how much he'd hurt her. He honestly hadn't planned to seduce her, but she wouldn't believe him. She was hurt and shocked and outraged. Probably she'd been taught that premarital sex was a sin, and now she was going to punish herself for falling victim to demon lust.

He turned the lock on her door so that it would engage when he went outside and pulled the door shut.

He stood on the porch, feeling the cool breeze touch his sweaty face, cooling him. He'd never lost control like that in his life. He was furious at himself.

While he was debating his next move, the ranch truck pulled up beside his car. Tony leaned out the window.

"She okay?" he asked his boss.

"She's fine," Jared lied, unlocking the Jaguar. "Let's go home. I want a drink. It's been a damned long day."

"You can say that again," Tony replied. "You won't believe the hell Max raised at the airport."

He'd believe it, he thought. His whole evening had gone from bad to worse, and he wasn't about to tell Tony any of the details. Two women in his life, and he couldn't deal with either of them. He wished that this whole charade was over.

Eight

Sara didn't sleep at all. She took a shower and changed into a clean nightgown. Then she sat in front of her mirror and looked at the fallen woman there. Her grandfather would be ashamed of her. So would her father. They hadn't raised her to be careless with her morals.

She wasn't sure what to do. She knew there was a morning after pill, but she'd have to go to a doctor she knew to ask for it. Everybody in town would know what she'd been doing. The shame was too great for the risk. But what if she conceived? She was only at the beginning of her cycle. Wasn't that a bad time to get pregnant? But some women weren't regular. She wasn't. Would that make a big difference?

Jared hadn't even asked first. He'd taken what he wanted. Maybe she'd done something to make him think she was willing. She should have told him in the car that she was innocent. She'd thought he meant that he wanted to have a nice petting session in her house, not that he expected her to go the whole way with him. Had he thought she was agreeing to sex?

She was sickened by her lack of protest. It had been so sweet to lie in his arms and feel him wanting her. Nobody had ever wanted Sara, not in that way. Her grandfather had cherished her, but she'd been in such a condition when she and her mother first came home from overseas that she wasn't really expected to live in the first place. The group that had sponsored the family's trip had been kind enough to arrange for a medical flight back to Texas for Sara. As a result of her injuries, she had slight brain damage. People who knew her were aware of it. They never made fun of her when she couldn't match socks or clothes, when she forgot little things as soon as she learned them. She had trouble remembering much of the past as well. The doctors had said she was very smart and that she would be able to compensate. But now she wasn't so sure.

Maybe, she comforted herself, nothing would happen. She really hadn't enjoyed what Jared had done to her. Didn't that mean she wouldn't conceive?

She should have read more books, she told herself firmly. She knew too little about her own body, or what men and women did in the dark. At least she knew now what women had been talking about in whispers all her life. Sex was painful and quickly over with. It was only fun for men. Women endured it to have children. Now she knew that she'd never want it again. She knew the truth.

She went to bed. For the first time in years, though, she didn't have nightmares.

Jared felt guilty all day. He was shocked at his loss of control. He was sorry for the things he'd said to Sara, but she should have told him up-front that she had no experience of men. Most women knew how to take care of themselves in intimate situations. If he'd known Sara was completely innocent, he'd have used something and he wouldn't have hurt her so much.

He laughed coldly. Sure he would have. He hadn't had control of himself for those few, electrifying minutes on her sofa. He'd wanted her so much that he couldn't contain it.

Tony hadn't said anything to him about it, but he kept looking at Jared as if he suspected something. It didn't help to remember how fond Tony was getting of Sara. Sara liked Tony, too.

"You aren't yourself today," Tony commented at lunch, for which they had a nice paella that he'd concocted.

Jared moved restlessly, but he didn't reply.

"Max didn't leave town."

That got his boss's attention. "What?!"

Tony compressed his lips. "She's upstairs."

"I told you to take her to the airport!"

"I did," Tony said shortly. "But short of bodily carrying her onto the plane, I couldn't think of a way to get her out of the terminal."

Jared almost exploded. Just as he started to speak, Max lounged into the dining room in a gray silk pantsuit.

"Lunch? I'm starved."

"I told you to leave," Jared shot at her.

"You didn't mean it," she said complacently. "You're always throwing me out. Then the next day you call to apologize and ask me back again. I saved you the steps in between."

She was right, and Jared hated knowing it. She helped herself to paella and coffee. Nobody said anything else at the table.

Jared wasn't a drinker. He hardly ever touched alcohol. But remembering what he'd done with Sara sent him to a liquor bottle. Halfway through the afternoon, he was well on his way to staggering.

Max cornered Jared in his study, surprised at the amount of whiskey he was consuming. It had to be something rough, she thought. He hadn't had this much to drink since his daughter's death. "Something's gone wrong, hasn't it? Come on," she coaxed. "Tell me."

He glared at her. "I can handle this myself."

"Handle what?" She pursed her lips. She knew him very well. There was a pattern to his behavior that she recognized. A new woman. The hunt. The seduction. Then the need to extricate himself from the woman. "Don't tell me," she purred. "You let that hick girl seduce you, didn't you?"

He looked shocked.

"I thought so," she continued. "It was easy to see that she was after you. She watched every move you made. She wore seductive clothes. She did everything except wear a sign to show you that she was willing. No man could have resisted her."

She made him feel less guilty. She was right. It was Sara's fault. He'd been seduced, not the reverse. The alcohol helped him see the truth.

She saw the wheels turning in his mind. "And now you're worried about consequences."

He gave it away without knowing.

She nodded. "Don't worry. I'll take care of everything. You just attend to your current situation and leave it to me."

"Don't hurt her," he said as an afterthought.

"That's a joke. I won't have to."

"Okay." He went to find Tony. He felt a weight lifted from his shoulders. It would be all right. If Tony noticed that his boss was half lit, he was kind enough not to say anything about it.

* * *

Sara was back at work on Monday morning, feeling guilty and ashamed, as if what had happened showed on her face.

"Bad weekend?" Dee asked gently. "We all have them, from time to time."

"I went to the barbecue at the Parks's place," she replied. "The food was great."

Dee grinned. "Did Harley have a good time, too?"

"Harley had to go run an errand for his boss just after the dancing started," Sara said sadly. Harley would have saved her if Cy hadn't separated him from Sara.

"Mmm-hmm," Dee murmured.

Something in her tone disturbed Sara. She glanced at her boss. "What?"

"Did you know that Jared and Cy Parks grew up in the same town?"

Sara dropped the stapler she was holding and scrambled to pick it up again. "How do you know?"

"My cousin works for Cy on his ranch. He knows all the gossip. Yes, Cy had a place in Montana, and so did Jared Cameron." She stopped putting used books into boxes for resale. "Jared asked Cy to remove Harley from the field," she added.

Sara had always liked Cy Parks, until now. But he couldn't have known what a near-tragedy he'd contributed to. He probably thought Jared was seriously interested in Sara. According to Max, Jared was never seriously interested in any woman. Especially, she recalled sickly, once he'd had her. Her eyes closed in misery.

"Harley was topping cotton he was so mad," Dee continued. "He almost quit his job. He said you were a babe in the woods and Jared was a wolf in disguise."

"Jared was a perfect gentleman," Sara lied, and made it look convincing.

Dee stared at her for a minute and then visibly relaxed. "Thank goodness. I was worried…silly of me. I have to run to the bank to get some change for the drawer. Want coffee from the doughnut place?"

"Yes, please, black. No cream or sugar."

"That's new. You're sure?"

"I'm getting back to the basics, even in coffee. I'll hold down the fort."

Dee smiled gently. "Okay."

After Dee left, Sara felt as if the world was collapsing around her. It was a crisis that compared in intensity only to that episode in her past. She'd survived that, she reminded herself. She could survive anything, after that.

But minutes later, Max parked one of the ranch trucks outside the bookstore and strolled in, looking smug and arrogant. "Jared sent me," she said curtly. She took out an envelope and handed it to Sara. "It's a check for ten thousand dollars. He said there had better not be any complications from what happened Saturday night." She nodded toward the envelope. "There's more than enough in there to pay for a termination. And if it's not necessary, then you've still got a nest egg for the foreseeable future. Jared won't be here much longer."

"Won't…be here," Sara stammered, shocked by the unfolding nightmare.

"He's been down here waiting for the authorities to get their hands on three illegal aliens who came up from South America to kidnap Jared and hold him for ransom."

"Ransom?"

Max pulled a magazine from her briefcase. It was a national financial journal. There, on the front cover, was Jared Cameron. The story inside was revealed in a sentence: Oil magnate target of terrorists after firefight at South American pipeline…

Sara gasped.

"You can keep it," Max said easily. "To remember him by."

"But why did he come here?" Sara asked blankly.

"Because some of the team of mercenaries that helped him destroy the original terrorist cell that targeted his oil pipeline two years ago live here," she replied. "The survivors aren't willing to give up. They figure if they can nab Jared, they'll recoup what they lost when they failed to hold on to his oil pipeline in South America. They demanded millions for it, and he sent in mercenaries instead. He pulled out when the oil companies were nationalized, but the terrorists still want the money. Now they want revenge as well. They were just apprehended today near Victoria."

"Then he's safe," Sara said dully.

"He is. And he can go down to Cancún with me for a long holiday," she added. "His headquarters is in Oklahoma, but he has another house in Billings, Montana, and vacation homes all over the world. He's worth millions. The terrorists knew that his corporation would pay any amount of money to get him back. He's something of a financial genius." Her eyes narrowed as she smiled. "Hardly a match for a little bookseller in outback Texas, is he?"

Sara just looked at her, with the anguish she couldn't hide all over her face.

Max's expression hardened. "You'd better realize that he means business. If you turn up pregnant, you'd better get a termination. You don't want to know what he could do to you and your reputation."

Sara didn't answer her. She couldn't. She just stared.

Max shrugged. "You've been warned." She stopped at the doorway. "You shouldn't look so tragic. Women have fought their way into his bed for years."

"What for?" Sara asked with deliberate scorn.

Max looked as if she'd been doused with water. "You don't mean that you didn't enjoy…?"

"I'd rather stay single for the rest of my life than go through that again, ever," Sara said with a sob in her voice.

Something in Max that had been buried for a decade sat up and shivered. She searched for the right words. "You've never…?"

Sara swallowed hard. "My grandfather said that women who give their bodies cheaply are bound for purgatory."

Max's thin eyebrows pulled together. "Sara," she began hesitantly, "how old are you?"

"What does that have to do with…?"

"How old are you?"

Sara swallowed. "Nineteen."

Max felt the blood going out of her face. She was using a cannon to shoot a bird. She drew in a long breath. Well, at least it hadn't been statutory rape. But she was sure Jared didn't know how old this child was. He'd never have touched her.

"I'm sorry," Max told her. "I'm really sorry."

She turned and went out the door.

Sara dried her tears and went back to straightening the books on their shelves. Jared was a multimillionaire who owned an oil corporation and he was only here at the ranch to set a trap for the terrorists who wanted him for ransom. Sara had thought he was here forever. When he held her close and kissed her, she thought he wanted her forever. She was wrong on both counts. He could buy as many women as he wanted. Sara wasn't even in the running, except that he'd wanted her. Or, maybe he'd just wanted a woman and she was handy. She really did need to grow up.

Max was solemn and quiet when she went back to the ranch. Jared noticed.

"What's wrong?" he asked.

She looked up at him. "She's nineteen, Jared."

He had to sit down. Nothing had ever hit him quite so hard.

She sat down across from him in an armchair. "I told her what was necessary…"

"You what?" he asked, aghast.

She held up a hand. "Being kind to her isn't an option. What if she decided to accuse you of forcing her? You could lose millions. Your reputation would be in ashes. What sort of life would it be for a child, if she had one, living in this small town asylum with a mother who barely made minimum wage and could hardly afford to clothe her?"

Jared wasn't thinking about money. He was remembering the throb in Sara's voice in the darkness. She hadn't been leading him on. She hadn't realized what he meant. She didn't know that she was agreeing to have sex with him. And she was nineteen years old. He felt guilt like a rush of hot acid in his gut.

"When are we going to Cancún?" Max asked, to divert him.

He turned and looked at her, but he didn't see her. "I haven't thought about it."

"A few days on the beach would do you good," she coaxed. "You can put this place behind you."

He was staring at her. "Why Cancún?" he asked.

She hesitated. "It's got lovely beaches. There are Mayan ruins nearby."

His eyes had narrowed. "You'd better come clean."

She frowned. "I'm not doing anything dishonest," she said. "There's a consortium that handles pharmaceuticals. They want to invest in our corporation."

"Name them."

She frowned more. "Well, I don't really have just one name. They call themselves the Reconquistas."

"When did you speak with them?"

"Last week. Why?"

"Law enforcement just apprehended three terrorists in Victoria, heading this way," he said furiously. "And you don't know why?"

She looked stunned. "You can't mean…!"

"They're part of the consortium that smuggles narcotics, Max," he told her flatly. "If you'd come to me in the first place, I would have told you. But you were seeing dollar signs, weren't you?"

She flushed. "It never hurts to make more money."

"It never hurts to fire people, either," he said pointedly. "You'd better start looking for another job."

"You're not serious," she laughed. "You fire me all the time, but you always call me back."

He looked resolute. "Not this time," he said in a cold tone. "You've done enough damage."

"Me?" She stood up, fuming. "I've done enough damage? What would you call seducing a nineteen-year-old virgin?"

The last word drifted away as she noticed Tony standing fixed in the doorway, with eyes that promised mayhem.

Jared saw him and grimaced.

Tony marched right up to him. "Is it true?" he demanded.

Jared couldn't even find the words.

"That sweet woman," Tony said coldly, "who never hurt anybody, after the tragedy of her past almost destroyed her, and here you come to put the last nail in her coffin!"

"What do you mean, the tragedy of her past?" Jared asked.

Tony didn't reply. He looked more dangerous at that moment than Jared had ever seen before. "I'll never tell you. And the minute this standoff ends, I'm through. I won't work for a man like you."

He turned on his heel and went right back to the kitchen.

Max swallowed the hurt. She and Tony had both hit rock bottom, it seemed. "Well, it looks like you and your conscience will have a long time to get to know each other, doesn't it?"

She stopped by the kitchen to ask Tony to drive her to the airport. He agreed curtly. Jared went back into his study and slammed the door. He'd never felt so ashamed in his life.

The next morning, when Sara went to work, she noticed a strange beat-up van in the parking lot. It had been there just as she drove out of the parking lot the day before. In fact, it had pulled in just after Max walked into the bookstore. Sara hadn't seen anybody in it the day before, and she didn't see any people in it now. Maybe it broke down there and the owner had left it until he could get a mechanic to tow it. She went into the bookstore.

"Hi, Dee," she called.

Dee smiled. "Hi, yourself. I'm off to the bank. Want coffee?"

"I'd love it."

"I'll pick us up a doughnut apiece, too." She stopped at the door. "That old van's still there."

"Maybe it broke down," Sara murmured.

"I'm amazed anyone would risk driving it in the first place," Dee chuckled. "I'll be quick."

"Okay."

She'd no sooner driven away than three foreign-looking men walked into the bookstore. They glanced at Sara and nodded before they walked down the aisles, one of them peering into Dee's open office.

Sara didn't usually have premonitions, but she felt something odd about the men. She remembered what Max had said about terrorists. These three were tall and swarthy and disreputable-looking. They were wearing jeans and T-shirts, and they had very prominent muscles. She was in the bookstore alone, with no weapons except the pocketknife she used to open boxes with. She wouldn't stand a chance against even one of them, much less three, despite Chief Grier's handy self-defense for women course. She could scream, of course, but the bookstore was temporarily the only business in the strip mall.

They might have been arrested in Victoria, but it was obvious that they'd made bail. She knew the look of the people who lived in her area. These three were from overseas. And she didn't need a program to know why they were in town. They were after Jared. Max had come to the bookstore in a ranch pickup and had a solemn conversation with a woman. They might have had high-tech listening devices. If they knew who Max was, and they'd overheard what she said to Sara, maybe they figured Sara was a softer target than Jared, with his bodyguard.

She pretended not to see them, while her mind worried over possible courses of action. There was one. It was a long shot. If she stabbed herself with the pocketknife and they could see blood, and she pretended to be unconscious and tried to look dead, they might be startled into leaving. It would be risky to carry a wounded woman off for ransom, wouldn't it? Especially if she looked as if she were dying…it would slow everything down.

I'm probably crazy, she told herself. They're just tourists or ranch hands searching for something to read. Right, she added, and that's why they're looking outside to make sure nobody's coming and heading straight for me!

She knew where the appendicitis incision was. It was her best hope of missing any essential organs. They came around the counter, towering over her.

"You come with us," one of the men said in accented English. "We see you with the lawyer. You are Cameron's woman. He will pay for you."

"I am nobody's woman. I will die before I go with you!" she said, and, giving up a silent prayer, she jabbed the pocketknife into the incision, through her blouse. "Oooh!" she cried, because it did hurt.

She crumpled to the floor with blood on her hands and shirt. She sighed heavily and held her breath. She looked dead.

The men hesitated. They'd planned well, and now their hostage had committed suicide right in front of them!

While they hesitated, Harley Fowler got out of his truck and headed for the bookstore. He was wearing a sidearm, a six-gun that he carried when he was working fence lines, in case he encountered a rattler or some other dangerous animal. The men made a quick decision. They ran for it. They ran so fast that they almost knocked Harley down in the process.

Harley didn't understand why three men were running for the van. Then he thought about robbery. Sara and Dee were here alone. He darted into the bookstore.

Sara was on the floor, blood pouring from her side. She looked up at Harley, gasping for breath. "It worked," she mumbled. "I hurt myself, though. Can you call 911 please?"

He grimaced as he saw the blood. "Yes, I can." He flipped out his cell phone and pushed in the code, holding it to his ear with his shoulder as he pulled Sara's shirt aside and looked at the wound.

He put pressure on it to stop the bleeding and spoke into the cell phone between his shoulder and his ear. He had an ambulance sent to the bookstore. He managed to hold one hand on her wound and close the phone with the other and slide it back into his pocket.

"You'll be all right, Sara," he told her. "Any man who'd do this to a woman should be shot! I should have stopped them!"

"They didn't do it, Harley, I did," she said weakly. "They were going to kidnap me. They thought Jared Cameron would pay ransom for me. What a joke!"

"Why would they think that?"

"His lawyer, Max, came to buy me off yesterday," she said miserably. "They must have followed her here."

"You aren't making sense."

The wound hurt. She moved and flinched. "Look at the magazine on the counter, Harley," she told him. "You'll see."

"When the paramedics get here, I will," he replied, but he didn't move his hands. He didn't dare.

Dee and the ambulance arrived at the same time. She ran into the store, red-faced and fearful.

"Oh, my goodness!" she exclaimed. "Sara!"

"Three men. They were in that old van, I think," she told Dee. "They were going to kidnap me for ransom."

"Ransom? Dear, you must be feverish…"

Harley picked up the magazine and looked at it, frowning as he handed it to Dee.

They exchanged a worried glance.

The paramedics loaded Sara on the gurney.

"I'll go with her," Harley said. "Dee, you'd better call Cash Grier, in case they come back."

"I'll do it right now." She picked up the store phone.

"I'll be all right. Honest," Sara assured Harley.

He didn't answer. He was too worried.

The wound wasn't bad. Dr. Coltrain had to sew her up. He did it, after giving her a local anesthetic, shaking his head. "Couldn't you have dialed 911?" he asked.

"I'd never have made it to the phone. There were three of them, heavily muscled, with accents, and not Spanish ones. I heard accents like that in Africa," she whispered.

"Why were they after you?" he asked.

"They were going to take me for ransom."

"Oh. Who do you know with that kind of money?" Coltrain teased.

"They followed Jared Cameron's lawyer into the bookstore," she murmured, feeling drowsy now that the excitement was all over. "I guess they thought I had a connection to him that they could exploit. There's an article about him in the new financial magazine. His photo's on the cover. He's down here trying to avoid being kidnapped by South American terrorists who made a try for his oil pipeline."

"The excitement of living in Jacobsville, Texas," he replied as he stitched her up. "When I was a kid, this place was like the end of the world. Never any excitement."

"Maybe he'll go away and we'll get back to normal."

He only mumbled.

Sara was sitting up on the examination table when Cash Grier walked in.

"Harley said three men attacked you in the bookstore," he said without preamble. He looked solemn. "Three prisoners escaped from the Victoria jail yesterday about noon. They were Arabic, according to the police chief up there. At least, they spoke what sounded to him like Arabic."

"Yes," she replied. "They were in a ratty old van. They followed Jared Cameron's lawyer to the bookstore in one of the ranch trucks. They thought I was important to Mr. Cameron. What a joke!"

He didn't laugh. "Did they say anything to you?"

"Only that they thought I had a connection to him. They must be really desperate for a hostage."

"Did one of them stab you?" he asked.

She grimaced. "You aren't going to believe this."

"Try me."

"I stabbed myself. I made them think I was committing

suicide. They hesitated when I fell on the floor and pretended to be dead. Then Harley showed up and they cut their losses and ran for it. Good thing Harley was wearing his .45 on his hip today!" she added. "He always does when he rides fence lines."

Cash's dark eyebrows arched and he smiled gently. "Well, aren't you the mistress of improvisation?" he said with respect.

She grinned. "It seemed the only chance I had. There were three of them. You always said there was no shame in running if you were up against impossible odds."

"Yes, I did. You spooked them, I gather."

"Want to hire me?" she asked saucily. "You can teach me how to shoot a gun and next time I won't have to resort to stabbing myself. I can shoot them instead."

"We've put out a BOLO on the van," Cash assured her.

"It will stick out," she said. "It really is ratty."

Harley stuck his head in the door. "How are you?"

She smiled. "Dr. Coltrain sewed me back up. I'm fine."

"You couldn't have screamed?" he asked.

"Who would have heard me?" she retorted. "We're the only business left in the strip mall."

"She has a point," Cash told the younger man.

Just then, his radio beeped. He talked into the radio mike on his shoulder. "Grier."

"We got them," Assistant Chief Judd Dunn told him. "We're bringing them in now."

"On my way," Cash replied. "Clear."

He turned to Sara, grinning. "And that's a nice day's work. Stop stabbing yourself," he added firmly. "I'm sure there's a law against attempted suicide."

"Never again. I promise," she assured him.

He winked and left. Harley moved into the cubicle and held Sara's hand.

"What a relief to find you in one piece," he said gently.

Sara smiled at him. He wasn't the only person who was relieved.

There was a terrible commotion in the corridor. Seconds later, Tony the Dancer walked into the cubicle.

Nine

Tony glanced at Harley, who was holding Sara's hand in his.

"I heard those three assassins went after you," Tony told her, worried. "They followed Max, didn't they?"

"I think they did," she admitted. "But how did they know her?"

"Our Web site mentions all the people who work for the corporation," he replied. "I'm sure the would-be kidnappers are computer literate. Most terrorists are these days. You okay?"

She smiled at him. She nodded.

"What did they do to you?" he asked, noting the dried blood on her blouse.

"They didn't do anything. I stabbed myself where I had the appendectomy and played dead on the floor. They didn't want a dying hostage, I figured. Then Harley showed up with his .45 and spooked them while they were deciding what to do about me. They ran. Chief Grier said his men just stopped them and they're under arrest."

Tony let out a breath. He glanced at Harley and smiled. "You do look like a gunslinger," he said.

Harley chuckled. "I never get any practice on living targets," he said. "Pity they ran."

"Wasn't it just?" Sara murmured. She grimaced.

Copper Coltrain came back into the cubicle, raising his eyebrows at the newcomer.

"This is Tony Danzetta," Sara introduced him. "He works for Mr. Cameron."

Coltrain nodded. So did Tony.

Harley checked his watch. "Damn! Sara, I was on my way to pick up some butane and fencing for Mr. Parks when I stopped by the bookstore for a minute to see you. I've got to go."

"Could you call Dee and tell her I'll be there as soon as Dr. Coltrain releases me," she began.

"In a pig's eye you will," Coltrain snapped, his red hair seemed to flare up. "You'll go home and stay in bed for two days. You'll start an antibiotic as well, to protect against that wound getting infected." He hesitated. "You don't need to be on your own."

"Chief Grier and his men have the would-be kidnappers in custody," she repeated.

"Sara, that isn't what I mean," he replied.

"She won't be alone," Tony said quietly. "I'll take her home and get the prescription filled. Then I'll take care of her until she's well."

"But, your boss," Sara began.

"I'm quitting today," he returned, avoiding her eyes. "If they've got the kidnappers, he won't need me. He doesn't need protection anymore. If he does, he can hire somebody else. He's rich enough."

Sara sensed a confrontation, and she was sure she didn't

want to know why Tony had quit. She was almost certain it had something to do with her.

She flushed scarlet as she considered what Tony might have found out from Max.

Coltrain saw the flush and Tony's tight lips and drew a conclusion. "Mr. Danzetta, I need to take one more look at the incision. Will you wait outside, please? You, too, Harley."

"I'm just going. Get better, Sara," Harley said softly, smiling.

"I'll do my best. Thanks for what you did."

"It wasn't much. See you."

"I'll be right outside," Tony added, following Harley out into the hall.

Coltrain closed the door of the cubicle. His eyes were quiet and intense. "You don't have to say it. I read faces very well. What do you want to do?"

She started to deny it. She knew better. Coltrain was a force of nature. "I can't kill an ant," she said.

He scowled. "Who asked you to?"

She pulled the envelope with the check out of her pocket and handed it to him, nodding when he started to open it.

Tony the Dancer heard the curses outside in the hall. He opened the door and went back in, daring the doctor to throw him out.

"What?" he asked.

Coltrain, red in the face with bad temper, handed him the envelope.

He cursed as darkly as the doctor had. "A firefight in Africa that damned near killed her, and now this," he muttered.

Sara and the doctor gaped at him.

He cleared his throat. He looked at Sara. "You don't remember me, do you?" he asked.

She shook her head, feeling again the sadness that came with remembering her past.

Tony moved a step closer and stuck his hands in his pockets. "I was with a group of American mercs who were fighting to restore the rightful government in the province where your parents were missionaries," he said quietly. "We'd just driven into town, chasing after a rebel group that killed two of our men. We saw the explosion. And we found you and your parents."

She stared at him, trying to reconcile her memories. "Yes. Some mercenaries buried my…my father," she said huskily. "And one of them carried me to a truck and got me and my mother to safety, to the mission headquarters."

"That was me, Sara," Tony replied quietly.

She smiled sadly. She hadn't recognized him. But then, she couldn't remember much of that long-ago life. "I lost some of my long-term memory. I can't quite match colors, and I forget names…"

"You're smart, though," Tony replied. "It doesn't show. Honest."

Coltrain drew in a long breath. "It's a small world, isn't it?" he asked.

Tony nodded. "Cy Parks was in another group of mercs, working with us. He walked right into the gunfire of a machine nest and took it out. One of the men who died had set the explosion in the mission that killed Sara's father and injured her."

Sara was spellbound. "I never knew," she said softly.

"You never needed to," Tony told her. He looked at Coltrain. "When can you tell if she's pregnant?"

Sara gasped.

Coltrain took it as a matter of course. "In a couple of weeks," he replied. "Maybe three. I could do a blood test now, but we might get a false positive. You need to shoot your damned boss," he added without missing a beat.

"I'm tempted," Tony said curtly. "But it's too late now. What's done is done. I'll take care of her, no matter what."

Sara fought tears and lost.

Tony pulled her face to his shoulder and held it there while she cried. "Now, now," he said gently. "It's all over. Everything's going to be fine."

Coltrain clapped Tony on the shoulder. "I'll write the prescriptions for an antibiotic and some pain medication. You can make sure she takes it properly."

"You bet I will," Tony replied.

Sara felt like royalty. Tony was a wonder. He cleaned the place until it shined like a new penny, rearranged her uncoordinated shelves in the kitchen and made dinner. He also doled out pills and did the laundry.

Afterward, he called Dee and gave her a progress report.

Sara was aghast when he told her, late that night. "You told her you were staying with me?" she asked.

He glowered at her. "At least Dee doesn't have a dirty mind," he informed her.

"I do not have a dirty mind," she protested.

He drew the covers up over her, in the plain, discreet pajamas she was wearing. "I want to tell you a story," he said, sitting down on the edge of the bed beside her. His dark eyes were quiet and sad. "I had a sister, who was three years younger than me. We lived in foster care. Our old man drank and knocked us around a lot. Our mother was long dead. They took us away from the old man and we shuttled from foster home to foster home, where we were mostly barely tolerated. At one of the homes," he added coldly, "there was an older boy who liked the way my sister looked. I warned him off, but he was persistent and she was flattered that a boy liked her. She was only fourteen, you see." He drew in a long breath and looked down at the floor. "Long story short, he got her pregnant. She was so ashamed, so scared, that she didn't know what to do. The boy found out and told her he'd make her sorry if she didn't get rid of the kid. He wasn't going to be rooked into paying child support for sixteen years because she was too stupid to get the pill and use it."

"What a nasty boy," she muttered.

"She was too ashamed to tell the foster parents what she'd let him do, and too afraid of the boy to have the child. I was moved to another foster home while all this was going on, so she couldn't tell me, either. So she went out one night, after everybody was asleep. They found her washed up on the riverbank the next afternoon."

"Oh, Tony," she said gently. She touched his arm. "I'm so sorry."

He grimaced. "She was all I had."

She slid her little hand into his big one and smiled at him. "No. I'm your family now," she replied. "You can be my big brother."

He looked down at her with eyes that were suspiciously bright. "Yeah?"

She squeezed his hand. "Yeah."

He drew in a steadying breath. "Well, we'll be part of one amazingly dysfunctional family, if you still consider Jared part of it."

She glared. "He became a stranger when Max handed me that check. And we're not going to let him be in our family anymore, either."

He didn't believe that she'd stopped caring about Jared. She was just hurt. So he smiled and nodded his head. "Suits me."

He squeezed her hand and let it go. "You need to get some sleep," he said, standing. He smiled down at her. "I'll be a better family to you than my ex-boss was," he added coolly. "That's for sure."

The memory of how close she and Jared had become, until the end, made her sad. She'd cared for him more than she wanted to admit. His betrayal was almost more than she could bear.

"Don't brood," Tony said firmly. "It won't change anything. We'll deal with whatever happens."

"I'm not getting rid of a child, if the test comes up positive."

He smiled. "I never thought you would."

"We won't tell him," she muttered. "He can go back to his houses all over the world and have fun with Max."

"Nobody has fun with Max," Tony told her. "She's got a one-track mind. All she thinks about is money."

"That's sad. I mean, it would be nice to have money. But I'm happy living the way I do."

"So am I, kid," he told her. "Money's poor company if it's all you've got."

She smoothed the cover over her belly, wondering. "He loved his little girl," she said out of the blue, and felt sorry for him all over again.

"He did," Tony had to admit. "But he discovered it far too late. Now he's alone and afraid to risk having another child. He'd be vulnerable."

She laid back against the pillows. "Everybody's vulnerable. You can't escape life."

"Yeah," he had to agree. "I know."

She didn't expect to sleep, but she did. It was comforting having Tony down the hall. People would probably gossip about her, but she'd live with it; with the pregnancy, too, if she had to. Her friends wouldn't snub her, and it didn't matter if her enemies did. She frowned. She didn't have enemies. Well, unless you counted that conceited rancher who couldn't take no for an answer.

Tony brought her breakfast and went to work baking them

a nice pound cake. But just before lunch, he walked in with her portable phone, his big hand over the mouthpiece.

"Who do you know in New York City?" he asked, curious.

"No one… New York? Give me that!" She was almost on fire with excitement as he handed her the phone. She wrenched her newest set of stitches grasping for it and groaned before she spoke into the receiver. "Sara Dobbs," she said at once.

"Miss Dobbs, I'm Daniel Harris, an editor with Mirabella Publishing Company. I wanted to tell you that your story is delightful, and the drawings are exquisite. We'd like to publish your book!"

Sara sat there with dreams coming true. Tears rolled down her cheeks. She fought to find her voice. Yesterday her world had felt as if it were ending. Today…today was magic!

"I'd love that," she managed finally, and then listened while he outlined the process that would ensue, including an advance against royalties that would be forthcoming.

Tony lifted his eyebrows while he listened unashamedly to her conversation. She was so animated that he wouldn't have been surprised to see her levitate right up to the ceiling.

She hung up, finally, and handed him back the phone. "They bought my book. They bought my children's book! They're going to publish it! And I get paid!"

He laughed. "Well!"

"I can't believe it!"

"What's this book about?" he asked, curious.

She told him, going into detail about the puppies and their adventures. "I have to call Lisa and tell her. She'll be so thrilled. I'll call Tom Walker, too," she added. "His dog was their grandfather—old Moose, who died just recently."

"I'd love to see this book," Tony replied.

"I just happen to have a copy," she told him, and pointed

to the small desk in the corner of her bedroom. "I made a duplicate, in case it got lost in the mail."

He sat beside her and went through the drawings, exclaiming over their beauty. "I never knew anybody who could draw like this," he murmured. "You're really good."

"Thanks, Tony. I'm overwhelmed. I never dreamed it would even sell, and certainly not so quickly."

He glanced at her. "You know, life evens out. Something bad happens, and then you get something good."

"My grandfather used to say that." She leaned back against the pillows. "My mother hated him. He talked my father into the mission to Africa, something he'd always wanted to do, but never could. Mama didn't want to go. She thought Africa was too dangerous, but my grandfather and my father made her feel guilty enough to back down. She blamed Grandad for everything that happened. She went out of her way to embarrass him, to make him pay for Daddy's death." She shook her head. "The only person she really hurt was herself."

"You poor kid," he said gently. "I thought I had a bad life."

"Everybody has a bad life, up to a point," she replied, smiling. "But somehow we survive, and get tougher."

"So we do."

She'd just finished a cup of coffee when the door opened and Jared Cameron stalked in. His face was unshaven. His eyes were bloodshot. He looked worn-out and irritated. He wasn't smiling.

He stood over her, glaring. "Why didn't you call me? Why didn't Tony call me? You were targeted because of me!"

She felt uncomfortable with him, after what had happened. She couldn't meet his eyes. "We didn't think you'd want to know."

He cursed fiercely. "The police chief said the kidnappers followed Max to your bookstore. I didn't send Max to see you!" he raged.

Her sad eyes managed to meet his. "I guess she forged your name on the check, huh?"

He went very still.

That did make her feel a little better, but not much. She pulled the envelope out of the bedside drawer and tossed it to the foot of the bed where he was standing. "You'd better have it back," she said. "I don't take bribes."

His high cheekbones went a ruddy color as he picked it up and looked at it. "Damn Max!" he said under his breath.

"And I'm not having a termination," she added fiercely. "You have no right to try to force me to jeopardize my soul!"

He looked at her as if he didn't understand what she was saying. But slowly it came to him, and he seemed even more ill at ease. "I don't want another child," he bit off.

"Then why didn't you stop?" she demanded hotly.

The flush got worse. "I didn't mean it to go that far," he said curtly. "I swear to God I didn't."

It didn't help much, but it helped a little.

"I thought you were older," he added heavily. "Nineteen years old. Dear God!"

That helped a little more.

He stuck his hands into his pockets. "I fired Max."

"I'm not surprised."

"Which one of those SOBs stabbed you?" he added abruptly.

She blinked. "None of them," she said. "I stabbed myself. It was the only thing I could think of. I was alone and there were three of them. I thought they wouldn't want a dying hostage."

"You did what?" he exploded, horrified.

"I had a pocketknife. I stabbed myself where Dr. Coltrain

did the appendectomy. It bled a lot, but I didn't hit anything vital. It was all I could think of."

He winced. "If Max hadn't taken it on herself to interfere, they'd never have tracked her to you," he said. "I could have choked her when she told me."

"She didn't tell you about the check, I guess?"

"No," he replied curtly. "If she had, she'd never work again. I make a bad enemy."

She knew that already, from personal experience. She studied him quietly. "I thought you were just a comfortably well-off rancher," she said slowly. "That magazine story said you own oil corporations."

He frowned. "What magazine?"

"Max showed it to me," she said. "You were on the cover."

He let out a short breath. "It just keeps getting better and better," he gritted.

Tony came into the room, angry. "How did you get in here?"

"I walked in the front door," Jared shot back. "You should have called me!"

Tony glared at him. "Wouldn't you be lucky if I did?"

Jared glanced from Tony's hard face to Sara's hard face. He grimaced. "It isn't doing your reputation much good to have Tony hanging around here day and night," he said.

"See? He's got a dirty mind, too," Sara told Tony.

"I have not!" Jared gritted. "I hate to see you being gossiped about."

"Then don't listen. It's a small town," she pointed out. "There's usually not much excitement going on around here. Gossip is how we get through life."

Jared seemed to draw inside himself as he looked at Sara. All his regrets were in his green eyes. He glanced at Tony. "Give us a minute, will you?"

If he'd demanded, Tony would have dug in his heels. But

it was hard to argue with politeness. He shrugged. "Okay. I'll be in the kitchen, Sara."

"Okay," she replied.

Jared stuck his hands deeper in his pockets and looked down at her. "When will you know for sure?" he asked.

She fought a scarlet flush. "Dr. Coltrain says it's too soon to be sure. Two or three more weeks, I think."

"Damn the luck," he cursed through his set teeth.

She glared at him. "You go right ahead and curse," she said. "But all of this is your fault."

His eyes were sad and full of guilt. She was so young. "I know that, Sara," he said quietly. "It doesn't help much."

She sagged back against the pillows. She didn't know what she was going to do. Her conscience wouldn't let her take the easy way out, although she was pretty sure that he wanted her to.

"Don't torment yourself," he said after a minute. "You did nothing wrong, except trust me. That was a mistake. I haven't had a lot to do with women in the past few months. I just lost it. I'm sorry, if it helps."

It did, a little, but it was too late for an apology to be of much use. "Nobody ever made such a heavy pass at me," she murmured, not meeting his eyes. "I thought you just wanted to kiss me."

"I did," he said heavily. "But kisses lead to other things. I thought you were older, more experienced."

"You wish," she said curtly.

He sighed. "Well, we'll deal with it when we have to," he said after a minute. He looked down at her quietly, his green eyes searching, curious. "I should never have let them talk me into coming here," he told her. "Tony wanted the extra protection that some of his old comrades could provide. I didn't expect to have you drawn into this."

"Neither did I," she said. She stared at her fingers. "I guess it was hard on you, living in a little hick town, with no suitable women around to date."

He made a rough sound in his throat. "Stop that," he said shortly. "You weren't a substitute, Sara."

"Max said you love women until you seduce them, and then you just throw them away," she returned, staring straight at him.

His high cheekbones colored. "Damn Max!"

"If you're filthy rich, I expect you can buy as many women as you want," she continued conversationally.

"I don't buy women," he informed her. "I just don't want to get married."

"I don't think there's much danger of that, with Max carrying payoff checks around to all your girlfriends."

"I told you, I didn't tell Max to do that! It was her idea," he added. "She said she'd handle everything, and I was drunk enough not to care how."

Her eyebrows arched. "Drunk?"

He looked rigid. "You asked me to stop, and I couldn't," he growled. "How do you think I felt? I read the situation wrong and threw my conscience to the wind. Then Max told me how old you were." He winced. "Nineteen. Dear God!"

"Well, I'm not exactly a child," she shot back, growing angry herself. "And I'm no stranger to violence."

"People hit you with books in the bookstore, do they?" he asked, in a condescending, faintly amused tone.

She looked him in the eye. "A rebel paramilitary unit in Sierra Leone tossed a grenade into the clinic where my father was dressing wounds," she replied, watching the shock hit him. "I was standing beside him, holding a bowl of water. I was just ten, it was the only way I was able to help. My father died. I was concussed so badly that I had brain damage. That's why I can't match socks and earrings," she added. "I was right in the path of the grenade. Fragments penetrated my skull. One's still in there," she told him. "They were afraid to try to take it out."

His face was white. Absolutely white. "Why were you there?"

"My grandfather talked my father into doing a stint at missionary work. Dad had been a medic in the army and he was a lay preacher. He and my grandfather forced my mother into going. I begged to go, too. I thought Africa had to be the most exciting place on earth," she added in a dull, quiet tone. "Well, it was exciting, I guess."

"What happened to your mother?"

"She drank herself to death, after she used every low trick she could think of to embarrass my grandfather, to make him pay for Daddy's death. She grew famous locally. It's why I was innocent," she added bitterly. "I was afraid to go out with local boys, because she'd slept with some of them. Everybody thought I was like her. Everybody except Grandad."

Jared winced. "You didn't tell me any of this," he accused.

"We were friends," she replied heavily. "Just friends. I knew you'd never want somebody like me for keeps. I'm nothing like Max, or the women who chase after you. I don't care about money, I don't like diamonds, I'd never fit into high society and I'm brain-damaged. It would never have been my idea to get involved with you physically," she added coldly, "because I knew from the outset that there would be no future in it."

His teeth were grinding together. He'd felt bad before. Now he was sick to his stomach. Somewhere along the road to get rich, he'd lost his way. He had everything he'd ever wanted, but he had no one to share it with. He was alone. He would always be alone, surrounded by women who liked expensive jewelry and travel. And by bodyguards hired to protect him from people who wanted his money enough to risk anything to get it.

"It's going to ruin your reputation, having Tony live here with you," he pointed out.

"What reputation?" she muttered. "Thanks to you, I'm a fallen woman. If I do get pregnant, it's not something I'll be able to hide. Everybody who sees me will know what I've been up to. You'll be off in Las Vegas gambling, or sailing a yacht in the Mediterranean. At least Tony cares about me."

"There are things about Tony that you don't know," he said flatly.

"Yes, and there are things about Tony that you don't know, either," she retorted. "Tony got me to the hospital in time for them to save my life in Africa. I don't remember him, of course. A lot of my childhood was removed along with the damaged tissue in my brain."

His face was almost frozen in place. Nothing had gone right for him since the death of his daughter. He'd destroyed the life of the young woman in that bed. He'd disgraced and shamed himself. He didn't know what to do. But he knew that he needed to do something. He couldn't walk away and let Sara face this alone, not even with Tony for company. He'd have to have a nice talk with Tony, who hadn't bothered to tell him what he knew about Sara. All this misery might have been prevented.

"Don't you have a board meeting or a conference or a yacht race to go to?" Sara asked when he didn't speak. "I'd hate to delay you in any way from your business."

His eyes almost glowed red. He was just about to open his mouth and let her have it with both barrels when Tony walked in, carrying the phone.

"Sorry, Sara, but it's that guy from New York again," he said, handing it to her.

Jared frowned. "And just who the hell do you know in New York?" he demanded suddenly.

Ten

His own words shocked Jared. He was jealous. He didn't want to be.

Sara, oblivious to his thoughts, was torn between telling Jared to mind his own business and talking to the editor who was going to buy her book.

"Hello?" came a voice from over the telephone.

She put it to her ear. "This is Sara," she said.

Jared glared at her.

"Miss Dobbs? It's Daniel Harris here, at Mirabella Publishing Company."

"Yes, Mr. Harris?"

"I wanted to ask if you could do us a colored drawing of just one of the puppies to use in advertising. Also, we're going to need some ideas for a title. The contract will be on its way to you later this week. You aren't agented, are you?"

"No, I'm not," she said worriedly. "Do I need to be?"

"Of course not. You can have an attorney look over the contract for you, if you have any worries. We're offering you a standard royalty contract, with an advance—" he gave her the figure, and she gasped "—and then thereafter you'll get a percentage of the royalties when the book is on the shelves. We would also like for you to do some publicity, signings and so forth; but that will be when the book is published. Tentatively we're scheduling it for next spring. Sound okay?"

"Oh, yes," she said, beaming. "Mr. Harris, I'm just overwhelmed. I don't know how to thank you."

"It's a good book," he replied. "We're proud to publish it. If the terms are okay with you, we're sending the contracts down by courier. If you could send us the single drawing by next week or the week after, that would be fine."

"Yes, I can do that," she agreed, without mentioning her condition. She gave him her street address, trying not to let Jared's black scowl unnerve her.

"We'll be in touch."

"Thanks again," she replied, and hung up.

"Who's Daniel Harris?" Jared demanded.

Her eyebrows levered up. "What business is it of yours?"

The scowl darkened. "You're living with an ex-mercenary and handing out your home address to strangers in New York."

"Well, I am getting to be quite the vamp, aren't I?" she asked, and blinked her long lashes at him.

His teeth set audibly. "Who is he?"

She just glared, but he didn't back down an inch. "All right! He's an editor. I sold my children's book to him."

"Book?"

"The one I was working on? Lisa Parks's puppies?"

"Oh."

"They bought it. They're sending me a contract to sign."

"I'll have an attorney look it over for you," he offered.

She sat up. "Max isn't touching my book! Or my contracts!"

His expression lightened. "You're jealous."

She flushed. "So are you!"

He looked odd for a minute. He blinked. "Yes," he said finally.

That floored her. She just looked at him, dumbfounded.

"You might be carrying my child," he said after a minute, and something odd flashed in his eyes. "I'm territorial."

"It's my child, if there is one," she shot back. "You're not taking me over."

He was thinking, scheming, planning. It was in his expression. "I'm good at hostile takeovers."

"Remember me? The uncouth savage from Outer Cowpasture?" she prompted. "Imagine showing me off at cocktail parties! Think of the embarrassment when I open my mouth and drawl at your circle of friends."

"I don't have friends," he said coldly.

"Why not?"

He shrugged. "I never know if they're seeing me or my money."

"Fortunately I don't have that problem. Being poor has its advantages." She thought for a minute. "Well, I won't be as poor as I was, I suppose. If the book sells, I mean."

"If it's publicized enough, it will sell."

She gave him a wry look. "Don't even think about it. I can do my own publicity."

"I have a firm of publicists working for me, making up ad campaigns for the corporation and its divisions," he said.

"I don't work for your corporation."

"I thought we were family," he began.

"Tony and I are family. We just voted you out," she told him.

He moved closer to the bed. "You'd leave me alone in the world, with nobody?"

"You've got Max."

"I fired Max."

"I'm sure she won't be hard to replace," she said cattily. "And I'm sure you have a whole houseful of beautiful women ready to step into her shoes in other ways," she added meaningfully.

He avoided her eyes. "I'm a man," he said curtly. "Men have needs."

"Yes. I noticed," she said deliberately.

He moved restlessly. "I told you, I didn't mean for that to happen!"

She colored. "Great! If there's a baby, we can tell him he was an accident."

"Don't you dare!" he exploded.

She felt embarrassed at the statement, which she hadn't meant. He just made her mad. "I like babies," she said slowly, putting her hands flat on her stomach. "But it's scary, thinking about having one. They're so little…"

"When Ellen was born," he recalled quietly, "they put her in my arms. I'd never seen anything so tiny, so perfect." A sad smile touched his hard mouth. "I counted little fingers and toes, kissed her little nose, her feet. I never loved anything so much…"

He stopped and turned away, walking to the window. He looked out over the kitchen garden. It took him a minute to get his emotions under control.

Sara felt guilty. He'd loved his little child. He was afraid to have another one, afraid of losing it. He was closing up inside his shell for safety.

"Lisa and Cy lost their first baby," she said softly. "It was born with several rare birth defects. The doctors couldn't save it, and they had specialists all the way from Dallas. Lisa said it wasn't meant to be. They grieved for years. They were afraid to try again, too. But when she got pregnant again, everything went perfectly. She and Cy are like children themselves. They're crazy about this child and talking about having more. You can't hide from life," she concluded quietly. "I know. I've tried to. I have nightmares, remembering how my father died. I blocked it out for years, but sometimes now I can see it. I was conscious for just a few seconds after the concussion hit me. He was blown apart..." She had to stop. The memory was nightmarish.

He came back to the bed, standing over her. "I wish you could have told me about it," he said softly. "You haven't had it easy, have you?"

"Neither have you," she replied.

He drew in a slow breath. "I've lost my nerve," he said after a minute. "I don't think I could cope with losing another child."

"Neither did Lisa and Cy, but it didn't stop them from trying again. Life doesn't come with guarantees. Sometimes you just have to have faith."

"Faith," he scoffed. His face was hard, closed. "I hated God."

"He doesn't hate you," she said gently. "He doesn't punish people, you know. We have free choice. He doesn't control every second of our lives. Bad things happen. That's just the way life is. But faith is how we cope. Especially in small towns."

"You're only nineteen," he said quietly. "How did you come to be so wise, at such an age?"

"I had a hard life as a child," she replied simply. "It teaches you things you wouldn't learn in a protected environment." She searched his eyes. "I had a best friend at the mission in Africa. I watched her die of a fever. All the medicines we had couldn't cure her. One of our best workers, a nice boy named Ahmed, was gunned down two feet from his front door by rebels. He was smiling when he died. He said he was going to heaven now, and we weren't to grieve." She shook her head. "In Jacobsville, you can walk down the streets after dark and not get shot. I think of that as miraculous. People here just take it for granted."

He sat down beside her on the bed. "Where we sunk wells in South America," he said, "there were people living in conditions that you couldn't conceive of if you hadn't been there. Women were old by the age of forty, men were missing fingers, teeth, eyes. Children died in infancy of diseases we can prevent here. I felt guilty for making a profit from oil, when all those conditions were going on around me. I set up a foundation, to provide small grants to people who wanted to start businesses of their own. Women, mostly, who could weave cloth and keep chickens and a cow so they had eggs and milk and butter to sell. You'd be amazed at how far that little bit of money went."

She was fascinated. "But they sent kidnappers after you," she said.

He nodded. "The government nationalized all the oil companies. I pulled my people out. I'd already foiled one kidnapping attempt when I went down with our corporate attorneys to try to work the situation out. Do you know what a narco-terrorist is, Sara?"

"Yes. I've read about them. They grow coca and process it in factories on site, and sell coca paste to drug lords who market it in the U.S. and elsewhere," she said. "They control politicians."

"They always need money, for bribes and weapons," he said. "They've discovered that kidnapping wealthy foreigners is a quick, easy way to get cash. It's a bold move, sending people up here to try to nab me. But there was a raid just recently that cost them several million in operating cash. They thought I'd be easy to kidnap. Their mistake."

"Tony said that's why you came here," she replied. "A lot of his former comrades live in Jacobsville."

He nodded. "But it didn't work. They tracked me here without attracting attention. They might have succeeded, if you hadn't been canny enough to panic them." He shook his head, smiling softly down at her. "You're brave, Sara. I don't know a single other person, except maybe Tony, who'd have had the nerve to do what you did."

She felt warm inside. She shouldn't. He'd said terrible things to her. Besides, there was the possibility of a child. She looked up at him steadily. "So the kidnappers are in custody. Those worries are over. Right?"

His lips made a thin line. "They didn't actually kidnap anyone," he said. "Cash Grier is holding them right now on a weapons charge."

She felt her heart skip. "A weapons charge?"

"They had an AK-47 in the van and no permit," he replied. He frowned. "Actually I don't think you can get a permit for an automatic weapon as a private citizen. I'll have to ask Cash. Anyway, it's illegal in their case. But they didn't carry you out of the store or even lay hands on you." He sighed. "So there's a good chance that they're going to get out on bail as soon as their high-priced American attorney gets them to a bail hearing."

"The judge can set a high bail, if he or she is asked to," she began.

He smiled cynically. "Drug lords have so much money that even a million dollars is like pocket change to them. It won't help."

"But if they get out, won't they just try again?"

His expression changed. "Worried about me?" he asked in a soft, deep tone.

"I can worry, even if you're not family anymore," she returned pertly.

He laughed softly. The trap didn't feel like a trap. Maybe he'd been too grief-stricken to think of a child on his own, but this one had fallen right into his lap. Well, he'd helped it to, and he shouldn't feel happy about losing control with Sara, all the same.

She was watching his expression change, unable to follow what he was thinking. He seemed to be more comfortable with her now than he had several minutes ago. That didn't mean he was happy about their situation.

"What will you do?" she asked, because she really was worried.

"I don't know," he replied. "I think I'll go talk to the police chief." He frowned. "Now there's an odd bird," he said conversationally. "Someone said he was a Texas Ranger once."

"He was something else, once, too," she mused.

"The sniper thing?" he scoffed. "Gossip, I imagine."

"No," she said. "It's not. A Drug Enforcement Administration agent's little girl was kidnapped by the former head of one of the Mexican cartels last year. They threatened to kill her if the feds didn't back off their raid on a local drug warehouse. Cash Grier took out two of the kidnappers and the DEA agents got the rest and rescued the child. He made the shots in the dark from over six hundred yards away." She lowered her voice. "They say he was a covert assassin once."

His eyebrows lifted. "And he's a small town police chief?"

"He's happy here," she told him. "His wife, Tippy, used to be a model. They called her the 'Georgia Firefly.'"

"Well!"

"They have a little girl named Tris." She gave him a smirk. "So, you see, not everybody dislikes living in Outer Cowpasture."

"Touché," he replied.

"Maybe he has friends who could get those three guys on some sort of terrible federal charge," she murmured. "We never found out who the DEA agents were," she added. "One of them does undercover work, so he wasn't identified. The other, the child's mother, was a DEA agent, too. Her husband bought property here, but they're living in Houston until the end of the school year because of their daughter. They didn't want to put her into a strange school midyear."

"Do you know everything about everybody here?" he asked curiously.

"Sure," she told him. "Everybody does."

He glanced at the door, where Tony was just entering with soup and sandwiches on a tray. He glared at his ex-boss. "She needs to eat her lunch."

Jared got to his feet. "I was just leaving." He smiled down at Sara. "Eat it all up, like a good girl."

She flushed. "I'm not a kid."

He sighed. "Compared to me you are," he said quietly, and he looked lost.

"My mother was nineteen when she had me," Tony said abruptly.

Jared glanced at him, curious.

Tony shrugged. "It isn't the age, it's the mileage," he clarified, meeting the other man's eyes. "She's got almost as much mileage as you have. She just looks younger."

"I suppose so."

"I like babies," Tony said, setting the tray across Sara's legs.

Jared withdrew into his safe shell. He didn't say a word.

"Try not to get killed," Sara told him. "I'm in no condition to go to a funeral."

He laughed. "I'll do my best."

Tony glanced at him. "They'll try again," he said. "The minute they make bail, and they'll make it."

"Yes, I know," Jared replied. He pursed his lips. "I've had an idea."

"What?" Tony asked.

Jared glared. "Oh, sure, I tell you, and you tell her, and she tells everybody in Jacobsville."

"I only gossip about people I like," Sara protested.

"And pigs fly," he returned. "I'll come by tomorrow and check on you."

"I'll be fine," Sara protested.

He glanced at her belly with an unreadable expression. "I'll come by anyway."

He turned and left without another word.

"We could have offered him lunch," Sara told Tony. "Even if he isn't part of our family anymore."

"He'd curdle the milk," Tony muttered.

Sara laughed and finished her soup.

Jared went straight to Police Chief Cash Grier's office when he left Sara's house.

Cash was on the phone, but he hung up when Jared walked in and closed the office door.

"I haven't let them out yet," Cash told him, anticipating the reason he'd come.

"They'll skip town the minute they can make bail," Jared replied.

"In the old days, I'd have thrown them out the back door and charged them with attempted escape."

Jared glowered at him. "Civilization has its price."

Cash sighed. "Spoilsport."

Jared sat down in the visitor's chair without being asked. "They'll be as much a danger to Sara as they are to me," he said. "We have to find a way to prove they're kidnappers."

Cash's dark eyebrows went up. "We could stuff you in their van under a blanket and catch them at the city limits sign," he suggested dryly.

Jared chuckled. "That's just what I had in mind."

"It would be entrapment, I'm afraid," Cash replied, leaning back in his chair. "We'll have to find a legal way to keep them locked up."

"Suppose we have Tony the Dancer arrested for breaking and entering?"

Cash blinked. "Are we having the same conversation?"

"You could put him in the cell with the three kidnappers," he continued. "Tony could offer to help them get me, for revenge."

Cash whistled. "And I thought I was the only dangerous person in town."

"I didn't inherit what I've got," Jared told him. "The first company I started was a security business. I hired my men and myself out to oil companies as protection against terrorist attacks. An elderly oil tycoon with no dependents took a liking to me, taught me the business and left his company to me when he died. Eventually I sold the security company and parlayed the oil business into a worldwide corporation."

"So that's how you know Tony the Dancer."

Jared nodded. "He was the first man I hired, in the days before he worked for a legitimate authority. He still does odd jobs for me, from time to time."

Cash pursed his lips. "Then I suppose you know about his real background?"

Jared chuckled. "I check out everybody who works for me. His dossier was, to say the least, impressive."

"Yes, and how fortunate for him that he's not wanted in the States," Cash replied. "The only man I know who's a target for assassination in more countries than Tony is an undercover DEA agent named Ramirez."

"I know him," Jared said unexpectedly. "He worked for me, too, in the early days."

"He worked for a lot of people. He's involved in a case right now, so if you see him anywhere, pretend you don't know him."

"Isn't it risky for him to go undercover again?" Jared asked, curious.

"It is in Texas. He helped bring down the late drug lord,

Manuel Lopez. But he's not known locally, except by a few of us with ties to mercenaries. His name was never mentioned when his partner's child was kidnapped by drug smugglers here last year."

"I understand you brought down some of the kidnappers."

Cash nodded. "Some skills never get rusty." He leaned forward. "Who talks to Tony, you or me?"

"It had probably better be you," Jared said heavily. "He'd enjoy cutting my throat right now because of Sara."

"You didn't put Sara in the hospital," Cash replied, misunderstanding.

"No, but I may have gotten her pregnant," he said uncomfortably.

Cash's good humor eclipsed. His black eyes flashed at the man across the desk.

"We're all capable of making ungodly mistakes," Jared said quietly. "I don't think I've ever been around an innocent in my whole life. In recent years, women are as aggressive as men when it comes to sex."

"Not all of them," Cash said in an icy tone. "And Sara's only nineteen."

"I didn't find that out until it was too late," he said. "She seems older than she is."

"Considering her past, that isn't surprising."

Jared nodded. "I didn't know about that, either." His eyes held a sad, faraway look. "My daughter died eight months ago," he said. "I've grieved until it was an effort just to get out of bed in the morning. I don't understand how, but Sara brought the sunlight back in for me. I never meant to hurt her."

"I'm sorry," Cash said. "I know what it is to lose a child."

Jared met his eyes. There was, suddenly, a bond between them, forged of grief.

"Tony seems very fond of Sara."

Jared's face hardened. "Well, I'll take care of that when the time comes. If she's pregnant, that's my child. No way is he raising it."

Cash's eyebrows arched.

Jared cleared his throat. "He's not going to be able to settle down, anyway."

"You need to meet a few people around town," Cash told him. "Starting with Eb Scott."

"Eb Scott lives here?" he exclaimed.

"Yes. He's got a state-of-the-art training center for military and government resources," he said. "A lot of ex-mercs work for him."

"I'd never have expected Scott to be able to settle down."

"Most people said the same about me," Cash replied, smiling. "I think it comes down to what's important to you. It used to be work, for me. Now it's Tippy and our baby. And Rory," he added. "My brother-in-law." He chuckled. "He's twelve years old."

"It's still work that gets the major portion of my time," Jared replied. "But just recently I've begun to wonder if I don't have my priorities skewed." He studied his boots. "There aren't many women around like Sara. Of course, she's years too young for me."

"Judd Dunn, my assistant chief, is married to a young woman who was twenty-one at the same time he was thirty-two. They have twins and they're very happy. It depends a great deal on the woman. Some mature sooner than others."

"I guess they do."

Cash got to his feet. "I think I'll go have a word with Tony."

"I think I'll stop by the flower shop and start working on my campaign."

"Campaign?"

"Tony's not marrying Sara," Jared said shortly.

"That would be her decision," Cash cautioned.

"Yes, well, he can't afford as many roses and chocolates as I can, so let's see him compete!"

Cash knew when to shut up.

Sara was curious to see Cash Grier at her door. It must have something to do with the would-be kidnappers, she thought.

"How's it going, Sara?" he asked, smiling. "Feeling better?"

"A lot, thanks. Why are you here?"

"I have to talk to Tony." He moved closer to the bed. "You wouldn't mind having someone else stay with you for a couple of days, would you?"

"Why would you ask that?"

"Well, I'm going to have to arrest Tony for breaking and entering," he began, "and I don't want you to be here alone."

"Arrest…?"

"Now, calm down," he said. "It isn't for real."

"What isn't for real?" Tony asked, carrying two cups of coffee. "We can talk in the living room," he told Cash. "Sara, will you be okay for a few minutes?"

She couldn't put two words together.

Cash put his finger to his lips, walked out with Tony and closed the door, leaving Sara worried and quiet.

"But I didn't do it to steal anything," Tony was protesting. "I had to feed the cat!"

"It isn't for real," Cash insisted. "We want you to have to be thrown in with the kidnappers. Jared's having you arrested. You're furious at him. You want to get back at him. They'd love to help, I'm sure."

Tony put his coffee cup down. "Okay, now, you're starting to scare me. Have you been drinking?"

Cash chuckled. "Not today." He leaned forward. "Here's

the deal. I have to turn the men loose. All I'm holding them on is a weapons charge. I can't convince a sane judge to set a million dollars bail for a weapons charge. They're going to skip town the minute the cell door opens. If they do, they may try to grab Sara again, or they may go after Jared. Either way, it's going to lead to tragedy."

Tony pursed his lips. "Oh. I get it. You want me to lead them into a trap so that you can charge them with kidnapping."

"That's exactly what I want."

Tony's eyes narrowed. "Jared put you up to it."

"He did," Cash confessed. "He's worried about Sara."

"Not enough to keep himself from seducing her," Tony said angrily.

"I heard about that, too. He's sorry he did it. But if you have plans to help her raise the baby—if there is a baby—you're in for the fight of your life," he added. "He's just starting to feel possessive about her."

Tony scoffed. "He goes through women like a sword through tissue paper," he said coldly.

"Like a man who's afraid to risk his heart twice, I would have thought," Cash replied solemnly. "He told me about his little girl."

Tony's hard demeanor softened. "Yeah. That was rough. She was a sweet kid. He didn't spend nearly enough time with her, but he loved her. She loved him, too. Hell of a tragedy."

"Let's not have another one," Cash said. "Help me get these guys off the street before they do something stupid. Sara might not be so lucky a second time. And they wouldn't hesitate to kill her, after she foiled their plan so deftly."

"I thought about that, myself."

"It's only going to be for a couple of days," Cash said, "but we need somebody to stay with Sara. I thought maybe Harley Fowler…"

Tony's dark eyes twinkled. "Did you? I was thinking that Jared might be willing to sacrifice himself."

"Let him stay with Sara?"

Tony nodded. "It might be just the thing to get them both to sort out their priorities. And you could have extra patrols on the house, too. Just in case."

Cash grinned. "I like the way you think."

Tony just chuckled.

If making the decision was easy, telling it to Sara wasn't.

She looked utterly tragic. "But you can't put Tony in jail!" she cried. "I thought you were my friend!"

Cash grimaced. Tony was standing beside him in handcuffs.

"It isn't what you think, Sara," Tony agreed.

"Jared Cameron put you up to it, didn't he?" she demanded, and Tony grimaced, too.

She was almost in tears when the front door opened and Jared walked in carrying a suitcase. Sara spotted him, picked up a vase on the bedside table, drew back and flung it at him past the two stunned men. It shattered near Jared's shoulder.

"You get out of my house!" she yelled.

Cash looked at Tony. "Are you sure asking him to stay with her is a good idea?" he asked.

Eleven

Jared managed to look disgusted. "Is that any way to treat the father of your child?" he demanded.

"I'm not having a child!" she yelled, red-faced.

"How do you know?" he retorted. "It's too early for a pregnancy test."

"He's got you there," Cash interjected.

"You shouldn't be getting so upset, Sara, it's not good for you," Tony said worriedly.

"He's absolutely right," Jared said, putting down the suitcase. "I'm going to take care of you while Tony's away."

"You make it sound like he's going on vacation," Sara muttered. "He's going to jail!"

"Yes, I know."

She frowned. "You know?" She looked from him, to Tony, to Cash Grier. She wasn't stupid. "Oh."

"It's the only way," Tony told her. "Otherwise, you'll never be out of danger."

"You're sure you aren't going to keep him?" she asked Cash.

Cash smiled. "I'm sure. We'd better get going."

"I'll be back before you know it," Tony told Sara. He paused beside Jared. "You be careful, too. There may only be three of them, or there may not."

"I know that, too," Jared replied. He smiled wryly. "Don't forget who taught you surveillance techniques."

Tony chuckled. "I wouldn't dare. See you, Sara."

"See you, Tony."

Cash nodded and walked him out the door.

Jared watched them leave, his hands deep in his pockets.

"What did you mean about surveillance techniques?" she asked.

He turned. His green eyes were mischievous. "The first business I ever owned provided private security. Tony and I worked together until we could train assistants."

She studied him quietly. "And what did you do before that?" she asked.

"I was a cop in San Antonio."

Her lips fell open. "For heaven's sake! And you own an oil corporation now?"

"I've had a lot of help along the way. Most of it from Tony," he told her, stepping gingerly around shattered pottery. "We were always best friends until you came along."

"Well, you know why that happened," she muttered.

"Yes, I do. No need to remind me." He accidentally stood on a piece of ceramic that broke again. "Where's a broom?"

"In the closet in the kitchen," she began, but he was gone before she could ask anything else.

He came back with a broom and a dustpan and cleaned the floor as naturally as if he'd done it all his life.

"Were you in the military, before you were a policeman?" she asked, curious about him.

"Army," he said. "I was in special forces. So was Tony." He poured the broken pieces of what had been a vase into a nearby trash can and propped the broom and dustpan beside it. "He was best man at my wedding."

He'd never talked to her like this before. It was fascinating. "Did you love your wife?"

"Yes, when I married her," he said. "We both came from ranch families. My father got kicked in the head by a bull and died soon afterward. My mother grieved herself to death. Marian's parents died in a tornado outbreak. We'd known each other most of our lives. We were friends. I suppose we thought friendship was enough. It wasn't."

"Why did she leave you?"

"She found someone she loved," he said simply. "She took our daughter, Ellen, with her. She was a wonderful mother. Ellen was happy with her. I wasn't home much, but when I was, Ellen was always welcome to come and stay with me. My permanent home is in Oklahoma," he added, "where my corporation headquarters is."

"But you bought a ranch here," she said, mystified.

"I told you at the cemetery that I needed a change," he said. "I meant it. I was grieving for Ellen and upset over Marian's suicide just afterward. I thought new surroundings would help me get past the depression."

"The surroundings don't matter much," Sara said gently. "Pain and grief are portable. They go with you."

He glanced down at her and smiled warmly. "There's that odd insight again. You really are old for your age."

"And getting older by the day," she replied.

He moved to the bed and sat down beside her. He was

wearing jeans and a chambray shirt, open at the neck. He looked very sensual with his hair faintly ruffled and his nice tan.

Without warning, his big, lean hand pressed gently on her flat stomach. "I made a hell of a fuss about it. But maybe it wouldn't be a bad thing, if you're pregnant. I'll be a better father this time around."

"You can come and visit anytime you like," she told him.

He frowned. "My child isn't being born out of wedlock."

"Well, he won't have much choice, because I am not marrying you," she said firmly.

"Why not?" he asked, and seemed really intent on her reason.

She colored and averted her eyes. "Because I don't ever want to have to do that again."

He lost color. He knew his heart had stopped. "Sara, it was your first time and I was in too much of a hurry," he said softly. "I hurt you because I rushed it."

Her face was red by now. She couldn't possibly look at him. She clasped her hands together and picked at her thumbnail nervously.

He tilted her embarrassed face up to his. "I won't ever hurt you again," he promised. "It gets better. Honest."

She grimaced.

She was so young, he thought sadly. Probably he should never have touched her. But she made him feel young and vital and full of fire. She brought feelings of nurturing and possession to him. He'd never wanted a woman for keeps. Even his wife had been a footnote in his life. But this woman was magic. Sheer magic.

He thought back to their first meeting, and inspiration struck. "You could have your own bookstore," he said.

Her eyes widened. "My own…?"

"We could even build a child activity center into it. The baby could play while you worked. And if customers with children came in, they could play there while their parents browsed. There could be a snack shop with fancy coffee."

She was melting. Just the thought of her own place was tantalizing. "Really?"

He smiled at her enthusiasm. She couldn't even hide it. "I could delegate more, and travel less. We could have more than one child."

She looked into his eyes with all her longings showing there. Children. A home. A business. Max. She scowled and glared at him.

"What?"

"Are you sure you fired Max?" she wondered aloud. "Tony says you're always firing her, but she always comes back."

"This time it's permanent," he assured her. He drew in a long breath. "I'm through with the playboy life as well. I thought a few encounters would be a cure for loneliness. It wasn't. It only made me feel cheap."

That was a powerful admission, she thought. And he did seem sincere.

His big hand pressed gently against her stomach. He looked at it, his eyes quiet and full of wonder. "You know your body better than I do. What's your gut feeling?"

"I...I don't know," she faltered. "Really. It's too soon."

He smiled. "Well, either way, we'll cope. If you aren't pregnant, we'll spend some time getting to know each other before we start a family. We'll have plenty of time." He pursed his lips. "And Tony will have to find himself a new source of entertainment, besides looking after you and cooking," he said, and felt guilty and elated all at once. If she really was pregnant, Tony was right out of the running as a potential husband.

She frowned. "Tony will be all right, won't he? There are three of those men. They're all big and muscular, and they can't watch them all the time while they're in custody at the county detention center." Which was where they would be taken, because the city didn't maintain a jail.

He chuckled. "I've seen Tony take on six guys and walk away grinning," he told her. "It's the best idea we could come up with," he added, tugging the sheet up over her belly tenderly. "We can't risk having them make bail and come after you again."

She grimaced. "Life used to be so uncomplicated until you came along," she sighed wistfully.

"You're too young to appreciate monotony," he returned. He bent and kissed her gently on the forehead. "Try to get some sleep. I have a few phone calls to make, then we'll talk some more about the future."

She could have argued that there might not be one, but it was sweet to pretend. She smiled at him and agreed.

Tony was muttering, furious, as he was put into the general quarters in detention, wearing an orange jumpsuit and flip-flops. He glowered at everybody around him.

"I didn't even take anything!" he yelled at the guard who'd delivered him. "I was just feeding the cat."

"Tell it to a judge," the deputy replied wearily.

"You bet I will!" he raged. "He just wants me out of the way, so he can walk off with my girl. You tell Jared Cameron that when I get out of here, I'm going to drive a truck over him!"

"Terroristic threats and acts carry a felony charge," the amused deputy called over his shoulder.

Tony gave him a four-fingered salute.

One of the men in the dormitory was giving him odd looks. Tony stared at him belligerently. "You got a problem?" he demanded.

The man was about his own age, tall and muscular, with a mustache and tattoos over both arms. "Sounds like you got one," he said with a hint of a foreign accent. "Somebody locked you up for nothing, huh?"

Tony moved to a chair and sat down. "Something like that."

The man took a chair beside him. "Jared Cameron? I think I heard of him."

"Most people have," Tony muttered. "God, I wish I had a smoke!"

"Can't have cigarettes in here, my friend," the other man chuckled. "But I could get you some weed, if you got anything to trade."

"Do I look like I got anything to trade?" Tony demanded. "What are you in here for?"

"Weapons charge," the man said easily. "But me and my boys, we'll be out as soon as we have our bail hearing."

"Lucky you," Tony told him. "I'm in for breaking and entering. It's a felony."

"Not a big one," his companion said.

Tony stared at him. "It is if you're out on probation," he said.

The man grimaced. "Ah. I see. Too bad."

"Yeah. Too bad." His eyes narrowed angrily. "Jared Cameron better hope I get the death penalty for it, because the day I get out of here, he's a dead man. I know his routine, the layout of his house, everything!"

"How is that?"

"I was working as his bodyguard," Tony scoffed, "until he took a fancy to my girl and stole her from me. Now he wants me out of the way."

The man looked down at the floor. The room smelled of foul odors. Tony wondered if any of these people had ever been introduced to soap. One was obviously coming down from a drug-induced high, shaking and threatening people. Another was staggering drunk. Nobody looked as if he was a stranger to the criminal justice system.

"You know," the other man began casually, "you could make a lot of money and get even with Cameron at the same time if you wanted to."

Tony was all ears. "I could? How?"

"I know some people who would pay a lot of money for him."

"He's no pushover," Tony warned.

"Yes, but he is now lacking his bodyguard," the man persisted. "Before he can hire another one, it would be a good time to apprehend him."

Tony stared at the man. "Yeah. It would, wouldn't it?"

The man got up. "I got to talk to my friends about it. But I think I could get you in on it, if you're interested."

"I got no money for a lawyer and Cameron didn't even offer to help me," Tony muttered. "In fact, I think it was him who told the police I broke into the girl's house. Some boss!"

The other man was grinning now. "You want to get even, yes?"

"Yes."

"We will talk more later."

Tony shrugged. "Well, I'm not going anywhere. Not right away, at least."

That night, the jailer came and took Tony out, mumbling something about an attorney wanting to talk to him about his arrest.

Cash Grier was waiting in the interrogation room. He turned as Tony was escorted inside and the door closed, with the guard standing on the other side of it.

"Any luck?" Cash asked him.

Tony grinned. "Their ringleader wants me to help them put the snatch on Jared. He's been talking his two companions into it. One of them thinks I'm a plant. The other has, basically, the IQ of a plant."

Cash chuckled. "So you're in?"

"Seems so. I expect them to double-cross me the instant they see Jared in their sights, of course."

Cash thought for a minute. "We'll have Sara call a bail bondsman for you. We'll pay him without letting anyone else know. When you and the three outlaws get out, we'll have you wired and a homing device placed in their van. As soon as they grab Jared, we'll have them for attempted kidnapping and give them to the feds."

"Not a bad plan."

"You really think so? Thanks," Cash said with enthusiasm. "I don't actually know any feds, you understand, but I can look them up in the phone book."

Tony was laughing. "And they give you real bullets, do they?"

"I haven't shot anybody in a year, at least," Cash said with mock dismay.

"Just don't shoot me, when you show up to get those other guys. I weigh five pounds more than I should because of bullets they can't take out."

"I have a couple of my own that never left," Cash replied. "Okay. I'll go. I'll talk to Jared and have a couple of my officers standing by. Don't do anything until they actually have Jared in their van," he added cautiously. "We have to have charges that will stick."

"You keep an eye on Sara as well," Tony told him. "These guys don't act like they're hitting on all six cylinders. There's no telling what they may try next."

"I noticed. You know," he added seriously, "you look pretty good in orange."

Tony's eyes narrowed. "No fair picking on innocent victims of crime."

"Oh, that's rich, coming from you," Cash chuckled. "I'm leaving."

"Tell Sara not to worry about me."

"I can tell her, but it won't do any good. She likes you."

He shrugged. "I like her, too."

"We'll find a way to separate you from the kidnappers at the bail hearing so we can get you wired. I've already done their van."

"They may look for a homing device," Tony pointed out.

"They can look all they like," he replied. "They'll never find this one. See you."

"Yeah. You, too."

It was a very good plan. Tony was wired just before he left with the three men, now dressed again in their civilian clothing as Tony was. They seemed to trust him.

But once they were in the van, the driver spoke in an Arab dialect on his cell phone, blissfully unaware that Tony spoke that particular dialect.

The leader of the kidnappers told his contact that they were on their way to get the woman Jared loved. Somehow they'd found out that Jared was staying with Sara. They were going to hold her long enough to make him give himself up to them, then they were going to kill her. They would kill Tony, too, because he could become a liability once the girl was dead. They would kill Jared eventually, the minute they had the ransom in their hands. They already had airplane tickets. It would be a matter of hours. The contact could meet them at the airport in Belize where they usually hooked up.

Tony cursed the change of plans. He couldn't warn anybody. If he repeated what the kidnapper had said, they'd know he spoke Arabic and he'd be dead. If he didn't, Sara would be in terrible danger. Jared was with her. It would be an easy matter to take both of them.

He had to pretend that he hadn't understood a word and

act nonchalant. "Don't you guys kill Cameron," he cautioned belligerently. "He's all mine!"

"Be assured, we have no plans to kill him. We only wish for the ransom he will bring." He told the driver to slow down as they approached Sara's house.

"Hey," Tony murmured, looking out the windshield. "That ain't Cameron's house!"

"He isn't in his house," the leader of the three men replied. "Cameron is with your girlfriend."

"Don't you hurt her," Tony warned.

"Relax, my friend!" the other man laughed. "We intend only to take Cameron hostage. Then you and the girl will be free. I give you my word."

Which was as good as his sense of fashion, Tony thought sarcastically, but he only nodded and pretended to believe the man. While he was nodding, he was considering his options. He was not only wearing a wire, he had a hidden gun in an ankle holster and a commando knife in a sheath inside his slacks. He had a watch with a pull-out garrote. All that, combined with advanced martial arts training, should stand him in good stead if he had the opportunity to act.

"You taking Cameron out of the country after you nab him?" Tony asked.

The three men were intent on the sparse lighting of the small house just ahead. "Yes, yes," the leader said, distracted. "We have a base in Peru, where we can hold him until the ransom is paid."

Tony doubted that Jared Cameron would be alive after the ransom was in their hands.

"Stop!" the leader told the driver. "You stay and wait for our signal," he added. "We will take the bodyguard with us. Be vigilant."

"Of course," the driver replied.

The leader slid open the side panel of the van and motioned the shorter man and Tony out behind him.

"You will go first," he told Tony. "Knock on the door and pretend that you have come to check on the woman."

"Not a bad plan," Tony said, grinning, because this plan would give him room to act. "You guys are smart."

"You must not harm Cameron," the leader told him firmly. "We need the ransom very badly. Later, we will give him to you, once we have the funds."

Tony pretended to mull over the suggestion. "Okay. But you better give me a crack at him."

"We will. Of course we will," the leader said. He was now holding an automatic weapon. So was his companion.

It was going to be tricky, Tony mused, but he'd been in tighter spots. "You guys better get out of sight," Tony told them, hoping Cash Grier was listening closely to what he said to the hidden microphone.

"We will be just around this corner," the leader said. His face went hard. "We will have you in our sights, also. For insurance."

"In other words, I get shot if I try anything funny," Tony replied. "Hell, I want the guy as much as you do!"

The leader seemed to relax, a little. "Very well." He motioned to the second man and they went, light on their feet, around the corner of the porch.

Tony knocked on the door. He heard footsteps coming. They weren't Jared's footsteps. He would have known them anywhere. He had to hide a grin.

The door opened. Tony dived through it as Cash Grier slammed the door. Outside there was gunfire.

"Quick reflexes," Cash remarked to Tony.

"I've, uh, had a little practice over the years. How about Jared and Sara?"

"When we heard your plan over the wire," Cash replied,

"we got them out of the house. They're at Jared's. Nobody here but old Morris the cat, and we put him in a closet, just in case."

The shooting ended.

"All clear!" a voice called.

Cash and Tony went out onto the porch, where four Jacobsville police officers and a man in a suit were leading the two would-be kidnappers toward the front door. In the yard, the wheel man was standing in front of his van, handcuffed, with two other men in suits holding guns on him.

"Nice operation," Cash told his men. "I knew that extra training in hostage negotiation would come in handy."

"Hostage negotiation?" Tony exclaimed. "They've all got guns!"

Cash looked sheepish. "Well, you negotiate your way and I'll negotiate my way."

The officers chuckled. So did Tony.

They had tape of the kidnappers confessing. Federal marshals were escorting them to Dallas, where they'd face federal charges. Their kidnapping days were over.

Tony was back at the ranch the next day, but Jared was sending him on to Oklahoma to make sure the house was ready for occupants. And also to make sure no more would-be kidnappers were lurking around.

"You take care, Sara," Tony told her gently, and bent to kiss her on the cheek. "I expect we'll see each other again."

"I hope so." She hugged the big man and kissed his lean cheek. "Thanks for everything."

"No problem."

He shook hands with Jared. "I'll put Fred and Mabel to work getting the house set to rights. I assume you're not coming home alone," he added with a grin.

"You assume right," Jared said with a tender, possessive

look toward Sara, who was just going back inside the house to make sure old Morris was all right. Tony had brought him over after all the excitement was past.

Tony stuck his hands in his pockets. "I've got to go back to my day job," he said. "I'm tempted to give it up, but it's comfortable."

"You're too young to want to be comfortable," Jared replied. "Besides, you have to keep those reflexes honed." He smiled mischievously. "You might be the next target for kidnappers looking for ransom." He looked past Tony at the sleek Jaguar sports car that had been lodging in the huge garage with Jared's classic automobiles. "That car could get you some unwelcome attention."

"You're just saying that because you don't want me to take it away," Tony shot back.

"You could always get a newer one," Jared suggested.

"I don't like the newer ones. I like that one."

"Damn!"

"Listen, we signed papers," Tony reminded him. "It isn't as if I stole it."

Jared pursed his lips. "There's a thought," he began.

Tony wagged a finger at him. "You report this car stolen, and you'll never make it home to Oklahoma without being arrested for possession of at least one Schedule I substance. I swear!"

"All right, all right," Jared muttered. "You did see it first at the auto show."

"Damned straight, I did." He hesitated. "You take care of yourself. And if there is a baby," he added, "I get to be the godfather."

Jared opened his mouth to speak.

"I know at least one shaman who can do nasty spells back home in North Carolina," he interrupted.

"You're from Georgia," he shot back.

"My foster parents are from Georgia. I was born in Cherokee, North Carolina."

"Yes, but your real father wasn't."

Tony gave him a glare. "We don't talk about him."

"You need to," Jared said solemnly. "You have to deal with it one day."

"I'm going to Oklahoma." Tony put his sunglasses on. "Right now."

"Nice shades."

"That's what my boss said."

"You didn't! You wouldn't swipe his sunglasses…?"

"Of course I didn't swipe them. I won them."

"How?"

"He had a full house, I had four aces," he said smugly. "He threw the deck at me and walked out."

"Serves him right for getting suckered into playing poker with you," Jared said. He held out a hand. "Be safe."

Tony shook it. "You, too. I'll be in touch."

Sara came back with Morris in her arms, just in time to watch him drive away in a classic red sports car which, Jared told her, belonged to Tony.

"If Tony's leaving, why am I still here?" she asked Jared worriedly. "The bad guys are in Dallas by now, and I'm very fit."

He drew her to him, quiet and somber. "You're still here because we have things to talk about."

"Such as?"

He was oddly hesitant. "Come here."

He picked her up, Morris and all, and carried her into the living room, dropping down onto the sofa with her. Morris, uncomfortable, jumped down and went in search of food.

"We haven't known each other for a long time," Jared began quietly. "But I think we're basically the same sort of people. You're no doormat, and you're smart. You'd fit right in back in Oklahoma. Most of my friends are working people, just as I used to be. I don't travel in high social circles. In the past I spent a lot of time on airplanes, but that's going to stop. Whether or not you're pregnant doesn't matter right now. I'm going to delegate authority and start living my life for something other than making money."

"That sounds serious," she said, and her heart was hammering away in her chest. His eyes held a warmth she hadn't seen there before.

"It's very serious. I'm a good deal older than you," he began, "and I've had, and lost, a family. You could stay here and marry someone younger. Harley Fowler, maybe."

"I don't love Harley," she said softly, searching his eyes. "He's my friend. As for our ages," she added, "I'm more mature than a lot of women, because of what I've gone through."

He traced her mouth with a long forefinger. "Yes, you are," he agreed quietly. "Which leads to the next question."

"Which is?" she probed.

"Will you marry me, Sara?"

Twelve

Sara just looked at him, with her heart plain in her eyes. "Do you love me?" she asked, hesitating.

He smiled tenderly. "Yes," he said. "Of course I love you." He hesitated. His dark eyebrows lifted. "Well?"

"I loved you the minute you walked into the bookstore," she replied breathlessly. "I didn't really think you were an ogre, you know."

"Maybe I was, sort of," he returned, smiling. "But you've reformed me. So what do you think about getting married here and moving back to Oklahoma?"

"I don't mind where we live, as long as we're together," she told him. "But Morris the cat has to come with us." She paused. "Do you have pets?"

He laughed. "Do I! I've got saddle horses, cattle dogs, two huge Persian cats, an emu and an Amazon parrot."

"Oh, goodness," she exclaimed. "Why do you have an emu?"

He traced her mouth. "Ellen wanted one," he said simply. "I'd never even seen an emu, but a rancher I know was experimenting with them. We got Ellen a baby emu. She was crazy about him. We named him Paterson, after the Australian poet, and raised him with two border collies. The collies chase cattle, and the emu runs right along with them." He laughed. "It's quite a sight."

"I imagine so."

"We'll have cat furniture set up for Morris. After a few days of being spoiled, he'll adjust."

"What about your cats?"

He shrugged. "They'll all spit and fuss for a week, then they'll curl up and sleep together at night."

She smiled. It was usually the case when two sets of cats met. "We could be married here?" she asked, still having trouble believing it.

"Of course."

"I could wear a wedding gown, and carry a bouquet?"

"You can even have a photographer," he replied. "So that we have nice pictures to prove that we're married."

"That would be nice."

"We'll fly up to Dallas. You can have a gown from Neiman Marcus."

"I could buy something off the rack," she protested.

He brought her small hand to his lips and kissed the palm. "I'm fairly notorious," he said. "There will be news coverage. You wouldn't want me to look like a cheapskate on national television, would you?" he asked reasonably.

She laughed. "Nobody would think such a thing."

"Ha!"

Her head was spinning. She couldn't believe how quickly it had all happened. But there was that other thing, that worrisome thing...

He was watching her expression closely. He knew what the problem was. They were alone in the house. Old Morris had wandered off into the kitchen. He was safely established, for the time being. He pursed his lips as he looked down into Sara's worried face.

"There's no time like the present," he murmured.

"Excuse me?"

He bent and drew his mouth tenderly against Sara's. "Don't think," he whispered. "Don't worry. Just let go."

While he was talking, his hands were moving over her in soft, light caresses that made her mind overload. She wanted to tell him something, but he'd unbuttoned her shirt and his mouth was already on her breasts.

She gasped at the sensations. They weren't like last time. He was insistent, and expert. As the heated minutes sped past, she was as frantic to get her clothes out of the way as she had been to escape him the last time he'd touched her this way. But the sensations she was feeling now were explosive, overwhelming. She arched up to his ardent mouth and sobbed as his hands found her under the concealing cloth and created exquisite waves of pleasure.

She was under him. She felt the cold leather under her bare back, the heated weight of his body over and against hers. His mouth trailed down her body and back up again, in soft, arousing kisses that trespassed in all sorts of forbidden areas.

He asked her something, but she was already too far gone to hear him. Shivering, aching for satisfaction, she drew her legs up to ease his path, she arched up to his devouring mouth. It was the closest to heaven she'd ever imagined.

When she finally felt him, there, she dug her nails into his hips and held on for dear life as he buffeted her on the sofa. She was aware of the ceiling overhead, and the sound of his rough breathing, of her own frantic little gasps, as the pleasure began to build.

It was like climbing, she thought breathlessly, from one level to the next and the next and the next, and the pleasure increased with every fierce downward motion of his hips. She was dying. She couldn't survive. The pleasure was so deep and throbbing that it was almost pain. She strained for some goal she couldn't quite reach, her hips darting up to meet his, her body arched in a strained posture that was painful. She was almost there, almost there, almost…there!

He pushed down, hard, and she felt the world drop out from under her as a wave of white-hot pleasure racked her slender body and held her, motionless, in its vise-grip.

He lifted his head seconds later, drenched in sweat and barely able to get a whole breath. She was shivering in the aftermath. Her soft eyes were drowned in tears of joy as she lay under him, satiated.

"Now do you understand what was missing, the last time?" he whispered tenderly.

"Oh, yes." She locked her arms around his neck. She was trembling. "Is it always like this?"

"No," he murmured, smiling as his hips began to move again. "It gets better."

"You're kidding…!"

It was the last remark she was able to make for some time.

The wedding was beautiful, Sara thought, amazed at the media that gathered to watch Jared Cameron merge his oil empire with an unknown little bookseller in Jacobsville, Texas. One of the newswomen just shook her head, having covered stories that Jared featured in years ago. This little retiring Texas rose didn't seem at all the type of woman he'd marry. But then he looked down at his new bride, under her veil, and the look they exchanged made everything clear. Love, the reporter thought, was truly an equalizer.

Harley Fowler congratulated them with a bittersweet smile. Sara hugged him and thanked him for all he'd done, especially scaring away the kidnappers in the bookstore. He wished them well. Sara was very fond of him, but she'd never felt romantic toward him. He knew it, and accepted it.

All the mercs showed up at the wedding, along with just about everybody in town. Sara felt like Cinderella at the ball. And now she was going away with her very own version of Prince Charming. She'd never been so happy.

Several days later, Sara had packed up everything, including Morris the cat, and Tony had arranged for Sara's possessions, plus Morris, to travel to the house in Oklahoma City, where Jared lived most of the time. Morris rode in a chauffeured limousine, with one of Tony's old comrades, and Jared's new bodyguard, Clayton, at his side.

"Morris will never get over that," Sara told her new husband.

"It was the safest way I could think of," Jared replied, smiling. "Clayton will take great care of him. Tony trained him. He's good."

"We won't have to worry about kidnappers again, will we?" she worried.

He drew her gently into his arms. "*We* won't worry. We'll let Clayton worry. That's what he gets paid for."

"I thought Tony worked for you all the time," she commented.

"He was borrowed, for this assignment," he told her, and didn't offer any further information.

"He's rather mysterious, in his way," she said.

Jared raised an eyebrow. "You have no idea how mysterious," he assured her.

"Tell me."

He chuckled. "Not now. We've got work to do. You have to help me pack, now that we've got you covered."

"I'll miss Jacobsville," she said.

"I know you will, honey," he replied. "But you'll get used to it. Life has to be lived. You can't sit by the road and watch it pass."

"Maybe when we're old," she began.

He nodded. "Yes. Maybe when we're old."

"It was sweet of Dee to give us those rare World War II memoirs for a wedding present, wasn't it?" she asked.

"Yes, it was. And sweet of you to pack up all your grandfather's collection to bring with us. I'll only read one a week, I promise," he said when he saw her expression.

She frowned. "That reminds me, are you a sports fan?"

"I love soccer," he replied.

She beamed. "It's my favorite sport!"

"In that case, we'll make plans to go to the next World Cup."

"We could? Really?"

"Yes." He drew her against him and kissed her. "I love you."

She smiled. "I love you back."

"No regrets?"

She shook her head. "I'm going to take very good care of you."

He kissed her eyes closed. "And I'm going to take very good care of you." He rocked her in his arms. "Just for the record, any unusual nausea?"

She drew back and looked up at him, grimacing. "I'm afraid not. In fact, something monthly started up this morning. I'm sorry."

He kissed her. "We won't rush things," he said gently. "We'll grow together before we start a family. We'll travel. We'll go shopping. We'll find a nice location for a bookstore."

"You meant that?" she exclaimed.

"Of course I meant it," he said, smiling. "You can have anything you want, Sara."

She moved into his arms and pressed close. "Most of all, I want you, for all my life. I love you very much."

He swallowed hard and his arms closed around her. Grief had almost destroyed him, but this sweet, gentle woman had brought him back into the sunlight. She was his world now. He rested his cheek on her soft hair. "I love you, too, baby. I'll make you happy and keep you safe, all my life," he promised.

And he did.

* * * * *

SEDUCED BY THE
RICH MAN

by
Maureen Child

Dear Reader,

In this book, you're going to meet Janine and Max.

I probably shouldn't admit this, but Max Striver is one of my favourite heroes ever. He was so fun, so arrogant, so very British that I just adored spending time with him. And introducing him to Janine, an American woman with plenty of attitude, just made this story sing for me.

Writing a book about an island paradise in the middle of winter is always a good thing! Of course, California doesn't do winter like the rest of the world, but I really enjoyed my imaginary trip to the islands. In designing Fantasies, I built a place I would love to stay – of course, I also added a lot of little things I've personally experienced while on holidays.

Though my favourite kind of trip is driving down back roads in Ireland and Scotland, a beautiful tropical island has plenty of appeal, too!

So come back to Fantasies resort. Visit with old friends, meet new ones and be sure to order the house margarita. It's not to be missed!

Happy reading!

Maureen

MAUREEN CHILD

is a California native who loves to travel. Every chance they get, she and her husband are taking off on another research trip. An author of more than sixty books, Maureen loves a happy ending and still swears that she has the best job in the world. She lives in Southern California with her husband, two children and a golden retriever with delusions of grandeur.

You can contact Maureen via her website www.maureenchild.com.

To Romance Readers everywhere.
Thank you all for your support. Without you,
we would have no one to share our stories with.

One

Max Striver picked up his drink and let his gaze sweep the room. The club at Fantasies resort was packed with people drinking, laughing, dancing. The music was loud, and colored lights speared from the ceiling onto the writhing mass on the dance floor. A wall of windows overlooked the ocean and a bright moon spilled out of a black sky.

He leaned one elbow on the bar and took a sip of his single-malt scotch, letting the smooth liquor slide down his throat in a wash of heat. It had been so long since his last vacation, he felt out of place in the room full of partying people. And that wasn't a feeling he was comfortable with. Maybe it had been a mistake to come at all. Maybe he should have stayed in London.

He smiled to himself. But the chance to steal away his old friend and competitor's executive assistant had just been too appealing to ignore.

Still, he'd had no actual hope of hiring Caitlyn Monroe away from Lyon Industries. The woman was too loyal. But it had been fun to torment her boss, Jefferson Lyon. Max took another drink and laughed at the mental image of finding Jefferson sleeping on a chaise beside the pool that morning. Seeing the great Lyon brought so low was entertainment enough to keep Max chuckling for a long time.

"What's so funny?"

Max shot a look at the brunette sitting two seats down from him at the bar. Her dark brown hair was short and spiky and her big brown eyes shone. Her skin was the color of warm honey and her body looked curvy under a pale green tank top and white shorts.

His own body tightened as he felt a stir of pure sensual interest. "Just thinking about a friend," he said.

"And this friend's funny?"

"Not purposely," Max admitted, then asked, "Are you alone tonight?"

She shifted on the high red cushioned bar stool and swiveled it around until she was facing him. Tipping her head to one side, she smiled. "I was."

Intriguing, he thought. He liked a woman who was up-front and not afraid to let her interest in a man show. He liked even more that his own interest was spiking. He'd been spending too much time with work lately.

Hell, it'd been months since he'd had a damn date. But that looked as if it was all about to change.

"Can I get you another drink?"

She glanced at her nearly empty glass, then back at him. "I think that would be a good start."

He signaled the bartender, then speared his gaze into hers. "Would you like to dance while we wait?"

She smiled at him and he loved the way her mouth moved.

"Another good idea," she said and slid off the stool.

As if prearranged, the music shifted from pulsing rock to slow and smooth. Max guided her through the mass of people to a shadowy corner of the dance floor and pulled her into his arms. She fit against him just right, the top of her head hitting at his chin level. And when she swayed into him, Max felt his blood start to pump.

It had been far too long since he'd been with a woman. Far too long since he'd allowed himself a chance to relax.

The music poured over them in a silky wave and she tipped her head back to look at him. "I like your accent. British?"

His arm tightened around her waist. "Yes. You?"

"California."

That explained the lovely tan, he thought and stared down into her deep, dark eyes. "And what brings you to Fantasies?"

"My friends." Janine Shaker felt a ripple of something hot and swirly move through her. That accent of his was really doing a number on her hormones. Or maybe it was just him. Tall, with broad shoulders, a squared-off jaw and black hair that was long enough to brush across the top of his collar, he also had eyes the color of chocolate and a mouth that just begged to be kissed.

Oh, boy.

"So, not alone then."

"My girlfriends," Janine clarified.

She'd come to Fantasies with her two best friends, Caitlyn and Debbie. It had been her idea, though heaven knew, she couldn't really afford this trip. But she and her friends had *all* been dumped by their fiancés over the last few months and this trip was supposed to be a life-affirming-screw-men kind of thing.

So Janine had taken the money she'd put aside for the wedding that had never happened and splurged it on a three-week trip to Fantasies. She'd go home broke, but she'd worry about that later.

At the moment, a man who was the perfect distraction had his arms around her and that was all she wanted to think about.

"Girlfriends, eh?" He smiled down at her and tightened his grip around her waist. "I'm relieved to hear it."

"Are you?"

"Oh, yes."

Seriously, that accent seemed to ripple up and down her spine with delightful results. She was probably making a mistake. Heck, she was sure of it. But she'd lived most of her life being a good girl. Doing the right thing at the right time. Never taking a risk.

And still her world had imploded around her.

Maybe it was time to stop being careful.

At least while she was at Fantasies. After all, the very name of the resort conjured up all kinds of wonderful images.

"Are you flirting with me?"

He thought about it for a moment, then grinned. "Yes, I believe I am."

"Well, good," Janine said. "I think I like it."

His hand on her back slid up and down in a slow motion that might have been considered soothing, except for the flash of heat zipping through her body. "Then we're well on our way to a beautiful new friendship, aren't we?"

"Is that what you're looking for? A friend?"

One dark eyebrow lifted. "For the moment."

"And after this moment?"

"Let's be surprised."

Wow. He really was good at the flirting thing. A quiet but insistent voice in the back of her mind whispered a warning that a man like this wasn't one to take chances with. He was too gorgeous. Too smooth. Too…everything. But it wasn't as if she was looking for forever, was it? She'd tried that with John Prentiss, her former fiancé. She'd believed all of his lies. Believed him when he'd promised to love her forever.

She'd believed right up until the moment three days before their wedding when he'd disappeared, leaving behind only a note that read *Sorry, babe. This isn't for me.*

So she was through with love. But that didn't have to mean she was through with men. She was here. On vacation. In the splashiest, sexiest resort in the world.

Was she really going to lock herself up in her tiny room and be a good girl? Or was she going to do just what she'd told Caitlyn and Debbie they should *all* do? Find a gorgeous man and have mindless, meaningless sex?

With the feel of this man's arms around her, Janine knew exactly what she wanted to do.

When the music stopped and shifted into another drum-driven number that had everyone on the floor jumping into action, Max steered her through the crowd, back to the bar and their waiting drinks. He sat down beside her and said, "I propose a toast."

"To what?" She picked up her drink.

He clinked his glass gently against the rim of hers. "To possibilities."

"I can drink to that," she said and did.

"Are you going to tell me your name?" he asked, his beautiful brown eyes looking directly into hers.

She thought about it for a second, then shook her head. "I don't think so."

"Why not?"

"Because," she said, swallowing her trepidation with a big gulp of her Cosmo, "if we introduce ourselves, then this becomes ordinary. No names means no expectations."

He reached out and stroked the top of her thigh with the tips of his fingers. Goose bumps raced across her skin and she shivered in response.

"No names, then," he agreed, leaning in closer to her. "So, mystery woman, would you like to join me for a walk on the beach?"

"Yes," she said, still shivering at the soft touch of his hand on her leg, "I really would."

The beach was nearly deserted, and the music from the club floated on the cool ocean breeze. Stars flickered on a blanket of black and the moon's pale light shone down like a wash of silver.

As romantic settings went, Janine thought this one was an A-plus.

She should have been nervous. After all, this wasn't like her in the least. Taking long, romantic walks at night on a beach with a perfect stranger. And yet, all she felt was the quickening of expectation. A flicker of heat inside that was as dazzling as the look in his eyes.

"How long are you here for?" he asked and his deep voice was almost lost in the sigh of the wind coming off the ocean.

"Three weeks," she said. "You?"

"I don't know." He stopped, stared out at the water and tucked both hands into the pockets of his slacks. "Coming here was a whim."

She bent down, picked up a broken seashell and fingered it for a moment before tossing it into the incoming tide. "Nothing you have to rush back to in your life?"

He glanced at her and smiled. She really did have an amazing mouth. "Not particularly."

"Must be nice," she said, staring out at the sea. "I practically had to give blood to get my boss to agree to three weeks off."

"What do you do?"

She glanced at him and plucked windblown hair out of her eyes. "I'm a floral designer. You?"

"A little of this. A little of that." He reached out and tucked a strand of her hair behind her ear.

"Well, that was vague," she said.

"Do you really want to discuss our careers?" he asked.

"I guess not," she conceded. "But at least tell me you're not some jewel thief or something."

He laughed and the sound rolled out around her.

"No," he said. "Not a thief. Just a businessman, I'm afraid."

"There are worse things to be," she said, thinking of John Prentiss...liar, thief, con man.

"Besides," he said, "isn't talking about our work the same as exchanging names?"

"No. Work's generic. Names are specific."

"Ah, rules to this, then."

"Aren't there rules in everything?" She looked up at him briefly, smiled, then turned her gaze back on the ocean.

"Should be," he conceded. "Though I confess, I'm enjoying the mystery you suggested."

"Why's that?"

"Because," he said on a sigh, "there aren't nearly enough mysteries in the world."

When he took her hand and pulled her into the circle of his arms, she went willingly. Eagerly. He dipped his head low, tasted her mouth once, twice, and then devoured her.

Janine felt all of the air rush from her lungs and her heart pounded frantically in her chest. His kiss was electric. Dazzling. She felt every cell in her body leap to attention and shout for mercy.

But she didn't want him to show mercy. She wanted him to touch her, taste her, hold her.

She didn't care what his name was. Didn't care that she knew nothing about him. Didn't care that only hours ago, she hadn't known he existed.

All that mattered now was his next touch. His next kiss.

His tongue parted her lips and she opened to him. Wrapping her arms around his neck, she held on tight even as she went up on her toes to meet his advances. His arms vised around her body, pulling her close enough that she could feel the pounding of his heart against her own.

His hands moved up and down her back next, sliding over her clothes, slipping beneath her shirt to caress her bare skin. Every touch inflamed; every stroke made her want another.

He kissed her deeply, passionately and Janine's head spun. She'd never felt anything like this. Hadn't known she *could* feel like this. She trembled and moaned gently when he tore his mouth from hers to rake his teeth and tongue along the line of her throat.

"Lovely," he whispered against her skin, "just lovely. I must have you. Now. Now."

"Yes," she said, tipping her head back so that she could afford him greater access to her body. She wanted his mouth on her, his hands on her. She wanted to feel his body push into her own and she wanted, more than anything, to experience the wild rush of an orgasm ripping through her system. Because she had a feeling this one was going to be a beaut.

He groaned deep in his throat and his hands slipped beneath her shirt, lifting it up and off her too-warm body. Instantly, the cool ocean wind slid across her skin, and became just another sensation whirling together her mind, her blood.

Bending low, he took first one pebbled nipple into his mouth and then the other. Janine could hardly draw breath. She couldn't make herself concentrate on even *that*. All she could focus on was the feel of his hands and his mouth. The rush of her senses, the pulse of her heart.

One corner of her mind screamed at her that they were too close to the resort. That someone might wander down this deserted beach and stumble across them. But a part of her found that thought exciting. And she cringed away from that admission.

The simple truth was, though, that she didn't care where they were. She knew if she didn't feel him on her, in her in the next few minutes, her body was going to explode.

Stepping back from her, he lifted his head and glanced around them, assuring himself that they were still alone. Then he tore off his shirt, spread it out on the sand and lowered her onto it. The cool of the cotton felt good against her back, and when he undid the button and zipper of her shorts, Janine lifted her hips, helping him to rid her of the clothes that felt too tight, too uncomfortable.

The wind stroked her naked body and only made her feel more wanton. More wicked. She'd never been the kind of woman to do something like this. And now that she was, she found she *liked* being this kind of woman.

She stared up at him as he quickly shed his clothes, then knelt between her thighs. His hands roamed up and over her body, tweaking her nipples, sliding over her skin, dipping down into the warm cleft between her legs. He touched her there, intimately, and Janine jolted, hissing in a breath.

He loomed over her until all she could see were his eyes. The depths of them. The glittering shine of a hunger as fierce as her own.

Reaching up, Janine cupped his face in her palms and pulled him down for a kiss. She opened her lips for him; her tongue met his and they tangled together in a furious dance of desire and pleasure. She sighed, heard the heavy sound of it and did it again. Perfect. He was perfect.

She was still kissing him when he plunged his body into hers. Hard and thick, he claimed her, delving in and out of her heat with a passion that stole her breath. Again and again he took her, pushing her higher, faster, than she'd ever been before.

The quickening of her own desire enflamed her and Janine lifted her hips into him, over and over. Meeting each of his thrusts with a wild abandon that took him deeper and deeper inside her.

"I have you," he said, his voice tight with need that still crouched between them like a hungry tiger. "And I want more. I want *all*."

She gave him everything she had and took from him the same. His body pumped and hers kept pace. She raced with him to the precipice that nestled just out of reach.

So close, she felt it. So very close to the edge. Her nails scored his back, digging for purchase as if holding on to him was the only thing that mattered. And in that moment, it was. It was everything.

Janine felt the first spiraling flex of her muscles and knew what was coming. She braced for it, and still was unprepared for the gut-clenching, overwhelming rush of sensation crashing through her. She held on tight and groaned as she took that wild ride into oblivion.

And a moment later, he buried his face in the curve of her neck and followed, his hoarse shout muffled against her skin.

A moment later, Max came back to himself and couldn't believe what he'd done. He'd taken her with no thought to their surroundings. No thought to safety.

He was still buried deep within her hot center and he knew he should be feeling bad about all of this. But he just couldn't manage to.

Instead, he wanted her again.

As fiercely as he had the first time.

"That was—" she stopped, took a deep breath and exhaled again before finishing "—never mind. I don't even have a word for that."

"Nor do I." He smiled and shifted on her, pleased when her eyes closed and a sigh slipped from her mouth. His body was hard and ready again, and from her reaction, he knew she was feeling the same need.

Music from the club drifted down to them and that was enough to make Max say, "I'm not finished. But I'd like to suggest we adjourn to my room."

She licked her lips, sighed a little and said, "Oh, yeah. Good idea."

Two

He opened the door of the Presidential Suite and Janine tried not to gasp.

Fantasies was great, no question, but she had reserved one of their smallest and least expensive rooms for herself. This...she couldn't even take it all in.

Walking past him into the living area, she was struck first by the wall of tinted windows that overlooked the ocean and the beach below. The view seemed to go on forever. The carpet was thick enough for her feet to sink into as she turned in a slow circle, admiring the rest of the place.

Crystal vases filled with bright flowers rested on top of glass tables. Bright red couches and chairs created conversation areas at each end of the room and there was even a fireplace—she was guessing more for ambience than necessity. Soft puddles of lamplight shone in the darkness and she spotted a door on either side of the room. Leading to bedrooms, no doubt.

She shivered as he wrapped his arms around her, and she felt the warmth of him seep into her bones. "Amazing place," she said, leaning her head back against his chest.

She heard the smile in his voice when he said, "It'll do until something better comes along."

Turning her head slightly, she looked up at him. "You sure you're not a jewel thief?"

He laughed and she caught the sparkle of delight in his eyes. "Very sure. Just a boring businessman, as I told you."

"Business must be good," she muttered.

His arms dropped away from her and he moved silently to a bar tucked into a corner of the big room. "Well enough."

"Wow. Just got cold in here," she said, reacting to the sudden chill in his tone as much as his abrupt absence.

He flicked her a glance and for a moment, she saw wariness in his eyes, then it was gone. "Sorry. I just don't feel like talking about—well, to be honest, I don't feel like talking at all."

"Me, neither." Janine walked across the room and sat down on one of the red cushioned bar stools. "Boy, the guy who owns this place really does like red, doesn't he?"

The gorgeous man pouring her a glass of wine smiled. "Does seem to be a theme."

"Do you know him?"

"I beg your pardon?"

"The owner. Do you know him?" Janine took the wine he offered and tasted a small sip. Cold and delicious, the wine was, naturally, perfect.

"As a matter of fact, I do."

"Thought you might," Janine muttered. After all, rich guys tended to hang in packs, didn't they? At least, John always had. Of course, as it turned out, John hadn't actually *been* rich. He'd only been pretending to have money. Just as he'd pretended to love her.

He lifted his own glass of the pale gold wine and took a drink before setting it down on the bar top again. Laying both hands flat on the gleaming wood surface, he looked at her and said, "Before this goes any further, we should talk about what happened on the beach."

Janine squirmed a little on the stool. Doing it was one thing, talking about it another. "Why?"

"Because we took no safety precautions."

Six simple words with the power to rock her world on its axis.

"Oh."

"Yes," he said, picking up his wine for another taste. "Oh."

"Well." Janine thought fast. Surprising actually, since her stomach was suddenly full of lead balls, rolling around erratically. "First off, I can tell you I'm healthy."

"Nice to know. As am I. However, there is an even bigger question to be concerned about."

"Yeah." Okay, lead balls a little bigger now and clanking together in the pit of her stomach, making her sorry she'd had such a big lunch. But she took a deep breath, and said, "We'll just have to wait and see, I guess. But it'll be okay. I'm sure. It was only the one time."

One black eyebrow lifted high on his forehead. "I wonder," he mused, "just how often that line of reasoning has been employed over the centuries."

"Wow. When you're worried, you sound way more British."

"I suppose I do. Still, as you say, we'll simply have to wait and see."

Janine felt like an idiot. She couldn't believe she'd made love with a stranger on a beach with no protection. For heaven's sake. She wasn't a stupid woman. But right now, she felt as though she had a huge *L* stamped in the middle of her forehead. *Loser.* Or maybe an *I. Idiot.*

Her fingers stroked up and down the crystal stem of the wineglass until finally he said, "Unless you want a repeat of our earlier performance, perhaps you could stop doing that."

"Huh?" Her gaze shot to his and found fierce hunger shining at her. And just like that, her worries dissolved into a puddle of want. What in the heck was going on here? She'd never been that into sex. Never really craved it as she did now.

And maybe, she told herself, that was because the men she'd been with before hadn't exactly been world-class lovers.

But her mystery man surely was.

Deliberately, she stroked the stem of the glass again and watched flames flash in the depths of his eyes. He came around the end of the bar, plucked her off the stool and lifted her clean off her feet.

At five foot seven, she wasn't exactly a tiny pixie of a woman, and having a man lift her with such obvious ease was really more of a turn-on than she would have guessed. He swung her up into his arms, looked down into her eyes and said, "This time, we'll do it right."

She linked her own arms around his neck, smiled up at him and said, "I thought we were pretty good the last time."

"Mystery woman," he said, heading for the bedroom, "you have no idea."

As good as his word, the second time had been even better than the first. Thankfully, condoms had been readily available, too. And just when Janine was sure they'd outdone themselves, he took it to another level.

She'd never been more relaxed. More completely and totally sated. Every cell in her body was humming with satisfaction, and when she rolled over and opened her eyes to a stream of sunlight, she didn't even mind.

Then she looked beside her at the empty space on the bed and wondered where her handsome stranger was. The sheets were cool to the touch, so he'd been up for a while. She grabbed a robe he must have laid out for her and slipped into the silky material, loving the feel of the fabric as it skimmed over her flesh.

She left the bedroom, walked into the main room and noticed for the first time that there was a balcony jutting off from the living area. She hadn't seen it in the dark the night before. But now, the sun splashed across the flagstone floor and the scrolled iron railing. There was a glass table set under a red-and-white striped umbrella and sitting at the table, drinking a cup of coffee and staring out at the sea, was her lover.

Smiling, she tasted that word again in her mind. *Lover.* She liked it. It felt decadent. Sexy. And the fact that she still didn't know his name was somehow even more wicked.

He was already dressed, wearing black slacks and a dark blue long-sleeved shirt with the sleeves rolled back to the elbows. He should have looked relaxed, unguarded. Instead, he looked like a prince, surveying his kingdom from atop his castle.

She stepped out onto the patio and he looked up at her, offering a smile. Automatically, he reached for the thermal pot in the center of the table and poured her a cup of rich, steaming coffee.

"Thanks," she said. She took her first glorious sip and added, "You were up early."

He shrugged. "London time I'm afraid. Couldn't sleep, but didn't see the sense in rousing you."

"I appreciate it."

"Have you plans for the day?"

God, he even looks spectacular first thing in the morning was all she could think. His black hair was tousled by the soft wind coming in off the ocean and his deep brown eyes were sharp on her. His mouth, that incredible mouth, was curved into a small smile and her stomach did the twisty thing just looking at him.

"Um, no." What she wanted to do was sit right here. Or maybe sit here for a while and then go back to the bedroom. And then come out here again and watch the waves while sneaking long looks at him. But, what she *should* do, as a caring and concerned friend, was go down and see how Caitlyn was doing after her big blowup with her good-for-nothing boss. "But I should check on my friend. See what she's doing."

"Of course." If he was disappointed, he hid it well. Then he leaned across the glass tabletop and covered one of her hands with his. "But I'll see you later."

It wasn't a question; it was a fact. And they both knew it. Turning her hand under his, she held his hand briefly and said, "Yeah. I think that's a good idea."

"Brilliant." He gave her a smile designed to knock her socks—and whatever other clothing she might be wearing—off. "How will I find you, Mystery Woman? Without your name I can hardly ask at the desk."

She glanced back through the open French doors into the plush suite behind them. Then turning her gaze back on him, she said, "You're a lot easier to find. How about if I meet you here around six?"

"Six it is, then." He gave her hand another friendly squeeze and stood up. "If you'll excuse me, I have some business to attend to. Please, take your time here. Enjoy the view. Have some coffee. There's no need for you to rush off."

"Thanks," Janine said and tipped her head back to meet his gaze. "I will."

He bent down and speared his fingers through her short, wildly tangled hair before dipping his mouth to hers to claim a brief kiss. When he pulled his head back, his eyes met hers. "I'll see you at six."

She watched as he turned to leave. Let's face it, he was a much better view than the ocean. Her heart fluttered and her stomach spun just enough to make her smile. Amazing how a night of incredible sex with a gorgeous man could turn a girl's outlook on life around.

When he was gone, she curled up in the comfortably cushioned chair, lifted her coffee and took a long drink. She didn't know where this was going or how it would end. But for the moment, she was going to stop questioning everything and simply enjoy.

It was a gorgeous day in paradise. She was sitting on a balcony that boasted a bird's-eye view of the world and she had a date with a fabulous stranger.

It seemed the resort called Fantasies was earning its name.

The following day, Max had lunch with Gabriel Vaughn, the owner of Fantasies. They were served at the rooftop restaurant, open only for dinner under most circumstances. But when the owner wanted a private lunch, things changed.

"Saw you with your friend at the bar last night," Gabe said, leaning back in his chair.

Max finished off his coffee and kicked his legs out in front of him, crossing his feet at the ankles. "I saw you, too. Thanks for not interrupting."

"No problem. You looked a little too cozy for interruptions."

True. Max thought back on the night before. After some spectacular sex, he'd taken his mystery woman to the club to dance. And after watching her trim, curvy body move sinuously on the dance floor, he'd been all too eager to get her back into his suite. He hadn't felt like this in years. The sharp teeth of sexual hunger were tearing at him continually. Even now, he wanted her, though he'd had her—over him, under him—only a couple of hours ago.

"So who is she?" Gabe asked.

"I have no idea," Max told him with a wry smile.

"What?"

"Nothing," he said, reluctant to explain to his old friend the silly game he and his mystery woman had been playing. Shrugging one shoulder, he said, "I appreciate the lunch, Gabe. But I've a feeling there's something else on your mind besides just catching up with an old friend."

Gabriel Vaughn was usually the very epitome of unruffled cool. Max couldn't remember a time when his old friend had been as tense as he looked at that moment. Five years ago, when they'd met on Max's first visit to Fantasies, the two men had struck up a friendship that had survived both time and distance.

Gabe sat up, braced his elbows on his knees and

speared his green gaze into Max's. "Actually, there's something going on that has…surprised me."

"And not happily, I see."

"Not particularly," Gabe admitted, then shook his head. "But that's not what I wanted to talk to you about."

"Right then. What is it?"

"Elizabeth."

Max blew out a breath. His ex-wife, Elizabeth Bancroft Striver. The once love of his life and current pain in the neck. "What about her?"

"She's coming." Gabe winced and added, "Her assistant called this morning. Made a reservation in Elizabeth's name."

"Bugger." Irritated, Max scowled thoughtfully as his brain raced through scenarios. There was no chance Elizabeth had chosen to come to Fantasies on a whim. She was coming because *Max* was here.

He'd caught her with a lover more than a year ago and had initiated divorce proceedings almost immediately. He wouldn't stand for being lied to. And damned if he'd keep a woman who would cheat on him. Then, to infuriate him even further, he'd discovered that Elizabeth had married him solely for the Striver fortune. She'd had her lover on the side almost from the get-go.

But for the last few months, she'd been dropping by his office once or twice a week, arranging to "bump" into him when he was out, and phoning him at night to tell him how much she "missed" him. He didn't believe it for a moment, of course, but he knew Elizabeth. She wasn't a woman who enjoyed losing. And that was exactly how she would appear on their divorce papers.

Now, she was pretending to want a reconciliation and, worse yet, she'd enlisted Max's father in her battle strategy.

The old man was of the opinion that you never trusted a woman anyway, so why not stay married to the woman you'd chosen and keep her on a tight leash? Max's father wanted grandchildren and he wanted them now. Plus, he believed that Elizabeth would be the perfect mother for the heirs of the Striver dynasty. Her bloodline was lofty enough to dismiss the annoying adulteress accusations.

"My father probably told her I was here. Isn't that perfect?"

Gabe gave him an understanding smile. "I can have the desk call. Cancel her reservations."

He paused to think about that for a moment. Max appreciated the gesture, but they both knew Elizabeth would never allow that to happen. She would come anyway and make quite a scene, perhaps costing Gabe more trouble than he deserved.

"No," Max said, biting back the annoyance. Damned if he'd give Elizabeth the satisfaction of becoming that important to him again. "Canceling her reservations wouldn't stop her in any case. No point in you losing business over my marital…problems."

Nodding, Gabe ran one hand through his shoulder-length brown hair and said, "Your father is still trying to convince you to take her back?"

Max snorted. "You could say so. He takes the trouble

to tell me at least once a week that 'the devil you know' is easier to handle."

"Some would agree."

"I wouldn't be one of them," Max said flatly. Idly, he straightened up and rested his left foot atop his right knee. Smoothing his thumb over the knife-edge crease on his slacks, he added, "I don't make the same mistake twice."

Something in Gabe's eyes shifted, darkened. "Neither do I," he said in a grim voice.

"We're agreed then. Elizabeth will be arriving… when, exactly?"

"Two days," Gabe said. "Are you going to be staying on, or are you going to be gone when she gets here?"

That would be easiest, Max told himself. Leave, go back to London. Ruin whatever plans Elizabeth was counting on. But that was the coward's way out and Max Striver was no coward. And why the bloody hell should *he* have to leave? Especially when he was finding this vacation so…enjoyable.

No, he wouldn't be leaving. He would find a way to put a stop to Elizabeth's plans. It was there somewhere. All he had to do was find the right way to deal with his ex-wife and convince her once and for all that she had no chance at a reconciliation.

Glancing at Gabe, he said, "You've never been married, have you?"

His friend's features tightened perceptibly before relaxing into their more usual expression of easy good humor. "No. Came close once."

"What happened?"

"The lady changed her mind." Gabe grabbed up his water glass and chugged down half of it as though his throat were on fire.

A story, Max mused. And one his friend had no intention of sharing. But then, a man was entitled to his privacy, wasn't he?

"I only wish that I could say the same," Max said at last after a long bristling moment of silence. "Unfortunately, though, I cannot. But I won't run just because Elizabeth has decided she needs to see the tropics." A small smile curved his mouth. "I'm staying."

"Have to say," Gabe told him, "I'm glad to hear it. Didn't think for a minute that you'd run."

Max gave him a quick smile. "Thanks for that. I'm not looking forward to playing Elizabeth's game though, I must admit."

"Maybe what you need to do," Gabe offered, "is to change the rules of the game on her."

"A good idea in theory. But how?"

"I have every confidence in you, Max. You'll think of something."

"Yes. I will." He had two days to come up with a way to thwart Elizabeth. Max knew his ex-wife. She was beautiful and devious. She wouldn't be put off easily. He would need to be at the top of his game to convince Elizabeth to find greener pastures.

Surely he could find some rich, brainless fool for her here at the resort. One who would be as blinded as Max had once been by Elizabeth's physical charms. Or maybe, he thought suddenly, *he* could find someone for *himself*. Someone to make Elizabeth believe that Max had moved on.

Intriguing idea.

"Max. Isn't that your friend, down there?"

He looked past the railing to the swimming pool below and spotted his mystery woman stretched out on a red-and-white flowered chaise. He stood up for a better view. Her tanned, lithe body looked wonderful in a lemon-yellow bikini. As he watched, she sat up, turned to look at the woman beside her and laughed in delight.

Even from a distance, she looked good enough to make his blood hum and his body tighten. She set her hands behind her on the chaise and leaned back, arching her body into the slanting rays of the hot sun and something inside Max twisted hard.

"Beautiful, isn't she?" he mused.

"Yeah." Gabe stood up, leaned on the railing and stared down at the two women laughing together at poolside. "The blonde with her's not bad, either."

Max only glanced at his mystery woman's companion. "I suppose. I hadn't actually noticed her to be honest."

"Really? I did," Gabe said and the flat, hard tone of his voice told Max he wasn't very happy about that fact, either.

Another story, Max thought, but dismissed it almost immediately. As his gaze focused on his mystery woman again, the idea that had begun to bubble in his brain came to fruition.

The answer to his problems, it seemed, had been in his bed all along.

Three

"**Y**ou're *engaged?*" Janine's voice hit a note so high even she winced. She told herself there had to be some kind of mistake, but staring at Caitlyn's glowing face and beaming smile, she had to discount it. "Seriously engaged. To *Lyon?*"

"This is huge," Debbie muttered and grabbed for her margarita glass. She took a gulp of the frozen concoction, shivered and set it back down. "You just got *un*-engaged like a week ago, for God's sake."

Janine couldn't believe this. Cait had been down-in-the-dumps miserable when Lyon had left the island a few days ago. Now he comes back and everything's great again? Was it just her, she wondered, or had the world sort of tipped over onto its side?

"I know," Caitlyn said and wasn't able to stop grinning. "But Peter breaking off our engagement was the absolute right thing to do. I know that now. Heck, I knew it when he did it." She picked up her raspberry martini, took a sip and kept on smiling. "I think I'm going to have to thank Peter when we go home."

"You're leaving, then?" Janine asked it and was sorry to think about it.

Debbie's former love had been exposed as a bigamist. Caitlyn's ex-fiancé had broken their engagement because he'd claimed she was in love with her boss. Which, Janine supposed, made him a pretty smart guy, since that was how it had turned out.

Janine's ex, though, was in a class by himself. Even her best friends didn't know the whole story of her dissolved engagement. John Prentiss hadn't only ended their engagement three days before their wedding…he'd stolen nearly every dime she had.

"Actually," Caitlyn said, taking another taste of her drink, "tomorrow, we're going to Portugal for a couple of weeks."

"Ah." Janine nodded. "The business trip you told him you weren't going to go on."

"The very one." Cait grinned. "It's different now. We'll go to Portugal, take care of business, then we're coming back here for a week. When we go home, we'll get married."

"At least your mom won't be so pissed off anymore about missing out on the whole mother-of-the-bride experience." Debbie shrugged and stirred her drink.

"I'll call her tonight," Caitlyn said. "She can plan all she wants to. But she's going to have to do it fast. We want to get married as soon as possible."

"Amazing," Janine said. "I never would have guessed that Lyon would be so damn romantic."

"I'm *so* happy, you guys." Caitlyn sniffled and her eyes welled up.

Janine handed her a napkin with Fantasies scrawled across it in red ink. "Don't go getting weepy. Lyon will think we tried to talk you out of marrying him."

As she'd hoped, Caitlyn laughed. "Coming here was the best idea you've ever had, Janine."

"Amen," Debbie added with another slurp of her margarita. "I haven't felt this relaxed in forever."

"It does seem to be working out," Janine said and leaned back in her chair.

She'd worried about coming, even though staying at Fantasies had been her suggestion. After all, this place was costing each of them a bundle. They were all spending the money they'd hoarded to pay for the weddings that had never happened.

But her friends weren't broke. Janine was. Oh, she still had her condo in Long Beach, California, but the equity was gone, since she'd listened to John and taken out a second mortgage for him to "invest." Turned out all he'd been investing in had been himself.

Still, she thought bravely, she still had her job as head floral designer at a very chic flower shop in the exclusive beach community of Naples. And she had hopes that the police would eventually track John

Prentiss down and squeeze him until he coughed up every last cent of her money.

A sentiment she could drink to. At the thought, she downed the last of her Cosmo and turned her mind away from the man who'd cheated her to the man who was currently lighting up her sex life. If she hadn't come to Fantasies, she never would have met her mystery man. And she never would have known just how incredible she could feel under the hands of a master lover.

So, she thought, well worth the price of the vacation.

"Well," Debbie said, "if Cait's leaving tomorrow, I say we all go to the hotel spa and get the works. Massage, manicure, pedicure, facial."

Cait smiled again.

Janine thought about meeting her mystery man later that evening and decided she could use a little pampering, too. "Great idea."

"You smell wonderful." Max dipped his head, took one of her nipples into his mouth and rolled his tongue across the sensitive tip. She squirmed beneath him and his body reacted in a white hot flash.

"It's the lotion," she whispered. "Or the massage oil. Or maybe the seaweed wrap."

He smiled against her breast and nibbled gently. She cupped the back of his head and held him to her breast, as if silently asking him not to stop. No worries there, he thought and kept his attention solely on the task at hand. He was a man of great concentration and at the moment, his legendary focus was intent on exploring every square inch of her amazing body.

She was a feast for a man. Soft curves and toned muscles, she wrapped her long legs around his hips and silently urged him to take her. He already had, of course. And would again, he thought, every chance he got.

Finding her here at Fantasies had been a gift.

In more ways than one.

He knew everything about her now. Knew who she was, where she lived, how she lived. And he knew that if he played this right, she would be the one to help him thwart Elizabeth.

Max lifted his head, looked into her passion-glazed brown eyes and smiled to himself. That talk was for later. Now there was only this moment. This woman. She was insatiable. Nothing like the cold woman he'd married and divorced. Elizabeth had accepted his lovemaking as a task. One she'd carried out with efficiency if not desire.

But this woman came to him eagerly. This woman opened herself to him and gave as much as she took.

"What're you thinking?" she said and inhaled sharply as he dipped two fingers into her tight, hot center.

His body thickened, tightened until it was nearly painful to keep himself from her. But he wanted to wait. Wanted to watch her eyes as he sent her over. Then, and only then, he would take that ride with her.

"I'm thinking that a woman like you is a treat for a man."

She smiled, then tipped her head back into the

pillows and moaned softly. His thumb caressed one sensitive nub as his fingers dipped in and out of her heat in a rhythm designed to bring her to the edge.

"Inside me," she whispered and licked lips gone dry. "Inside me, please."

"Soon," he said and dipped his head to taste her pulse beat at the base of her throat. "Soon. But first, come for me and let me watch. Let me see your eyes as you take the fall."

She slid one hand to the side of his face. Max turned his head, kissed the center of her palm and stroked her center again.

She choked out a half laugh mingled with a groan and managed to say, "You're killing me here."

"No, mystery woman. I'm *filling* you."

He ached for her. Ached for the feel of his body sliding into hers, her body holding on to him like a tight, slick fist. He wanted nothing more than to bury himself within her heat. But first…

She inhaled sharply and her eyes flew open. He saw the jolt of passionate surprise flicker there. As if her body, even knowing what was coming, was somehow shocked to find it arrive.

Her hands slid to his shoulders and he felt her short, neat nails digging into his skin as the first slam of release hit her hard.

She cried out, unable to help herself. Her hips bucked, her back arched and she stared directly into his eyes as wave after wave of soul-shattering sensation ripped through her body.

And when the last of those ripples were just dying away, Max entered her with a quick, smooth thrust that had her gasping for air. Her legs tightened around his hips. Her arms held on to him tightly, as if her hold on him were the only thing keeping her centered.

He moved within her. Fast, hard, impatient now to feel what she had felt. To go over the edge as completely as she had. To join her in that nebulous half-world of satiation and desire. And as he quickened his pace, he felt her body tighten, her inner muscles flex.

Her hands slid up and down his back adding to the clamoring sensations jolting through him. And when he reached the peak, when he felt her join him at the very precipice, he thrust one last time and sent them both flying.

Janine's hands dropped from his shoulders and her arms flopped onto the mattress. She felt completely used up. Spent. And yet, she knew that given a few moments' time to recover, she would want him again.

Sex had never been like this with anyone but him. She'd never suspected that she *could* experience such complete abandon. He brought out something in her that Janine hadn't expected. And she could only be grateful to him for that.

As he rolled to one side and lay flat on his back beside her, she looked slowly around the plush bedroom. A lamp in the corner threw soft golden light into the shadows. The sheer white drapes hanging across the French doors leading to the terrace that ran the length of the suite fluttered wildly in the breeze sliding in off the ocean.

From the main room came the soft sounds of classical music streaming from the stereo, and the fresh flowers on the chest of drawers scented the air with a sweet spice. It was perfect. Everything about this place, this man, was perfect.

Janine smiled to herself and enjoyed the limp, lovely feeling sliding through her body. Who would have guessed she would find such wonder on a vacation she couldn't afford?

"I'm not done," he said softly from beside her.

She laughed, turned her head on the pillow and met his gaze. "Me, neither."

His amazing mouth quirked at one edge and Janine instantly felt a quick flash of something warm dart through her insides.

He rolled toward her, propped himself up on one elbow and said, "I think it's time we exchanged names."

"Do you?" She wasn't sure how she felt about that. True, she did want to be able to call him something other than Amazing Lover Boy. Especially to his face. But, if they introduced each other, wouldn't the magic be lost?

Then he took that decision away from her.

"I'm Max. Max Striver."

She watched him, savoring the name. The short, sharp name suited him—with his chocolate eyes and hard jaw and that mouth that could quirk in an unexpected smile and kiss her until she wanted to whimper.

Okay, magic not gone.

"I'm Janine Shaker."

He reached out and trailed one finger along her jawline. "I know."

She blinked. "You know? How do you know?"

"It wasn't difficult to discover your name, Janine."

Now the magic was dissolving as quickly as sugar in water. They'd had a bargain. They'd promised to keep their names a secret. "So you cheated."

One shoulder lifted in a shrug. "I changed the rules."

"Typical." Funny just how quickly all those lovely warm feelings could just drain away. Rich men, she should have remembered, had their own ideas on what was fair and what wasn't. Even pseudorich men, like John Prentiss. He'd rewritten the rules every time he'd needed something more from her. And she'd never caught on.

Well, she wouldn't be that slow again.

She sat up, scooted off the edge of the wide bed and looked for her clothes. They'd been in such a hurry, her things were scattered all over the damn place.

"What are you doing?"

She spotted her white lace panties hanging off the arm of a chair and snatched them up. Hopping on first one foot, then the other, she tugged them on and up. "What's it look like?"

"I'm not sure," he said lazily and shifted to drag his robe off the end of the bed. "But if I must hazard a guess, I'd say you were getting dressed."

"Bingo," she muttered, still not finding the pale green sundress she'd worn to dinner with him earlier. "Where's my damn dress?"

"I believe you'll find it in the living area," he said

smoothly with just a touch of—blast him for it anyway—humor.

She shot him a glare at the satisfied tone in his voice and then headed for the other room. Her bare feet sank into the pale blue carpet but she hardly noticed. Neither did she pay any attention at all to the romantic music, the soft lighting, or the table on the terrace, set with champagne for two.

He was only a step or two behind her.

"Why are you so upset? I've told you my name," he said in such a placating tone she wanted to kick him. But first, she wanted to find her shoes. Those pointy-toed high heels would really hurt his shin far more than her bare foot would.

"Yes," she snapped and rolled her eyes when she spotted her sundress tossed across the end of the bar. Oh yes. Now she remembered. He'd undressed her the moment they'd stepped into the suite. Not that she'd minded at the time, of course.

But now.

Now, he'd changed the rules on her. He'd gone behind her back to find out her name when they'd agreed to be sexy strangers. Why? Why would he do it? She grabbed her dress, shimmied into it and while she struggled with the back zipper, asked him outright. "Why did you have to do that? Why'd you sneak around and find out my name? Why'd you have to ruin everything?"

"I really don't see why you're so upset," he reasoned. "Didn't you only a moment ago *tell* me your name yourself?"

"Yes, but that was *my* choice." Why do clothing designers put zippers in the back? Why were they so difficult to do up you needed to find help? Was a single person, alone, supposed to go ask a *stranger* to zip them up?

"You're overreacting." He came up to her, turned her around and quickly zipped her dress, managing to stroke her bare skin with the tips of his fingers as he did so.

It simply wasn't fair that his touch could make her shiver. Make her *want* all over again. As soon as she could, Janine eased away from him and continued her search. All she needed now were her shoes and her purse.

"Overreacting?" she repeated. "I don't think so. We had a deal. I didn't try to find out who you were."

"But I did tell you."

"Sure. *After* you knew who I was." She flashed him a quick, angry glance. Okay, one corner of her mind argued, maybe she was overreacting a little. But she'd been enjoying this. The sexiness of it. The mystery of it. And he'd cheated. He'd lied.

And damn it, she'd had enough of men's lies for a lifetime.

"If you're looking for your shoes," he said from behind her, "I've got them right here."

She whirled around, glared at him and charged. "Hand them over."

"Not quite yet, I think." He held them high above her head, out of her reach, and had the nerve to smile at her. "Janine, I only want to talk to you."

"Uh-uh. Done talking. Shoes. Now."

He smiled and damned if that amazing mouth couldn't make her insides quiver whether she wanted them to or not. "Fine," she snapped. "Talk."

She folded her arms across her chest, tapped her bare toes against the carpet and tilted her head to one side, giving him a look that should have set fire to the deep red robe he was wearing.

"I think this calls for some champagne," he said, completely unmoved by her fierce show of temper.

"I don't want any champagne."

"A pity. But I do and I have your shoes."

"What're you, twelve?"

"If I were, you would have been a very bad girl only moments ago."

She blew out a breath and followed him as he strolled out onto the terrace. Out there, the wind was soft and cool; the ocean glittered beneath a pale moon and stars twinkled like far-off lights hung in celebration.

"Will you please give me my shoes?" She squeezed the words out through gritted teeth.

"In a moment." He kept her heels firm in one grip and motioned her to a chair with the other. "Sit. Have a drink with me. I'll explain everything and then, if you want to, you may certainly leave."

"Why thank you, your majesty." She sneered at him, yanked the chair out and plopped down onto it with her temper still riding her hard.

He smiled again and even chuckled a little as he uncorked the no doubt unbelievably expensive champagne and poured each of them a glass.

"I do enjoy you."

"Isn't that special?" She crossed her legs and reached for her glass. Taking one long drink, she let the bubbles soothe her throat.

"If you'd let me explain," he said, sitting down opposite her. In the moonlight, his dark eyes shone. "I have an offer I'd like to make you, if you think you could refrain from tapping your toes so loudly against the flagstone."

Instantly, she stopped the tapping and took another sip of her champagne. Be reasonable Janine. Be calm. "If I listen to this offer, will you give me my shoes?" She heard herself and realized just how stupid that sounded. But it couldn't be helped.

"Of course." As if to show how relaxed he was, he hooked the heels of her shoes over the scrolled iron-worked railing. "Now, as I said, I found out who you were easily enough."

"Congratulations." She gave him a sneer. "You must be so proud."

His lips quirked again. *Fantastic.* She was amusing him, she thought.

"And, once I had your name, I was able to find out…other things as well."

Her eyes narrowed on him. "What're you talking about?"

"I'm talking about your former fiancé and the fact that he stole from you, leaving you—I believe the phrase is 'in desperate straits.'"

Janine gulped down the last of her drink, set the

empty glass down on the table and slowly pushed herself to her feet. Her temper before had been full of fire and heat. Now, she felt cold. Right down to the bone. Wasn't it enough that John Prentiss had made a fool of her? Did she really have to stand here and have another man throw her mistakes in her face?

"You know what? Screw the shoes. *You* keep 'em."

She turned to walk away from him, but he was already there. Moving incredibly quickly, he grabbed her upper arm and held on tightly. "But you said you'd listen and I haven't finished."

"I changed my mind."

"That's merely your temper speaking." He smiled down at her. "As I said before, Janine. I have an offer I'd like to make you. One that, should you agree, would solve all of your financial problems."

She stared up into his eyes and couldn't believe what she was hearing. Of course, why she should be surprised was beyond her. What did she expect? She'd slept with him the night she'd met him. She'd had sex with him almost continually for the last few days. And she hadn't even asked him his name.

Why shouldn't he think she was cheap and easy? Why wouldn't he expect her to leap at the chance to be his mistress? No doubt, he was used to buying and selling people with a flick of the wrist. And now that he knew how badly she needed money, he figured she was easy pickings.

But darn it, it stung.

"I don't believe this."

"What?" He smiled again and this time, his smile didn't stir a thing inside her. "I haven't made my offer yet."

"And you don't have to," she said, tearing her arm from his grasp and looking at him as though she'd never seen him before. "I can guess all too well what you're going to offer me."

"Is that right?" He gave her a nod. "Well, I'm fascinated. Why don't you tell me what you think I'm going to say?"

"You're going to ask me to be your mistress." When he didn't say anything, Janine was sure she was right. "I swear, rich men are all alike. Whatever you want, you get. Is that it? What's the plan? Set me up in a sweet little apartment somewhere? Visit me twice a week?"

"What an interesting mind you have," he said finally, as he shook his head. "And one day, I'd love to hear your reasons for hating men with money. I'm sure they'll be just as fascinating. But no. That is not the plan, as you say."

He had looked surprised when she'd leveled her accusation, so she'd apparently been wrong about what he was up to. She couldn't imagine anything else though that he would need to pay her money for. Confused now, she fought against her own temper and indignation and finally surrendered to simple curiosity. "Then what?"

"Why, I want to hire you to be my wife."

Four

"Your *wife?*" Janine staggered back a step or two, her balance completely dissolving. But he reached out, grabbed her arm and steered her back into her chair. She sat down gratefully and sipped at the glass of champagne he handed her.

"I can see I've surprised you."

"You could say that," she muttered, setting the glass back down and staring at him as he sat opposite her again. "Why would you need to pay anyone to be your wife?"

His features tightened and that mouth of his briefly flattened into a thin, grim slash. Then he smiled again, though it never reached his eyes. He poured more champagne, shifted his gaze to the ocean, and spoke quietly, in a cool, controlled voice. "Actually, I need you to 'pretend' to be my wife."

"Fine. Question still holds. Why?"

"My ex-wife will be arriving on Fantasies in two days," he said, his British accent becoming more snooty and pronounced with every word. A frown tugged at his features. "She is trying to reconcile with me and I'm afraid I'm simply not interested."

Janine took a deep breath. "And this involves me how?"

He turned his head and those chocolate-brown eyes of his speared into hers. There was calculation there. And determination. "I need you to play the part of my wife for the next two to three weeks."

"Again, I say, why?"

"Because," he said softly, "if I'm already married, Elizabeth will have to search out greener pastures."

Janine leaned back in her chair, crossed her arms over her chest and watched him. "Why not simply tell her you're not interested and to take a hike?"

"Ah, what a clever idea. I wonder why I hadn't thought of it?"

"Sarcasm doesn't suit you."

"Really?" he said, amused again. "I thought I did it quite well. At any rate, I have told Elizabeth to 'take a hike' as you so elegantly put it. She refuses to. She seems determined to win me back. I won't be won."

"I'm getting that." Janine saw the hard flash in his eyes and heard the steel in his voice. A part of her sympathized with him. Not a very big part, but still. "Fine. You've got issues with Lizzie."

He chuckled at the name.

"But I don't see how this becomes *my* problem."

"Not your problem," he said, refilling her champagne glass. "Your opportunity."

She waited, sensing he was going to continue, and she'd rather have all the information before she started firing back.

"As I said, through a few inquiries, I was able to ascertain that you've had some financial difficulties lately."

Now it was her turn to laugh shortly. "Difficulties. Yeah. I guess you could call it that."

"Your former fiancé stole from you, taking, I believe, most of the equity in your home and then disappearing shortly before your wedding."

"How did you find out all this?"

He shrugged. "It wasn't at all difficult, I assure you."

"Meaning money talks."

"Actually," he corrected with a smile, "it sings and dances."

"I'll bet." She knew he was right, of course. Hadn't she seen enough proof of it from the customers at the flower shop where she worked? The rich and spoiled always got what they wanted. Enough money could smooth any path.

But she really didn't like knowing that her own life, her own privacy and secrets, were open game to anyone with a hefty bank balance.

"My point is," he said, cutting into her thoughts, "if you agree to play the role of my loving wife for the next few weeks, at the end of our bargain, I will pay you three hundred thousand dollars."

Janine goggled at him. She actually *felt* her jaw drop and had to wait a few seconds for her brain to recover from the shock and kick back into gear. When it did, she said, "Are you nuts?"

"Not at all," he assured her, sipping his champagne with the air of a man who knew his place in the world and was quite comfortable with it. "I assure you, that sum of money is insignificant to what Elizabeth would be trying for. I believe you lost two hundred thousand dollars to your erstwhile fiancé. This bargain with me would net you a tidy profit. And if I do say so myself, you've already seen that the task would hardly be an onerous one."

She was shaking her head and couldn't seem to stop. This was all so bizarre. So completely out of left field. "I don't even know what to say to this."

"Say yes."

She huffed out a breath, stood up on shaky knees, walked the two steps to the terrace railing and curled her fingers around the cold metal. A cool wind brushed her face and tousled her short, spiky hair. Below her, the ocean rumbled in a continuing heartbeat of sound.

This was crazy.

All of it.

She glanced back at Max and found him staring at her, watching her expression with the idle concentration of a man who was confident of getting his own way. Janine didn't know how to feel about that, either. Was she so predictable? Was he so sure that she would agree to this nutso plan?

"Is it really such a terrible idea?" he asked.

"That's what I'm trying to figure out," she muttered, turning her gaze back to the black sweep of ocean and the sky full of stars.

Then her brain started working through the shock. If she agreed, her money troubles would be over. She wouldn't have to worry about losing her home. She wouldn't have to think about taking on a second job.

And best of all, no one would have to know what an *idiot* she'd been to trust John Prentiss in the first place.

All appealing points.

On the other hand, if she agreed to this, she'd be forced to live with Max twenty-four hours a day for the next few weeks. She'd have to pretend to be in love with him. Not so great a hardship, when you considered how she'd spent the last few days.

Still, if she took money for having sex with him, what did that make her?

She winced at the thought.

God, she'd never believed herself capable of being bought. But here she was, seriously considering just that. Her fingers tightened on the railing. Ordinarily, she would have thrown his "offer" back in his face.

But this was no ordinary situation, was it?

She was desperate, and he knew it. *There* was a hard pill to swallow. She really had no choice. Not if she wanted to keep everything she'd worked for. And he knew it.

Max Striver was like every other rich man she'd ever known. Under the elegant manners and smooth charm, he was basically a sleaze. He manipulated people into doing what he wanted by offering them the one thing they needed.

And damned if he hadn't found the right button to push on her.

Turning to face him, she kept one hand on the railing, as if to steady herself. "Let's say I agree…"

"Happy to hear it."

"This is a pretend marriage. Just to fool Elizabeth."

"Yes."

She nodded, swallowed hard and said, "So then we don't have to let sex be a part of this."

His eyebrows lifted. "I beg your pardon?"

"Well, it's not like Elizabeth will be in the bedroom. We don't have to keep sleeping together just because we'll be 'married.'"

"I disagree. Sex will be a part of our bargain," he said, stretching his long legs out and crossing his bare feet at the ankles. "There's an intimacy between couples who share a bed that is lacking in others. Elizabeth is quite perceptive enough to deduce the difference. And," he added, his gaze locked with hers, "we've already proven that our time in bed together is mutually satisfying. Why would we want to deny ourselves?"

"Uh-huh." She lifted her chin. "But if I let you pay me for sleeping with me, that makes me—" She just couldn't say it out loud.

"It makes you a smart woman," he said tightly, obviously fully aware of her thoughts. "Don't insult us both. I'm not paying you for sex, Janine. I'm paying you a large sum to help me in a difficult situation."

Well, it really did sound a lot better said his way.

"Okay." She nodded, grateful he'd put it like that. "How do I know you'll keep your word?"

His eyes flashed briefly with offense. "Once given, I don't break my word."

"I've heard that before," she said, unimpressed. "From the man who said he loved me and then disappeared with everything I owned."

"I don't appreciate being compared to a thief, Janine."

"And I don't appreciate you dodging the question. How do I know?"

"I'll sign a note," he offered. "And at the end of three weeks, I will have the money wired into whichever account you prefer."

She thought about it and even while she did, she could hardly believe she was actually considering this. She knew that if she was smart, she'd grab her shoes and purse and stomp out of the room. She'd like to tell him she wasn't interested in being his paid-for playmate. She'd like to wipe that smug expression off his face by refusing his offer entirely.

But she wouldn't.

She couldn't.

And he knew it.

While she watched him, Max stood up, walked around the table and came toward her. Even though her mind was a whirling, churning mass of thoughts and emotions, her body responded to his nearness with a quick burst of heat. Oh, the next three weeks were going to be interesting.

"So," he said, a smile on his face, "do we have a bargain, then?"

She inhaled sharply, blew the air out again and nodded. "Yeah. I guess we do."

"Brilliant." He cupped her face in his palms and said, "Well, wife…why don't we seal this bargain with a kiss?"

She scooted back and held out her right hand. "It's a business deal, right? Let's seal it the old-fashioned way."

His mouth quirked, but he inclined his head in a gracious nod, then folded his fingers around hers.

So. Had she just made a deal born in heaven?

Or hell?

Money, as Max had told Janine, did indeed sing and dance.

A couple of hours later, after a few gifts in the right quarters, and the help of Gabe Vaughn, Max was able to get official-looking paperwork, which would be more than enough to convince anyone who might inquire, that he and Janine Shaker were husband and wife.

He stood on the terrace of his suite and looked out at the gloriously bright, sunny day. From below came the muted sounds of laughter and the quiet drift of music. And somewhere in the crowds of people, Janine was telling her friends about her change in plan, packing up her things and getting ready to be his Three-week Wife.

He hadn't had a single doubt that Janine would go along with his plan. After all, she needed money desperately and he was here offering it to her. Of course she would take it. Like any other woman, she was willing to do whatever she had to—to gain access to the Striver fortune.

He glanced at his left hand and the intricately carved gold band he'd purchased at a jewelry store in the village. He had a matching one for Janine—to complete the picture. Irritated that it had come to this, Max idly thumbed the ring on his finger. He didn't like the idea of using one woman to shield him from another. But, needs must. With any luck, this ruse would rid him of Elizabeth. When she found out about the marriage, she would be furious. Furious enough to grab hold of the first unsuspecting male who crossed her path.

Then all Max would have to do was pay off Janine and go back to living his life the way he liked it best.

His way.

Janine would go back where she came from and Elizabeth, hopefully, would be some other poor bastard's problem.

"And the very best of luck to him, whoever he might be," Max muttered.

Gabe came up behind him, stood on the terrace of Max's suite and looked down on the grounds below. "You're set. You're now officially listed in the hotel register as Mr. and Mrs. Striver."

Max shot his friend a quick grin. "Gives a man cold chills, doesn't it?"

Gabe grinned right back, leaned one hip on the railing and folded his arms across his chest. "Seems extreme, arranging a marriage to avoid a marriage."

"Sometimes extreme is the only way to handle things." He took a drink of his coffee and added, "When Elizabeth sees that she's lost, she'll complain to my father and I'll have him off my back as well. Thanks for your help with the paperwork, too."

"Not a problem." Gabe glanced over his shoulder at the world he'd created. "Easy enough to do when you own the damn island."

"True enough."

Gabe pushed his hair back from his face and frowned at Max. "So do you think your 'wife' is really going to be willing to go through with this?"

"She'll do it."

"Why?"

Max looked at his old friend and shook his head. He wouldn't be sharing Janine's secrets. Not even with Gabe. This was a private bargain and it would remain that way. "She has her reasons."

"Okay then. I just hope you know what you're doing."

Max chuckled. "I always know what I'm doing, Gabe. You should know that."

"You should have told us."

"Debbie's right," Caitlyn said and her voice carried a note of hurt. "Damn it, Janine. You should have let us help."

She fought the twinge of guilt. She hadn't told her

friends about John because she'd felt like such a fool.
But now she felt like a bad friend.

"There was nothing you could have done."

"We would have tried," Debbie said, frowning at her.

"Exactly," Janine retorted. "And I didn't want you
to try. I got into this. I'll get out of it."

"Honey, you don't have to do this." Caitlyn plopped
down onto Janine's bed.

"Yeah, I really do." Janine smiled at her friend,
shrugged and continued her march between the narrow
dresser and the bed, carrying her neatly folded clothes
to her suitcase.

She'd finally told both Cait and Debbie the whole
truth behind John's canceling their wedding. Since they
were such good friends, they'd immediately offered to
hunt John down like a dog and beat him to death for her.
But when she'd let them in on Max's proposition, they
were stunned.

And still trying to talk her out of it.

"We can loan you the money you need," Debbie said
from her spot in the only chair in the room. "I mean, I don't
have all of it, but between me and Cait, we could—"

"Nope." Janine stopped her before she could finish
the offer. "This is exactly why I didn't tell you guys in
the first place," she said, looking from Debbie to
Caitlyn. "I'm not asking either of you for anything.
Besides, you can't afford it any more than I can."

"Jefferson can."

Janine turned her gaze to Caitlyn, who was sitting
on the bed, watching her. "What?"

"Jefferson. Janine, I'm marrying the man in a few weeks. I'm sure he'd loan you whatever you needed. All I have to do is ask."

"Don't." Janine scowled and scrubbed both hands across her face. "God, I don't want Lyon knowing I'm an idiot. It's hard enough that you two know."

"You're not an idiot," Debbie defended her instantly. "You trusted a man you thought loved you. What's wrong with that?"

"Plenty, as it turns out," Janine said, but managed a smile. "Thanks, though." Looking back at Caitlyn, she said, "Seriously, Cait. Don't tell Lyon. I don't want to borrow the money from him. I don't want to owe friends. Bad enough I'm in a hole, I'm not dragging you guys down with me."

Cait blew out an impatient breath. "Okay, I can see what you're saying, and to be fair, I've known Max a few years now and he's always been a nice guy. But that's surface stuff. I mean, I dealt with him because of Jefferson's business with him. I don't know how he's going to be to live with—let alone to be 'married' to."

"Well, I'll have three weeks to get to know him, won't I?" Janine moved to the small closet and took down one shirt after another. She laid them out on the bed, then folded them, one by one. "And we're not really married, remember."

"That's the part that worries me," Debbie said quietly. "I just don't think it's a good idea. You're trusting a guy who's hired you to lie to his ex-wife. Not exactly a testament to his reliability."

"He's signing a note," Janine argued. "I'm going to have someone at the hotel business center notarize the damn thing. Trust me when I say I'll make sure he sticks to his end of the bargain."

"I'm not worried about that," Cait said and when Debbie sniffed, she said, "honestly. Max isn't a thief, unlike some John Prentisses who shall remain cursed for all eternity. It's just sort of…creepy all the way around. Don't you think?"

"I'm with you," Debbie told her.

"Well, I can't say I'm feeling fabulous about it, but I've already agreed," Janine told them. "I don't go back on my word, so I'm in this. And look at it this way…Max is a *great* lover—"

"Oh, I so didn't need to know that," Cait muttered.

"Well, I'm intrigued, and a little jealous," Debbie said.

Janine grinned. "There you go. And Max and I get along well enough. How hard could it possibly be to pretend to be in love with him?"

"Guess you'll find out," Debbie said.

"I will." Janine finished packing, took a quick look around her small, viewless room and then zipped her suitcase closed. "I'm supposed to meet him at his room in an hour," she said with a quick glance at her silver wristwatch. "So until then, how about my two best friends give me a real send-off? Margaritas for three?"

"Oh," Cait said, scooting off the bed, "I think this definitely calls for a margarita or two."

"We can think of it as a mini bridal shower," Debbie said and stood up, shaking her head. "We'll toast the bride, worry about the groom and stay close enough to catch you if this blows up in your face."

"That's the spirit," Janine said, forcing a nervous laugh. "To me. The temporary Mrs. Max Striver. God help us both."

Five

"This closet is as big as the room I just checked out of." Janine hung up her shirts, looked at the miles of empty closet rod and almost felt guilty for not having enough things to fill it.

Not Max's problem, she conceded as she shot a quick glance at the other side of the huge walk-in closet. The man had brought enough clothing with him to stock a small exclusive men's shop.

"Aren't you fortunate to have traded up then?" Max said from the open doorway.

He leaned one shoulder against the side of the door and kept his gaze fixed on her until Janine wanted to fidget. Silly really. She'd been naked with the man almost continuously for the last few days. And now she got nervous?

"You're enjoying this, aren't you?"

"Shouldn't the question be why aren't *you* enjoying it?" he countered with an easy smile that tugged at her insides.

"Hmm. Let me think." She ran one hand through her short, spiky hair. "Could it be because I'm being paid to pretend to be married to a man I've only known a few days?"

He shrugged. "Consider it a job, with exceptional fringe benefits."

"No ego problems with you."

"None at all," he agreed.

What had she gotten herself into? There he stood, looking like an orgasm on legs and Janine could feel her insides melting. And she wondered, did he feel anything at all for her? *Did he even like her?* Or was she just a handy tool? In the right place at the right time?

She didn't suppose she'd ever really know for sure.

She walked out of the closet, skirted past him and headed for the suitcase open on the wide bed. "Look," she said softly, "I'm just a little nervous. I've never done something like this before."

"I already know you're not a virgin," he said and humor colored his tone.

"Funny." She flipped him a quick look over her shoulder. "I *meant,* I've never had to act a part before. Pretend to be someone I'm not."

"Haven't you?"

"No. And I don't know if I'll be able to pull it off."

"You'll be fine. I'm not asking you to behave like a duchess. Simply like a woman who's madly in love with me."

"Oh, well then. That makes it much easier." She watched as he pushed away from the wall and walked toward her. Reaching into his pocket, he pulled out a small maroon velvet jeweler's box and opened it.

Janine sucked in a gulp of air. A gold band, wide, thick, intricately carved with leaves and sprinkled with tiny chips of diamond, winked up at her. "Whoa."

Smiling, he took the ring from its bed, lifted her left hand and slid the band onto her finger. It felt heavy. And oddly right. She shut that thought down quickly and instead concentrated on the weirdness of the situation.

"There," he said. "Now it's official."

"Swell. An official lie."

He held up his own left hand and she saw the matching ring on his finger. "We're in this together, Janine. And believe me, it will all work out just as it should."

Her heart fluttered in her chest and her stomach took a nosedive. Suddenly, she was more nervous than ever. Having great sex was one thing. Living here with him, pretending to be his wife, was something else.

"Max…" She shook her head and stared at the ring. "I don't know how to be a rich man's wife. I mean…I don't do operas and fancy restaurants. I'm more the movie-and-tacos kind of girl."

"I love the movies," he said and tucked a strand of her hair behind her ear.

His touch skittered heat through her like buckshot. "And tacos are delicious."

"Uh-huh." She reminded herself to breathe, which wasn't easy since he kept touching her. Why did he have to keep touching her? "But Elizabeth will never believe that a guy like you married someone like me."

He frowned and his eyes narrowed. "Why wouldn't she?"

"Because…" She stepped back, out from under his hand that kept caressing the back of her neck. "Because girls like me don't end up with men like you, Max. We just don't. How many of your friends' wives are florists? How many of 'em live in condos in Long Beach? How many of 'em are still making payments on a four-year-old car?"

"When this is over, you can buy a new car. For cash."

"That's not what I meant." That bubble of nerves in her stomach had suddenly become a roaring, fizzing tide of bubbles, making it hard to catch her breath. "You and I are way too different, Max. Your ex is never going to buy that I swept you off your feet."

"But you did," he said, his voice a low rumble of sound that rippled over her skin. "You absolutely did. From the moment I met you in the bar. I looked into your deep, dark eyes and knew I was lost. You touched me and I fell. I kissed you and knew I never wanted to taste anyone else."

Janine swallowed hard. Her mouth was dry, her palms damp and the bubbles in her stomach frothed and churned. Where was this coming from?

He slid the tip of one finger along her cheek and down to the line of her jaw. His gaze on hers softened. "Your sense of humor, your laughter, your sighs, fill me more completely than anything I've ever known."

"Max…" She was being swept away by a tidal force of something she hadn't expected. Something she hadn't seen coming. She'd had no idea he'd felt like this. No idea *anyone* could feel this way about her. She didn't know what to say. Didn't know what to do.

"You're everything to me, Janine. That's why I married you. That's why I'll keep you."

Her knees wobbled and her head spun. She smiled, took a breath and then blew it out when he spoke again.

"You're *very* good," he said, stepping back from her and giving her an appreciative nod.

"Excuse me?"

"I don't know why you believe you're not a good actress. There's no reason at all for you to be nervous, Janine. You're reacting perfectly." He smiled. "You're the very picture of blushing romance. Excellent job. Now, if you'll just do the same thing in front of Elizabeth, all will be well."

"Perfectly," she whispered.

"Why, if I didn't know better, I would swear that you were wildly in love with me." Max dipped his hands into the pockets of his slacks.

"You were practicing."

"Naturally," he said. "I wanted to prove to you how well this is going to go. I hope you're convinced."

"Oh yeah. I'm convinced." She needed to sit down.

She dropped to the edge of the bed, staring up at him. She looked into his eyes, eyes that only a moment ago had been filled with emotion, and now she saw only cold calculation. What did that say about him?

That he was an excellent liar.

"And you saw how easy that was. Simply look at me the way you just did and Elizabeth will believe everything we want her to."

"Right. Elizabeth." Well, why wouldn't the other woman believe it? Janine almost had. And she *knew* that none of this was real.

Slapping his hands together, he rubbed his palms in gleeful anticipation. "We'll do very well together, Janine. You'll see. Now. Elizabeth is due to arrive in just a day or so. And the woman cannot be counted on to be timely, which means she could arrive earlier than expected."

"So?" God, she felt stupid. Her head was still filled with a romantic haze, and her limbs still felt weak and rubbery. *When* was she going to be immune to good liars?

"So, we must be ready."

"I'm as ready as I'll ever be," she said.

He stepped closer, tipped her chin up with his fingertips and looked into her eyes. "Not quite yet. Before my ex-wife shows up, I'm going to take my present wife shopping."

"Shopping?" She pulled her head back, away from the distraction of his fingers on her skin. "I'm not going shopping with you."

His eyes narrowed and his features went grim. "You agreed to this, Janine. Now I expect you to fulfill your part of our bargain."

"You never said anything about shopping." She'd never liked shopping. Maybe that was an affront to her feminine genes, but to Janine's way of thinking, a mall was practically the seventh level of hell.

He sighed. "As my wife, you'll be expected to dress a certain way. To have certain things."

"I don't want new things."

"A pity. You'll have them anyway."

"You're enjoying this, aren't you?"

The gleam of victory shone in his eyes briefly. "Very much."

"Fine." Janine stood up and lifted her chin, like a warrior princess facing down her executioners. "I made the deal. I'll stick to it. Do your worst."

"You're very brave indeed."

"Like I said, sarcasm doesn't suit you."

"On the contrary," he said, coming to her and tucking her arm through the crook of his. "It suits me down to the ground. Now, buck up, wife. You're about to make quite a few shopkeepers in the village very happy."

"Whoopee."

He'd never had so much trouble spending money on a woman.

In Max's experience, women given free rein to his financial coffers always reacted like a child on Christmas morning. There was glee and greed.

There was neither with Janine.

She went along with his choices, grumbled some about spending so much time in the shops, but never so much as hinted at a choice of her own. She couldn't have been less interested and, despite his best intentions, he was intrigued. She didn't seem to care about his money—beyond the agreed-upon sum he was paying her to go through with this ruse.

In fact, before they'd left the hotel for the village, she'd insisted that they stop at the hotel business office, where he'd written her a promissory note and had gotten it notarized. Though it stung Max's pride that the woman clearly didn't trust him to follow through with his end of their bargain, he could at least admire her thoroughness.

And yet, watching her as she tried on one outfit after another in an exclusive clothing store, he thought she looked more miserable than anyone he'd ever known.

When they were at last finished, he arranged to have their purchases delivered to the hotel and then steered Janine down the narrow village street. He held her left hand in his right, and his thumb idly moved over the gold ring on her finger.

She tried to pull her hand free, but stubbornly, Max just tightened his grip. "We're married, remember? Try to look happy."

She laughed shortly. "Were you happy the *last* time you were married?"

"Hmm. No," he allowed. "But this is different, isn't it?"

"It is for me."

"Me as well," he assured her and caught her when she tripped on a loose cobblestone.

"Thanks." She tipped her face into the wind and he watched as she sighed with pleasure. "You didn't have to buy so much."

"You're the first woman I've ever heard make that particular complaint," he admitted, and glanced down at her.

"Then you're hanging with the wrong women."

"Perhaps." He guided her around a young couple, arms wrapped around each other and oblivious to the world around them. If he felt a pang of envy, it was quickly buried. He'd tried once to find happiness with one woman and it had ended in disaster. "The point is I'm *hanging* around with you, now. What else would you like to do in the village?"

"No more shopping," she said quickly.

"Yes, I guessed as much." And since it still surprised him, Max smiled. "Shall we have lunch, then?"

"Some posh restaurant with a wine list and cloth napkins?"

He smirked. "You prefer paper?"

"Don't look now, but you're sounding snooty and British."

"I *am* snooty and British."

"Right." She actually laughed and he enjoyed the sound of it. "My bad. I forgot. But if we're doing lunch, we're going to a place I found a few days ago. And, it's on me."

One eyebrow lifted. "Really?"

"Don't look so surprised. Hasn't a woman ever bought you a meal before?"

"Actually, no."

"Then I'm happy to be your first."

She led him off down the street and Max could admit, if only to himself, she was his first in many things.

"That won't do at all."

"I'm sorry ma'am, that's the best we can do."

The tall, slim, elegant woman wore a cream-colored silk shirt, pale green trousers and heels that looked as uncomfortable as they did expensive. Her wheat-colored hair was up off her neck and twisted into a knot that was studded with what were probably real pearls.

Janine stood beside Max in the hotel lobby and watched the woman she was willing to bet was his ex-wife as she made the desk clerk's life a living hell. The minute they'd walked in through the front door, Max had stiffened and come to a complete stop.

Now, he draped one arm around her shoulder and Janine could sense the irritation swimming through him. She fought down her own sudden spurt of nerves as she realized that she was about to start playing her role, whether she was ready for it or not.

And a part of her wished she were wearing one of the fabulous new outfits Max had just purchased for her. Because, standing there in a simple red sundress and flat black sandals, she felt severely underdressed for the confrontation to come.

The wide, plush lobby of Fantasies was dotted with people, gathered at the small knots of red furniture placed around the tiled room. Glass tables held crystal vases filled with bright flowers and the walls of windows allowed views every way you turned.

But Janine couldn't enjoy any of it. She was way too busy watching Max's ex-wife. Only a few minutes ago, she'd been laughing. After enduring the forced shopping trip, she and Max had had lunch at a tiny café near the island harbor. The two of them sharing fish tacos, which she'd insisted on, had made her feel more in charge than she had in the exclusive dress shops.

But now, faced with the coldly imperious woman just a few feet from her, Janine was once again feeling way out of her league. And she didn't like it.

"Do *not* call me *ma'am*," the woman said, her cultured, British voice biting off every syllable. "My assistant arranged these reservations and I was assured of a luxury suite."

"Yes ma'am—I mean, miss," the young clerk muttered, flushing red to the roots of his blond hair. "But you did arrive early and all I have available is a junior suite."

"Do I look as though I would be satisfied with a *junior* suite?" Elizabeth impatiently tapped her long French-manicured nails against the top of the glass registration desk.

"Well gee, Max," Janine whispered, "she's a real sweetheart."

"As quiet and unassuming as ever," Max muttered.

Then he turned his head and looked down at Janine. "Are you ready to begin?"

"As ready as I'll ever be, I guess," she said, instinctively lifting her chin.

"Excellent. Let's bell the cat then, shall we? Before she tears that young man's throat out."

"Remove the people currently in my suite," Elizabeth was saying as they approached the desk.

"I—I can't do that, ma'—miss."

Amazing. Janine listened to the elegant woman issue commands with every expectation of having them followed and wondered how people achieved that kind of arrogance. Were they born into it, or was it something they worked at? Despite the thread of nerves whipping through her, she braced herself. No way was she going to let Max's ex get to her.

The desk clerk was still stammering and looking as though he wished he were anywhere but there. "I'm sorry, really, that's simply impossible, Miss—"

"Mrs.," she corrected. "Mrs. Elizabeth Striver."

"Ex Mrs. Striver," Max said, his quiet, steely voice slicing through the temper-filled air like a sword made of ice.

Elizabeth whirled around, a wide smile on her face that never came close to warming up her cool blue eyes. "Max! You've come to greet me in person. Thank you, darling. That was so thoughtful." Her gaze slid quickly to Janine and then away again. "Max darling, you must help me deal with this person."

Janine watched the kid behind the counter scrape

one hand across his face and she felt a tug of sympathy for him. Then saved the rest for herself. After all, *she* was the one who was going to have to be dealing with the queen of the universe.

"Elizabeth," Max said, "if there is no room for you, you'll simply have to wait."

She pouted prettily and slapped one hand gently to his chest. "Now Max, don't tease. Why, one would think you didn't care."

"One would, wouldn't they?" His voice was thick and tight with repressed anger, and Janine marveled that the other woman either didn't hear it or didn't care enough to pay attention to the warning.

"Well," Elizabeth said, once again glancing at Janine and then away again, as if she didn't want to dirty her eyes by looking for too long, "if it can't be helped, it can't be helped. I'll tell you what we'll do," she said, eyes brightening and mouth curving into a delighted smile as she turned to the hotel clerk. "If my suite's not ready, I'll just stay with my husband until it is. Knowing Max, he has the Presidential Suite. I'm sure there's room for me."

The clerk's eyes got a deer-in-the-headlights look to them as he shifted a glance at Max.

"No, you won't," Max said, with a decisive shake of his head. Speaking directly to the desk clerk, he added, "This lady is my *ex*-wife and she is not to have access to my suite under any circumstances, is that understood?"

"Now Max, don't speak so. This poor man will think

you a very poor husband indeed. And surely you won't sentence me to a life of gritty misery in a junior suite when you've more than enough room for a 'guest.'"

"I don't have the room as a matter of fact," Max said, and ran his hand up and down Janine's right arm, drawing Elizabeth's attention to the motion. "My *wife* and I would prefer to be alone."

"Your what?"

Whoa. Janine felt the frost in the air and wondered if her breath would puff in front of her face.

"Wife."

Now, Elizabeth's blue eyes fixed on Janine and it was all she could do to keep from squirming. Here we go, she thought, gathering up every ounce of nerve she'd ever had. Weird, but she'd never been daunted by the rich and tacky before. She'd gone toe-to-toe with more than one society queen who expected her floral orders to take precedence over say, the rest of the world.

But dear God, if looks could kill they'd have been able to bury Janine right there in front of the registration desk. And maybe there'd be a small, tasteful plaque. Here Lies a Woman who Should Never Have Said Yes to a Rich Man.

"Wife?" Elizabeth repeated and Janine was pretty sure she could actually see icicles forming in the air between them. Oh yes, the next three weeks were going to be a lot of fun.

"Yes, my wife." Max, ignoring Elizabeth's irritation, said, "Janine dear, this is Elizabeth. My former wife."

"Nice to meet you."

"Oh," the cool blonde said, "I'm sure it is." She looked at Max and cooed, "Darling, whatever game you're playing at, I don't find it amusing."

"Oh," Janine said quickly, plastering a phony smile on her face, "it's no game, Lizzie…"

"Elizabeth—"

Janine wrapped both arms around Max's middle and cuddled in. "We got married just yesterday. It was sooooo romantic. Sorry you missed it."

"Oh, as am I," Elizabeth muttered. "Yesterday, you say. Awfully sudden, wasn't it?"

"Max just swept me off my feet, isn't that right, Max?" She blinked innocently up at him and returned the smile he gave her.

"Absolutely," he muttered and dropped a quick, hard kiss on her mouth.

"How very…nice for both of you," Elizabeth said.

"Isn't it?" Janine blew out a breath and said, "I'm really sorry, Liz, but Max just tired me out last night. I think my new hubby and I need a nap."

"Elizabeth," the woman said with a snarl.

"Right. Sorry." Janine shrugged and leaned closer into Max. Looking up at him, she said, "What about it, honey? How's a nap strike you?"

"Brilliant idea, my love," he murmured, stroking one hand up and down her spine. Then he looked at the blonde watching them through slitted eyes. "Elizabeth, good luck with your reservation trouble."

They walked arm in arm to the bank of elevators on

the far side of the lobby and, just as they turned the corner, Janine chanced a quick glance back. Elizabeth was watching them.

And she didn't look happy.

In that moment, Janine knew she was going to earn every penny of the money Max had promised her.

Six

Max waited until they were in his suite before speaking. His temper spiked, settled and spiked again on the elevator and during the walk down the hall. By the time they were in their suite, he was ready to answer all of the questions he expected Janine would have. "Should have known she'd arrive early."

"You could have warned me that she's a witch." Janine dropped onto the deep red sofa and curled her legs up beneath her.

Max glanced at her as he walked to the bar and stepped behind it. "If she were a nice woman, chances are, I'd still be married to her, wouldn't I?"

Janine's eyebrows lifted. "Cranky much?"

He frowned, poured a short glass of scotch and drank

it down like medicine. Then, setting the tumbler back onto the bar top, he looked at her. "She's a way of getting under my skin like no one else."

"Why do you let her?"

"Excuse me?"

Janine shrugged, wrapped her arms around her middle and said, "She's your *ex,* Max. Why do you care what she does or says?"

"I don't." He really didn't. There'd been a time, of course, when Elizabeth had occupied a good deal of his thoughts. Back then, though he hadn't loved her, he had been attracted. Interested. Though that time was long over, he found she could still grate on him. Something like salt in a wound. "Having her a constant thorn in my metaphorical paw is irritating."

"So, why'd you marry her in the first place?"

He poured another drink, then opened a chilled bottle of chardonnay and poured Janine a glass of the cold white wine she preferred. After carrying it to her, he took a seat on the sofa, stared down into the amber scotch in his glass and said, "Many reasons. The main one being her family and mine wanted the match."

"An arranged marriage?" She took a sip, shook her head and said, "Jeez, I knew you were British. Didn't realize you were medieval."

"What's that old saying, *the more things change, the more they stay the same?* Some traditions, shall we say, die hard in England." He sipped at his scotch, then leaned his head against the back of the couch. "Marriages in some circles are, even today, generally more about lineage than love."

"That sucks."

"It does indeed," he said, sliding a look and a half smile at her.

"So why doesn't Lizzie just find some other lineage to lay claim to? Why's she so hot on getting you back?"

He lifted his head, looked at her. "Elizabeth doesn't like losing any better than I do. Her pride took a beating when I insisted on a divorce."

Cradling her wineglass between her hands, Janine watched him for a long moment. "And you really think a woman like that is going to give up and go away just because you have a 'new wife'?"

"I do." He pushed off the couch, shoved one hand into his slacks' pocket and walked to the French doors leading to the terrace. "Because I plan on throwing you into her face at every opportunity."

"Wow. Lucky me."

He whipped his head around and speared her with suddenly hot, flashing eyes. "You agreed to this bargain, if you'll remember."

She held up one hand in surrender. "I know what I agreed to. I'm not trying to weasel out of anything."

"Good." He turned his head back to the terrace doors and the evening beyond. The sun was sliding into the sea, swirling the sky with shades of gold and scarlet that clung to the drift of clouds like brilliant paint on sailing vessels. The first star winked into life as he watched and he forced a calm he didn't feel into his bones. When he knew he could speak without snarling, he said, "There will be no 'weaseling' of any kind. We're both in this to the finish. And by the end of it, Elizabeth will be only a bitter memory."

She sighed behind him and Max almost wondered what she was thinking. But he could guess well enough. He presumed she was regretting stepping into this little bargain. But wishes were useless as he knew only too well. So best she understand now that he wouldn't be releasing her from this task.

Turning his back on the incredible view, he faced the woman who was his temporary wife and spoke softly. "For the next three weeks, you're going to be my wife. That means you will conduct yourself accordingly at all times." He walked toward her, stopped when he reached the sofa and looked down at her. "No more spending your evenings drinking with your friends, or dancing at the club unless I'm with you."

"Now just a minute…" She set her glass of wine on the nearest table and stood up. But even pulling herself to her full height, she was forced to look up to meet his gaze. "I agreed to this, but—"

"No buts." He cut her off neatly, tossed back the last of his scotch and said, "From here on out, who you were is gone. You're no longer a single woman on holiday. Now you're my wife. And you'll do as I say."

She looked him up and down, and then folded her arms across her chest. "You know, Max? If you acted this much of a bastard with Elizabeth, I can't imagine why she wants you back."

He reached out, cupped the back of her head and pulled her close. He ground his mouth over hers in a hard, fierce kiss and he didn't stop until he felt the gentle sway of her surrender. Then he lifted his head, cocked a brow and asked, "Can't you?"

"I knew going in that I was going to regret this," Janine said the following afternoon. "But damned if I knew how much I'd want to kill him."

"Honey," Debbie said, "all of us end up wanting to kill a man sooner or later."

"Yeah, but look at me!" Janine waved one hand down the front of herself, to indicate the deep violet silk dress with the scooped neck and elegant cut. She had diamonds at her throat and sparkling in her ears. Her makeup was perfect and even her spiky hair had been tamed into what looked like tousled curls instead. "He's turned me into someone I'm not. This isn't me. This silk and the makeup and *diamonds*."

"Poor little you. Forced to dress up and wear pretty things. He should be shot."

"Very funny." Janine smirked at her. "Fine. I'm not exactly being chained to a wall, but you know I hate this stuff, Deb. I'm a jeans and T-shirt girl. I don't wear diamonds. Hell, I don't *own* diamonds."

"You do now," Debbie pointed out, with only a slight touch of wistful envy.

"No way. I'm not keeping any of this stuff," Janine vowed. She broke off a small corner of the hot bread sitting in the middle of their table. Popping it into her mouth, she said, "I don't want his damn jewels. Or the stupid clothes. Where would I wear them back home? Can you see me, standing in the flower shop wearing this getup?"

"Actually, yeah. You've always had the confidence to pull off anything." And Debbie'd envied that self-assurance more than once over the years.

Janine blinked, smiled a little and said, "Thanks, but this is so not me."

"Well, if it makes you feel better, give it all back," Debbie said. "I just don't get why you're so pissed off about it. Most women wouldn't complain about a man spending a fortune on them."

Scowling, Janine drank the last of her mimosa and set the glass down again. "I think what bugs me most is Max *expects* me to want all this stuff. Like because I accepted his damn bargain, he can *keep* buying me. That doesn't even make sense, does it? No wait. It does. He gets this look on his face—"

"What?"

"I can't even explain it. It's like tired and bored. We went into those shops and the women there fawned all over him, racing around in circles, trying to sell him as much as they could before he slipped away again."

"Seems natural."

"Yeah, but the looks he gave me weren't. Like he couldn't figure out why I wasn't into it. Like why I wasn't drooling over his credit card."

"He doesn't know you," Debbie said and reached out to pat her friend's hand. Janine had never really cared about money. And Debbie had never understood it. For Janine, all that was important was a home. Having her home and a place to work with the flowers she loved was enough. The only reason she'd accepted this deal with Max was so she could replace what John had stolen, return to her everyday world and not be afraid to lose it.

For Debbie, money was more important—not spending it, squandering it, or lording it over everyone who didn't have it. But she liked knowing it was there, as a safety net. She'd worked hard, had built up her travel agency and had carefully tucked away every spare cent, all to ease the constant, niggling fear that lived inside her. Janine and Cait teased her about it, naturally, but then, neither of her best friends had ever really been *poor*. Had never gone to bed hungry, or worried about not having a place to sleep.

Well, Debbie had and it sucked.

"Max doesn't know you, that's all," she said as Janine continued to glower at the table.

Debbie shrugged, signaled for their waiter and ordered another two mimosas. Champagne and orange juice. People should drink it all the time, she thought. It would seriously improve their dispositions. Of course, it wasn't doing much for Janine's at the moment.

Still, who could blame her? She'd been cheated out of everything she owned by the man she'd thought loved her and then forced to pretend another love, just to try to hold her own world together. A lot of crapola in a very short time. No wonder she was feeling a little less than chipper.

A shame though, Debbie thought, glancing around the crammed restaurant at the well-dressed crowd. They'd come to Fantasies looking for escape and so far, both Cait's and Janine's pasts had arrived to haunt them.

Debbie's mom used to say that bad luck came in threes.

Which, if truth were told, was making Debbie just a little bit nervous.

"If it's that bad," she spoke quickly, more to shatter her thoughts than anything else, "quit. Walk away. He can't stop you."

"That's what you think." Janine leaned back in her chair and folded her arms across her chest, like a petulant child, pouting. "He'd find a way. Besides, I can't quit and you know it as well as I do."

"The money."

"Exactly. I can't risk losing my home, Deb. I worked too hard to get it. So I'll stay with Max and I'll play the part. But that doesn't mean I won't complain about it to you."

"Understood."

Janine blew out a breath, glanced over the railing at the pool beyond the restaurant and shook her head. "I feel like I'm in a play and they keep changing the script on me."

"What do you mean?"

She sat up, braced her arms on the glass tabletop and scowled. "Last night, his majesty informed me, there'll be no hanging with you at night. Or going dancing. I'm his 'wife' and I'll do as he says."

Debbie winced and took a sip of one of the mimosas a handsome waiter delivered. "Did he make you salute?"

"It was close."

"Okay, but you had to know that would be part of it."

"I suppose, just hadn't really considered it." She sighed and picked up her fork to stab at the chef's salad in front of her. "And now I feel guilty."

"About what for heaven's sake?"

"About you. Bailing on you," Janine said. "Cait's off in Portugal with Lyon of all people, I'm trapped with my British jailer and you're on your own." Disgusted, she dropped her fork again. "This was supposed to be a trip for *us*. The three of us. To party. To relax. To have fun, for Pete's sake."

Debbie sighed. Sure she missed hanging with her friends, but she was still enjoying herself. How could she not in a place like Fantasies? Even if she did, every once in a while, feel as though she were being watched.

She shivered a little, rolled her shoulders and dismissed the notion. At the moment, she wasn't feeling anyone's eyes on her and that was good.

"Look, Cait'll be back in a week or two. With any luck, Max's ex-wife will get tired of being snubbed early and we can go back to having fun."

"You think?"

"Why not? Would *you* stick around if your ex was rubbing your nose in his new relationship?"

"I guess not."

"So." Debbie picked up Janine's mimosa, handed it to her, then held her own out, waiting for her friend to clink glasses with her. "Let's keep with that good thought, have a toast to the Queen Witch leaving in a snit and enjoy what's left of our lunch, okay?"

Shrugging, Janine agreed. Their glasses touched with the music of crystal and both of them took long, satisfying drinks. When she set her glass down again, Janine said, "You're right. Maybe, if I play this part well enough, I could actually chase her off faster."

"That's the spirit," Debbie crowed, glad to see a sparkle back in her friend's eyes.

As Janine tucked into her lunch, she started talking, telling Debbie all about the Presidential Suite, about the mountain of clothes and jewelry Max kept heaping on her....

And Debbie heard only about every other word. That creepy sense of being watched was back. It was probably nothing, but it was enough to make her signal for the check and hurry her friend along.

Three nights later, the live band on stage created hot, bluesy music swirling around the crowd gathered in the club at Fantasies. Tables of gleaming oak and sparkling glass dotted the room, circling a wide dance floor that shone beneath winking colored lights.

Candles rested in the center of every table and soft lighting from seashell sconces on the walls kept the atmosphere to a soft glow. Crystal clinked laughter bubbled and conversation swam through the air with a muted hush that rose and fell with the rhythm of the band's melody.

Janine swept one hand through her softly curled hair and accidentally sent a swag of diamonds at her ear swinging. She'd never get used to it, she thought. Not the glamour, not the lies. Not any of it.

"Mrs. Striver?"

She jolted in her seat, then smiled at the waiter who'd spent half the night hovering near their table. "Yes. I'm sorry. What?"

"I've a message for you, from your husband." He held out a folded piece of paper and when Janine reached for it, the waiter smiled. "May I freshen your drink?"

"Um, sure. Marg—"

"Margarita on the rocks, no salt," he said quickly. "I remember."

She nodded as he moved off into the crowd. Just one more thing she couldn't seem to get used to. As the "wife" of a very rich man, she had the entire staff of Fantasies practically leaping to attention whenever she was around. No one could do enough for her.

"Just weird," she muttered and opened the note from Max.

Had to take a phone call. Will be back soon—M.

"Short and sweet," she said and folded the note away. She would have tucked it into her elegant evening bag, but before she could, someone snatched it from her.

"Ah, love notes," Elizabeth purred as she slid into the

booth with Janine. "I wonder what the happy bride-groom has to say…."

"Back off, Lizzie." Janine grabbed for the note, but the other woman held it out of reach.

When she'd read it, she turned a sympathetic glance on Janine. But her smile was pure mean as she handed the note back. "Such passion. I wonder now the paper didn't simply erupt into flames."

"Funny."

"No, dear. Quite sad, actually." Elizabeth held up a finger for a waiter and when he scuttled up, said only, "Vodka. Your best. Chilled."

Janine just looked at her. "Well, please. Sit down. Get comfy."

"I believe I will." Elizabeth crossed her legs with a slide of silk, stretched one arm out along the back of the deep red leather booth and said, "You and I should really talk, you know. We could be friends."

"Oh, I don't think so."

"But we share so much."

"Such as?" Where was her damn drink? Janine scowled into the crowd of partiers and wished fiercely that she were one of them.

"Max, of course."

"We don't share Max, Lizzie." Janine speared her with one long look. "I have him. You don't."

Score one for me, she thought, enjoying the flash of fury in Elizabeth's eyes. For the last three days, every time Janine turned around, there she was. Elizabeth took every opportunity to try to drape herself across

Max and, at the same time, edge Janine right out of the picture.

So far, she hadn't had much luck.

"It's Elizabeth," she said, her mouth barely moving. "And I have to wonder if you do indeed 'have' Max, as you put it."

Janine waved her left hand, letting the candlelight flash off the thick gold band she was actually getting used to wearing on her ring finger. "This says I do."

Of course, the ring lied, too, but Lizzie didn't have to know that.

Elizabeth sniffed dismissively. "That tacky little band says *temporary* to me."

"Tacky?" Janine glared at the woman, glanced at her ring, and then focused on the blonde across from her again. "It's not tacky. It's beautiful."

"And if you look closely, you can almost see the tiny, baby diamonds," Elizabeth said, not bothering to hide a sneer. "Now, the ring Max bought *me* was a five-carat yellow diamond solitaire. *That* was a ring."

"Sure," Janine said, rolling her eyes, "if you're trying to signal ships at sea. Talk about tacky."

"It was elegant."

"And showy."

"Beautiful."

"Vulgar."

"Why you little—"

The waiter showed up, carrying a tray with both drinks. Janine smiled a thank-you while Lizzie barely registered his existence.

Blowing out a long, infuriated breath, Elizabeth smiled grimly and inclined her head. "We'll leave the discussion of the ring for now."

"Why don't we leave *all* of it?" Janine shook her head and said, "Max'll be back in a minute or two. Do you really want him to see you here…*again*…looking all pitiful and doe-eyed? Where's your dignity?"

"My dignity is not at issue," Elizabeth informed her and took a sip of her iced vodka. "My future happiness *is*."

"Give it a rest, Lizzie. He doesn't want you. He wants me. And hey, look at the ring again. He's *got* me."

"For now, perhaps. But I think you and I both know that what you have with Max won't last."

If she only knew, Janine thought. Sure, the marriage was temporary, but that didn't mean that Janine was going to lie down so Lizzie could walk across her forehead. No way. She'd agreed to this little bargain with Max and she was going to do everything she could to hold up her end of it.

No matter *how* annoying it got.

"And I suppose you're the expert on lasting relationships?" Janine taunted. "No, wait. You're the *ex*-wife. I'm the new wife."

"Or current wife," Elizabeth said, "which is probably closer to the truth."

"What's your point? Even if Max and I split up in a year, we're together *now,* which should be plain enough even for you to understand."

"Unfortunately, you're not together, dear. Not in any possible sense of the word."

The band kicked it up a notch and the colored lights flashing on the dance floor seemed to pulse a little brighter.

"What's that supposed to mean?"

Elizabeth sipped at her vodka and leaned in over the table. Candlelight flickered in her pale blue eyes and it was like watching a spotlight dance across ice. "Of course, being a man, Max is blinded by your…charms. For the moment. But you can't possibly believe you're capable of being the kind of wife Max needs."

"And you were?" Janine snorted, despite the thread of irritation unwinding inside her. "I don't think he appreciated you dangling your lover under his nose."

"A miscalculation," she admitted. "But at least I knew how to be his wife. Have you ever entertained heads of state, dear? Pulled together a dinner party for a hundred?"

Janine squirmed a little, took a sip of her icy drink and told herself none of this mattered. She wasn't really Max's wife, so she didn't have to be any of the things Elizabeth was so enjoying pointing out that she wasn't.

"Hey, I do parties. I'll learn," she said stubbornly.

"I'm sure. With time and effort, you might even one day become adequate. But I wonder if Max will wait that long."

"Max wants me, Lizzie. Not you. Get over yourself."

Her features tightened, but she didn't quit. "Now, certainly. But once you've proven to him that you're nothing at all like the kind of wife he needs, I wonder if he'll still want you?"

"The point is he still *won't* want you," Janine said and watched that barb hit home. So, this little match could be considered a draw. Sure, she'd been stung at a few of Lizzie's taunts, but she'd had the last laugh.

Finishing off her vodka, Elizabeth fluffed at her blond hair until it swung loose around her shoulders like a golden cloud. "You're a fool, dear. A poor, simple fool. Max can hang all the diamonds he likes on you. But you'll never be worthy of them. And I think you know that as well as I do."

Janine took a gulp of her margarita. "Did you know you've got something green stuck in your front teeth?"

Elizabeth whipped her head back, ran her tongue over her teeth and then practically hissed at Janine. "Very amusing."

"Thanks, I thought so." Feeling better already, she took another sip of her drink and looked at the wide doorway to the club. Max was there. Looking gorgeous in black slacks and a white shirt, open at the collar. His black hair swept back from his forehead and his dark eyes stared directly across the room at her.

She felt the slam of heat rock through her and smiled to herself. Temporary or not, there was a very real connection between her and Max. Even as she looked at him, she could see his eyes darken from across the room.

"There's Max, now." Gathering up her bag, Janine scooted out of the booth, eager to get some distance between herself and the rabid dog Max used to be married to.

"Yes, run along like a good little peasant." Elizabeth nodded, then sighed suddenly. "My goodness. Who is that man coming in the door behind Max?"

"Watch it, Lizzie," Janine whispered, "your adoration of Max is slipping."

"Silly girl. Admiration of a handsome face costs me nothing."

Shaking her head, Janine stared across the room, smiled at Max, then shifted a curious glance at the man just now striding into the club. Tall, he had wavy blond hair, dark blue eyes and the tan of a perpetual beach lover. She knew his walk. Knew the confident air he wore as he cruised the crowd.

John Prentiss, one-time lover, full-time thief, walked into Fantasies and ruined what was left of Janine's vacation.

Seven

Janine actually took a half step toward John before she caught herself and stopped dead. Her instinct was shrieking at her to race up to that cheating snake and shake him like a cheap piggy bank until the money he'd stolen from her fell out. But she couldn't.

Not with Elizabeth standing right beside her.

The tall blonde was practically quivering with interest as she watched John stroll through the club like a great white shark in a school of guppies. But why should that surprise her, Janine thought. She herself hadn't seen John for what he was. Why would Elizabeth?

Nope. Janine couldn't afford to meet John here and now. She was supposed to be Max's wife. Which meant she couldn't be chasing down some other man while Elizabeth watched and plotted.

Damn it. She'd never thought she'd see John again. What kind of weird twist of fate was it to have him walk in when she couldn't confront him? Fine. She couldn't talk to him now. But that didn't mean she wouldn't face him down the minute she could shake loose of Max and his ex-wife.

Turning away quickly, so John wouldn't get a glimpse of her, Janine slipped through the crowd, leaving both Elizabeth and John far behind her. When she reached Max's side, she nodded and would have kept going, but his hand on her arm stopped her cold.

"Where are you going?"

She avoided looking into his eyes. "Outside. Need some air."

"Awfully sudden, this need for night air, isn't it?"

"Yeah, well…" She shrugged, forced a bright smile and said, "I'm a spontaneous kind of person."

His hand on her arm gentled, his thumb stroking her skin as if to soothe. "It's Elizabeth, isn't it?"

"No, it's not."

He clearly didn't believe her as he turned a frown on the woman across the room from him. "She's a stubborn thing when she's made up her mind about something."

"Oh, she's a pain in the behind all right," Janine said, pitching her voice to carry across the music and the low rumble of conversation behind her. "But Lizzie's not scaring me off. Don't worry about that."

"Glad to hear it. But if she's not worrying you, then what is?"

She pulled her arm free of his grasp, took a breath and turned around to look at the room she'd just crossed like an Olympic sprinter. Pointing as discreetly as possible, she aimed her index finger at John as he oozed up to the bar and zeroed in on a curvy redhead. "Him," she said. "My problem is him."

Max followed her gaze. "Did he say something to you?"

Janine smiled slightly in spite of the situation. The difference in men, she mused. John used women and Max instinctively moved to defend. Even his "temporary" wife. "No. In fact, he didn't even see me."

"Then…"

"That's John Prentiss," she said, watching her former fiancé turn on the charm. Sighing, she noted that the redhead was leaning in toward him now, smiling up into eyes that would be full of fascination. Janine remembered just how mesmerizing the man could be. How special he could make her feel just by giving her his complete attention.

And she hoped for the woman's sake that the redhead had her money under lock and key.

"*The* fiancé?" Max asked, interest in his voice.

"The very one." Janine turned her back on the crowd, looked up at Max and said, "So if you don't mind, I think I'm going to disappear before he spots me."

"Probably best," he said, "all things considered."

She turned to go again, but once more, Max stopped her with a hand at her shoulder.

"Max, come on," she said, irritation spiking. "I don't want him to see me and you shouldn't, either. Especially with Elizabeth out there, antennae quivering."

"Fine. We'll both go." He laid his right arm around her shoulders and steered her out of the club and down the wide tiled hall toward the lobby.

The music followed them. Candlelight glimmered on every table in the lobby, giving the room a flickering warmth that dazzled every bit as much as the fabulous views did during the day. And when Janine would have headed for the elevators, Max instead turned to the front doors.

"We'll take a walk."

She wasn't in the mood, but it wasn't worth arguing about, either. So she walked beside him and saw their reflection in the glass doors as they approached. They looked well together, she thought. Anyone on the outside would think that Mr. and Mrs. Max Striver were a handsome couple.

Which only went to show how wrong it would be to judge anything on appearances only. The doors slid open automatically and the cool ocean wind greeted them as they turned to walk across the grass, headed for the beach. The air smelled of flowers and the sea. The whispered hush of the ocean reached for them and above the sky was scattershot with stars that looked brighter here, somehow, than they did at home in the city.

And with every step, Janine felt her tension melt

away. Max didn't speak and she was grateful. After all, what was there to say? But the strength of his arm around her shoulder eased her stress level down several notches.

She stepped out of her heels at the edge of the sand and walked barefoot away from Max and onto a beach that still held the warmth of the sun. The wind here was sharper, colder and she welcomed the sting of it. Turning to look at the man still standing on the grassy verge, she said, "Thanks. Guess I really did need the air."

He tucked his hands into his pants pockets and studied her for a long moment before saying, "What do you plan to do about your fiancé's arrival?"

"I'd like to shove him back on a plane. Or better yet, underwater."

"Yes, I'm sure. However, it would be best if you simply avoided him."

She'd thought of that already, in the last few frenzied moments while her brain raced and her heart thumped hard in her chest. "It's a small island, Max. Going to be hard not to run into him."

"Will he believe you're married to me?"

"I don't know. Maybe." How could she possibly know what John would or would not believe? Clearly, she didn't know him as well as she'd thought she had. Or she would have spotted the whole "thief" thing in time to save herself.

"This is unfortunate."

She snapped a look at him. "Don't go all British on me, Max."

"That can hardly be helped," he pointed out, calm reason in the face of her rising fury.

God. What were the odds of John Prentiss showing up here? Was fate just playing with her mind? Or was this her chance to get back at the man who'd cost her so much? Was she being offered an opportunity here?

Or just another disaster?

"If he doesn't believe we're married, he could upset this situation before Elizabeth is convinced."

"I know that, Max." She dropped her heels into the sand, reached up and shoved both hands through her hair. "Why do you think I wanted to get out of the club so fast? But at the same time, I'm asking myself why I should have to be the one to avoid him. I'm not the thief. I'm not the one who did the lying and stealing."

Even in the moonlight, it was easy to see his features tighten and his brows lower over narrowed eyes. "Confronting him wouldn't gain you anything. Thieves don't usually make a habit of returning their spoils."

"I know that but—"

"And, you're in the process of earning back the money he stole from you."

"Yeah, but—"

"Do you really want to risk losing it all again for the momentary pleasure of facing him down?"

"Shouldn't I?" Janine took a step toward him and stopped. "He didn't just steal from me, Max. He lied to me. He—" She broke off and left what she might have said drift away. No way was she going to admit that John had broken her heart.

Fine, her heart had mended. She hadn't been emotionally shattered. She'd bounced back. But it had been a hard climb, pulling herself up out of the pit John had left her in. It wasn't just about the money. It wasn't even only about the lies.

It was, mainly, that he'd made her feel like a fool.

And damn it, she resented that most of all.

"Your motivation isn't in question," Max said, his voice low enough that she barely heard it over the pounding of her own heart. "What you have to consider is this. Do you really want this man to be the cause of more loss for you? Do you risk ending our bargain simply for the satisfaction of looking him in the eye and telling him you know what he is?"

She inhaled sharply, drawing the cold air into her lungs. She wished she knew what she was going to do, but she simply didn't. She couldn't promise *not* to talk to John. Sooner or later, they would run into each other—Fantasies just wasn't that big. But what she'd say when that time came?

She had no idea.

The following afternoon, Janine sat down beside Debbie's poolside chaise and listened to her friend's fury.

"He's *here?*"

"Yes, he's here."

"I can't believe it," Debbie said, whipping her head around, staring at the people crowding the area as if she could spot John Prentiss in the mix and fry him with a glare. "That lying, cheating, no good…"

Janine lifted her head, looked at her friend and grinned. God, it made everything better when you had someone ready to go to bat for you. Someone who understood, completely, how it felt to be made a fool of. To be lied to.

"Thanks, Deb."

"For what? I haven't found him and kicked his butt for you. Yet."

"No, but you want to and that's good enough for me."

Debbie swung her short, tanned legs off the chaise and reached out one hand to cover Janine's. "Where'd you see him?"

"In the club last night. Cruising the room, looking for his next victim, no doubt."

"What'd you say to him?"

"I didn't." Janine sighed, glanced over at the beautiful people splashing in the pool with enough care that no one's hair got wet. "I sneaked out before he saw me."

"You sneaked out? For God's sake, why?"

Looking back at her friend, Janine shrugged. "I couldn't talk to him. Elizabeth was there. And I'm supposed to be married to Max. Remember?"

Debbie drew her head back and stared at her as if she were nuts. "So because you've got a new man, you're not supposed to care about the lying, cheating snake who stole from you? On what planet does that make sense?"

"This one, as far as Max is concerned." Janine propped her elbows on her knees and her chin on her fists. "We talked last night. I told him John was here and Max doesn't want me talking to him. He thinks the creep will figure out that we're just pretending to be married and tip off Elizabeth."

"Oh, very nice."

"Can't really blame him," Janine said, though in a way, she did. He should understand, she'd told herself all night. She'd wanted him to be as angry for her as Debbie was. Which was unreasonable, she knew. After all, he didn't know her that well. He hadn't been around when John was taking her for a ride. Hadn't any personal interest in the fact that Janine's life had been shaken right down to the ground.

"So you're not going to say anything?"

"I didn't say that," Janine admitted. Max practically ordering her to avoid John didn't really sit well with her. After all, she'd done the good "wife" thing. Played by his rules. But this was important to *her* and he should know it.

She'd never be able to live with herself later if she didn't confront John when she had the chance. He'd stolen more from her than her money. He'd chipped away at her belief in herself. That wasn't something she could accept. Wasn't willing to accept.

And Max didn't even have to know about this. She could meet John, say what needed saying and then slip right back into being Mrs. Striver with no one the wiser.

Leaning in closer to Debbie, she whispered, "I have to. I have to at least stare him down and call him a thief to his face. I'd like to make him pay back every dime he stole from me, but even if all the satisfaction I get is telling him what I think of him, then that's what I have to do."

"Atta girl."

"I knew you'd get it," Janine said, smiling. Then the smile faded as she bit down on her bottom lip. "Max won't, though."

Debbie shrugged. "Why does he even have to know?"

"God, this is why we're friends. That's just what I was thinking a second ago."

"Good." Debbie smiled grimly. "Besides. Do you really think if someone had cheated Max he wouldn't take care of it? He wouldn't want some closure?"

Thinking about the man she'd come to know over the last week, Janine shook her head. "Not a chance. He'd do whatever he had to do. And so will I."

There was no reason she had to tell him she was going to hunt John down like a dog. No reason for him to be concerned with any of this. She could take care of John and still keep up the pretense of her "marriage."

She just had to be careful.

"What is this nonsense I hear about you having a wife?"

Max rolled his eyes and listened to his father's quiet fury bristling over the phone. He should have been more prepared for this conversation but in truth, he hadn't thought Elizabeth would move so quickly to spread the word around. "It was very sudden, Father."

"Too sudden to inform me?"

"Actually," Max said smiling, "yes."

"Who is she? Who's her family? Elizabeth tells me she's a very common-looking woman."

"Elizabeth would," Max said and felt a whisper of anger for the woman he'd once convinced himself he loved. Janine didn't look common. She simply wasn't as elaborately made up and artificial as Elizabeth. "Not that it's any concern of hers. Or yours, for that matter."

"I'm your father—"

"Not my keeper." Max's voice was steel and his father must have noticed. Stalking to the bar at the far side of the room, Max poured himself a short glass of single-malt scotch and tossed the liquor back quickly.

There was a long pause while the older man struggled to control his own temper before he said, "True, and yet, I find myself wondering why you didn't bother to contact your family about this hasty marriage."

"Sudden, not hasty," Max corrected. He wouldn't explain his relationship with Janine to the old man any more than he had explained his divorce from Elizabeth. Max was willing to concede that he had a duty to get married, have children. But he would do it in his time. Not his father's. He'd made that mistake once, in surrendering to family pressure to marry Elizabeth. And look how badly that had turned out.

"Fine, fine," the older voice rumbled in Max's ear. "You've put Elizabeth in a difficult position though, son."

"She's done that to herself. With your help." Pacing the length of the room, he continued, "Why the bloody hell did you tell her where I'd gone?"

His father cleared his throat, hemmed and hawed a

moment or two, then said, "She seemed eager to mend fences, whatever they might be."

Translation: Elizabeth had badgered the old man, then had cried to *her* father until he had gone to Max's father and demanded he do something. Elizabeth wielded tears like a broadsword in the hand of an expert.

"The only thing Elizabeth is eager for is to get more money out of me," Max said. "She's not happy with the divorce. Or with her settlement."

"Ah, that's a woman for you," his father said on a short, sharp laugh. "Of course she's looking out for herself. Any woman would."

Janine didn't, Max thought. Oh, she'd agreed to their bargain, but every time he presented her with jewelry or more clothing, she protested. She wasn't interested in Max's bank balance. She wasn't actively trying to bleed him for more than they'd agreed on. In fact, she'd outright told him all she expected from him was their agreed-on deal.

"That's damned congenial of you to be so forgiving of Elizabeth's mercenary nature."

His father grumbled into the phone. "Most marriages have difficulties, you know. At least you and Elizabeth share a background. Interests in common."

"Yes," Max allowed with a tight grimace, "we both enjoyed my money."

"Your mother and I had an arranged marriage," his father reminded him hotly. "And it worked out well in the end."

True. But then his mother hadn't been the kind of woman to take lovers on the side. Still, not something Max wanted to admit to another man. Not even his father.

"My arranged marriage did not," was all he said.

"No. But perhaps if you tried again…"

The elder Striver hadn't built the family business into one of the biggest in the world by giving up easily. This wouldn't be the first or last time he and Max butted heads.

"I'm already married, Father. Not to Elizabeth."

"Yes, yes." A gruff sigh of impatience came loudly across the line. "As you say. Well. It is your life, after all. But I want to meet this wife of yours. Soon."

Well, meeting Janine wasn't likely, he thought. Not when she would be returning to her own life in just a couple of weeks. Of course, Max would have to tell his father the whole truth about his sudden "marriage" once he went back to London. No doubt the old man would have plenty to say on the subject, but Max didn't have to think about that now.

He drew a breath, fought down a rising tide of frustration and blurted a change of subject. "Have you heard anything from the shipyard? Is the cruise liner going to be finished with the refit soon enough for the season?"

"Ah well, that is why I called and yes, they say the ship will be finished in…"

Max followed the slanting rays of the sun across the floor to the French doors where white sheers danced in a soft ocean wind. And, while the old man nattered on about a coming negotiation with a competitor, Max wandered out of the suite to stand on the terrace.

The sun was hot, streaming down from a cloudless blue sky. That slight ocean wind ruffled his hair and eased back the sting of the heat. Out on the sea, boats with brightly colored sails darted across the ocean's surface. On the beach, couples strolled hand in hand while two or three surfers rode the rush of waves to shore.

Max set one hand on the iron railing and stared down at the pool area below him.

There was a crowd of people gathered around the infinity pool. Lush, flowering plants edged the tiled patio and the sound of laughter drifted on the air like music. It wasn't difficult to spot Janine talking with her friend. And as Max's gaze locked on his counterfeit wife, he began to think about everything he'd told his father about her.

He smiled when she laughed and then wondered if perhaps life wasn't handing him an opportunity.

His gaze moved over Janine and even from this distance, his body stirred. She attracted him like no one else ever had. And he actually liked her. She made him laugh. Didn't take herself, or him for that matter, too seriously.

Added to that, seeing her with Elizabeth over the last couple of days had only underlined the two women's differences. Where Elizabeth was cool sophistication, Janine was open, warm. In bed, Janine heated his body until he felt as though he were being swallowed by an inferno, and he'd never known anything close to that with anyone else.

Though they were only pretending a relationship, what he and Janine shared was far more real than anything he'd had with his ex-wife. In fact, Janine played her part of wife so well—in public as well as in private—that even Max was convinced that she actually cared for him.

All of which led him to consider the "opportunity" erupting in his mind. What if he suggested their arrangement become permanent? What if they were truly married?

While his father talked business, Max thought about his life. He and Janine got on well. As lovers, they were an excellent match. And, over the last couple of days, she'd shown that she could play the part of his wife with ease.

Why not make it legal? It would work for both of them. She wouldn't have to worry about financial difficulties—not to mention, there would be no reason for her to concern herself with John Prentiss any longer. And Max would have a marriage and one day, a family—without having to add emotions into the mix.

"Are you paying attention?" his father demanded.

Max smiled. "Of course." But as the old man continued with his one-sided conversation, Max turned his mind instead to possibilities.

Eight

A few days later, Janine was still looking for her chance to approach John Prentiss.

She had to be alone to do it and as if he knew just what she was waiting for, Max made sure she was never alone. As if he were attached to her side, he was always there, insisting that as "newlyweds" they should spend as much time together as possible.

Not that she minded his company—God knew, she was really enjoying this time with him. More than she had thought she would. This faux marriage of theirs was getting easier to pull off, too. They were actually becoming a couple, which was something Janine hadn't counted on. Sure, she'd gone into this arrangement with her eyes wide open. But she hadn't thought she'd come to care for Max so much. Hadn't thought that she'd get so used to having him with her during the day—and beside her at night—that the thought of never seeing him again would tear at her so.

"You'll survive," she whispered, as if saying the words aloud would make her believe. And of course she'd survive losing Max. What they had wasn't real. She knew that.

She just wished it didn't *feel* real.

And, she thought with a sigh, added to everything else going on in her world, Lizzie was never far away. The woman couldn't seem to take a hint. And she showed no signs of surrendering gracefully to Max's new "wife."

Sitting under a red-and-white striped umbrella on the poolside patio, Janine took a sip of her iced tea. "Speak of the pain in the rear and in she walks," she muttered as she watched her "husband" and his ex-wife thread their way through the crowd to join her.

Another typically beautiful day at Fantasies, there were at least a hundred people scattered around the patio, having lunch or a drink, or simply enjoying the setting. As Janine had been, up until she'd spotted her elegantly dressed nemesis closing in on her.

Even from a distance, she could see Max's frustration and Lizzie's determination. The woman was practically sprinting trying to keep up with Max's long strides and while she ran beside him, she never stopped talking. Though she couldn't hear her, Janine would have been willing to bet that Lizzie was delivering yet another tirade on how unsuitable Max's new wife was and how much better off he'd be if only he went back to Lizzie.

"What kind of woman," she wondered aloud, "works so hard to get the attention of a man who clearly isn't interested?"

Was it the challenge? Maybe. But in Lizzie's case, Janine was willing to bet it was ego run amok.

Lizzie simply was *not* the kind of woman men walked away from. At least, she didn't think so.

Max gave Janine a tight smile as he walked up to the table and stopped beside her. His eyes rolled as Lizzie rushed up behind him. Ignoring her, he quipped, "Lovely day."

"For some of us," Janine said, letting her gaze slide to Lizzie.

The woman's hair was mussed, and a sheen of dainty perspiration shone on her face. Not a good idea to run in the sun if you were trying to maintain the aura of perfection.

"Gee, Lizzie," she said, "you look all worn out. Would you like some iced tea?"

The other woman sneered at her, took a deep breath and then ran one hand over her hair, tucking the few escaped strands back into formation. "Thank you, no. Max and I were having a private conversation, if you don't mind, so why don't you…" She waved a hand to indicate that Janine could take herself off anywhere at all and Lizzie would be happy.

"We were not having a discussion at all," Max said,

placing a kiss on Janine's forehead and taking the seat beside her.

"And even if you were," Janine pointed out with a smile, "it didn't look private. Not with the way you were doing the Olympic sprint and shouting after Max."

Max smiled and Elizabeth went into frosty mode.

"I do not shout."

"If you say so," Janine said and had to admit, if only to herself, that she was sort of beginning to enjoy these little sparring matches with Lizzie. And she wondered what that said about her.

"Max," Elizabeth said, ignoring Janine entirely now, "I think it would be best if you and I spoke privately."

"I'm sure you do," he said and dropped one arm around Janine's shoulder. "But I need a moment alone with my wife, so I'm sorry to say I'm unavailable to you."

The sleek blonde was still struggling to catch her breath but she managed to huff out a spare burst of air. "Really, Max. Your wife can do without you for a moment."

"Wow. First time you've said the word *wife* without a sneer," Janine said. "Kudos."

Now the sneer appeared.

"There it is after all."

"Isn't there somewhere else you need to be?" Elizabeth urged.

"Hey," Janine pointed out with a lazy wave of her hand, "I was here first. You came to me."

"I didn't come to you—I was following—er, I came with Max."

"Elizabeth," Max interrupted. "If you don't mind…?"

"And even if you do?" Janine smiled.

Straightening up, Elizabeth lifted her chin, fingered the strand of pearls at her throat then managed a smile that only partially resembled a grimace. "As you wish. But Max, I do need to speak with you. Perhaps tonight. Dinner?"

"That's sweet of you to ask, Lizzie," Janine said, completely ignoring the fact that *she* hadn't been included in the invitation. "But Max and I will be having dinner alone. In our suite."

"How very cozy for you both."

"Yes, isn't it?"

"Perhaps tomorrow then." Elizabeth smiled at Max, glared at Janine, then slunk elegantly away, moving through the crowd like a benevolent queen through a throng of ungrateful peasants.

"You're getting very good at handling her," Max said.

A cool wind off the sea ruffled Janine's hair and teased the fabric of the umbrella she sat under into a quick dance.

"It's not that hard, really. I treat her like I would a spoiled three-year-old. Plus, she gives me all the openings I need." She picked up her iced tea, took a sip, then offered it to Max.

He took a quick drink then frowned. "Why don't you use sugar?"

"And spoil the taste of the tea?" she countered. "Just what kind of British guy are you?"

"The kind," he said, leaning in closer and teasing the ends of her hair with his fingertips, "who has to attend a business meeting in Florida tonight."

A swirl of something she was afraid to admit might be disappointment surged through her and Janine quickly battled it down. If she was going to miss the man for a few hours, how would she ever do without him once they returned to their own lives?

Stirring the tea with her straw, she listened to the soft click of ice cubes hitting crystal before she said, "How long will you be gone?"

"Only overnight." He leaned back in his chair now, shifted his gaze over the crowd briefly and then looked back to her. "I couldn't get out of it. One of our accounts needs to see me about some plans for expansion."

"Sounds important."

"It is." He stretched out his long legs, crossed his feet at the ankles and studied her. "If it weren't, I wouldn't go."

"Well then," she said, forcing a smile. "What time's your flight leave?"

He grinned at her and Janine felt a straight shot of something sizzling rush through her. The man really could get to her as nobody else ever had. Probably not a good thing, she decided, since this whole relationship was so temporary. How in the hell would she ever be able to date some average Joe at home without mentally comparing him to Max?

And how would any man ever be able to measure up?

"*My* plane is gassed up and ready to go whenever I arrive at the airfield."

Of course it was. How foolish of her to have forgotten even for a minute that Max ruled his own little world. A world where flight schedules meant nothing because he could call up his own jet on a moment's notice. A world Janine had no place in.

"Right. Wasn't thinking. So, when do you leave?"

"Now." He straightened up in his chair, rested his forearms on his thighs and leaned in toward her. "I just wanted to see you before I left. Make sure you'd be all right dealing with Elizabeth on your own."

"Please." Janine laughed, set her tea down and reached over to lay one hand on his. "Lizzie doesn't worry me."

He nodded, frowned, then asked, "And you'll stay away from Prentiss, as we discussed."

It wasn't a question. It was a simple statement of fact. Which was exactly why it irritated her.

"Max…" She sighed, lifted her hand from his and only sighed again when he caught it and held it trapped between his palms. Staring at him, she said, "Let it go, okay? What's between John and I is none of your business."

"It is now that we've got our own bargain running, Janine. And I won't have it spoiled by a petty need for revenge."

"Petty?" Now she yanked her hand free of his grasp and tried to remember why, only moments ago, she'd been sorry to hear he was leaving. "It's not petty. He lied to me. Used me. Stole from me. If someone did that to the great Max Striver, no way would the guy just walk away unscathed."

He glanced around as if to assure himself that no one

was paying attention to them. Then, when he looked back at her, his eyes were narrowed and his voice was low and tight. "Whatever he did to you, it's over now. You survived it. Let it go and move on."

She shook her head at him and knew he would never understand. Irritation warred with disappointment, and disappointment won. "Wow. You should put that on a T-shirt. Great advice, Max."

His voice was low and somehow more British with the sting of banked temper in it. "You're making this more difficult than it is."

"I'm not making it anything. You're the one with the bug up the wazoo about it."

"The—never mind," he said. "I don't want to know."

She sat back in her chair, folded her arms over her chest and tapped the toe of her ridiculously expensive leather sandals against the tile. "Just as well."

"As I thought," he said. "You're being very short-sighted about this, you know."

"Oh, am I? And how's that?"

"You're so interested in confronting this man, you've forgotten that you're already beating him." When she frowned at him, he kept talking before she could interrupt. "He thought to leave you broken and bleeding. He thought to ruin you. To shatter your life. But he didn't."

"Damn right he didn't," Janine said, remembering though, how she'd cried, how she'd mourned and how she'd felt the fool once she'd understood that John'd slipped out of town with all of her money.

He reached out again, grabbed the sides of her chair and turned her around so that she was facing him squarely. She didn't want to look into his dark eyes. Didn't want to feel anything but the anger churning within.

"You hung on," Max said. "That took guts. And now, you've found a way to earn back what he took from you. You can go home now and rebuild your life into exactly what it was before he entered it."

Logical. Completely logical. She knew that.

But she didn't care.

She wanted to look into John's lying eyes and tell him she knew him now for what he was. She wanted to demand her money back because she knew that was the only way she'd earn back her self respect. But she couldn't tell Max any of that because he didn't know. Could never know how it felt to have your heart torn out of your chest and tossed at your feet.

So she kept her thoughts to herself and let him talk.

"But if you face him now, you lose everything. You prove that you are the foolish woman he thought you to be." His gaze was dark, and steady. "Is that what you want?"

"No," Janine said tightly and shifted her gaze from his. "I don't appreciate you talking to me like I'm a child, either, by the way."

"You're not a child, Janine," he whispered, going down on one knee and leaning into her. He turned her face with the tips of his fingers until she was looking into his eyes again. "You're a woman with a sharp, clever mind. A woman who is, I believe, too smart by half to make the same mistake twice. Don't let John ruin you again. Don't give him the satisfaction."

"You're pretty clever yourself," she said, trying to ignore the tiny pinpoints of heat his fingertips engendered on her flesh. "Turning this all around to put it on me. Did you take psychology in college or something?"

He grinned fiercely. "Or something."

"Fine," she said. "Don't worry about me. I'll be a good little wifey. I'll stay away from John and I'll try to keep from punching Lizzie dead in the face."

"Much appreciated," he said, laughing.

"But don't expect me to think about this the way you do, Max." She pulled her head back, stared at him and said, "I can't. I won't."

He sighed and his brow turned into a frown. "You're a stubborn woman. I believe I may have mentioned that before."

"A time or two."

Nodding, he stood up, rested one hand on her shoulder, then bent down to kiss her.

His mouth moved on hers and despite the anger churning within, Janine couldn't help but be moved. It was her damn body's fault. Everything in her lit up for Max like a fireworks show on the Fourth of July. Her blood sizzled, her heartbeat pounded and her brain went a little fuzzy as his lips and tongue teased her.

Finally, he pulled his head back, smiled at her and said, "I'll try to hurry through the meeting."

"No rush," she quipped, but damned if she didn't

hope he came back fast. Not fair to heat her up only to leave town.

He grinned, as if he knew exactly what she was thinking. "Take care."

She watched him walk away and noticed that several other women were watching him, too. Well, she thought, why wouldn't they? All they saw was a tall, amazing-looking man with a great behind. They didn't know how pushy and bossy and overbearing he was to live with.

They didn't know that the man understood *nothing* about women. They didn't know that he'd just given her a direct *order* for Pete's sake.

And they, like Max, had no way of knowing that she had no intention of following his order.

Later that night, Janine was ready. She wore yellow capris, a white shirt and brown sandals. She wasn't dressed like Mrs. Striver. No diamonds. No silks. To face John, she wanted to do it as herself.

Besides, if John got a look at some of the jewelry Max had given her, he'd find a way to steal it.

Walking out the hotel's glass front doors, she fought down the nerves battling to take over. Her stomach churned and her blood raced. She'd seen John heading for the beach just a half hour ago. If she moved fast, she could catch him, hopefully alone, and say what she had to say with Max never being the wiser.

Her steps were quick, light as she moved through the darkness. Her heartbeat was pounding, her stomach still spinning but her course was set. She'd waited too long for this chance to pass it up now. Janine crossed the lawn, continued down the slow slope of grass to the edge of the sand. Once there, she stepped out of her sandals and carried them as she walked toward the water.

He was there. Watching the sea, as if he knew exactly the kind of picture he painted. A gorgeous man on a starlit beach, waiting for a lover.

Or, in this case, a furious ex-lover.

"John."

He turned, saw her and just for an instant, cool deliberation flickered across his face. Then a moment later, his expression eased and a practiced smile curved his mouth. "Janine. I didn't expect to speak to you again."

His voice rippled through her and she remembered so much she didn't want to recall. The way he'd whispered to her in the night. The first time he'd told her he loved her. The night he'd proposed.

Then she remembered his all-too-brief goodbye note—and the empty echo inside her savings account. Pain was still there and that surprised her. But it was quickly drowned by her simmering anger. "I bet you didn't."

"What're you doing here?" He turned his back on the ocean to face her, tucked his hands into his pockets and kept that smile in place.

"I'm on vacation," she said, walking closer.

"Oh, I knew that," he told her. "I've seen you a couple of times with your *husband.*"

She swallowed hard. The emphasis on the word *husband* told her he knew something—or thought he did.

"I didn't come to talk to you about Max," she said. "I want the money you stole from me."

"Janine," he said, his voice holding a note of disapproval. "You *wanted* to give me that money. An investment."

"Uh-huh. And how's it going, my investment?" Her nerves were gone and in their place was a cool detachment. God, how could she have ever believed him? How could she have looked at him, loved him, and not seen the truth of him? "How about some dividends?"

"There've been some setbacks," he admitted with a shrug. "Unfortunate downturns."

"Right." She lifted both hands to encompass the resort, the fact that he was there and hey, probably on her money. "Looks like you've had some setbacks, all right."

"Investing is risky."

"For some more than others. Look, John, I'm here to tell you that you'd better find that investment for me."

He pulled his hands free of his pockets and held them out helplessly. "Sorry, babe. No can do."

She'd expected that. Known he'd fight her. And was prepared.

"If you don't," she said, moving closer, "I'll tell everyone on this island just what you are. A thief. A liar. A man who romances a woman until he can steal everything she's got. Be a lot harder to find the next woman to fleece."

MAUREEN CHILD 125

His eyes narrowed. "I wouldn't do that."

"Really. Why's that?"

He grinned again and even managed a short, amused laugh. "Well, *Mrs.* Striver, I figure you've got a few secrets of your own to keep quiet."

Janine rocked backward on her heels. He knew. How? A cold wind whipped off the ocean, making her eyes tear.

"You're the talk of the resort, babe," he was saying. "The whirlwind romance of a nobody and the very important Max Striver. Congrats, by the way."

Fury choked her, held a tight fist around the base of her throat and made even breathing difficult.

He didn't wait for her to say anything; he just kept talking. "See, I know you, Jan. You don't do anything without a plan. There is no way you would have been swept off your feet by anybody. Unless you married him for his money, in which case, what makes you better than me?"

"You—"

"So, I figure this puts us at a stalemate, Jan honey."

"Don't call me that."

His grin widened. "You say anything about me, I'll blow the whistle on you."

"There's nothing for you to tell."

"Oh, come on. A man like him? Marries someone like you in an overnight romance? I don't think so. There's something there. I don't even have to know what it is, though if you want to tell me, I'm all ears." He paused. "No? That's okay. Like I said, I don't have to know. All I have to do is start the wheel spinning. Gossip. Rumor. A few whispered questions and people will talk. Speculate. It'll ruin whatever it is you've got going and you know it."

He was right. Gossip didn't need facts. Rumors didn't have to be based in reality. He could ruin her again if she allowed it. Then she'd be right where Max had said she would. Nowhere.

"You're a real bastard, aren't you?"

"Sticks and stones," he said, clearly enjoying himself now.

Before she could even think about it, she charged. Swung her hand back to slap his face and he grabbed her wrist with one lightning-quick move. Yanking her up close to him, he looked down into her eyes and said quietly, "You back off, I back off, Jan honey. We go our separate ways and call it a draw."

Pressed up against him, she felt as though her skin was crawling. How had she ever cared about this man? How had she made love to him and not seen what he really was? And how had she thought, even for a minute, that she'd be able to outwit him? John made his living by lying and cheating. She was only an amateur.

"Let me go."

"We have a deal, then?"

"Yes," she blurted, disgusted with him and with herself. God, she should have listened to Max. Should have stayed away from John. Because now, she'd allowed him to make a fool of her twice.

"Glad to hear it," he said and let her go. Smiling congenially, he suggested, "Now you really should be going. I'm expecting someone any moment."

"Your next victim?"

"That's a little harsh."

She choked out a laugh that felt as though it were torn from her throat. "Fine. I'll go. Hell, she probably wouldn't believe the truth about you even if I told her. Poor woman."

"As I recall, you didn't have any complaints."

"Maybe not then. I've got plenty now." She was furious. And humiliated. And disgusted. More with herself than him. She'd walked into another mess with her eyes wide open. She'd allowed John to win. Again. Damn it.

"Then you should probably hurry on back to your 'husband.'" His gaze left hers, looked past her, and that smile she remembered so well touched his face. "My date's arrived, so I really think our time together is over, Jan."

She glanced over her shoulder and saw Lizzie mincing her way across the sand on impossibly high heels. For God's sake. This just kept getting better and better.

"Janine?" Elizabeth said when she was close enough. "If you've decided to start taking a lover already, you might take one who's not already spoken for."

"Trust me on this, he's all yours."

She turned to hike back up to the hotel, grimacing tightly as she heard Lizzie's delighted laughter floating on the air behind her. Just perfect. She'd been humiliated by both John *and* Lizzie.

Could this night *get* any worse?

Nine

Max saw it all.

He'd rushed through his meeting in Miami and flown back earlier than expected to surprise Janine. As it turned out, he was the one surprised.

He watched, hands fisted at his sides, as Janine met with John Prentiss in the moonlight. He was too far away to hear what was said, but fury choked him when the tall blond man grabbed Janine and held her pinned to him. Jealousy spiked inside him, an emotion he was unfamiliar with—one he'd never experienced before. But the jealousy was nothing compared to the urge to rescue Janine from the man handling her so roughly.

Before he could rush to her aid though, she tore herself free and in another moment or two, she turned from the man just as Elizabeth strode clumsily across the sand toward them.

While one corner of his mind noted that his ex-wife was suddenly focused on a man other than himself, Max was too fixated on Janine to enjoy Elizabeth's distraction.

His gaze caught and locked on the woman who was his temporary wife. A dizzying mix of emotions churned inside him, and he fought to sort them through. Fought to maintain the icy calm for which he was known. But even as he grasped at the slippery ends of his control, he muttered, "Why the bloody hell did she meet with the man directly after I expressly told her not to? What was she thinking? Damned woman never listens."

When Janine started back over the sand, heading quickly toward the resort, Max stepped out of the shadows. He watched her face, saw the anger glittering in her eyes, saw the pinched look to her mouth and could practically feel the fury radiating off her in thick, hot waves.

Until she saw him.

Then she stopped dead, glanced guiltily over her shoulder at the beach she'd just left and took a long, deep breath before shifting her gaze back to his. "Max. I thought you were in Florida."

"I was." Betrayal chewed at his insides. He knew the feeling well. Remembered it all too clearly. And now, here he was again. Once more, his woman was out meeting another man. Perhaps Janine hadn't made vows, but she had made a promise. And perhaps the reasons were different, but the sting of deception was just as sharp. Somehow, he'd expected better of Janine and that made this all the more irritating. He'd actually considered making her his *real* wife. He'd come to think rather highly of her only to find she was, in effect, no better than Elizabeth.

The wind ruffled her short brown hair, tossing the unruly curls into a waving, dark halo. She scraped her palms over her hips, then folded her arms defensively across her chest. "I didn't know you were coming back so soon."

"Yes." He bit the word off, hardly trusting himself to speak. "I can see that."

"Fine. You're pissed." Her arms dropped to her sides, then she reached up to shove both hands through her hair with impatience. "Go ahead and say it."

"Where shall I begin?" He silently congratulated himself on keeping his voice level and his fury tamped down. "I told you to stay away from him."

Now her restless hands moved to her hips. "I don't take orders from you, Max."

He bristled. "Clearly."

"I had to see him."

A couple strolled out the front doors of the hotel, their whispered conversation and laughter somehow making Max even more angry.

"Bloody hell, Janine." He stepped toward her, grabbed her upper arm in a firm grip and practically dragged her away from prying eyes, farther into a moonlit garden. The grass was damp, the flowering shrubs flavoring the air with a tropical sweetness.

But the beauty of the place was lost on him. Anger pumped through his body and Max felt himself nearing the ragged edge of restraint. Deliberately, he let her go, took a step away, and then turned to look at her. "You've risked a lot," he told her. "By meeting with another man, you've put everything in jeopardy. Was it worth it?" he wondered aloud. "Did you find satisfaction? Did he promise to repay you?"

"No," she said and began to wander the enclosed garden. She walked to a hibiscus plant and gingerly ran her fingers over a soft pink flower. She didn't look at him as she continued. "No to all of it. There was no satisfaction. It wasn't worth it and of course he won't pay the money back."

Stuffing his hands into the pockets of his slacks, Max gritted his teeth. "You knew that. You knew bloody well he wouldn't before you ever faced him and yet, you simply couldn't help yourself. Why? Why when you're in the position of earning back what he stole, why was it so damned important to demand restitution from him?"

At last, she turned her head to look at him. In the moonlight, her complexion looked softly bronzed. Her dark eyes flashed and the mouth he usually found so tempting firmed into a grim line. "Because it wasn't just about the money, Max. That's what you don't get."

"Of course I get it," he snapped, unwilling to traipse back over the same blasted argument they'd had the last time they'd discussed her former fiancé. "We've been over this."

"But you don't understand." She stalked toward him and stopped directly in front of him. "He took something from me you can't compensate me for."

He huffed out a breath, shook his head and pinned her with a dark gaze. Janine met that stony stare with one of her own. Fine. She felt guilty. She shouldn't have met with John. She felt terrible that Max had caught her red-handed while breaking her promise to him. But damned if she'd feel *badly* about facing John. It was simply something she'd had to do. She only wished she could make Max understand.

"This wasn't about the money," she said and willed him to listen. To really hear her. "This was about what he did to *me*." She slapped one hand to her chest and felt the thudding of her own heart beneath her palm. "He took my sense of self from me. He stole that as surely as he did the money. He took away my pride. He scampered off with my belief in myself. And that's something our little bargain won't earn back for me, Max. I had to find it on my own."

A silent, tension-filled moment passed before he asked, "And did you? Did you find what you needed?"

"Truthfully? I don't know." Janine lifted her chin and kept her gaze fixed on his. "I feel better for having looked him in the eye and told him what I think of him. I feel less used, somehow. Less a victim."

"And I'm supposed to applaud now, I suppose? Say

well done, Janine? I'm expected to commend you for breaking your word to me. For going behind my back?"

"I don't want your applause, Max," Janine said, suddenly tired as adrenaline drained away, leaving her a little shaky. Why was she bothering to explain herself? Clearly, all Max was concerned with was the bargain they'd made and how her confrontation with John would affect it. And still, she said, "I would like you to at least try to understand."

"Yes. I expect you would." Then he turned around, walked into the hotel and left her, standing alone in the moonlight.

"Well, forget him," Debbie said the next day as she and Janine walked on the beach. "I mean seriously, what an ass. How could he *not* understand about you needing to face down John the Jerk?"

"Thanks, pal," Janine said and bent to pick up a broken seashell tossed ashore by the blue-green waves. She ran her thumb across the ridged surface, then turned and threw it back into the water.

The rush of foam-topped waves continued relentlessly toward shore and the wet sand beneath their feet sank with every step. Seagulls whirled in a noisy dance overhead and several surfers sat on their boards, waiting for their next ride. Farther out to sea, sailboats skimmed the water's surface, sails bellied out in the wind. Janine squinted into the brilliant sunlight to focus on the beauty around her. Anything really, to help take her mind off her own problems.

"He didn't even come to bed last night," she said softly.

"Max?"

"Of course Max, who else?"

"Well, sounds like he was really pissed. And you should have been, too," Debbie pointed out. "Did you really *want* him in bed with you?"

The answer to that question should have been a resounding *no*. But it wasn't and Janine knew it. She *had* wanted him with her. She'd wanted his arms around her. Wanted his body moving into hers. Wanted him to whisper in her ear that he did understand. That she'd done the right thing.

Ha!

And she might as well have wanted to be crowned Queen of the Known Universe.

"Oh," Debbie said, then winced. "Ouch. So you still wanted him even though he acted like a supreme idiot."

"Yeah. So what's that say about me?"

Debbie shrugged, threaded her arm through the crook of Janine's and said, "It says you like him. A lot. Even when he's an idiot."

Janine snorted. "Well hell. If we only liked men when they *weren't* idiots—"

"Good point." Debbie grinned and shook her long blond hair back from her face. "So. What're you gonna do about it?"

"Why should I have to be the one doing anything about it?"

"Because, as you just pointed out…men…idiots."

"He's seriously pissed, Deb."

"And you care?"

Janine just looked at her friend.

"You *do* care. How much?"

"Too much."

"Hell, honey. Why'd you have to go and fall in love with him?"

"I didn't say *love*—" She stopped herself, took a breath and blew it out again. Who was she kidding? This had been coming on since she'd first met Max. She'd known the danger going in and she'd risked it by putting herself in the position of pretending that what they had together was real. And now, she'd gone and made the dumbest move of her life. "Fine. Okay. I do love him. So who's the real idiot here?"

"Still him," Deb told her and gave her a nudge with her shoulder.

"Thanks." Janine stopped, looked back at the resort behind them, standing on a knoll like a castle. And inside that castle was her very own prince. The only problem was he didn't know he was the prince. And he wouldn't care that she loved him.

Lousy fairy tales.

"What in the hell am I going to do?"

"What you always do," Debbie told her. "Lead with your heart, no matter what happens."

"Yeah, and that worked out so well the last time."

"Sure. But John was a JERK, capital letters, and Max is just an idiot. There's hope."

Janine laughed, and felt better than she had since Max had left her alone in the darkness. God, what would she do without her friends? Didn't even want to think about it. But was Debbie right? Was there really any hope where Max was concerned? He'd made it plain going in that he was only interested in a temporary setup. Love had never been mentioned and she had the distinct feeling he wouldn't like it mentioned now, either.

Besides, he didn't trust her.

She'd seen his eyes clearly enough last night to see past the anger and identify the mistrust glittering there like glass shards.

And she had no idea how to get past that.

The main bar at Fantasies was on the lobby level. A wide open space, it was filled with glass tables dotted with small ruby vases boasting tiny white flowers. Sunlight was muted through the tinted glass walls that surrounded the room, providing a view of the grounds, the beach and the ocean.

Max, though, wasn't noticing the ambience. Instead, he kept his gaze fixed on his untouched glass of thirty-year-old scotch. His fingers idly played with the crystal tumbler, moving it in slow concentric circles on the table. His mind couldn't settle any more than his hands could.

He kept thinking about Janine. About the talk they'd had the night before and how he'd walked away from her. Well bloody hell, what else did she expect? he wondered, silently fuming. She'd gone behind his back. Betrayed him. Was he supposed to then turn about and be the understanding male?

Not bloody likely.

He was still furious and, in keeping with that feeling, had continued to avoid Janine. He'd slept in the second bedroom of the suite—and didn't want to admit even to himself that he'd slept badly because she hadn't been there—and he'd left the suite as early as possible, to elude her again. No doubt, like every other female he'd ever known, she would want to "talk" about what had happened.

Well, they'd talked enough, he told himself. And he wasn't nearly ready to let go of the fury crouched inside like a snapping beast.

"You look like you're ready to break something."

Irritated, Max looked up, then smiled at his old friend. "Gabe. Don't worry. Your crockery's safe."

"Glad to hear it." Gabe sat down opposite him, signaled a waiter for some coffee, then leaned back in his chair. "So. What'd you want to see me about?"

Max had almost forgotten about calling Gabe and asking him to meet him in the bar. But now that the man was here, he found himself hesitant to say what he'd come to say. Still and all, who better to ask. "You have a guest here. John Prentiss."

"All right." Gabe took his coffee from the waiter, nodded his thanks and then lifted the cup for a sip.

"What do you know about him?" Max asked the question knowing that Gabe was the kind of man who made it his business to know whom his customers were. To hear if there were complaints.

"Offhand? Not much." Gabe shrugged, set the cup

down and said, "Seems to be popular with the ladies. Plays a lot of high-stakes poker in the casino every night. What else do you need to know?"

"No grumbling or grievances about him from anyone?"

"Not yet." Gabe's features tightened perceptibly. "Should I be keeping an eye on him?"

Max thought about what he knew of John Prentiss. What Janine had told him. He had only her word and the information he had gathered from her background check. But… "It might be wise."

"I'll look into it," Gabe said as he stood up and walked off.

Thoughtful now, Max remembered the look on Janine's face the night before. When he'd left her, so wrapped up in his own sense of annoyance that he hadn't wanted to admit even to himself just how damned…regal she'd looked in the moonlight. But now he couldn't stop thinking about it. And about what she'd said. And perhaps she was right. Perhaps he couldn't understand what her former lover had done to her.

Disgusted now, he lifted his gaze to take in the bar area. Doing a quick scan of the room, he spotted John Prentiss at a table and instantly made up his mind to talk to the man. He wanted to see for himself if the man was everything Janine insisted he was. Standing, he carried his drink with him to John's table. "Mind if I join you?"

The blond man looked up, seemed to take him in at a glance and then said, "Sure. Be my guest."

"Thanks." Max sat down and watched as John

tucked away the newspaper he'd been reading. "John Prentiss, isn't it?"

"That's right. And you'd be Max Striver."

"I would. I wondered if we might talk."

"About Jan?"

Why hearing the other man call Janine by an intimate-sounding nickname should strike him so wrong was beyond him, but Max shut those feelings down and cut right to the heart of the matter. "My wife tells me you took advantage of her."

John smiled winningly, spread both hands out as if in supplication and shook his head slowly. "Now, that's simply not true."

"Really?" Max took a sip of his drink, then set the glass aside. Folding his hands on the glass table, he cocked his head, studied his adversary and said, "Why don't you tell me what really happened, then?"

John leaned back in his seat. Lacing his fingers together loosely atop his abdomen, he said, "I hesitate to spread stories about another man's 'wife.'"

Catching the emphasis on that last word, Max lifted one eyebrow, stared hard into the man's clear, watery blue eyes and encouraged him. "I'm sure it's distaste-ful to all of us. And yet…"

"Fine then." John nodded, sat up and lowered his voice into a tone of sympathetic regret. "I'm sorry to say that your wife once tried to blackmail me into marriage."

"Is that so?" Something tightened inside him, but Max kept his features carefully blank. He was known in the business world for his poker face and it stood him in good stead.

"Oh, yes." John nodded, lifted his martini glass and took a sip. Setting it down again, he stared directly into Max's eyes and said, "When I tried to end our relationship, I'm afraid Janine became hysterical. Why, she even pretended to be pregnant—in a blatant attempt to get me to marry her. Told her friends we *were* engaged. Sad, really."

"Yes, I'm sure." Max's mind raced while the other man talked. Janine? Hysterical? Those two words didn't seem to fit well together. Though granted he'd only known her a little more than two weeks, he'd seen enough of her moods to know that hysteria wasn't one of them.

"Fortunately, I found out at the last moment that she wasn't pregnant." John smiled and shook his head again, as if sorry for the poor, pitiful woman who'd tried to cheat him. Max didn't know whether to believe him or punch him.

Yet…a small corner of his mind wondered. While John continued talking, Max asked himself if any of this could possibly be true. Though he didn't like the look of Prentiss—the man had a weak chin and a gaze that continually shifted to one side—Max had to admit that he was wondering about Janine. Asking himself what the real story was. Yes, he'd investigated her and she seemed to be all she claimed to be. But even seeing proof on paper wasn't enough to completely convince him to trust Janine. Once burned, it seemed, forever shy.

He wanted to trust her. But the truth at the bottom of it all was that he didn't.

After all, why would a woman who was willing to take money to pretend to be married, hesitate to lie her way into a real marriage?

Still, his instincts told him to be wary. Both of Janine—and the man she had once been in love with.

"I spoke to John today."

"What? Why?" Janine turned on him in the bedroom of the suite they were sharing.

"I wanted to see what he had to say for himself," Max told her and adjusted the fit of his black suit coat. Catching her eye in the mirror, he said, "After all, I'd only heard your side of the story."

"My side. That's great. Thanks for your support." Janine bent down, grabbed a red silk high heel and shoved it onto her right foot. Balanced on that slender heel, she used her left foot to turn the matching shoe over before stepping into it.

Turning his back on the mirror, he faced her, shoving both hands into his slacks' pockets, idly jingling the change. "Aren't you curious as to what he had to say?"

Yes.

"No," she snapped and grabbed her red clutch purse. She couldn't believe they were going down to dinner together. He was still furious with her and she was still sure there was no reaching past the mistrust hanging between them. And yet, Max insisted they continue their charade. Appear at the crowded rooftop restaurant and behave as any other "happily married couple."

How was she supposed to act *happy?*

"He tells quite the different story," Max said.

"Not surprising," Janine muttered, fluffing her hair with one hand and walking to the mirror to check her makeup one more time. "He'd hardly admit to you that he's a thief and a liar."

"On the contrary. He says you tried to blackmail him into marriage by pretending a pregnancy."

"He *what?*" She turned around to look at him so quickly, her heel caught on the throw rug and she was forced to grab hold of the dresser to stay upright. Fury, rich and hot, raced through her. She felt the heat of it on her skin, in her blood. And when she looked up into Max's eyes, she wanted to shriek. "You *believed* him?"

A very long moment passed before he said, "No."

"Gee. Feel the warmth."

"Wear the rubies tonight," Max told her blandly.

"Wear the—I don't care about jewelry and how can you when you're telling me something like this?"

He reached past her, flipped open the lid of the jewelry box atop the dresser. Snatching up long gold-and-ruby drop earrings, he passed them to her.

They felt cold in her hand.

God. She felt cold. The fury was gone, replaced by an emptiness she had the feeling would never completely leave her. How had this all turned out so badly?

"You know what, Max, I can't do this anymore." She dropped the earrings onto the dresser and shifted her gaze from his. "I can't pretend to be your wife. Can't play at your game and make it believable. Not when you think so little of me. Not when I know that you think I'm capable of—God."

He laid both hands on her shoulders and waited until she looked at him again. "You're not backing out of this now, Janine," he said tightly and his eyes were unreadable. "You'll play the part you've chosen to play. And when Elizabeth leaves Fantasies, I'll pay you what we agreed upon and then you can go home. Back to your flower shop. Find your next rich fool."

His words slapped at her. "You said you didn't believe him."

"That doesn't mean I believe *you*." He handed her the earrings again. "Now finish getting ready. We have reservations."

Ten

The next few days limped past.

Janine felt more alone than she ever had, despite sharing a bed every night with a man she loved.

Max was cool, withdrawn. There was no snuggling in the dark. No reaching for her to pull her close to his hard, warm body. There was polite chitchat instead of laughter and hard feelings on both sides instead of the "we're in this together" attitude they'd shared at the beginning of this little adventure.

And Janine was pretty pissed off about the whole situation.

"This is just wrong," she complained for what had to be the tenth time in as many minutes. "I'm the one who did *nothing* wrong and I'm being made to look like a money-grubbing fortune hunter or something!"

"Well," Debbie said from the pool chaise beside Janine, "you *did* go to meet with John right after Max asked you not to."

"*Told* me not to," Janine corrected, then practically snarled, "and whose side are you on, anyway?"

"Yours!" Debbie held up both hands in surrender. "Totally. Your side. Completely."

"Okay, then." Janine sat up, grabbed her water bottle and took a long drink. Her head was pounding and her stomach was doing a weird spinny thing. She drew in a deep breath and ignored the off feeling. "Deb, he looks at me like I'm trying to pick his pocket or something."

"Then why are you staying?"

Someone in the pool screamed in delight and droplets of splashed water landed around her like fat raindrops from a bright blue sky.

"Huh?" She picked at the label on her water bottle with her thumb.

"I said, why stay?" Debbie sighed, swung her legs off the edge of the chaise and sat up. "Cait'll be back from Portugal any time now. And she's already told you she'd get Lyon to loan you the money that Max is going to pay you. So why stay when you're obviously miserable?"

Good point. She'd asked herself the same question several times over the last few days. And she only came up with one answer. Because she'd given her word. And she wouldn't break it again.

The truth was she *had* broken a promise when she'd gone to meet John. Sure, Max had ordered her not to go, but she'd agreed, then gone right ahead and done what she'd wanted anyway. Look how well that had gone. So she wouldn't break her word again. She'd stay because she'd promised him she would. Because she wasn't going to give him another reason to think she was a liar.

"No." She took another drink of her water and gritted her teeth. "I said I'd stay and I'll stay. I gave my word on it, Deb. Only a few days left anyway. And you know what? I *earned* that money from Max and damned if he's going to get out of paying it."

"Man, you're stubborn."

"Yeah, guess I am." She screwed the lid back onto the empty water bottle and set it aside on a nearby table. "One upside to this is Lizzie's spending so much time with John lately, she's leaving me and Max the hell alone."

"Well now," Debbie mused, "John and Lizzie. There's a match made in hell. I guess Karma's alive and well and Lizzie's going to get what's coming to her."

"Yeah." Janine frowned and shifted her gaze to the crowded pool where tanned, hard bodies frolicked in warm water. "I admit, a part of me's thinking, *Good. Lizzie's getting what she should.* But there's another voice in my head telling me I should warn her about John."

"She wouldn't listen."

"Not the point, is it?" Janine looked at her friend again. "Shouldn't I tell her anyway? It's the right thing to do, isn't it?"

Debbie just stared at her for a second or two. "Both Lizzie and John have tried to screw with you and you *still* want to be the good girl?"

"It's a curse."

"I'll say." Debbie leaned in closer, lifted her sunglasses and peered hard at Janine. "You're awful pale. Are you feeling okay? You look sort of…off."

She swallowed hard. "Actually, I'm not feeling very well. My stomach's a little upset."

"Not surprising."

"I suppose." Blowing out a breath, Janine picked up her towel and stood up. "I think I'm going upstairs to lie down for a while. I'll catch up with you later, okay?"

"Sure, sweetie." Debbie stood up, hugged her quickly, then let her go again. "Go take a nap. Forget about Max for awhile."

It wasn't that easy, Janine thought as she headed inside. Because even when she slept, her dreams were filled with Max.

That night, Max dropped in on the casino. He didn't much care for gambling ordinarily, but then that night, he wasn't there for the games.

Taking a seat at a high crystalline bar, Max ordered a drink and watched the crowd. Elegantly dressed people moved in and out of the table games, laughed and shouted at the slot machines, and over it all, rock music flowed from overhead speakers. The lights in the casino flashed and dazzled and winked off the diamonds worn by the women wandering the packed floor.

From his seat, he had a view of the high-stakes poker room, and Max focused his attention on one of the players. John Prentiss, wearing a well-tailored tuxedo, held court at one of the tables. Even from a distance, Max could see that the man bet wildly. Extravagantly. His manner was exuberant, over-the-top, and Max wondered how a woman like Janine could ever have thought herself in love with such a clearly shallow individual.

Why would she try to "trap" this fool into a marriage?

And as he wondered, he had to ask himself if any of what John had told him was true. Max took a drink of his scotch, set the glass down onto the bar and wondered if he'd been entirely fair to Janine. Or had he been susceptible to John's side of the story because of his own experiences with a woman's betrayal?

"He's up tonight."

Max turned to look at Gabe as his friend walked over to join him.

"Prentiss, you mean?"

"Yeah." Gabe leaned one elbow on the bar, shook his head at the bartender, silently telling him he didn't want a drink. Nodding in John's direction, Gabe said quietly, "He plays fast and hard. Last couple of nights, he's had some heavy losses, but looks like his luck turned tonight."

"Do you always pay such close attention to your guests' gambling records?"

Gabe lifted one eyebrow and smiled. "Nope. I only watch the ones I hear talk about."

"And people are talking about Prentiss?"

"Oh, yeah." Gabe turned his back on the crowd, braced his elbows on the bar top and turned his head to look at Max. "I've had three different people tell me about some 'investment' opportunities Prentiss is offering."

"Is that right?" Max's voice was thoughtful, his gaze piercing as he stared at the man raking in stacks of chips.

"Uh-huh. One of my regulars said it sounded shifty to him, but a couple of others are interested." He swung around now to face the poker table again. Keeping his voice low enough to be barely heard over the clattering noise of the casino, he said, "I'm keeping an eye on him. I don't allow thieves to make their next mark in my place."

"Thief? There's proof?" Max ground his teeth together and thought about how he'd been treating Janine the last few days. He'd allowed John Prentiss to sway his opinion of her and for that he wanted to kick his own butt.

"Not much. But there's talk. And when you run a place like this," Gabe said, a proud smile flashing across his face, "it pays to listen."

"Good policy," Max mused, remembering now that he himself had checked into John Prentiss before he'd ever offered Janine the bargain she'd agreed to. He'd discovered then that the man had disappeared with her money. And yet, even knowing that, he'd been prepared to believe John's practiced lies over Janine's furious indignation.

What kind of man did that make him?

Had he really become so distrusting that even when faced with truth, he would rather believe a lie?

"Isn't that your ex?"

Following the direction of Gabe's gaze, Max saw Elizabeth enter the casino like a goddess awaiting worshippers. She stood in the entrance, wearing a column of white silk that kissed the floor at her feet. Her hair was twisted into an elaborate knot on top of her head and her features were cool, detached, as she looked about the room.

"Yes. That's her." Max saw the flash of delight in her eyes when she spotted John Prentiss and he knew that his fondest wish had come true. Elizabeth had finally shifted her attention to someone else.

They had nothing but bad blood between them now, and yet, he briefly considered going to her. Warning Elizabeth about John Prentiss—even knowing she would never believe him.

Then that decision was taken from him.

"Well, this can't be good." Gabe's voice broke into Max's thoughts, and he saw Janine walk into the casino and stop alongside Elizabeth.

Janine wore red. Red-hot enough to inflame him even at a distance. Her one-shouldered gown sleeked along her curvy body like a song. Her short dark hair looked casually tousled, and her features, as she addressed Elizabeth, looked strained.

"Why is she deliberately talking to her?" Max wondered aloud even as he stood up and prepared to cross the room in as few steps as possible to reach the women.

"Are you nuts?" Gabe grabbed Max's forearm to

hold him in place. "Any man who purposely gets into the middle of that is certifiable."

Max was forced to agree as he watched the two women begin what appeared to be a heated exchange.

"Leave me alone," Elizabeth said in a command filled with her usual venom.

Janine wouldn't be ignored, though. She'd decided only an hour ago to talk to the other woman. Warn her about John. Whether or not Lizzie deserved a warning didn't come into it. Janine couldn't simply stand by and watch another woman be victimized by an expert.

"Look, Lizzie," she said, keeping her voice low enough to be nearly swallowed by the clatter and rush of the casino, "I'm trying to do you a favor, here."

"Ah yes," the other woman said with a short laugh. "Because we're such chums. Of course you'd want to help me in any way possible."

"Fine. I hate you. You hate me. This isn't about us."

"Rest assured," Elizabeth said, her eyes narrowed dangerously, "I'm no longer interested in Max, so we don't have that to discuss, either."

"I didn't come to talk about Max."

"Then what could we possibly have to say to each other?" She moved to step past her, but Janine was quicker and blocked her path. *"What?"*

"It's about John Prentiss." Janine took a quick breath, ignored the flash of anger in the other woman's eyes and kept talking. "He's not what he seems to be. He's a thief and a liar and if you're not careful, he'll take you for as much as he can before he dumps you on the side of the road."

A long sizzling minute passed before Elizabeth snorted in disgust. "This is pitiful."

"I'm sorry?"

"As you should be." Elizabeth lifted her chin and looked down her patrician nose in a manner that told Janine the woman had been learning that particular move since she was a child. "John told me what you might say about him."

"John—"

"He told me exactly what kind of woman you are," Elizabeth said, leaning in now, so her voice could be a whisper of sound and still be heard. "Trying to trap him into a marriage with the threat of a false pregnancy. I knew the first time I saw you that you were beneath contempt. This only proves me right."

Janine felt a flush of heat and fury race to fill her cheeks and only hoped that Lizzie wouldn't think it was embarrassment. "For God's sake, of course he'd tell you lies about me. Do you think he'd be *honest* about setting you up?"

"Pitiful." Elizabeth shook her head and gave Janine a dismissive glance. "I find you to be completely pitiful and frankly I don't know what Max saw in you in the first place. But if my ex-husband was foolish enough to be ensnared where John would not be, then shame on him."

"Lizzie, you don't understand…."

"On the contrary, I understand completely," the other woman said with a sniff of distaste. "You couldn't trap

John and now you're trying to see to it that no one else will find the happiness with him that you were denied. It's all quite simple, really."

Janine felt a swell of regret. She wasn't going to be able to get through to Lizzie. Why had she even tried? Stupid really to think the woman would believe her about anything.

"Fine." Janine nodded, swallowed hard and said, "You've made up your mind. I wish you luck with him. You're going to need it, Lizzie."

"If I were you," Elizabeth told her, "I would be more concerned with my own welfare than that of others. I assure you, I have no compunctions against telling anyone who will listen just exactly what type of woman Max has married. Whatever you think you've gained will be smeared with your own unsavory reputation."

Janine took a breath but before she could speak, the other woman cut her off neatly.

"John and I will be leaving, going to my home in London the day after tomorrow. Until then, I would appreciate it if you could refrain from being in my presence."

"No problem," Janine muttered as Elizabeth sailed past her and walked smiling toward the man who would, eventually, break her heart as well as her bank account.

Well, Max would be pleased. He wouldn't have to worry about Lizzie hunting him down like a trophy anymore. Just two days, she thought as John smiled at Elizabeth and drew up a chair for her to join him. Two more days and this bargain would be over. She could go home. Reclaim her life. Go back to the flower shop and work to forget everything that had happened on the vacation she'd wanted so much.

Max walked out onto the dimly lit patio and slipped up behind Janine quietly. She stood at the stone railing that edged the terrace and looked out at the black sea, glittering in the starlight. Her chin was lifted, her eyes focused on the horizon and her hands were curled tightly over the balustrade.

"You tried to warn her, didn't you?"

She didn't jolt at his surprise intrusion, merely turned her head and looked at him, as if she'd been expecting him to appear. "Yes."

"She wouldn't listen."

"No." Janine lifted one hand to smooth her hair back from her forehead, and the diamond bracelet he'd given her flashed in the light. "John's much more convincing than I am. You should know that."

Max winced a little. "I suppose I deserved that."

"Yeah, you really did."

He stepped closer, turned his back on the sea and leaned one hip against the stone railing. The cold damp soaked through the fabric of his tuxedo, but he hardly felt it. He looked into her eyes and saw so many things. Regret, disappointment, anger, all churning together. And he knew he owed her something.

"I don't say this very often," he said quietly as her gaze fixed on him, "but I owe you an apology."

Her eyebrows lifted into delicate arches above her fathomless eyes. "About…?"

"You know very well about what," he said and reached out for one of her hands. Taking it between his, he felt the chill in her skin and wondered if it was from the air or what she was feeling. And he wondered how much of what she was feeling could be blamed on him. "I was wrong. About you. About Prentiss. About many things."

"Wow." She smiled all too briefly then shifted her gaze back to the ocean stretching out before them. The music from the casino was softer here, more muted, but there was enough to fill the silence building between them. "This is a moment we're having."

Now it was Max's turn to smile. He should have expected that apologizing wouldn't be enough. He'd hurt her. And that actually had never been his intention. Now, he was hoping that he might both win back her trust and do something that would benefit each of them.

He pulled her close, opened his thighs and held her, trapped between them, pressed tightly to him. "Janine, I'm telling you I believe you. More, I believe *in* you."

"That's nice, Max, but…"

"I understand that I behaved badly."

"Ah yes. Calling me a cheat and insinuating that I was willing to trap some poor rich man into marrying me. Yes, that was behaving badly, wasn't it?"

"*Very* badly," he amended and was pleased to see a tiny flash of humor spark in her eyes. "It was good of you to try to warn Elizabeth."

She frowned. "No woman deserves to be had like that."

"She'll make her own choices," he said, knowing

that Elizabeth had already charted her course. She'd decided to have John Prentiss and no one would be able to talk her out of it. And who knew? Perhaps they might even be happy together. After all, Elizabeth was a wealthy woman in her own right—she'd only wanted to add to her coffers by marrying Max. Perhaps John Prentiss would actually be satisfied with this woman and her money. "You couldn't dissuade her no matter what."

"No, I guess not. I didn't really expect to," she admitted, laying both hands on his shoulders. "But I had to try."

"And I respect you for that effort."

A soft wind caressed them, the sweet scent of tropical flowers floating on the air.

"Thanks."

"So I'm forgiven then?" His hands at her waist tightened, his fingers sliding over the silky red fabric of the dress he wanted to get her out of as soon as possible.

"Why not?" Janine shrugged, cupped his face in her palm and said, "You were just being you, Max."

He chuckled wryly. "I don't know whether to be pleased or insulted by that."

"Always good to leave 'em guessing," she quipped, then stepped out of his embrace and smiled. "You should know, Lizzie and John are leaving the day after tomorrow."

Max nodded and stood up to face her. This then was as good a time as any to tell her of his proposition. With Elizabeth gone, their bargain was almost at an end.

"I'd like you to think about something," he said,

then scowled when a clearly drunk couple staggered out of the casino and onto the terrace. Taking Janine's arm, he steered her around the edge of the balustrade and out onto the grassy area where they could be more private.

Here, the scents of the sea and the flowers surrounded them. The shadows hid them. And he used both as he drew her into his arms and looked down into her eyes.

"Max?"

"Janine, our time together is almost over," he began, letting his gaze move over her features. "And I think you'll agree that but for a couple of bumps in the road, we've done well together."

"Yeeesss…" She dragged that one word out into several wary syllables.

"I'd like you to think of extending our bargain."

"What?"

"No, not so much extending as redesigning."

"What're you talking about, Max?"

"It's very simple, really," he said, bending his head to plant a quick, hard kiss to her delectable mouth. "I think we should be married legally. The two of us get on well. We're very compatible, both in bed and out. It's perfect, really."

Her mouth fell open.

He rushed on. "You can have your own flower shop if you like, when we get to London."

"How nice for me."

Max frowned a little, but kept going. He wanted to get it all said. "Janine, we've both been badly burned at relationships based on so-called 'love.' This would be far better. We can both enjoy a marriage, children, a *family,* without risking emotional damage."

"You're serious, aren't you?"

"Never more so." He grinned now, staring down at her surprised expression, convinced that he was doing the right thing. For both of them. Surely she would see that. "What do you say?"

Eleven

Janine looked up at Max, noting the pleased expression on his face. Clearly he was delighted with himself and his clever proposal. He was also damned sure of himself. He had the air of a man who knew he was about to get what he wanted.

Too bad he was about to get shot down instead.

Hurt warred with wounded pride and anger, and surprisingly, the hurt won out. Her heart felt as if it had taken a hard slap and the sting of tears burned at her eyes. But damned if she'd cry for him. So she blinked the sensation away and shook her head.

"Sorry, Max. I won't be the bought-and-paid-for bride for you."

"I beg your pardon?"

She inhaled sharply, blew out a breath and watched as consternation, and then anger flitted over his face. "You're trying to buy a real wife, just the way you bought a pretend one. I'm not interested."

"I'm not trying to bleeding *buy* you for God's sake," he snapped.

"So the flower shop just for me isn't the bribe? It's the reward?"

He sighed heavily, like a man forced to endure far more than any man should. Shoving both hands into his pockets, he grumbled, "I only meant that you could do the work you love in London as easily as you could in Long Beach, California."

Another twinge of pain rippled through her, sending ribbons of misery to every corner of her body. Strange. She shouldn't be so wounded. She'd known full well that Max didn't have feelings for her. It wasn't his fault she'd fallen in love and ruined their perfect little deal.

But pain made her a bit less than understanding, she supposed.

"I'm not interested in a faux life, Max," she said with a slow shake of her head. "Three weeks of pretense is one thing. A lifetime is quite another."

"It wouldn't be a faux life, Janine. It would be *our* life."

"As long as nothing messy like real emotion, real depth of feeling gets involved?"

He scowled at her. "Bloody hell, woman. Haven't you already been down that road?"

"Yes," she said, taking another deep breath of the

floral air, "but I went down that road alone. I'd like to have someone with me the next time."

"I'm not interested in love, Janine."

"That's a shame, Max," she said. "For both of us. Because I love you."

His eyes narrowed and his jaw muscle twitched. She could only imagine he was grinding his teeth together hard enough to turn them into dust. "You don't."

Janine actually laughed, though the sound was harsh and it felt as though her chest was tightening around her shattering heart. "I probably shouldn't love you, it's true," she said. "God knows it would be a lot easier if I didn't. But I do."

"For God's sake, why do all women have to bloody well confuse things with *love?*" He stalked away from her a few paces, stopped dead, then turned to look back at her. "I didn't ask to be loved. I don't want to be loved."

"With that attitude," she managed to say, "don't worry about it. You won't be loved by many."

"But you do," he said, disbelief clear in his tone.

"Clearly, I like the crabby type." She walked up to him, each step measured. Her gaze locked on his and she saw the regret shining in his eyes along with frustration. "If you think I wanted to feel anything for you, you're wrong," she said quietly. Laying one hand on his forearm, she felt his muscles bunch and tighten beneath the elegant tuxedo jacket. "I didn't expect to fall in love, Max. And I don't expect anything from you, now. I'm just saying, I won't marry you. Not like that. Not with no feeling. With nothing more than a signed contract between us."

He didn't speak, but then he didn't have to.

Janine dropped her hand from his arm and smiled sadly. "If I did that, I'd end up hating myself for loving someone who *refused* to love me. And I won't do that, Max. Not even for you."

By the following afternoon, Janine was wishing she were already home in Long Beach. She'd had enough of the rich and fabulous lifestyle, thanks very much. She needed to be back at work. Back living the kind of life she understood.

Back where she could start forgetting about Max.

"I can't believe you didn't slug him for that," Cait muttered, obviously disgusted. "I've known Max for years and I cannot believe he could make such a stupid proposal!"

"He's a man, Cait." Debbie shook her head and took a drink of her iced tea. "You've only forgotten that because you're still in the 'glow' of new love."

"Thank you oh, wise woman," Cait said, then shifted her gaze to Janine. "How'd he take it when you said no?"

Janine leaned back in her chair. She and her friends were having lunch on one of the resort's patio restaurants. It was good to have Cait back, and it was great to have them both supporting her in this. But the truth was she didn't want to talk about Max and his stupid proposal anymore. She just wanted to get through the next day or so and then go home.

"He wasn't happy," she said and stabbed at her tea with a straw.

"Typical," Debbie said, taking a bite of her penne pasta. "He doesn't see that *you're* unhappy?"

"I don't know." Janine pushed her chef's salad to one side, suddenly not up to even looking at the crumbled blue cheese on top, let alone smelling it.

"Well," Cait said, as if guessing that Janine simply didn't want to talk about any of this anymore, "Jeff and I are going home early. Tomorrow, in fact."

"What?" Debbie asked. "Why?"

"My mom," Cait admitted. "She's calling me two or three times every day now to talk about the wedding."

"Bet Lyon's loving that," Debbie said.

"He's being very sweet," Cait told her.

Janine stayed out of it. She listened to her friends and told herself she should join in. Get involved. Not think about Max. But the hurt she'd been wrapped in since the night before wouldn't ease long enough for her to see beyond it.

"I'm going to stay an extra week," Debbie said. "I'm enjoying being pampered. I called home last night and told Trudy she could call or fax me if there are any problems."

"Must be nice to own your own business," Cait said with a laugh.

"It has its perks." Debbie reached over and squeezed Janine's hand. "You still feeling yucky?"

"A little."

"You're sick?" Cait leaned in, too.

"No," Janine said softly, swallowing hard against a small wave of nausea. "Just a little…bleh."

All around them, happy people chatted. Silverware clinked against fine china, and waiters and waitresses bustled through the crowd, keeping everyone content.

"Uh-oh." Cait stared at her long and hard, until Janine finally shifted uneasily in her seat.

"What?"

"Um…" Cait shot Debbie a worried look. "How long have you been feeling 'bleh'?"

"Just the last few days and—" She broke off, looked from Cait to Debbie and back again before finally seeing the unsaid questions in their eyes. "No way."

"I didn't say anything," Cait blurted.

"You didn't have to. You think I'm…I can't even say it."

"You mean pregnant?" Debbie asked.

"Thanks. Saying it out loud won't jinx me or anything." Janine's hands dropped to her flat belly. "I can't be pregnant. It's too quick."

"Hmm… How long's it supposed to take, then?"

"You're not helping," Janine said, glaring at Debbie.

"Fine. Go find out. Buy a test. Flunk it."

Cait shrugged and gave her a small smile. "She's right. Take a test. Then you'll know."

"That's the trouble," Janine muttered.

Early the next morning, Max watched as Elizabeth and John left Fantasies together. A mountain of luggage accompanied the smiling couple as they walked out to the waiting limousine. And with his ex-wife officially out of his life, Max took a long, deep breath and enjoyed the heady sensation of freedom that surged through him like a rising tide.

If Elizabeth was walking blithely into disaster, there was no stopping her. And she, unlike Janine, was no longer his problem.

He still couldn't understand why Janine had turned down his offer of marriage. Especially if she really did "love" him as she had insisted. Wouldn't she be happier with him than without him? Wouldn't she rather be a part of his life than live on separate continents?

Was her love so miniscule that unless it was reciprocated it would wither and die?

Of course she wanted to marry him, he told himself with a hard nod. She simply wanted to be wooed. Convinced. And he could do that. Why, this was even better than he had thought it would be. If she actually loved him, then he would at least be able to count on the fact that she wouldn't be dangling lovers in front of his eyes.

He would be a good husband and father.

All he need do is ask her again.

Couch his exceptionally reasonable proposal in such terms as to make her see the clear benefits to her.

Smiling now, he started across the lobby for the elevator, sure he could make his temporary bride see reason.

"No way."

Janine looked at the white plastic stick in her hand

and shook it as if it were a Magic 8-ball and would give her a different answer. But nothing changed.

She was still pregnant.

Slapping one hand to her forehead, she leaned against the bathroom counter and stared into the mirror at the face of a woman who was well and truly screwed. Then a small thread of hope showed on her reflected face. "The pharmacist said it was too early. That I might get a messed-up answer. That's probably it. I'm probably not pregnant. The test is just messed up. Debbie was wrong."

She let her forehead rest on the cold glass of the mirror as that tiny hope drained away in the face of what she *felt* to be true.

"Not Debbie's fault. My fault. Well, and Max's. Oh man. One time? That one time we forgot a damn condom and this is what happens?"

She opened her eyes, looked at herself and sighed. How was she supposed to tell Max about this? Their agreement was at an end. They were about to go their separate ways. And now she had to tell him she was pregnant?

In the harsh glare of the bathroom lights, she shook her head at her image in the mirror. "He'll never believe me. Especially not after the story John told him. He'll think I'm lying about a baby to trick him into marriage."

No.

Wait.

Maybe not.

Her eyes lit up and another spark of hope fitfully

clung to life inside her. "He asked me to marry him already, right? If I was willing to trick him into marriage, I wouldn't have to. I could have just said yes when he asked." She nodded, smiled woefully and said, "So he'll know this isn't a trick. A lie. He'll believe me. He won't be happy, but he'll believe me."

She slumped down onto the closed toilet seat. "What if he doesn't believe me?"

"Janine?"

She jolted and threw a quick look at the closed bathroom door. "In here!"

"Ah. Fine. When you come out, we have to talk. Elizabeth just left with John."

Janine sighed. Well, she had enough to worry about. She couldn't spare another thought for the bear trap Lizzie was stepping into. The woman was on her own.

"Okay," she called back, and congratulated herself on the steadiness of her voice. "Be out in a sec."

Staring down at the pink plus sign in the middle of the plastic stick, she muffled a groan, then buried the stick at the bottom of the bathroom trash can. No point in Max seeing the damn thing until she'd had a chance to tell him about this herself.

When she came out of the bathroom, Max was waiting with a welcoming smile on his face. "Congratulations are in order to both of us," he said. "Elizabeth's gone and our bargain convinced her to move on."

"Yay us," Janine said and walked past him, through the bedroom into the plush living room. Taking a seat in one of the well-cushioned chairs, she curled her legs up and watched Max as he came into the room behind her. "So then, the deal's complete. Task finished."

"Yes," he said softly and held out a single sheet of paper to her.

She took it, her mind racing, and tried to concentrate on the three lines of typed print on the page. When she'd read it, she looked up at him. "You've already wired the money into my bank account?"

"As agreed." He took the chair opposite her, leaned forward and braced his forearms on his thighs.

"Thank you," she said and folded the paper neatly, closing her fingers around it. No matter what else happened now between she and Max, at least Janine knew that she wouldn't lose her home. She'd be able to take care of her baby—alone if she had to.

Her *baby*.

Oh, God. Her stomach shivered and spun. She was going to have a baby. Max's baby.

"Janine," he said, his voice soft and easy, "I've been thinking about our discussion in the garden last night."

"Me, too," she admitted.

"Brilliant," he said, clearly pleased.

Obviously he had convinced himself that she'd changed her mind. That she was more willing now to talk about entering into a loveless marriage.

"But, Max…"

"Now, usually I prefer to say ladies first. This time however, I want to tell you what I'm thinking before you say anything. All right?"

"Fine." She swallowed the knot of nervousness clogged in the middle of her throat and fought to focus solely on Max. On what he might say. There was still a chance that he was willing to try to love her, wasn't there? Shouldn't she hear him out at least? Besides, she was just coward enough to appreciate having a few more minutes before she had to tell him her news.

"I want you to reconsider," he said, smiling at her with all the warmth she'd come to know he was capable of. "We're bloody good together, Janine. There's no reason to throw that away for lack of emotion."

"Oh, Max…" Disappointment welled inside her and only swelled as he continued to talk.

"You say you love me," he said, gaze fixed on hers. "Well then why not marry me? If love is important to you, you already have it."

"But you don't love me," she pointed out.

"I…care for you," he admitted and it sounded as though he'd had to grab hold of the words and drag them from his own throat. "And I find I will miss you when our time together is finished. Isn't that enough? For now, at least?"

Oh God, she was tempted. Especially now. Especially knowing she was carrying his child. But how could she risk living with a man who might never love her? How could she tie herself forever to a man who had no *interest* in loving?

No. Not even for the sake of the child she carried would she live with the emptiness of knowing that she loved alone.

"No, Max. It's not enough."

He sat back in his seat and his features slipped from congenial to angry in the blink of an eye. "You're being ridiculously adolescent, Janine. You know that, don't you?"

"No, I don't." She stood up slowly and looked down at him. "I need to be loved, Max. I deserve to be loved. If you can't or won't do that, then we can't be together."

"Love is for children. For fools who trust their hearts more than their heads."

"God, I hope not," she said on a sigh. Then she inhaled sharply, looked at him and said what she had to say before leaving him forever. "I'm going to pack, Max. I'm leaving on the first flight out I can get."

"Janine—" He stood up, looked into her eyes.

"But before I go, there's something you have to know." He waited and in the deafening silence, she said, "I want you to know that I seriously considered not telling you this at all. But that wouldn't be right. And now that I'm talking, I'm feeling a little nervous about the whole thing so I'm just going to spit it out. Get it over with. Throw it out there so you'll know the whole truth."

"At which point will you be imparting this news?" he wondered.

He was right.

She was stalling.

"Fine. Here it is. I'm pregnant."

A heartbeat, then two, then three passed before he took a step back from her, looked her up and down and snorted a harsh, disbelieving laugh. "This was unnecessary," he said tightly. "I'd already offered to marry you."

"This has nothing to do with—"

"Oh, of course not. It's simply a convenient twist of fate that finds you pregnant with my child." He laughed again, walked away from her as if he couldn't stand to be in close proximity any longer, then turned and glared at her. "The amusing part of all this is I believed you to be innocent. I thought John had lied about you trying to use an imaginary pregnancy to trap him into marriage."

"Max," Janine said, fighting the insult, fighting the hurt clamoring inside her, "I'm not lying."

"Damned if you're not quite good at this!" He laughed again and the sound was like knives slashing the air. "But you may as well realize, you won't be getting any more money out of me than the sum we've agreed on."

She swayed as if his words had been a physical blow. This was what he thought of her? At the base of it, the heart of it, he thought she was after his damned money? She looked at him and knew that in his mind, he'd lumped her alongside Elizabeth, and that not only hurt, it made her furious.

"I'm not asking for anything from you."

"You've overplayed your hand, Janine," he said and now his voice sounded weary. "I won't play this game. And by the way? You might think of developing a new routine. This stratagem is getting a bit frayed around the edges, don't you think?"

Janine stared at him and saw the hard glint in his eyes and the defensive posture in his stance. There was no bend in Max Striver. He went where he pleased, ran his life as he liked and dismissed anyone who got too close.

Well, fine. She'd leave. But she wouldn't go without telling him exactly what she thought of him.

"You're an idiot, Max."

"I beg your pardon?"

"You really should," she started, squaring her shoulders and lifting her chin. "You know what's wrong with you?"

"I'm sure you're about to inform me," he said with idle disinterest.

"Damn straight. You've spent way too much time in the rarified atmosphere of the rich and useless, Max. You look at those of us who don't have billions and think we're all after your money. Well the hell with your money, Max. I don't want it and don't need it. I made a deal. I earned what you paid me, but that's all I'll ever ask of you.

"I pay my own way. Live my own life. I don't need billions to survive, unlike *some* people."

"If you're finished…"

"Not even close," she snapped. "You can't see the truth when it slaps you in the face, Max. You're always ready for a lie because you trust no one. Fine. Maybe Lizzie did treat you badly. Get over it already."

He furiously sucked in air. "If you think you can—"

"I've more than earned the right to tell you off, Max, so just shut up and listen." Sunlight speared through the

French doors and gilded him in a wash of light that made him look so handsome, so completely amazing that it nearly killed her not to go to him. But that time had passed. "You think you're the only one who got stepped on? Take a look around, Max. Lots of people have a lot harder life than you do. But you know what? They go on anyway. They trust again. They love again. They *live*."

His eyes were no more than black slits watching her. "Have you finished *now?*"

She blew out a breath, looked at him one last time and realized that nothing she'd said to him had gotten through. "Yep. I guess I have."

Several long, quick strides carried him across the floor to the door. He opened it, turned and looked back at her with an icy gaze that sent shivers rolling along her spine.

"Then I'll say goodbye. And leave you to your packing."

Twelve

Max locked himself into his suite for the next two days. He spoke to no one, saw no one. He didn't allow housekeeping in and instructed room service to leave his meals outside the door.

And like a caged beast, he prowled the empty suite night and day. He couldn't sleep. Every time he closed his eyes, he saw Janine's face. Heard her voice. She was haunting him and he was suffering for it.

"Damned woman."

He stalked across the living area and cursed silently because Janine's shoes weren't there for him to trip on. He hated going into the master bath because her creams and lotions and hair things weren't scattered across the red granite surface. He hated taking a shower because her bottles of shampoo and conditioner weren't crowded alongside his own. He hated going to bed because her scent still clung to her pillow and the wide mattress felt too damned empty to give him any peace.

He kept the stereo on, trying to shatter the quiet that felt as though it were choking him. He missed the sound of her voice, the peal of her laughter.

Damn it all to bloody hell, he missed *her*.

And that made him furious.

"Ridiculous," he muttered. "She lied to me. Claimed a pregnancy only to try to manipulate a different sort of marriage than the one she'd already turned down." It made no sense. None at all. Why would she do it? Why would she claim to be pregnant? What was the point? Where was the win?

Bugger it. Even when she wasn't around, Janine was making him insane. "Enough. I'm not a man to be led around by a woman. I got along fine without her before, I will again."

He stalked across the room to the French doors leading to the terrace, flung them open, stepped outside and took a deep breath of the brisk ocean air. But it didn't help. Nothing seemed to help. He curled his fingers over the rail, stared down at the pool below and in his mind's eye, saw Janine stretched out on one of the chaises.

The ghost of the woman was everywhere in this place. Grumbling, he went back inside. Back to the quiet, where only the soft sounds of light jazz played through the stillness. He hated being here and hated the thought of leaving, as well. For the first time in his life, Max felt unsettled and didn't care for it.

But holing up in this plush cave was not the answer and he knew it.

"Time to go home," he said, more to break up that annoying silence than for any other reason. "That's what's needed here. Home. Work. Soon enough, I'll forget all about her."

Nodding, he marched off to the bathroom, reached in and turned the shower knob. As steam filled the room, he turned, glanced into the quickly fogging mirror and saw the face of a man who looked haggard. This was what he'd come to? He stepped in closer to the counter, kicked the small trash can and cursed when it toppled over, spilling its contents across the tile floor.

"Bloody perfect," he muttered, bending down to clean up the mess.

On one knee, he paused and stared at the white plastic stick that had fallen facedown from the trash. Pregnancy test. Everything in him went still and cold. He shouldn't even look, he told himself. There was no need. He knew she wasn't pregnant. Knew it was all a ploy.

And yet…

He reached for it, saw the plus sign and felt his world shift.

"She *is* pregnant." Max stood up slowly, staring down at the stick that had changed everything for him. She was carrying his child and he'd sent her away because he hadn't trusted her.

Behind him, the shower roared and steam billowed out into the room. He looked into the nearly completely fogged mirror and saw only a ghostly reflection of himself. Appropriate, he thought, because without Janine there, he was bound to admit that he felt only partially alive.

The pregnancy notwithstanding, it was *she* whose absence tore at him. She who lived in his mind, his thoughts. She who Max had treated so badly she'd run from him.

And the question facing him now was what was he to do about it?

Was he going to go back to England, let Janine and their child slip away from him? Or would he risk everything and take a chance on finding something worth having?

Max reached out, swiped one hand across the fogged mirror and stared hard into his own eyes. There, he saw the answer he was looking for.

A week back from Fantasies and Janine was finding her feet again. She'd slipped into her life and let the familiar rhythm of it all soothe away the sharp edges of her memories.

Of course, Max still zipped through her thoughts at every unguarded moment. Which was both sad and infuriating. Her heart hurt, reminding her always of the emptiness that she'd be living with for the rest of her life. But beneath that soul-deep ache was the realization that because of the baby she carried, she'd always have a piece of Max with her. The best part of him. And eventually, she told herself, she'd get past the sting of his rejection. The fact that he hadn't believed her. Trusted her.

The fact that he hadn't wanted her love.

"Okay, Janine, enough thinking. Just focus on the job," she whispered, reaching for a fishbowl-shaped vase from the upper shelf in the design room of the flower shop. The plain concrete floor was strewn with discarded leaves and dead flower heads. Small puddles of water formed in the corners and the overhead skylight allowed sunlight to pour in.

Grabbing fistfuls of lavender sweet peas, pink tulips and soft white baby's breath, she set them aside, picked up the floral Styrofoam and soaked it thoroughly at the sink. Then she aligned it in the bottom of the vase and set to work. This arrangement was only the first of fifty that had to be prepared for an elegant wedding the following day. She had plenty to do to keep her busy, keep her mind off the fact that the man she had wanted to marry hadn't been interested.

Music played and she danced in place to the rock music pulsing through the sound system. Smiling, Janine focused only on color, design, the art of what she did. The sweet scent of fresh flowers filled the air and she found peace, as she could nowhere else.

While she worked, she heard the clang of the cowbell that hung over the front door of the shop and, only slightly irritated, she dried her hands on a shop towel and headed to the front of the store. She was the only one there at the moment, since the owner was out to lunch and their second designer wouldn't be in until later.

"Can I help—" She stopped speaking as she rounded the corner and found Max standing in the center of the small elegant shop.

He looked fabulous, of course. Black slacks, dark blue long-sleeved shirt and God, she'd forgotten just how dark his eyes were. Surrounded by flowering plants, hanging baskets and huge tubs of single flowers, Max stared at her as if seeing her for the first time.

And she was so tempted to cross the room, throw her arms around his neck and feel him hold her. But what would that solve, really? The issues that had splintered their faux relationship still existed. Nothing had changed.

But then, she wondered, why was he here?

"Janine—"

"Max, you shouldn't have come."

"No, you're wrong," he said and took a single step before stopping again when she backed up. "I should have come sooner. Better, I should never have let you leave Fantasies without me."

"But you did."

"Yes," he said, nodding, grim faced, his eyes unreadable, his features closed to her. "I did. And I'll spend the rest of my life trying to make it up to you for that piece of shortsightedness."

Janine's insides twisted and her heart ached. Just looking at him reminded her of everything she could never have. Having him here would only make it harder for her to forget him.

"Max, what're you doing here?"

"I'm an idiot."

She laughed shortly.

Max took a breath and decided he'd accept that short laugh of hers as a good omen. He needed to tell her everything he was thinking, feeling. He needed to take the biggest risk of his life and hope to hell he hadn't bollixed it all up by being an ass.

"I know that already, but thanks," she said drily.

"I thought you should know that now *I* know it as well."

"Thanks for the share, but I have to go back to work."

"No, don't." He walked to her quickly, sensing that she was going to turn her back on him before he'd had the chance to try to make this right. "Wait. Please. At least hear me out."

She looked down at the hand on her arm and didn't look away until he'd released her.

"Fine," she said then. "Talk."

He scraped one hand across his jaw, pulled in air like a drowning man and blurted, "I should have believed you. Should have known all along that you weren't the kind of woman I was used to dealing with."

"Yeah, but—"

"But I didn't want to trust my instincts where you were concerned. I thought my desire for you was clouding my thinking." She only stared at him and Max wondered how he'd ever thought to live without looking into her eyes. "I didn't want to risk believing in you. In *us*."

"Max," she said, and her voice was so low, he nearly missed it entirely. "It's too late. Don't you get it? We had our shot and we blew it." Shaking her head, she fought a sheen of tears with furious blinking and said, "It wasn't all your fault. I never should have taken you up on that bargain. Because I did, you figured I was no better than Lizzie."

"No. No, that wasn't it," he said and he risked putting hands on her again. Laying both hands on her shoulders, he felt the tension in her and cursed himself for ever having hurt her. "It wasn't about you, Janine. It was me. I was just the type of man you accused me of being. I never looked beyond my own safety zone. Never wanted to trust because that would mean I would have to risk myself again. Never wanted love because I didn't feel lovable. Stupid, really. And not much of an apology. But there it is."

"Max…"

"I would've been here sooner," he blurted, when he sensed that she was going to tell him to go away. "But first, I went home. To London. I bought a flower shop—it's quite near my company's downtown headquarters. Lovely place, really. You'd like it."

"Why would you buy a shop, Max?"

"For you." He lifted one hand to smooth his palm over her cheek, feel the line of her jaw, the slide of her skin beneath his again. God, how he'd missed her. "I bought the shop for you, Janine. I can't stay in California. My business is in Europe. But I can't do without you, either. I want you to come home with me, Janine. To England. I want you to marry me. I want you to love me. And blast it, I want to love you."

She swayed in his grasp. "Max…"

"Let me finish, get it all said, then you decide." He bent down, kissed her hard and quick, then looked directly into her eyes. "I'm not doing this because of the baby—"

Her gaze flickered.

"Yes," he said. "I believe you. I found the test strip."

"Oh."

"But a part of me believed you even before I found it," he said quickly, desperately. "The part of me that wanted to love you. The part of me that recognized you as the other part of myself from that very first night."

A solitary tear rolled down her cheek and he smoothed it away with the pad of his thumb. "Don't cry, Janine. I don't want to make you cry. Ever again. Just say you'll believe me. Say you'll let me be a part of your life. Be a part of our child's life. Say you still love me."

She took a great gulp of air and blew it out in a rush. "I do, Max. Of course I do, it's just—"

"No," he said it quickly and framed her face with his palms. "Don't qualify it. You showed me that love's a gift, Janine. One I was almost too stupid to appreciate. I'll never make that mistake again. I swear it to you."

She watched him and as the seconds ticked past, Max held his breath. At last, she smiled up at him and whispered in a tear-choked voice, "I do love you."

He grinned and felt better than he ever had in his life.

This was what he'd been missing. This was what he had so needed. Janine. She was all. She was everything.

"And I love you. Come home with me," he urged, pulling her into his arms. "Come to London. Marry me. Be with me. I promise you, with your help, I'll be the husband you deserve."

Janine looked up at him, felt the solid warmth of his arms around her and knew that the love she'd found at Fantasies had become real. It was everything she'd ever wanted. More than she'd ever dreamed of.

Wrapping her arms around his middle, Janine stared up into those fathomless dark eyes and went with her instincts. "Yes, Max. Yes, I'll marry you. I'll live in London. And I will love you for the rest of my life."

"Thank God," he said with a smile. Lowering his head to hers, he claimed a kiss to seal their new bargain. Their Till Death Do Us Part bargain.

The bargain that had been born in Fantasies.

* * * * *

Don't miss Captured by the Billionaire,
available November 2008 from
Mills & Boon® Desire™.

Turn the page for a sneak preview of

Secrets of the Tycoon's Bride
by
Emilie Rose

A scandalous new story in
THE GARRISONS *series, available from*
Mills & Boon® Desire™ in November 2008

Secrets of the Tycoon's Bride

by

Emilie Rose

Lauryn Lowes would make him a perfect wife because he didn't love her and wasn't attracted to her.

Hell, Adam Garrison realized, he barely knew her.

Their bi-weekly meetings since she'd started working for him seven months ago had never allowed time for get-to-know-you chatter. She worked days when the club was closed, and he worked nights when Estate was open. He knew little about her except what he'd read on her job application.

A tap on his open door revealed the woman in question. "You wanted to see me?"

"Come in, Lauryn. Close the door. Have a seat."

She did as he instructed and perched on the edge of the visitor chair in front of his desk.

According to his lawyer, who happened to be Adam's best friend and someone whose judgment Adam trusted, Lauryn was the perfect wife candidate.

Adam's leather chair creaked as he leaned back to make his own assessment. Lauryn wasn't bad-looking. Bland. No make-up. Pale-blond hair which she always kept pinned up. An intelligent and independent worker. Otherwise he never would have hired her to handle his nightclub's multimillion-dollar books.

"Is something wrong? This isn't our usual meeting day." Lauryn pushed the narrow rectangles of her tortoiseshell glasses up her straight nose, and then with slender, ringless fingers adjusted the longish skirt of her boring navy suit.

He'd never noticed her hands before. But then he'd never considered those hands touching him. Intimately. Her short, unpainted nails were a far cry from the lacquered claws the majority of women in his life preferred.

Besides a manicure, she'd need new clothing to carry off this charade. Maybe contacts. Better shoot for a complete makeover. Otherwise no one would believe he'd chosen her out of all the fashion models and celebrities who frequented Estate and/or his bed.

He had his pick of women. Just not the type he needed for this assignment. The council already considered him a playboy. His female equivalent would not help his cause. Lauryn was far from a party girl. If she'd dated at all in the past months no one on the staff knew it. He'd asked. Discreetly, of course.

She shifted in her chair, reminding him he hadn't answered her question. That was something else he'd always admired about her. She knew how to be quiet instead of chattering endlessly.

"Nothing's wrong, Lauryn. In fact, I'd like to offer you a raise and a…promotion of sorts." He punctuated that with what he hoped would be a reassuring smile. Whether for her or for himself, he couldn't say.

God knows he had reservations about this plan. He was

only thirty and he *liked* being single. Between witnessing his parents' far-from-perfect union and his front-row seat to the nightly dating safaris at the club, he'd never planned to marry for any reason, but he couldn't see any other way to achieve his goals.

He wanted a bigger stake in the family business and there was only one way short of murdering his two older brothers to get it. He had to gain their respect. His father had died unexpectedly in June, and here it was the first of November, and Parker and Stephen still hadn't given Adam more responsibility in Garrison, Inc., because they didn't take him seriously. Frustration burned Adam's stomach.

Lauryn's smooth brow furrowed. "I'm confused. I'm Estate's only accountant. How can I get a promotion? Are you planning to hire an assistant for me? Because I assure you, Mr. Garrison, I can handle the workload. I don't need help."

"Adam," he corrected not for the first time. She never relaxed around him. In fact, she always seemed on edge, and he didn't know why. People—women in particular—liked him. More than one reviewer had attributed Estate's popularity to Adam's charm. He knew how to work a crowd, how to make guests feel welcome and want to return.

Of course, he'd never tried to charm Lauryn Lowes. She was an employee and that was a line he'd never crossed. But he would today.

"The president of the Miami Business Council is retiring next year. As you may have heard, it's a pretty conservative group."

She nodded.

"I've been an active member for years, but the council's not willing to entertain the idea of a single guy—especially one who runs a scandalous South Beach nightclub—being in charge no matter how qualified he might be."

"You mean *you* want to run for president?"

The surprise in her voice stung like salt in a fresh wound. "Yes. And the only way for me to have a chance at that nomination is to become the stable, settled guy they require. I won't give up Estate. That means I need to acquire a wife."

Her look of confusion grew. "What does that have to do with me?"

"You're the perfect candidate."

She blinked once, twice, a third time. "To be your *wife?*"

"Yes."

She sat back in the chair, her posture stiffer than usual. After a few moments an uncertain smile wobbled on her lips. "I—I— You're joking. Right?"

Nice lips, he noted. Pale pink. No lipstick. Not collagen enhanced.

Natural. That's it. Lauryn's a natural.

Too bad that would have to change.

"No." He leaned forward and pulled the file pertaining to this merger from the stack on the side of his desk. "Brandon Washington—you've met my attorney—has drawn up the necessary paperwork. I'll pay you five hundred thousand per year for two years plus reasonable living expenses. After that we'll quietly divorce. We'll have a contract and a prenuptial agreement. What's yours stays yours including any gifts I buy you. What's mine stays mine."

Extracting the relevant documents, he pushed the pages across the polished wood surface toward her. She didn't take them. "You're welcome to have your attorney look over the agreement."

Tightening her grip on the arms of the chair, she eyed the papers like she would a hungry gator. "You actually expect me to agree to this…proposition?"

"You'll be paid a million dollars to do nothing for two years. Why wouldn't you accept?"

"Because I don't love you?"

A little surprised by her reluctance, he shrugged. He could think of several dozen women who'd jump at this chance, but they weren't the type he needed.

"I don't love you, either, but it's an advantageous match for each of us and a sound business decision. You'll move into my loft and I'll buy you a new car. Maybe a Mercedes or a Volvo wagon. We need to give the impression we'd like to start a family soon."

Eyes wide with shock, she made a choking sound. "A family?"

"We won't of course, but we need to play the part."

"Part?" she echoed.

Lauryn's quick grasp of details was one of the things he'd liked about her at that first interview and in subsequent meetings. But she wasn't picking up quickly now. He stifled his impatience. "The picture of domestic bliss. Stable. Settled. Rooted in the community."

She shook her head as if bewildered. "I'm sorry. I just can't wrap my brain around this. You're seriously asking me to marry you?"

"Yes."

"Mr. Garrison—*Adam*—" Her lips stretched in a fleeting and clearly forced smile. "I'm not the woman for this…position."

"I think you are. You're poised, articulate and conservative. You're exactly what—who—I need, Lauryn."

Although she flushed at his compliments, the words didn't ease the starch from her spine. Biting her bottom lip between straight white teeth, she rose. Her fingers knotted so tightly at her waist that her knuckles gleamed white in the overhead fluorescent light.

"I am extremely flattered by your, um…proposal, but I'm afraid I'll have to decline."

"Lauryn—"

She gasped and worry pleated her brow. "My refusal isn't going to cost me my job, is it?"

"Of course not. What kind of jerk do you think I am? But if you marry me you'll be too busy doing whatever it is South Beach socialites do to put in a forty-hour workweek here."

He came around the desk and stopped just inches from her. For the first time he noticed her scent. She smelled like the night-blooming vines growing on his condo neighbor's patio with an additional kick of something spicy and alluring mixed in. "Consider it a two-year paid vacation. Pampering, shopping—"

"But I enjoy my job. And I like working. I'm sorry, but no thank you. I'm sure you can find someone else who—"

"I don't want anyone else. I want you."

MILLS & BOON
Desire 2-in-1
On sale 17th October 2008

Captured by the Billionaire *by Maureen Child*

Trapped on an island resort with the man she'd once jilted, she knew her sexy billionaire captor would like to teach her a lesson…

Sold Into Marriage *by Ann Major*

Can a wealthy Texan stick to his end of the bargain when he takes the very woman he vowed to blackmail to bed?

Secrets of the Tycoon's Bride *by Emilie Rose*

This playboy needs a wife and thinks his accountant the perfect bride-to-be…until she says no and her scandalous past is revealed.

The Executive's Surprise Baby *by Catherine Mann*

The father of her child-to-be is also her family's arch enemy, and Jordan Jeffries is determined to claim his baby and make Brooke his wife!

Series – The Garrisons

The Desert Bride of Al Zayed *by Tessa Radley*

She decided that her secret marriage to the sheikh must end… just as he declared the time had come to produce his heir.

Best Man's Conquest *by Michelle Celmer*

She had agreed to be a bridesmaid at her cousin's wedding…until she discovered that the best man was her gorgeous ex-husband!

Possessed by a passionate sheikh

The Sheikh's Bartered Bride by **Lucy Monroe**

After a whirlwind courtship, Sheikh Hakim bin Omar al Kadar proposes marriage to shy Catherine Benning. After their wedding day, they travel to his desert kingdom, where Catherine discovers that Hakim has bought her!

Sheikh's Honour by **Alexandra Sellers**

Prince and heir Sheikh Jalal was claiming all that was his: land, title, throne…and a queen. Though temptress Clio Blake fought against the bandit prince's wooing like a tigress, Jalal would not be denied his woman!

Available 19th September 2008

www.millsandboon.co.uk

M&B

Celebrate 100 years of pure reading pleasure with Mills & Boon®

To mark our centenary, each month we're publishing a special 100th Birthday Edition. These celebratory editions are packed with extra features and include a FREE bonus story.

Plus, you have the chance to enter a fabulous monthly prize draw. See 100th Birthday Edition books for details.

Now that's worth celebrating!

September 2008

Crazy about her Spanish Boss by Rebecca Winters
Includes FREE bonus story
Rafael's Convenient Proposal

November 2008

**The Rancher's Christmas Baby
by Cathy Gillen Thacker**
Includes FREE bonus story *Baby's First Christmas*

December 2008

One Magical Christmas by Carol Marinelli
Includes FREE bonus story *Emergency at Bayside*

Look for Mills & Boon® 100th Birthday Editions at your favourite bookseller or visit
www.millsandboon.co.uk

2 FREE

BOOKS AND A SURPRISE GIFT!

We would like to take this opportunity to thank you for reading this Mills & Boon® book by offering you the chance to take TWO more specially selected titles from the Desire™ series absolutely FREE! We're also making this offer to introduce you to the benefits of the Mills & Boon® Book Club—

- ★ FREE home delivery
- ★ FREE gifts and competitions
- ★ FREE monthly Newsletter
- ★ Exclusive Mills & Boon® Book Club offers
- ★ Books available before they're in the shops

Accepting these FREE books and gift places you under no obligation to buy, you may cancel at any time, even after receiving your free shipment. Simply complete your details below and return the entire page to the address below. You don't even need a stamp!

YES! Please send me 2 free Desire volumes and a surprise gift. I understand that unless you hear from me, I will receive 3 superb new titles every month for just £4.99 each, postage and packing free. I am under no obligation to purchase any books and may cancel my subscription at any time. The free books and gift will be mine to keep in any case.

D8ZED

Ms/Mrs/Miss/Mr ....Initials ....

BLOCK CAPITALS PLEASE

Surname ....

Address ....

....

....Postcode ....

Send this whole page to:
UK: FREEPOST CN81, Croydon, CR9 3WZ